# Sleuthing in the Shadows
## A Collection of Short Detective Stories
### By Layla A

# An Artist's Enigma Unveiled

## Chapter 1: The Stolen Masterpiece

The crisp evening air hung heavy with the scent of autumn leaves as art detective Isabella Rousseau stepped out of her black Mercedes-Benz. She adjusted her black fedora and tugged at the hem of her tailored trench coat. Isabella was known for her keen eye, impeccable taste, and a reputation for recovering stolen art, but tonight's case had an air of mystery that intrigued even her.

Before her loomed the grand entrance to the Strathmore Art Gallery, a beacon of opulence in the heart of New York City. Isabella's footsteps echoed on the marble floor as she entered, her high-heeled boots tapping a rhythm that resonated through the gallery's cavernous halls.

The theft of the priceless masterpiece, "The Enigma of Eternity" by reclusive artist Viktor Kozlov, had sent shockwaves through the art world. As Isabella made her way through the gallery, the atmosphere exuded a shimmering facade of glamour, wealth, and pretense that masked the chaos brewing beneath the surface. The stolen painting was the crown jewel of the gallery, a piece that had drawn countless art enthusiasts and critics alike.

The gallery's director, an elegant woman with a silver chignon, led Isabella to the crime scene. The empty frame on the wall was a stark reminder of the theft's audacity. Isabella examined the intricate details of the frame, a relic from the 18th century. A gloved hand carefully touched the remaining fragments of glass still clinging to the frame. Her gloved fingers traced the delicate brush strokes that had once captured the essence of "The Enigma of Eternity."

"It's not just a theft, Ms. Rousseau. It's a slap in the face to the entire art world," the gallery director sighed. "The painting is insured, of course, but its loss is a blow to our reputation."

Isabella nodded in agreement, her mind already racing with possibilities. She could feel the weight of the art world's expectations pressing on her, but she welcomed the challenge. "Tell me everything you know about the night of the theft," she requested.

As the director recounted the details, Isabella's eyes were drawn to a group of wealthy patrons mingling in the adjacent room. They sipped champagne and discussed the audacity of the theft, their gowns and suits shimmering in the dimmed light. She observed them with a critical eye, suspecting that beneath their sophistication and smiles, some might be harboring secrets.

After finishing her conversation with the director, Isabella ventured into the gallery's archives, where she knew she would find more clues. In the dimly lit room, she pulled out a file labeled "Kozlov" and began flipping through documents. She uncovered a series of letters exchanged between Viktor Kozlov and a mysterious collector named Anton Malakov. The letters hinted at a simmering feud, possibly over the stolen masterpiece.

Isabella's pulse quickened as she pieced together the puzzle. The theft was not merely an act of criminal audacity; it was personal, fueled by a deep-seated vendetta. She knew she had to find Anton Malakov, a man who had remained elusive in the shadows of the art world.

As she left the archive room, Isabella noticed a shadowy figure lurking in the gallery's dark corners. It was a man in a trench coat, with a fedora pulled low over his face, eerily reminiscent of her own attire. He seemed to be watching her, and a chill ran down her spine.

Isabella stepped out into the gallery once more, her eyes scanning the crowd. The mysterious figure had disappeared into the sea of patrons. She knew that the pursuit of the stolen masterpiece had just become infinitely more complex, and she was determined to unravel the web of forgeries, intrigue, and personal vendettas that lay ahead.

With her heart pounding and a sense of urgency, Isabella Rousseau embarked on a journey into the art world's glittering facade, where danger and deception lurked around every corner, and the stakes were higher than ever.

As the clock struck midnight, she received a cryptic message on her phone, a single word: "Beware." It was a message that left her with a sense of impending danger and uncertainty, setting the stage for a high-stakes investigation that would test her skills, her resolve, and her knowledge of art's darkest secrets.

## Chapter 2: Shadows of the Past

The Strathmore Art Gallery had transformed into a labyrinth of whispers and secrets as Isabella Rousseau delved deeper into her investigation. The echoes of footsteps seemed to whisper tales of deceit, and the hushed conversations among the well-dressed patrons only intensified the intrigue. The stolen masterpiece was more than just a painting; it was a key to a world of forgeries, vendettas, and untold mysteries.

Isabella's pursuit of Anton Malakov, the elusive collector linked to the stolen artwork, had led her to delve into his past. She discovered that he was a shadowy figure who had vanished from the public eye years ago. Rumors spoke of a reclusive lifestyle, hidden wealth, and a penchant for acquiring art at any cost.

The detective's first destination was a dilapidated building in the heart of Brooklyn, a former industrial space now housing a multitude of eccentric artists and bohemians. It was the rumored location of Anton Malakov's secret lair, an underground gallery of his most prized possessions. The place exuded an aura of creative chaos, with graffiti-covered walls and flickering neon lights.

Inside, the labyrinthine maze of art installations and hidden rooms was a testament to the collector's enigmatic taste. Paintings, sculptures, and artifacts from various cultures adorned the space, a captivating menagerie that spoke of obsession and wealth. Isabella's sharp gaze scanned the eclectic pieces, wondering if any of them held clues to the stolen masterpiece.

The smell of turpentine and aged wood wafted through the air as she ventured deeper into the heart of the space. Her eyes fell upon a life-sized sculpture of a veiled woman, her face hidden beneath a delicate, gossamer shroud. The intricate details of the sculpture were haunting, and it left an indelible impression on her. It seemed to embody the essence of the art world—mysteries concealed beneath a facade of beauty.

Isabella approached a local artist working in a corner of the room, his hands caked with paint. "I'm looking for Anton Malakov," she said, her tone a mix of determination and charm.

The artist, a wiry man with unkempt hair and a cigarette hanging from his lips, regarded her with a smirk. "You're not the first one, sweetheart," he replied, his voice dripping with cynicism. "Malakov's a recluse. No one knows how to reach him."

Isabella took a card from her pocket and handed it to the artist. "If you hear anything about his whereabouts or if you've seen him recently, please give me a call. There's a generous reward waiting for those who help."

The promise of a reward sparked the artist's interest. He nodded slowly and tucked the card into his pocket. "I'll keep an eye out. But you didn't hear it from me."

With a curt nod of thanks, Isabella exited the underground gallery, the thoughts swirling in her mind as she headed back to her sleek black car. She knew she had only scratched the surface of the enigma that was Anton Malakov. The stolen masterpiece was just the tip of the iceberg, a catalyst that had plunged her into a world of art, intrigue, and personal vendettas.

Her next destination was a modest brownstone in the heart of Greenwich Village, where she hoped to find more information about Anton Malakov's past. The brownstone was a stark contrast to the opulence of the Strathmore Art Gallery, with its aging brick façade and wrought iron gate.

Inside the dimly lit living room, Isabella met an elderly woman named Evelyn Patterson. Her frizzy white hair and sharp, intelligent eyes gave the impression of a woman who had seen it all. She had known Anton Malakov when he was still a promising young artist, a time when he was on the cusp of fame.

"Evelyn, I'm here to learn more about Anton," Isabella explained, her tone respectful. "Anything you can tell me might help solve the mystery surrounding the stolen painting."

Evelyn hesitated for a moment, her eyes distant as she recalled memories from long ago. "Anton was brilliant, you know," she finally said, her voice tinged with nostalgia. "But something changed in him. He became obsessed with collecting art, as if he believed it held the answers to some profound secret. He withdrew from the world, and his art became dark and cryptic."

Isabella leaned forward, her interest piqued. "Dark and cryptic in what way?"

Evelyn's gaze met Isabella's, and the weight of her words hung in the air. "He began to create art that seemed to hint at a hidden world, a place where secrets lay buried, and where vendettas were settled. His paintings were like puzzles waiting to be solved, but I never knew what they meant."

Isabella couldn't help but think of "The Enigma of Eternity" and the secrets it might hold. She knew that the stolen masterpiece was not just a random theft but a piece of a larger puzzle, one that Anton Malakov had been constructing for years.

As the conversation continued, Evelyn mentioned a name that sent shivers down Isabella's spine. "There was a man who used to visit Anton—Daniel Blackwood. He was his closest friend and confidant, but they had a falling out. I never knew the details, but it was something profound, something that changed them both."

The mention of Daniel Blackwood added a new layer to the mystery. Isabella knew she had to find him and uncover the truth about the strained friendship between him and Anton Malakov. It was a crucial piece of the puzzle that had the power to reveal the secrets behind the stolen masterpiece.

As she left the brownstone and headed back to her car, a sense of urgency gnawed at Isabella. She needed to find Daniel Blackwood and learn what drove the two friends apart, for it might hold the key to understanding the vendettas and hidden world that had entangled her in their dark web.

The night was shrouded in mystery, and Isabella Rousseau had only begun to unravel the enigma of the stolen masterpiece. She knew that the path she was on was fraught with danger and intrigue, and the secrets of the art world were more treacherous than she could have ever imagined.

## Chapter 3: The Broken Friendships

Isabella Rousseau's determination to uncover the truth behind the stolen masterpiece and the enigma of Anton Malakov's hidden world led her to an inconspicuous building nestled on the outskirts of Brooklyn. It was here that she hoped to find Daniel Blackwood, the estranged friend of the reclusive collector.

The building stood like a sentinel against the dimming evening light, its brick exterior worn and weathered, a reflection of the strained friendships and secrets it harbored within. Isabella approached the entrance, feeling the chill in the air as she pressed the buzzer for Blackwood's apartment.

The door creaked open to reveal a man with disheveled hair and a haunted look in his eyes. Daniel Blackwood's once-vibrant spirit seemed diminished, his eyes now betraying the weight of untold secrets. His surprise at Isabella's presence was evident.

"Ms. Rousseau, I wasn't expecting visitors," Daniel said, his voice tinged with unease.

"I hope you can spare a few moments of your time, Mr. Blackwood. I believe you might have information that can help me with an important investigation," Isabella replied, her voice a mixture of charm and authority.

Daniel hesitated but eventually stepped aside, allowing Isabella to enter his sparsely furnished apartment. The scent of old books and fading memories hung in the air. As Isabella took in her surroundings, she couldn't help but notice the multitude of paintings adorning the walls—masterpieces that seemed to hold their own stories.

"I'm trying to put the past behind me," Daniel admitted, his gaze lingering on the art that surrounded him. "Anton and I were close once, but things changed. He became consumed by his obsession with art, and I couldn't keep up."

Isabella's eyes drifted toward a particular painting—a haunting depiction of a desolate, moonlit landscape. It was a puzzle waiting to be unraveled, a testament to the darkness that had infiltrated their friendship. "Did you and Anton have a falling out over one of his paintings? Perhaps 'The Enigma of Eternity'?"

Daniel's shoulders slumped as he recalled the past. "We did. 'The Enigma of Eternity' was at the center of it all. Anton believed that the painting held the key to something profound, something that transcended art itself. I disagreed. It tore us apart."

Isabella leaned in, her eyes locked onto Daniel's. "What is it about that painting, Mr. Blackwood? What secret does it hold?"

Daniel's expression darkened. "I don't know, Ms. Rousseau. Anton never shared the details with me. He became reclusive, lost in his own world of art and obsession. I haven't seen him in years."

Isabella knew she had hit a dead end with Daniel. He was a broken man, haunted by the past and the strained friendships that had unraveled his life. With a promise to keep in touch, she left his apartment, her thoughts consumed by the enigma of "The Enigma of Eternity."

Back in her car, Isabella's mind raced as she pondered her next move. Anton Malakov remained a shadowy figure, and the stolen masterpiece was still at large. Her investigation had led her to fractured friendships, strained relationships, and secrets that seemed to transcend the world of art. She knew she had to find Anton, but the path to him was veiled in darkness.

The night was in full bloom as Isabella decided to pay a visit to the Strathmore Art Gallery once more. She felt the weight of the mystery pressing on her, and the need to find the stolen masterpiece and unravel the web of forgeries and vendettas consumed her every thought.

As she stepped into the gallery, she was greeted by the same opulence and pretense that had defined it. The patrons continued their hushed conversations, sipping champagne and discussing the audacity of the theft. But Isabella noticed something amiss—the gallery's director was speaking in earnest with a well-dressed man, and their expressions were fraught with tension.

Isabella approached the pair, her presence commanding attention. "Is there a problem, Director?" she inquired, her tone laced with authority.

The director turned to Isabella, her face pale with worry. "This is Anton Malakov's lawyer, Mr. Vincent Sterling. He claims to represent Mr. Malakov in the recovery of 'The Enigma of Eternity.'"

Vincent Sterling, a tall and imposing man in an impeccably tailored suit, regarded Isabella with an air of authority. "Ms. Rousseau, I've been instructed by my client to request your assistance in locating the stolen painting. Anton believes that it holds a profound secret, and he wishes to see it returned."

Isabella felt a knot of suspicion tighten in her chest. The sudden appearance of Anton's lawyer raised questions about his involvement in the theft and his true motives. "Where is Mr. Malakov, Mr. Sterling? I would like to speak with him directly."

Sterling's gaze remained unwavering. "My client is currently out of the country on urgent business. But he is eager to recover the painting and believes that your expertise can help."

Isabella couldn't shake the feeling that something was amiss. The lawyer's presence, combined with the web of strained friendships and dark secrets, left her with a sense of unease. The mystery deepened, and she knew that unraveling it would require more than just solving the theft of a priceless painting.

As she prepared to leave the gallery, the weight of moral and ethical dilemmas weighed on her shoulders. Anton Malakov was a man enshrouded in secrecy, and Vincent Sterling's motives remained questionable. The enigma of "The Enigma of Eternity" had become more complex than ever, and the pieces of the puzzle were scattered, waiting to be reassembled.

The night had fallen, casting a veil of darkness over the art world's glittering facade, and Isabella Rousseau was left with the unsettling knowledge that the web of forgeries, intrigue, and personal vendettas had only just begun to unravel.

With the weight of the mystery bearing down on her, Isabella couldn't help but feel that the key to solving the case lay within her reach. But as she continued her pursuit of the stolen masterpiece, she knew that danger and deception lurked around every corner, and the enigma of "The Enigma of Eternity" was far from being unraveled.

## Chapter 4: Secrets in the Shadows

The night hung heavy with mist as Isabella Rousseau returned to her office, her mind consumed by the enigma of "The Enigma of Eternity." The sudden appearance of Anton Malakov's lawyer, Vincent Sterling, had added a layer of intrigue to the case, and the mysteries seemed to multiply with each passing moment.

As she entered her dimly lit office, the glow of antique lamps cast an eerie light over the room. The shelves were lined with art books, and the walls adorned with photographs of recovered masterpieces, a testament to Isabella's impeccable track record. But tonight, her focus was on the stolen painting that had become the centerpiece of her most complex mystery yet.

Isabella's phone buzzed, shattering the silence. It was a text message from Vincent Sterling: "Meet me at The Royal Gallery, midnight."

The message sent a shiver down Isabella's spine. She couldn't help but wonder about Sterling's motives and the urgency of his request. Her encounter with the lawyer at the Strathmore Art Gallery had left her with a nagging sense of unease.

As the clock in her office ticked away, Isabella prepared to head to The Royal Gallery. The air outside was cool and damp, and the mist clung to her coat like a shroud. The Royal Gallery, a hallowed establishment in the art world, was known for its secretive dealings and exclusive clientele.

As she arrived at the gallery, the dimly lit exterior gave no hint of the treasures hidden within. The door creaked open, and Isabella entered a world of opulence and extravagance. The air was thick with the scent of rare perfumes and the hushed voices of patrons who had come to admire the gallery's private collection.

Vincent Sterling appeared from the shadows, his presence commanding attention. He led Isabella to a secluded corner of the gallery, where a painting shrouded in darkness awaited them.

"I have something to show you, Ms. Rousseau," Sterling said, his voice low and mysterious. "But it must remain our secret."

Isabella's curiosity piqued, and she nodded in agreement. The lawyer unveiled the painting, revealing "The Enigma of Eternity" in all its glory. The masterpiece, once stolen, was now bathed in the soft glow of a spotlight, its intricate details shimmering in the darkness.

"Anton Malakov believes that this painting holds a profound secret," Sterling began. "He wants you to examine it and find the answers it conceals."

Isabella approached the painting, her eyes tracing the enigmatic figures and symbols that seemed to dance on the canvas. The painting was a puzzle waiting to be solved, a testament to the darkness and intrigue that had surrounded it.

As she studied the artwork, Isabella noticed a series of hidden messages—subtle clues and symbols that hinted at a hidden world. The tension in the gallery's atmosphere was palpable, as if the art itself held a powerful secret.

"I need time to decipher this," Isabella said, her voice barely above a whisper. "The painting is a maze of mysteries, and I believe it may hold the key to unraveling the enigma that Anton has become."

Sterling nodded in agreement. "Anton is willing to cooperate with you in any way he can. He believes that the stolen painting is just the beginning, and that there are other pieces of this puzzle yet to be discovered."

As Isabella left The Royal Gallery, the weight of the enigma pressed on her. The stolen masterpiece had become a symbol of a hidden world, one that was shrouded in secrets and danger. She knew that her investigation had taken a new turn, one that would lead her to uncovering the truth behind Anton Malakov's obsession.

Back in her office, Isabella meticulously documented the hidden messages and symbols she had discovered in "The Enigma of Eternity." The painting seemed to contain a narrative of its own, one that held the power to unlock the secrets of the art world's glittering facade.

Her phone buzzed once more. It was a message from her trusted friend and art expert, Thomas Maddox. "Isabella, I've uncovered a series of cryptic letters exchanged between Anton Malakov and a mysterious figure known only as 'The Collector.' These letters might hold the key to the stolen masterpiece and the world of secrets it conceals."

Isabella's heart quickened as she read the message. The name 'The Collector' sent a chill down her spine, and she knew that the mysterious figure was a central piece of the puzzle. She needed to find out who 'The Collector' was and what role they played in the theft of the painting.

As she delved deeper into the letters, a pattern emerged. The Collector seemed to be a figure of power and influence, one who had been in contact with Anton for years. The letters hinted at a web of intrigue, vendettas, and hidden alliances.

With each new discovery, Isabella felt the tension and suspense of the case intensify. The stolen masterpiece was no longer just a painting; it was a key to a world of secrets, and the enigma that surrounded it seemed to grow more complex with every revelation.

The night was in full bloom, and Isabella knew that she was on the brink of uncovering the truth. The web of forgeries, vendettas, and hidden alliances was unraveling before her, and she was determined to see it through to the end.

But as she continued her investigation, she couldn't help but wonder about the moral and ethical dilemmas that lay ahead. The choices she would have to make, and the secrets she would have to confront, were far from simple. The enigma of "The Enigma of Eternity" had become a journey into the shadows, one that held the power to change the art world forever.

As she prepared to follow the trail of clues, Isabella knew that the road ahead would be treacherous, and the stakes higher than ever. The mysteries that awaited her in the art world's glittering facade were far from being solved, and the tension in the air was electrifying.

## Chapter 5: Veils of Deception

As the night's shadows deepened, Isabella Rousseau's determination to unravel the enigma of "The Enigma of Eternity" led her down a labyrinth of art and intrigue. The stolen masterpiece had become more than just a painting—it was a key to a world of secrets and hidden agendas.

Following her discovery of the letters exchanged between Anton Malakov and 'The Collector,' Isabella's next move was to uncover the identity of this mysterious figure. Her trusted friend and art expert, Thomas Maddox, had promised to assist in the investigation, but they needed more clues to unveil the Collector's true identity.

Isabella met Thomas at a dimly lit café, the scent of freshly brewed coffee mingling with the aroma of aged leather-bound books. The establishment was a haven for intellectuals and art aficionados, a place where ideas flowed freely.

Thomas slid a file across the table, his eyes reflecting the urgency of the situation. "Isabella, I've managed to gather more information about 'The Collector,' but the web of secrecy around this figure is formidable. The letters suggest a connection to an exclusive art society known as 'The Inner Circle.'"

Isabella took the file and began sifting through the documents, her fingers tracing the names of influential art patrons and collectors who were part of this enigmatic society. "The Collector seems to have powerful allies. They hold secrets that reach deep into the art world's glittering facade."

Thomas nodded in agreement. "The Inner Circle has always been shrouded in secrecy. It's said that its members influence the art market, dictating the rise and fall of artists and their works. But uncovering their motives and true identities is a daunting task."

As Isabella studied the documents, a thought struck her—a potential ally in her pursuit of the truth. "Thomas, I need to infiltrate 'The Inner Circle.' I believe that it's the key to uncovering the Collector's identity and the mysteries surrounding Anton Malakov."

Thomas hesitated for a moment, his expression one of concern. "Isabella, the Inner Circle operates in the shadows, and their members are fiercely protective of their secrets. Infiltrating the society will be dangerous, and the risks are high."

Isabella's gaze met Thomas's, her determination unwavering. "The stolen masterpiece and the enigma it holds are worth the risk. I need you to find a way to get me an invitation, Thomas. The answers we seek lie within the Inner Circle's web of intrigue."

As they parted ways, Isabella's mind was consumed by the enigma that had become her obsession. The Inner Circle held the answers she sought, and she knew that her path was fraught with danger and deception. The mysteries surrounding the art world's glittering facade were entangled in the secrets of influential figures.

In the days that followed, Thomas worked tirelessly to secure an invitation to the Inner Circle's exclusive gathering. Isabella's anticipation grew, and the moral and ethical dilemmas of infiltrating the secretive society weighed heavily on her mind.

Finally, the day of the gathering arrived. Isabella was dressed in an elegant gown that exuded sophistication and charm, her attire carefully chosen to gain the trust of the Inner Circle's members. As she entered the lavish mansion that hosted the event, the opulence of the surroundings was breathtaking, a stark contrast to the shadowy world of secrets she was about to enter.

The atmosphere within the mansion was charged with an air of prestige and power. Influential art collectors and patrons mingled, their voices a soft hum in the grand hall. Isabella knew that within this assembly of privilege and influence, her pursuit of the truth was fraught with danger.

She approached a group of members who were engaged in animated conversation. Their words hinted at a world of manipulation and power, and the tension in the room was palpable.

Isabella's gaze locked onto a woman with piercing eyes and an air of authority. She introduced herself as Vivienne Cavanaugh, a prominent art collector, and curator. Isabella seized the opportunity to engage her in conversation.

"Ms. Cavanaugh, I've heard that the Inner Circle holds significant influence over the art world," Isabella began, her tone measured and inquisitive.

Vivienne regarded Isabella with a scrutinizing gaze. "Indeed, the Inner Circle is a select group of individuals who shape the art market. But it's not an organization to be taken lightly. We value discretion and influence above all else."

As the evening progressed, Isabella moved through the crowd, her interactions revealing fragments of the enigma that was 'The Inner Circle.' Whispers of secret deals, manipulations, and betrayals painted a picture of a world where power and influence were paramount.

The tension and suspense in the room mounted, and Isabella knew that her pursuit of the Collector's identity was far from over. As the night drew to a close, she couldn't help but feel that the moral and ethical dilemmas of infiltrating this society were deeper than she had anticipated.

As she left the gathering, Isabella was aware of the risk she was taking, and the weight of secrets and danger that awaited her. The enigma of 'The Enigma of Eternity' had taken her deep into a world of shadows, where the complexities of the art world's glittering facade were intertwined with the agendas of influential figures.

Her phone buzzed with a message from Thomas: "The Collector is watching you. Be cautious."

The message sent a chill down Isabella's spine. The Collector's presence was closer than she had imagined, and the secrets that had eluded her for so long were on the verge of being unraveled. The web of deception and danger had tightened, and Isabella Rousseau's pursuit of the truth was about to take a treacherous turn.

## Chapter 6: Unmasking Shadows

The echoes of secrets reverberated through Isabella Rousseau's mind as she delved deeper into the enigmatic world of 'The Inner Circle.' The elusive Collector remained a veiled presence, a shadowy figure lurking on the periphery of her investigation. With every step, the complexities of the art world's glittering facade grew more intricate, and the tension in the air became nearly palpable.

Isabella had secured her place within the exclusive society, and the anticipation of unmasking the Collector had her pulse quickening. She knew that the risks were high, and the moral and ethical dilemmas of her actions weighed heavily on her conscience.

The gathering had reconvened, this time in a grand ballroom illuminated by a cascade of crystal chandeliers. The attendees exuded an air of privilege and influence, and Isabella couldn't help but feel like an interloper in their world of shadows and secrets.

As she mingled with the members, she couldn't shake the feeling that the Collector was watching her every move. The tension and suspense in the room was nearly unbearable, and the sense of danger loomed like a dark cloud.

Her interactions led her to a man named Lawrence Van der Meer, an art historian with an air of charisma and intrigue. Their conversation was filled with veiled references and innuendos, and Lawrence's eyes held a hint of knowledge that sent shivers down Isabella's spine.

"Ms. Rousseau," Lawrence began, his voice a velvet whisper, "you are not like the others here. I sense a different kind of ambition in you, one that seeks to uncover the shadows within the art world."

Isabella met Lawrence's gaze with a mixture of caution and curiosity. "The shadows conceal more than just secrets, Mr. Van der Meer. They hide the moral and ethical dilemmas that have plagued the art world for far too long."

Lawrence's smile was enigmatic, and he nodded in agreement. "You are a woman of principle, and that is a rare find in the world we navigate. But be careful, Ms. Rousseau. The Collector is not to be underestimated. Their power is as vast as it is hidden."

As the night progressed, Isabella's pursuit of the Collector continued, and the complexities of the enigma deepened. The atmosphere in the ballroom was charged with a sense of anticipation and danger, and she couldn't help but feel that her actions were drawing her closer to unmasking the shadows that concealed the Collector's identity.

As the evening drew to a close, Isabella discreetly excused herself from the gathering and returned to her apartment, her mind a whirlwind of thoughts and revelations. The moral and ethical dilemmas of her actions weighed heavily on her, and the choices she had made were far from simple.

As she settled into her dimly lit office, she couldn't help but reflect on the social commentary embedded in the art world's glittering facade. The power and influence of the Inner Circle were a stark reminder of the inequalities that persisted in the world of art. The Collector represented the hidden agendas and manipulations that shaped the market, and Isabella was determined to unmask the figure responsible for the theft of "The Enigma of Eternity."

Her phone buzzed with a message from Thomas: "The Collector's identity may be closer than you think. Meet me at the old warehouse by the waterfront."

The message left Isabella with a sense of urgency. The warehouse by the waterfront was a place of intrigue and shadows, a location that held the potential to reveal the Collector's true identity. She knew that her pursuit of the truth was far from over, and the tension and suspense that had enveloped her would only intensify.

As she arrived at the old warehouse, the air was thick with the scent of salt and decay, a testament to the secrets that lay hidden within. The space was dimly lit, and the echo of footsteps reverberated through the cavernous interior.

Thomas emerged from the shadows, his face etched with a mixture of determination and trepidation. "Isabella, I've uncovered a lead that could reveal the Collector's identity. But it's dangerous, and the risks are high."

Isabella met Thomas's gaze, her resolve unwavering. "The Collector's identity is the key to unraveling the enigma that has consumed me. I'm willing to take the risks."

Thomas led her to a collection of documents scattered on a weathered table. Among them was a series of coded messages and letters that hinted at the Collector's true identity. The documents spoke of a hidden alliance and a network of influential figures who had manipulated the art world for years.

As Isabella deciphered the codes and examined the clues, the vivid imagery of her investigation began to take shape. The complexity of the mysteries had reached a point where the pieces of the puzzle were slowly falling into place.

"The Collector is part of a larger network, Isabella," Thomas explained. "They've left a trail of secrets that reaches far and deep into the art world. But with these documents, we may finally have the upper hand."

As they prepared to leave the warehouse, Isabella knew that the next chapter of her investigation would bring her closer to unmasking the Collector's identity. The moral and ethical dilemmas that had haunted her were about to be put to the test, and the web of deception and danger was closing in.

Back in her apartment, Isabella's mind raced as she reviewed the clues and revelations that had come to light. The Collector's identity was within reach, and she was determined to expose the figure responsible for the theft of "The Enigma of Eternity" and the web of secrets that had plagued the art world for too long.

As the night deepened, the enigma that had consumed Isabella Rousseau drew her further into the shadows, where the complexities of the art world's glittering facade were intertwined with the agendas of influential figures. The reader was left with a sense of anticipation, knowing that the next chapter of the investigation would bring them closer to unveiling the Collector's identity, but also deeper into a world of intrigue and danger. The enigma of 'The Enigma of Eternity' had become a journey into the heart of deception, and Isabella's pursuit of the truth was reaching its zenith.

## Chapter 7: Unveiling the Enigma

The dark underbelly of the art world's glittering facade had never been more exposed than it was on the night Isabella Rousseau stood at the precipice of unveiling the identity of the Collector. With every revelation, the complexities of the mysteries surrounding "The Enigma of Eternity" had drawn her deeper into the enigma, where moral and ethical dilemmas weighed heavily on her shoulders.

The documents Thomas had unearthed in the old warehouse hinted at a hidden alliance, a network of influential figures who had manipulated the art market for years. The Collector, shrouded in mystery, had remained the enigma at the center of it all.

As Isabella pieced together the coded messages and letters, she couldn't help but feel a growing sense of resolution and closure. The Collector's identity was within reach, and her pursuit of the truth was reaching its zenith.

With the clues laid before her, Isabella embarked on a mission to confront the Collector. Her resolve was unshakable, and the tension and suspense that had surrounded her investigation had reached its peak.

She arranged to meet the Collector at an abandoned art gallery in the heart of the city. The setting was eerie, the walls adorned with faded remnants of forgotten masterpieces, a testament to the art world's hidden agendas and deceptions.

As Isabella entered the gallery, the atmosphere was thick with anticipation. She couldn't help but feel a growing sense of closure as the Collector's identity hung in the balance. Her phone buzzed with a message from Thomas: "Be cautious, Isabella. The Collector is a formidable figure, and their motives remain unclear."

The message served as a stark reminder of the danger that lay ahead. Isabella knew that she was stepping into a world of shadows and intrigue, and the moral and ethical dilemmas of her actions were more pronounced than ever.

In the dimly lit gallery, Isabella met the Collector, a figure cloaked in shadows and authority. Their voice was a whisper, their identity still veiled. "Ms. Rousseau, your pursuit of the truth has led you to this moment. But what do you seek to gain from unmasking me?"

Isabella met the Collector's gaze with a mixture of determination and curiosity. "The stolen masterpiece, 'The Enigma of Eternity,' holds a profound secret. I believe that by revealing your identity, I can uncover the mysteries that have plagued the art world for too long."

The Collector's enigmatic smile was a play of shadows and light. "The art world is a tapestry of deception and manipulation, Ms. Rousseau. I am but one thread within it. But the secrets of 'The Enigma of Eternity' are far greater than you can imagine."

As the Collector revealed their identity, Isabella couldn't help but feel a growing sense of resolution. The Collector was none other than Anton Malakov himself, the reclusive collector who had remained a shadowy figure throughout the investigation.

Anton's confession was filled with remorse and regret. "I believed that 'The Enigma of Eternity' held a secret that could change the world. I stole it to protect the painting from falling into the wrong hands. But in doing so, I became entangled in a web of intrigue and deception."

The revelation left Isabella with a mix of emotions—shock, compassion, and a growing sense of closure. The complexities of the art world's glittering facade had been exposed, and the moral and ethical dilemmas that had haunted her were now at the forefront of her mind.

Anton's voice grew somber as he continued, "The painting's secret is one of redemption and forgiveness. It has the power to heal the wounds of the past and reveal the truth behind the art world's hidden agendas."

As Isabella absorbed the weight of Anton's confession, she couldn't help but reflect on the social commentary embedded in the art world. The power and influence of figures like Anton had shaped the market, but the art world remained plagued by inequalities and deceptions.

With a sense of resolution and closure, Isabella's pursuit of the truth had come to an end. The stolen masterpiece was no longer a mystery, and the moral and ethical dilemmas that had defined her journey were now part of her past.

As she left the gallery, the weight of the mysteries and secrets that had consumed her lifted. The art world's glittering facade had been exposed, and the enigma of "The Enigma of Eternity" had been unraveled.

THE END

# Shadows of Legacy

## Chapter 1: The Vanishing Heiress

The grand ballroom of the Winslow Estate shimmered with the glow of crystal chandeliers, casting a dazzling array of sparkles on the gathered elite. The annual Winslow Gala was a spectacle of opulence, a testament to the family's centuries-old legacy. But tonight, the air was heavy with anticipation, for it marked a pivotal moment in the family's history. Evelyn Winslow, the sole heiress to the Winslow fortune, was to come into her inheritance at midnight.

As guests swirled in their finest attire, Detective Victor Sterling, renowned for his sharp mind and unwavering resolve, watched the proceedings from the shadows. He had been summoned to the estate with an envelope containing a singular message: "Meet me at the heart of the rose garden at the stroke of midnight." The note was unsigned, but the ink smelled of roses, a scent that clung to Evelyn Winslow like a second skin.

Evelyn was a riddle wrapped in an enigma. She had spent most of her life sheltered within the marble walls of the Winslow Estate, known for her beauty and rumored to be possessed of an untold fortune. Victor had heard whispers that some of the Winslow family harbored grudges and secrets that could rival the mysteries of ancient legends. Tonight, those secrets threatened to spill forth like a turbulent sea.

As the hours ticked away, Victor observed Evelyn's interactions with the partygoers. She floated through the ballroom with a grace that was breathtaking, captivating every gaze that met hers. He couldn't help but admire her presence, her bewitching allure. The heiress held the power to charm and command anyone in her vicinity, and Victor wondered if this magnetism was the source of the sinister invitation.

Midnight drew closer, and Victor felt the weight of the impending investigation pressing upon him. The guests began to gather in the rose garden, each step taken in hushed anticipation. The moonlight bathed the garden in a silvery glow, illuminating the blossoms in shades of palest white. In the center, a stone gazebo stood, adorned with intertwined roses that had been planted generations ago.

Victor slipped through the crowd, his footsteps masked by the soft rustling of evening gowns and tailored tuxedos. He reached the heart of the rose garden and waited in the shadows, his senses alert and every muscle tensed. The minutes ticked by, each one drawing out the tension and mystery of the night.

Then, the midnight bells chimed, and the world fell silent. The guests held their collective breath, their eyes focused on the gazebo. Evelyn Winslow was nowhere to be seen. In her place stood a silhouette, cloaked in shadows, barely distinguishable from the surrounding darkness.

A gasp swept through the crowd, and Victor's heart quickened. Was this the person who had summoned him? The shadowy figure stepped forward, revealing a mask that concealed their identity. It was a porcelain visage, as white as the garden's roses, with intricate filigree patterns that hinted at a hidden purpose.

"Ladies and gentlemen," the figure's voice rang out, clear and commanding, "I have come to claim what is rightfully mine."

The guests exchanged bewildered glances, and Victor felt the tension in the air ratcheting up another notch. Was this an imposter, or was this the real Evelyn Winslow, speaking from behind a mask?

Victor watched the heiress's closest confidantes, her family members, and her childhood friends. Suspicion and alarm crept across their faces, as if they too were uncertain of the figure's identity.

The figure continued, "Evelyn Winslow's legacy belongs to me, and I shall not rest until I've exposed the truth that the Winslow family has so diligently concealed."

The words hung in the night air like a thunderclap, and Victor knew that he had stepped into a web of lies, deceit, and treachery that threatened to unravel the very foundation of the Winslow dynasty. The heiress was missing, and a masked interloper had laid claim to her fortune.

## Chapter 2: The Unmasking

The silence that followed the shadowy figure's bold claim seemed to stretch on endlessly. The guests exchanged nervous glances, unsure of how to react. Victor Sterling, hidden in the garden's shadows, remained vigilant. This was a game, a high-stakes masquerade, and he was determined to uncover the truth.

The figure's porcelain mask gleamed in the moonlight, and for a moment, it seemed as if the entire world held its breath. Then, with a graceful sweep of their hand, the mask was lifted, revealing the face beneath.

Evelyn Winslow.

Victor felt a ripple of shock course through him. It was indeed the heiress, the center of attention, the jewel of the Winslow family. But there was something different about her. Her eyes, once radiant and full of life, now appeared distant and haunted. It was as if she had aged in a matter of minutes, her features etched with worry.

Evelyn's unsteady voice broke the eerie silence, "I am Evelyn Winslow, and I claim my rightful inheritance."

A murmur of disbelief ran through the crowd. Whispers and speculations raced from one guest to another. Victor watched the reactions carefully, sensing the tension rising. The heiress was missing, then reappeared masked, and now stood unmasked, claiming her own fortune.

Lady Beatrice Winslow, Evelyn's mother, stepped forward, her face a mask of astonishment and relief. "Evelyn, dear, you've given us such a fright! What happened? Why did you do this?"

Evelyn's gaze remained fixed on her mother, but she seemed not to register her presence. Her voice quavered as she spoke, "I've had enough of these secrets, Mother. It's time for the truth to be revealed."

The shadow of darkness that had clouded her eyes deepened. Victor, keenly observant, noted a bruise on her wrist, partially concealed by the folds of her evening gown. It was a small detail, but it told a story of captivity and struggle.

"I won't let you ruin this, Evelyn," Lady Beatrice hissed, her composure slipping. "This is our family's legacy, and you're not in a position to make such demands."

Evelyn's defiance seemed to grow, her gaze unwavering. "I know the family's secrets, Mother, and I know what you've done. The truth must come out."

The room's tension became nearly unbearable. Victor felt a weight in his chest as he sensed the magnitude of the family's hidden turmoil. Evelyn's revelation was just the tip of the iceberg.

But it was another voice, one from the gathering, that shattered the uneasy silence. "Enough of this!" Sir Reginald Winslow, Evelyn's father, bellowed. He was a man of power and influence, used to command. "Evelyn, it's time you come inside. We'll discuss this matter privately."

Evelyn hesitated for a moment, her gaze flickering to Victor in the shadows. There was an unspoken plea in her eyes, a plea for help. But before Victor could react, she was led away by her family, disappearing into the grand hall, the mask back in place.

The guests, bewildered and captivated by the unfolding drama, dispersed into hushed conversations. Victor, however, remained rooted in the rose garden, his mind racing. He knew he had to act quickly, for Evelyn Winslow was in danger, and the family's secrets were a ticking time bomb.

Victor decided to follow Evelyn's family into the heart of the Winslow Estate. With practiced stealth, he made his way to the mansion's opulent interior, navigating the labyrinthine corridors and dimly lit passages. The further he ventured, the more he uncovered the family's dark secrets.

In a dimly lit study, Victor discovered a trove of old diaries, letters, and photographs that painted a picture of treachery, deceit, and long-buried scandals. It seemed that the Winslow legacy was built upon a foundation of manipulation and betrayal, and Evelyn had become the key to exposing it all.

As he pored over the documents, a voice echoed down the hallway, shattering the silence. It was Lady Beatrice, her tone laced with desperation. "We need to find her and silence her, Reginald. We can't afford for those secrets to come to light."

Victor's heart raced as he realized the heiress was in imminent danger. He had to reach her before it was too late. Clutching the incriminating evidence he had found, he moved swiftly through the mansion, guided by the sound of voices and the urgency of the situation.

## Chapter 3: Midnight Pursuit

Victor Sterling moved through the mansion's dimly lit corridors, guided by the sound of hushed voices. The urgency of the situation gripped him as he realized that Evelyn Winslow's life hung in the balance. Her revelations about the family's secrets had placed her in grave danger, and it was clear that her family would stop at nothing to protect their legacy.

As he neared the source of the voices, Victor couldn't help but reflect on the intricacies of the case. The Winslow family's wealth and influence had created a web of deceit that spanned generations, but Evelyn had dared to pull at its threads. Her determination had transformed her from an heiress into a pariah, a threat to everything the Winslow family held dear.

The voices grew louder, and Victor's heart quickened. He knew he needed to reach Evelyn before her family silenced her. With each step, he was fueled by a relentless determination to uncover the truth and protect the heiress from harm.

The voices led him to an ornate, wood-paneled door, slightly ajar. He pressed his ear to the crack, listening intently to the heated conversation on the other side.

"I won't allow her to expose us, Reginald," Lady Beatrice's voice quivered with fear. "The family's secrets must remain hidden at all costs."

Victor couldn't see the room's occupants, but their words sent shivers down his spine. He could sense the tension, the palpable threat hanging in the air. The Winslow family's facades of elegance and sophistication were unraveling, revealing a darkness that had festered beneath the surface for far too long.

Sir Reginald Winslow, his voice heavy with authority, responded, "We must act quickly. Our reputation, our legacy, everything we've worked for—it's all at stake. Find her, bring her back, and ensure she remains silent."

With Evelyn's life in jeopardy, Victor knew he couldn't wait any longer. He pushed the door open slightly and peered into the room. Lady Beatrice and Sir Reginald Winslow stood near a large oak desk, their faces etched with desperation and resolve. But Evelyn was nowhere to be seen.

Victor's instincts kicked into overdrive as he scanned the room for clues. His gaze landed on an open window, a possible escape route for the heiress. He had to find her before her family did. Silently, he retreated from the doorway and made his way to the open window, scanning the moonlit grounds for any sign of her.

There, in the distance, he spotted a figure moving swiftly through the gardens. It was Evelyn, her gown billowing as she fled into the night, the mask once again concealed in her hand.

Without hesitation, Victor pursued her. The grounds of the Winslow Estate were vast and labyrinthine, filled with manicured hedges, stone pathways, and hidden alcoves. Evelyn's pursuit of truth had transformed into a desperate flight for her life, and Victor was determined to be her guardian.

As he closed in on her, he could hear Evelyn's ragged breaths and the faint sound of her footsteps. She glanced over her shoulder, her eyes wide with fear and uncertainty. "Who are you?" she cried out, her voice wavering.

Victor revealed himself, his presence intended to be reassuring. "I'm Detective Victor Sterling," he said, his voice steady and calm. "I'm here to help you, Evelyn."

For a moment, the heiress hesitated, her trust torn between the desire for safety and the fear of betrayal. She finally nodded, and Victor quickened his pace to reach her side.

The chase continued, their breathless pursuit through the moonlit gardens taking on an air of danger and uncertainty. As they weaved through the shadows and hidden alcoves, Evelyn began to speak, her voice trembling. "I had to expose the truth,

Detective Sterling. The Winslow family's secrets—they've caused so much pain."

Victor could hear the anguish in her words, and he knew that Evelyn was the key to unraveling the dark history of the Winslow dynasty. "I promise you, Evelyn, we will uncover the truth together," he reassured her.

But their pursuit was far from over. The stakes were high, and the threat of capture by her own family loomed large. The heiress's revelations had shattered the facade of the Winslow family's opulence, and now they would stop at nothing to protect their legacy.

As they raced through the garden, Evelyn suddenly stopped, her eyes fixed on a hidden alcove. "There," she whispered, her voice trembling. "I left something there that could expose them."

Victor nodded and urged her to keep moving while he investigated the alcove. There, hidden beneath a stone bench, he found a bundle of letters, diaries, and documents—the heiress's evidence. Clutching the trove of secrets, he rejoined Evelyn.

## Chapter 4: Hidden Allegiances

Evelyn Winslow and Detective Victor Sterling moved in the shadows, their every footfall muffled by the lush, moonlit gardens. The heiress's revelations had set in motion a desperate chase to expose the secrets hidden within the Winslow family, secrets that threatened to consume all in their path. As they hurried through the winding pathways, they were driven by a singular purpose: to reveal the truth.

In their pursuit, Evelyn led Victor to a secluded garden pavilion adorned with climbing roses, its architecture reminiscent of a forgotten time. The moon cast an eerie glow on the arched entrance, creating an almost ethereal atmosphere. It was here that Evelyn had hidden a significant piece of evidence that could expose the Winslow family's dark past.

Evelyn carefully pulled aside a curtain of rose vines and revealed a hidden compartment within the pavilion's stone structure. Inside lay a collection of aged journals and letters, their pages yellowed with time, written by ancestors long gone. The documents bore witness to a history of deceit, betrayal, and intrigue.

"Evelyn," Victor whispered, studying the documents, "This is an extraordinary find. These papers may hold the key to unraveling the family's secrets."

Evelyn nodded, her eyes reflecting a mixture of fear, determination, and sorrow. "I've known about these secrets for a long time, but I've never had the proof to expose them. My family has done terrible things, Detective Sterling, and it's time the truth came to light."

The heiress's voice trembled as she revealed her family's complicity in a web of lies and corruption. Victor's respect for her grew with each confession, as he understood the enormity of the burden she had carried. "We will ensure that these documents are protected and used to bring justice, Evelyn," he assured her.

Their moment of resolution was cut short by the sound of approaching footsteps. The darkness of the garden seemed to close in, and Evelyn's eyes widened in panic. Her family was closing in on them, and the threat of capture loomed larger with each passing second.

"We must leave, Evelyn," Victor urged. "We can't let them find us here."

Together, they gathered the documents and retreated deeper into the garden, seeking a place of refuge. Evelyn led Victor to a concealed passage that twisted beneath the mansion, hidden from the prying eyes of her family. The passage was dimly lit, with narrow stone walls that carried with them the whispers of history.

As they hurried through the labyrinthine tunnel, Evelyn's voice trembled as she recounted more of her family's secrets. "The Winslows have always been a powerful and influential clan, but that influence has been built on the suffering of others. Their fortune is steeped in dark deeds, from manipulations of the stock market to unsolved mysteries that have plagued our name for generations."

The heiress's revelations were like pieces of a puzzle, slowly coming together to form a chilling picture of a family that would stop at nothing to maintain their wealth and standing. Victor couldn't help but feel the weight of responsibility as he realized the enormity of the task ahead.

The passage led them to a hidden chamber deep beneath the mansion, filled with forgotten relics of the past. Evelyn explained that it was a place of refuge where she would often escape to reflect on her family's actions. It was here that she had hidden the most damning evidence—the final pieces of the puzzle.

Among the artifacts, Evelyn retrieved a series of intricate paintings, each a cryptic representation of long-buried crimes and betrayals. She explained that her family had maintained these symbolic representations as a secret code, only known to a select few. Evelyn had decoded the paintings, revealing the dark secrets they held.

"Look, Detective Sterling," she implored, her voice heavy with the weight of knowledge. "These paintings hold the answers, the truths that will finally expose the Winslow family's malevolence."

Victor examined the paintings, deciphering the hidden meanings within each brushstroke and intricate design. They revealed a network of connections, a tapestry of corruption that extended into the highest echelons of society. These discoveries had the power to dismantle the Winslow legacy and bring about the justice Evelyn sought.

Their moment of triumph, however, was interrupted by the muffled sounds of voices above them. The family was searching for them, growing closer with each passing minute. Victor and Evelyn knew that time was running out, and the path they had chosen was fraught with danger.

"We need to leave this place," Victor said, determination etched on his face. "We can use the evidence you've gathered to confront your family and expose their secrets. But for now, our priority is to ensure your safety."

Evelyn nodded in agreement, and together they made their way back to the hidden passage, their hearts heavy with the knowledge that their actions had set in motion a dangerous confrontation with the Winslow family. As they retraced their steps through the dimly lit tunnels, they were acutely aware that their pursuit of justice had placed them on a treacherous path, where hidden allegiances and buried grudges would come to light.

## Chapter 5: Family of Shadows

Evelyn Winslow and Detective Victor Sterling had managed to evade her family's pursuit, finding temporary refuge in the labyrinthine passages beneath the family mansion. The heiress had entrusted Victor with a trove of damning evidence, documents and decoded paintings that revealed the dark secrets that the Winslow family had guarded for generations. Now, with the weight of those secrets upon them, they had to decide their next course of action.

In the dimly lit underground chamber, the two of them huddled around a flickering candle, casting eerie shadows on the stone walls. Evelyn's eyes were filled with a mix of fear, determination, and a touch of desperation. "We can't stay here, Detective Sterling. My family won't stop searching for us."

Victor nodded, his mind racing to formulate a plan. The revelations they held had the potential to expose the family's corrupt dealings, but the Winslow family's influence was far-reaching. Their every move needed to be careful and calculated. "We need to find a safe place to go, somewhere your family won't anticipate. I have contacts who can help protect you."

Evelyn hesitated, glancing at the evidence they had collected. "But what about the truth? We can't simply hide and hope the secrets will disappear. The world needs to know what my family has done."

Victor understood her concern, the desire to bring justice and transparency to the forefront. "You're right, Evelyn, but we need to tread carefully. Exposing the truth will require a well-thought-out plan, and your safety is our top priority. Let me reach out to my contacts, and we'll decide on our next steps."

Evelyn nodded in agreement, and Victor proceeded to make discreet arrangements, reaching out to allies who could ensure her safety while keeping her whereabouts a closely guarded secret. The heiress, meanwhile, examined the decoded paintings once more, her fingers tracing the hidden symbols that held the key to unraveling her family's secrets.

Hours later, in a safe and undisclosed location, Evelyn and Victor reconvened to discuss their strategy. The evidence they had gathered was damning, but they needed additional support to expose the Winslow family's crimes. Victor had called in a favor from a trusted journalist, Laura Hastings, known for her dedication to uncovering the truth.

Laura arrived with a determination to help expose the corruption within the Winslow family. "I've read through the evidence you provided, Evelyn. It's compelling, but we'll need more to build a case. We should start by interviewing potential witnesses, people who may have been affected by the Winslow family's actions."

Evelyn agreed, her resolve growing stronger with each passing moment. "There are individuals who have suffered at the hands of my family, their lives ruined by the Winslow's greed. We must seek them out and gather their testimonies."

As they laid out their plan, they were unaware that their actions had not gone unnoticed. A shadowy figure loomed in the background, watching from the darkness. The family's secrets were their legacy, their power, and they would go to great lengths to protect them.

Over the following weeks, Evelyn, Victor, and Laura embarked on a journey to unearth the truth, reaching out to those who had crossed paths with the Winslow family. Their inquiries led them to individuals who had been financially ruined, businesses that had been manipulated, and once-promising careers that had been destroyed by the Winslows' insatiable ambition.

One such encounter was with Edward Henderson, a former business partner of the Winslow family who had suffered significant losses when their underhanded dealings had left him bankrupt. As he recounted his experiences, the trio could sense the anger and determination in his voice. "I've been waiting for a chance to expose the Winslow family for what they are. They've controlled my life for far too long."

Evelyn, Victor, and Laura began to collect statements and evidence from people like Edward, building a strong case against the Winslow family. But their actions were not without consequences. As they delved deeper into their investigation, their pursuit of truth brought them face to face with adversaries who were willing to go to any lengths to protect the family's secrets.

One evening, as Evelyn, Victor, and Laura huddled around a table, reviewing the growing body of evidence, a sudden crash echoed through the room. The door burst open, and a group of imposing figures clad in black suits stormed in.

Evelyn's heart raced as she recognized her family's security personnel. The situation had escalated beyond her worst fears. The lead figure, a man with cold, unyielding eyes, spoke in a chilling tone. "You've gone too far, Evelyn. The Winslow legacy will not be tarnished by your actions."

Victor acted quickly, positioning himself between the heiress and the menacing intruders. "You won't intimidate us. We have evidence that will expose your family's crimes," he declared, his voice unwavering.

The standoff was tense, and it was clear that the confrontation had reached a critical juncture. The choices made in that moment would determine the fate of Evelyn, Victor, and the secrets that had haunted the Winslow family for generations.

## Chapter 6: A Family Divided

The room crackled with tension as Evelyn Winslow, Detective Victor Sterling, and the imposing security personnel of the Winslow family faced off in a standoff that threatened to erupt into violence. The confrontation had reached a critical juncture, and the choices made in that moment would determine the fate of all those involved.

Victor Sterling's voice was resolute as he stood his ground, his gaze unwavering on the intruders. "We have evidence that will expose your family's crimes. We won't back down."

Evelyn, her heart racing, took a step forward, her voice steady despite her fear. "I won't let you protect the lies and corruption any longer. These crimes must be brought to light."

The head of the security team, a tall, imposing figure with an air of authority, raised an eyebrow, his tone dripping with menace. "Do you truly believe you can challenge the Winslow family, Miss Winslow?"

It was then that Laura Hastings, the determined journalist who had joined their cause, stepped forward, her eyes blazing with conviction. "The truth has a way of finding its way to the surface. We're here to ensure that it does."

The standoff continued, the room filled with a thick, palpable silence. The Winslow security personnel were relentless, their loyalty to the family unwavering. Evelyn, Victor, and Laura knew that they had to act swiftly to maintain the upper hand. They couldn't afford to let the evidence they had gathered fall into the wrong hands.

The security personnel were about to make a move when an unexpected voice echoed from the doorway. "That's enough."

All heads turned to find Sir Reginald Winslow, Evelyn's father, standing in the entrance. He had an air of authority, his features etched with a mixture of anger and concern. "Stand down, gentlemen."

The security team reluctantly obeyed, stepping back from the confrontation. Sir Reginald had always been the patriarch of the Winslow family, and his word was law.

Evelyn's eyes were filled with disbelief. She had expected her family to fight against the exposure of their secrets, but she hadn't anticipated her father intervening on their behalf.

Sir Reginald turned to Evelyn, his voice strained. "Evelyn, we need to talk."

In the tense silence that followed, Evelyn, Victor, and Laura followed Sir Reginald Winslow to a more private area of the mansion, a dimly lit library adorned with centuries-old books and antique furnishings.

Evelyn's father began, his tone a mix of urgency and despair. "You don't understand, Evelyn. The path you're on will lead to our family's destruction. You've unearthed secrets that are best left buried."

Evelyn remained resolute. "The truth must come to light, Father. The suffering that our family has caused—it's too much to bear."

Sir Reginald's face contorted with emotions that he couldn't quite mask. "You don't know the whole story, Evelyn. There are reasons for the actions we've taken, reasons that you cannot comprehend."

Evelyn's eyes glistened with unshed tears as she confronted her father. "I want to understand, Father. I need to know the truth, all of it."

Sir Reginald hesitated, torn between the loyalty to his family and the desire to protect his daughter. Finally, he spoke in hushed tones, revealing secrets that had been hidden for generations.

"The Winslow family was built on a foundation of manipulation and deception," he confessed. "But it was never about greed or ambition. It was about survival. The crimes we committed were born of necessity, not desire."

Evelyn, Victor, and Laura listened with rapt attention as Sir Reginald unraveled the intricate history of the Winslow family. He spoke of a past that had been plagued by a powerful adversary, one who had sought to destroy their family's legacy. To protect their name and fortune, they had engaged in shadowy dealings, leaving a trail of victims in their wake.

The revelation left them with a sense of unease, as the lines between right and wrong blurred in the face of a compelling family history. Evelyn realized that her quest for truth had taken an unexpected turn, leading to a family divided by secrets and survival.

As the night wore on, Evelyn, Victor, and Laura grappled with the weight of the revelations. They were no longer certain of their mission. The Winslow family's actions were no longer as clear-cut as they had seemed, and the choices ahead were fraught with complexity.

But even as they pondered their next steps, they couldn't ignore the lingering threats that surrounded them. The shadowy figure who had watched them before had not been vanquished. The family's secrets were still a target, and their determination to protect them had not waned.

## Chapter 7: The Unseen Adversary

The revelation of the Winslow family's past, a history tainted by a powerful adversary, had left Evelyn Winslow, Detective Victor Sterling, and journalist Laura Hastings in a state of disarray. The secrets that had driven their mission for justice had taken an unexpected turn, blurring the lines between right and wrong. But even as they grappled with the newfound complexities of their quest, they couldn't ignore the shadowy adversary that continued to lurk in the background.

Evelyn, her face etched with uncertainty, questioned her father, Sir Reginald Winslow, who had just unveiled the family's dark history. "Who is this adversary you speak of, Father? Why have we never known about them before?"

Sir Reginald, his gaze heavy with sorrow, chose his words carefully. "They are a force that has sought to destroy the Winslow family for generations, a power that we had to contend with in the shadows. We kept our struggles hidden to protect the family name."

The heiress's mind whirred with questions. "But what is their motive? Why do they want to destroy us?"

Sir Reginald's eyes held a mix of anger and fear. "It's a vendetta that has endured for centuries, one that traces back to a conflict our ancestors were involved in. The Winslow family has been marked as a target, and we've had to resort to desperate measures to protect our legacy."

Evelyn's determination was undiminished. "I need to know more, Father. I need to understand the full extent of our family's history."

Sir Reginald nodded and continued to divulge the details of the adversary's actions and the strategies the Winslow family had employed to protect themselves. He spoke of elaborate deceptions, manipulations, and alliances formed in the dark corners of society.

As Evelyn, Victor, and Laura listened, they realized that the family's secrets had not only concealed a history of deceit but had also formed the foundation of their survival. Their quest for justice had become far more intricate and multifaceted than they had ever anticipated.

The lingering threat of the unseen adversary had not dissipated, and the revelation of the Winslow family's history had only heightened the tension in the room. Their actions had not gone unnoticed, and their determination to expose the truth had provoked a response.

A sudden commotion echoed through the mansion, and the room was thrown into disarray as Evelyn, Victor, and Laura rushed to the window. A series of vehicles had pulled up to the mansion, and a swarm of suited figures emerged. The security personnel of the Winslow family had returned, and this time they were reinforced.

Victor's voice was urgent as he turned to Sir Reginald. "You need to tell them to stand down. We have to find a peaceful resolution to this."

Sir Reginald nodded, recognizing the gravity of the situation. He approached the security team, his words a mix of command and plea. "You must understand that we cannot continue on this path of violence. There's too much at stake."

But the security personnel remained unwavering in their loyalty to the family, and their response was to surround Evelyn, Victor, and Laura, their expressions cold and menacing.

As tensions mounted, Evelyn felt her heart pounding in her chest. The room seemed to close in around them, and the walls of the mansion felt like a cage. The unseen adversary, the shadowy figure who had watched from the shadows before, was inching closer, their motives and identity shrouded in mystery.

With the security personnel closing in, the room was thick with tension. Evelyn, Victor, and Laura knew they were at a critical juncture, their choices now carrying the weight of the family's secrets and the looming adversary.

But it was a sudden, unexpected noise that shattered the moment. A loud, echoing crash came from the entrance, followed by the sound of shattering glass. As they turned to face the source of the commotion, the room was thrown into chaos.

Through the broken windows, an unexpected savior had arrived. It was a mysterious figure, their identity concealed by a mask, their motives unknown. They had breached the mansion's defenses, and they were determined to intervene.

Evelyn, Victor, and Laura watched in shock as the newcomer's actions set off a domino effect of confusion and chaos. The security personnel scrambled to react, while the mysterious figure advanced, moving with grace and purpose.

In the midst of the turmoil, the masked savior approached Evelyn, Victor, and Laura, their voice a low, determined whisper.

"Come with me if you want to survive. There's no time to explain."

The choice before them was stark—stay and face the security personnel of the Winslow family, or follow the mysterious figure into the unknown. The reader was left on the precipice of suspense, eager to see how their decisions would unravel the intricacies of the family's secrets, the unseen adversary's presence, and the unexpected savior who had emerged from the shadows.

## Chapter 8: The Enigmatic Savior

In the midst of chaos and confusion, the masked figure who had burst through the shattered windows led Evelyn Winslow, Detective Victor Sterling, and journalist Laura Hastings into a maze of hidden passages and secret tunnels beneath the sprawling Winslow mansion. The intruders sent by the family were momentarily disoriented by the unexpected intervention, giving the trio a fleeting advantage.

Their enigmatic savior moved with a quiet and calculated purpose, leading them through a labyrinth of dimly lit corridors, stone walls, and secret chambers. There was an air of familiarity in their every step, as though they had traversed this clandestine network many times before.

Evelyn's heart raced as they fled through the underground labyrinth, her mind whirling with questions. "Who are you? Why are you helping us?"

The masked figure didn't pause, their voice a low, modulated whisper. "There's no time for explanations. We need to keep moving. Your lives are in danger."

The urgency of the situation pressed upon them, and they had no choice but to follow their mysterious savior. The winding tunnels led them to a hidden chamber adorned with ancient maps, documents, and an array of cryptic symbols. It was a clandestine sanctuary that had been hidden from the prying eyes of the Winslow family.

Evelyn, Victor, and Laura gathered around a massive oak table at the center of the chamber, each of them aware of the gravity of the situation. The truth they had sought was now entwined with the pursuit of an adversary whose motives remained shrouded in mystery.

The masked figure finally turned to face them, their mask concealing their identity. "The adversary you've uncovered is a formidable force, one that has pursued the Winslow family for generations. They are relentless, and they will stop at nothing to achieve their goals."

Laura, her eyes filled with determination, sought answers. "Who are they, and why do they want to destroy the Winslow family?"

The masked figure hesitated for a moment, as though considering how much to reveal. "The adversary's origins trace back to a conflict that took place centuries ago. It was a dispute over power, wealth, and a cursed artifact that has haunted our family for generations."

Evelyn's eyes widened with realization. "The artifact, the Mask of Shadows? It's at the heart of this conflict, isn't it?"

The figure nodded. "The Mask is the key to the adversary's power and their desire to eradicate the Winslow family. It carries with it a curse that has shaped our family's history."

Victor Sterling, always focused on the practicalities of their mission, interjected. "How do we confront this adversary? What's our next step?"

The masked figure leaned in, their voice resolute. "We must find the Mask of Shadows and destroy it. It is the only way to sever the adversary's connection to our family and put an end to this cycle of destruction."

But Evelyn was torn. "The Mask holds immense power, and my family has guarded it for generations. Destroying it may come at great cost."

The masked figure, their gaze steady, spoke with conviction. "The Mask's power has wrought too much suffering. It's time to break the curse, once and for all."

Determined to bring the truth to light and to protect her family's legacy, Evelyn reluctantly agreed. "We'll find the Mask and destroy it, but we must be prepared for the adversary's relentless pursuit."

Their savior nodded in agreement and produced a map, revealing a series of cryptic symbols and hidden locations that would lead them to the Mask of Shadows. The quest they were about to embark on was fraught with danger, and they were entering a world filled with treacherous secrets and ancient rivalries.

As they left the underground chamber and began their journey, Evelyn, Victor, and Laura couldn't shake the sense that their path was inextricably linked to a history that had been kept hidden for far too long. The adversary they were up against was powerful, cunning, and relentless, and their every move was fraught with danger.

Their quest would take them to ancient ruins, hidden libraries, and through a maze of cryptic riddles. Along the way, they would encounter a network of secret societies, each with its own motives and allegiances. The journey would test their resolve, their intelligence, and their ability to navigate a world of shadows and enigmas.

But there was one question that remained unanswered, one that weighed heavily on their minds: Who was the masked figure that had come to their aid, and what secrets did they hold?

## Chapter 9: The Labyrinth of Secrets

Evelyn Winslow, Detective Victor Sterling, and journalist Laura Hastings embarked on their treacherous quest to find and destroy the Mask of Shadows, the artifact at the heart of a centuries-old curse that had haunted the Winslow family. Their enigmatic savior, the masked figure, had led them to a world of shadows, secrets, and hidden alliances. The path they walked was laden with riddles, and danger lurked at every turn.

Their first destination was the ancient ruins of an estate, long abandoned and cloaked in a shroud of mystery. The ruins were overgrown with ivy, and the architecture held an air of foreboding. It was here that they believed they would find the first clue to the Mask's whereabouts.

As they explored the ruins, deciphering cryptic symbols and examining long-forgotten inscriptions, they stumbled upon a hidden chamber beneath the estate. The chamber was adorned with ancient symbols and held a mosaic of a masked figure. It was a chilling reminder of the adversary's connection to the Mask of Shadows.

Evelyn, her heart heavy with the weight of her family's history, examined the mosaic. "This is a clue, a sign that we're on the right path. But we must be careful; the adversary's influence is strong here."

Their savior, who had accompanied them on their journey, urged caution. "The adversary's presence is never far. We must proceed with care and precision."

As they examined the mosaic further, they discovered a hidden compartment that revealed a set of scrolls and a map, each filled with riddles and clues that would guide them on their quest. It was a cryptic puzzle, and they knew that time was of the essence.

Their first clue led them to a hidden library in an old, forgotten town, a place where rare and ancient texts were rumored to be stored. The journey took them through desolate landscapes, their surroundings echoing with an eerie stillness. The anticipation of what lay ahead weighed heavily on their minds.

The library was a dimly lit sanctuary filled with dusty tomes and forgotten knowledge. It was a place of quiet reverence, and the masks of shadow that adorned the walls served as a stark reminder of the Mask's enduring presence.

Evelyn, Victor, and Laura combed through the ancient texts, deciphering coded messages and piecing together the riddles. The Mask's curse, its history, and the extent of the adversary's power slowly began to unravel. It was a legacy that had lasted for generations, one that had been hidden from the world's eyes.

Their journey to uncover the Mask of Shadows led them to a hidden passage beneath the library, a labyrinthine network of tunnels that stretched deep into the earth. The passage was a maze of secrets, its walls adorned with inscriptions that revealed the steps to break the curse and expose the adversary.

As they delved deeper into the labyrinth, they encountered trials that tested their wits, their courage, and their unity. They faced puzzles that required intellect, and challenges that demanded bravery. At each juncture, they uncovered a piece of the Mask's history, the adversary's motives, and the extent of the curse that had bound the Winslow family for centuries.

Their journey was fraught with danger, and the presence of the adversary was an ever-lingering threat. The enigmatic savior was with them every step of the way, their guidance invaluable as they navigated the treacherous passages and deciphered the riddles.

As they ventured deeper into the labyrinth, their understanding of the adversary grew, and the burden of the Winslow family's history became increasingly apparent. The Mask of Shadows was not merely an object of power; it was a symbol of a conflict that had endured for generations, a battle between two forces that had remained concealed from the world.

But the labyrinth of secrets held more than knowledge and revelations. It held danger, and their pursuit of the Mask was not without consequences. As they reached the heart of the labyrinth, they discovered that they were not alone. The adversary had anticipated their arrival, and they had set a trap.

Evelyn, Victor, Laura, and their enigmatic savior found themselves surrounded by a group of figures, each wearing a mask of shadows. Their eyes were filled with an otherworldly malevolence, and their intentions were clear. They would stop at nothing to protect the Mask and to thwart the intruders.

## Chapter 10: Shadows Unveiled

In the heart of the labyrinth beneath the hidden library, Evelyn Winslow, Detective Victor Sterling, journalist Laura Hastings, and their enigmatic savior found themselves surrounded by figures cloaked in masks of shadows. The tension was palpable, and the air seemed to vibrate with an eerie malevolence. The adversaries were determined to protect the Mask of Shadows and maintain their dark legacy.

The leader of the masked figures, their voice laced with a haunting echo, addressed Evelyn, Victor, and their companions. "You tread on sacred ground, intruders. The Mask of Shadows belongs to us, and we will not allow you to disrupt the balance."

Evelyn, her eyes unwavering, met the leader's gaze. "The Mask carries a curse that has haunted my family for generations. We must destroy it to end the suffering."

The leader's response was a chilling laugh that sent shivers down their spines. "The curse of the Mask is not to be broken so easily. It is our source of power, and we will protect it at any cost."

As tensions mounted, the adversaries advanced, moving with an eerie grace that seemed almost supernatural. The confrontation was swift and brutal, a clash of wills, wits, and physical strength.

Victor Sterling, never one to back down from a challenge, engaged in a physical duel with one of the masked figures. Their movements were swift and precise, and it was clear that they were highly skilled in combat. Each blow and parry carried an otherworldly force, and the odds were stacked against Victor.

Laura Hastings, a voice for truth and justice, found herself in a battle of wits with another adversary, their exchange of words as dangerous as any physical confrontation. The masked figure sought to manipulate and deceive, their words laden with enigmatic riddles and half-truths. Laura's task was to navigate the treacherous verbal labyrinth and uncover the adversary's motives.

Evelyn, compelled to protect her family's legacy and the memory of her ancestors, confronted the leader of the adversaries. It was a battle of wills, a clash of determination and conviction. She needed to understand the Mask's history and the adversary's motives, and to do so, she had to delve into the heart of the enigma.

The enigmatic savior, whose true identity remained concealed behind their mask, played a pivotal role in the confrontation.

Their movements were agile and precise, their strategy a blend of physical prowess and strategic thinking. It was clear that they were an indispensable ally in the face of this formidable adversary.

The confrontation raged on, each battle revealing new layers of complexity and intrigue. The labyrinth was a crucible of knowledge, power, and danger, and the stakes were higher than ever.

As the adversaries were momentarily pushed back, Victor Sterling, with the aid of their enigmatic savior, discovered a hidden passage within the labyrinth. It was a door of shadows, concealed from the adversary's prying eyes. The passage led to a chamber filled with ancient relics, tomes, and a statue of a figure in a mask.

Evelyn's heart raced as she examined the chamber's contents. "This is it. The Mask of Shadows is here."

But the adversaries were not far behind, and the battle raged on. Their determination to protect the Mask had grown even stronger, and the confrontation was on the brink of becoming a dire battle of wills.

As Evelyn, Victor, Laura, and their enigmatic savior prepared to make their move, they couldn't ignore the sense that the labyrinth of secrets held more than knowledge and power. It held a connection to a history that had remained hidden for far too long, a legacy of shadows, and a curse that had haunted their family for generations.

The Mask of Shadows, a symbol of the adversary's power, was within their grasp, and the final battle to destroy it was imminent. But the adversary's true motives and the enigmatic savior's identity remained enshrouded in mystery.

## Chapter 11: The Unmasking

In the shadowy chamber deep within the labyrinth, the battle raged on as Evelyn Winslow, Detective Victor Sterling, journalist Laura Hastings, and their enigmatic savior fought to protect the Mask of Shadows. The adversaries were unyielding in their determination to safeguard the source of their power, and the confrontation had reached a critical juncture.

Evelyn, her heart pounding with the weight of her family's history, stood before the Mask of Shadows. It was an ornate, eerie artifact, its dark visage haunting and enigmatic. She had one goal in mind: to destroy it, to end the curse that had plagued her family for generations.

But the adversaries had other plans. The leader of the masked figures, their presence shrouded in a malevolent aura, approached Evelyn with a warning. "You underestimate the power of the Mask, Miss Winslow. To destroy it would come at a great cost."

Evelyn remained resolute. "The suffering that my family has endured must end. I am willing to pay that price."

Victor Sterling, who had fought valiantly to protect their group, joined Evelyn's side. He had seen the lengths the adversaries would go to maintain their power, and he was ready to confront them head-on. "We have come too far to turn back now. The Mask must be destroyed."

The adversaries advanced, their attacks relentless and otherworldly. Each blow carried an unnatural force, and the adversaries moved with an eerie grace that defied human capabilities. It was a battle of wills, and the outcome remained uncertain.

Laura Hastings, whose determination to uncover the truth had guided their journey, continued her verbal battle with an adversary who sought to manipulate her with riddles and half-truths. Her mind was a formidable weapon, and she refused to be swayed by the adversary's cryptic words.

The enigmatic savior, their true identity still concealed behind the mask, proved to be an invaluable asset. Their agility and precision allowed them to thwart the adversaries' advances, and their strategic thinking guided the group through the treacherous confrontation.

As the battle raged on, Evelyn and Victor managed to create an opening to reach the Mask of Shadows. It was a pivotal moment, one that would determine the fate of their quest and the future of the Winslow family.

Evelyn reached out to grasp the Mask, her hand trembling with a mixture of determination and fear. As her fingers made contact, a surge of energy coursed through her, and the Mask seemed to react to her touch. The adversaries let out a collective cry, their masks emanating an eerie, otherworldly glow.

In that moment, time seemed to stand still. Evelyn felt as though she had stepped into a different realm, a place where shadows and secrets held sway. The curse that had bound her family for generations felt tangible, an oppressive force that threatened to consume her.

But Victor, ever vigilant, stood by her side, ready to protect her from the adversaries and the power of the Mask. He called upon their enigmatic savior for support, their unity becoming their greatest strength.

Laura, in her unwavering pursuit of the truth, seized the opportunity to confront the leader of the adversaries once more. She sought answers, to understand the motives behind the curse and the adversary's relentless pursuit of the Winslow family.

The leader's voice was laced with an enigmatic, haunting echo. "The Mask of Shadows is a source of power that transcends time and space. It is a vessel of our existence, and it is our only connection to the world beyond."

As the confrontation unfolded, the adversaries' true motives began to unravel. They were a group bound by a curse of their own, one that had kept them tethered to the Mask for centuries. The curse was a double-edged sword, and it had driven their relentless pursuit of power and the Winslow family.

Evelyn, her determination unwavering, drew upon the strength of her ancestors, calling upon the legacy of her family. She felt a surge of power within her, a force that pushed back against the curse and the adversaries.

Victor, ever the protector, shielded Evelyn from the adversaries' attacks, his unwavering loyalty to her and their mission evident in his every move.

Laura, who had uncovered the truth throughout their journey, sought a resolution. "We must find a way to break the curse, to free both our families from this relentless cycle of destruction."

As the confrontation reached its climax, a blinding light emanated from the Mask of Shadows, and a forceful surge of energy filled the chamber. The adversaries let out an otherworldly cry, their masks shattering into pieces.

In that moment, the curse that had bound the Winslow family for generations was broken, and the adversaries' connection to the Mask was severed. The chamber seemed to shift, and the enigmatic savior's presence faded into the shadows.

Evelyn, Victor, and Laura were left standing before the now inert Mask of Shadows. The adversaries had been vanquished, their malevolent presence no longer a threat.

But as the dust settled and the echoes of the confrontation faded, a new challenge emerged. The Mask of Shadows, though no longer a source of power, held a secret that would reshape their understanding of their family's history.

Evelyn, her voice steady but filled with anticipation, spoke. "We must unmask the truth, to reveal the secret that the Mask holds."

## Chapter 12: The Unveiling of Truth

The moment had come to unmask the dark secret concealed within the Mask of Shadows. Evelyn Winslow, Detective Victor Sterling, and journalist Laura Hastings stood before the eerie artifact that had haunted their family for generations. With cautious determination, they reached for the mask, their fingers trembling with a mix of anticipation and trepidation.

As the mask was carefully lifted, it revealed an inner chamber adorned with a series of intricate carvings and symbols. The chamber held a hidden compartment, and within it lay a stack of ancient documents, parchments yellowed with age and adorned with cryptic writings.

Evelyn's eyes scanned the documents, her heart pounding with anticipation. It was as if the answers to a lifetime of mysteries lay within those ancient pages. She carefully selected one of the parchments and began to decipher the cryptic text.

The words revealed a shocking truth, one that would forever reshape the Winslow family's history. The curse, the Mask of Shadows, the adversary—they were all pieces of a puzzle that had been lost to time.

As she read aloud, her voice trembled with a mixture of disbelief and understanding. "The Winslow family's legacy is not one of malevolence but of sacrifice. Generations ago, our ancestors made a solemn vow to protect the Mask of Shadows, a powerful artifact that could be harnessed for great good or great evil. They took on the burden of the curse to ensure that it would not fall into the wrong hands."

Victor, who had been fiercely protective of Evelyn and her family, listened with a sense of realization. "The curse was a self-imposed burden, a means to safeguard the Mask and protect it from those who sought to misuse its power."

Laura, the relentless seeker of truth, nodded in agreement. "The adversary was a faction within the family that had lost sight of the original purpose. They had become consumed by the Mask's power and had forgotten the vow that had been made."

As the truth continued to unfold, it became clear that the curse had been a testament to the Winslow family's dedication to a cause greater than themselves. The sacrifice they had made had ensured that the Mask of Shadows remained hidden from the world, its true nature concealed.

The revelation left them with a profound sense of awe and a newfound respect for their ancestors' sacrifice. The centuries-old curse had not been a malevolent force but a guardian, a barrier that protected the world from the Mask's potential for great destruction.

Evelyn, her voice filled with reverence, spoke to her companions. "We have uncovered the truth, but we must ensure that the world knows of our family's sacrifice and the curse that has bound us."

The trio, united by their mission for justice and the unmasking of their family's history, understood that their journey was not yet complete. They needed to bring the truth to light, to reveal the sacrifice of the Winslow family, and to expose the adversary's misguided actions.

Their enigmatic savior, who had faded into the shadows during the confrontation, reemerged. They had been a guardian, a guide, and a source of strength throughout their journey.

The savior, their voice low and measured, addressed the group. "The truth has been unveiled, and the curse has been broken. It is time to bring the story to the world and ensure that the sacrifice of the Winslow family is recognized."

With the ancient documents and the Mask of Shadows in hand, they left the labyrinth and returned to the world above. It was a world that had remained ignorant of the family's history, a history that had been concealed by shadows and secrecy for far too long.

Their journey was far from over, but the revelations they had uncovered would serve as a foundation for the truth to emerge. The sacrifice of the Winslow family, the adversary's misguided actions, and the power of the Mask of Shadows would be revealed to the world.

The story of the Winslow family, once shrouded in mystery and darkness, would come to a close, and a new chapter would begin—one of recognition, redemption, and a legacy of sacrifice.

As they made their way back to the world above, they knew that their journey was not over, but the burden of the curse had been lifted, and the truth would now shine brightly for all to see. The Mask of Shadows, once a symbol of darkness, had become a beacon of enlightenment and understanding.

And with the weight of history and secrecy lifted from their shoulders, the Winslow family would finally find the resolution and closure they had sought for generations. Their legacy would be one of sacrifice, protection, and a commitment to safeguarding the world from the shadows of the past.

THE END

# City of Secrets

## Chapter 1: The Smoke-Filled Club

The night was drenched in a torrential downpour, washing the grimy streets of the city clean for a brief moment, only to leave them dirtier when the rain ended. As I stood in the entrance of the club, I couldn't help but think that this city had been corrupted long before the rain began to fall. The neon lights of "The Blue Note" flickered, casting an eerie, sapphire glow on the puddles that lay like liquid mirrors on the pavement. It was a jazz club, one of the last holdouts from the golden age of swing, and it was my destination on that rainy, unforgiving night.

Inside, the air was thick with the heady scent of cigar smoke, and the sultry notes of a saxophone danced through the room. The dimly lit space was packed with people, some lost in their own worlds, while others clung to their drinks like life preservers in a sea of melancholy. The crowd was as eclectic as the city itself – gangsters, artists, and dreamers, all searching for solace in the haunting melodies of the jazz band on stage.

I found a secluded spot at the bar, ordered a bourbon neat, and let my eyes scan the room. My name is Jack Malone, and I'm a private investigator, a grizzled loner in a city that thrives on secrets. I've been hired to find a missing jazz musician named Tommy "Satchmo" Davis. He was a regular here, a trumpet player whose soulful tunes had the power to make the angels weep. But for the past two weeks, he hadn't shown up for his nightly gig, and that had everyone in the club worried.

I couldn't help but notice the nervous glances exchanged by the club's regulars, the hushed conversations that stopped when I entered. Tommy Davis had a reputation for being a charmer, but also for getting mixed up with the wrong crowd. Word was, he owed a substantial debt to a dangerous gangster known as Marco "The Razor" Moretti.

My bourbon arrived, and I took a slow sip, savoring the warmth that coursed through me. Just as I was about to ask the bartender if he'd seen Tommy, a hand landed on my shoulder. I turned to see a tall, striking woman with raven-black hair cascading down her back. Her eyes, the color of emeralds, held a hint of desperation.

"You're Jack Malone, the private investigator, right?" she asked, her voice trembling.

I nodded, my curiosity piqued. "That's me. What can I do for you, sweetheart?"

She introduced herself as Lily St. Claire, a singer at the club. She'd been close to Tommy, and she knew he was in deep trouble. She lowered her voice, her eyes darting around the room.

"Tommy was mixed up with Moretti, the gangster," she whispered. "He owed him a big debt, and that's why he's been missing. Moretti isn't one to forgive and forget, Mr. Malone. He's dangerous."

I leaned in closer, captivated by her story. "Do you have any idea where Tommy might be? Or why he disappeared?"

Lily hesitated for a moment, then slipped an envelope from her purse, pushing it into my hands. "This is all I have," she said. "It's a letter he left behind. He was frantic, mentioned something about 'the blue notes' and a hidden melody. I don't understand, but I'm scared for him, Mr. Malone."

I opened the envelope and pulled out a handwritten note. The ink was smudged from tears, and the words were cryptic: "Follow the blue notes, Jack. Find the melody in the shadows."

I pondered those words for a moment. It was like a puzzle, a clue to Tommy's whereabouts. But the meaning eluded me, buried in the labyrinthine alleys of this corrupt city.

Lily's emerald eyes were filled with fear and hope, a dangerous combination in a place like this. "Please, Mr. Malone, find Tommy. I'll do anything to help you."

I tucked the letter into my coat pocket, assuring her I would do my best. A plan began to form in my mind, a plan that would lead me deeper into the heart of the city's shadows, where danger and deception lurked in every corner.

As I turned to leave the club, I couldn't shake the feeling that this case would be unlike any other, that it would lead me down a treacherous path of corruption and secrets, a path from which there might be no return.

The rain had stopped, but the storm was just beginning.

Little did I know, the city of shadows held more secrets than even I could fathom.

## Chapter 2: The Blue Note's Deception

The city's heartbeat pulsed with secrets, and I was determined to uncover them. Tommy Davis's cryptic note, "Follow the blue notes, Jack. Find the melody in the shadows," gnawed at my thoughts like a hungry rat. I couldn't afford to waste any time. As I stepped back into the rain-soaked streets, the neon lights reflected in the puddles, creating a distorted, surreal world.

The blue notes, I thought. What did they mean? The Blue Note jazz club was the obvious connection, but it had to be more than that. The rain had cleared, revealing a sliver of moon in the ink-black sky. My footsteps echoed through the desolate streets, my mind racing to decipher Tommy's message.

The first glimmer of understanding hit me like a lightning bolt as I approached a crossroads where a lone streetlamp cast its pale glow. I glanced up and saw a tattered poster clinging to a telephone pole, advertising an upcoming jazz festival. The poster's background was a deep, rich blue, and the notes floating above the musicians' heads were, unmistakably, blue.

The blue notes. I took a mental note of the festival's location and date, hoping it might lead me to Tommy. It was a long shot, but in this city, long shots sometimes paid off.

I returned to my office, a dimly lit, musty space in a run-down building that had seen better days. My desk was cluttered with open case files and empty whiskey bottles, a testament to the many sleepless nights I'd spent wrestling with the city's darkness. I slumped into my creaky chair and unfolded Tommy's letter, studying it once more. There had to be a hidden meaning behind those words.

I picked up my phone, dialed the Blue Note jazz club, and waited. The line crackled before a familiar voice answered, "Blue Note."

"Hey, it's Jack Malone," I said, leaning in. "I'm trying to find Tommy Davis. Can you tell me anything about the night he disappeared?"

There was a pause on the other end, and I could almost sense the unease in the voice of the club's owner, Freddie Russo. "Tommy left the stage after his set, said he needed to meet someone. That was the last anyone saw of him. We're all worried, Jack."

I thanked Freddie and hung up the phone, knowing I needed more information. I grabbed my coat and hat, the brim pulled low to shield me from the prying eyes of the city's watchful shadows, and made my way to the jazz club.

The Blue Note was quieter now, the late-night crowd thinning, and the air still hung heavy with the remnants of cigar smoke. Freddie Russo, a stocky man with a perpetual five o'clock shadow, welcomed me in, and we huddled in a corner to speak discreetly.

"I've been hearing rumors," Freddie admitted, his voice low. "Word on the street is that Tommy owed money to Moretti. He had a gambling problem, and he couldn't seem to shake it."

Moretti's name was a cold shiver down my spine, a powerful reminder of the danger lurking in the city's depths. "Did Tommy mention anything unusual before he disappeared?"

Freddie hesitated. "He was acting paranoid, Jack. Kept looking over his shoulder, like he thought someone was following him. He mentioned 'the blue notes,' but I didn't understand what he meant."

I nodded, the puzzle pieces starting to come together. "Freddie, I need to know if there's anything else you can tell me. Anything that might lead me to Tommy."

He rubbed his temples, deep in thought. "There was a guy, a regular, who was always hanging around the club. He and Tommy seemed close, but Tommy was never too open about him. Called himself 'Smooth Lou.' Maybe he knows something."

With Freddie's information, I left the Blue Note, determined to track down Smooth Lou. I'd seen him around before, a suave, silver-tongued character who was known to dabble in shady dealings. It wouldn't be an easy conversation, but it was a necessary one.

The city's alleys were darker, more menacing as I made my way to Lou's usual haunt, a backroom speakeasy where the underworld met to discuss their business. The moment I stepped in, I knew I was walking into a viper's nest. Lou was seated at a dimly lit table in the corner, surrounded by his loyal sycophants.

"Jack Malone, what brings you here?" Lou purred, sipping a glass of whiskey.

I didn't waste time with pleasantries. "I'm looking for Tommy Davis. He's missing, and I have reason to believe he might be in trouble."

Lou's gaze turned cold, his charming façade dropping like a mask. "Tommy got himself into a mess, Malone. You know Moretti isn't one to mess with."

"Tell me what you know," I demanded, my tone firm.

Lou leaned in closer, his voice barely a whisper. "Tommy had something, something Moretti wanted. A secret, Jack. A secret that could bring the entire city to its knees."

The revelation sent a chill down my spine. Moretti's thirst for power and control was boundless, and Tommy had stumbled upon something that could change everything. The moral and ethical dilemma lay before me: should I pursue the truth, risking my life and the city's, or should I turn a blind eye to the darkness that festered beneath the surface?

But before I could make a decision, the backroom door swung open, and the room plunged into darkness. A gunshot rang out, shattering the silence, and chaos erupted.

As the smoke cleared, I realized that the room had fallen silent. Lou lay lifeless on the floor, a bullet hole in his chest. The message was clear: someone didn't want me digging deeper into Tommy's disappearance.

The city's shadows had just grown darker, and the game had become deadlier. I was caught in a web of corruption and murder, and the only way out was to untangle the truth.

Tommy's secret was the key, and I had to find it before Moretti's henchmen did.

As I reached for my gun, the room's ominous quiet was broken by a chilling voice from the darkness.

"Malone, you should have stayed out of this. The Blue Note's melody will be your requiem."

## Chapter 3: The Melody of Deception

The dimly lit backroom speakeasy remained shrouded in the aftermath of chaos. Lou's lifeless body lay on the floor, a dark pool of blood forming around him. The scent of gunpowder hung heavily in the air. The menacing voice that had spoken moments earlier had retreated into the shadows, leaving a bone-chilling sense of foreboding in its wake.

I kept my hand on my gun, my senses sharpened, scanning the room for any sign of movement. But the darkness remained impenetrable, concealing the identity of the shooter. The city of shadows had a way of revealing its secrets in its own time, and patience was a virtue I'd learned the hard way.

The speakeasy's patrons and Lou's sycophants had scattered like rats fleeing a sinking ship, leaving me alone with the dead man, the unsolved mysteries, and a question burning in my mind. Who had killed Smooth Lou, and why was I still breathing?

I couldn't afford to stay at the scene of the crime. Sirens wailed in the distance, drawing near, signaling the approach of the city's finest. It wouldn't be long before they arrived to investigate, and I had no intention of answering their questions. I slipped out through the back door, disappearing into the labyrinthine alleyways of the city.

As I navigated the rainy, slick streets, a relentless determination coursed through my veins. The cryptic message from Tommy, "the blue notes," had led me down a perilous path of deception and danger. The Blue Note jazz club, Smooth Lou's ominous words, and now Lou's untimely demise – all pieces of a puzzle I was determined to solve.

My office became a sanctuary of silence once again. The rain tapped rhythmically against the windowpane, and the desk lamp cast a warm, golden glow on the cluttered room. The letter from Tommy Davis still held its secrets, and I unfolded it once more, studying the words etched in anguish.

"Follow the blue notes, Jack. Find the melody in the shadows."

The melody in the shadows. I ruminated on those words, their meaning eluding me like an elusive tune. What was the secret Tommy had uncovered, and why had it drawn the attention of Moretti and, quite possibly, whoever had silenced Smooth Lou?

The puzzle was complex, the stakes high, and I needed more information. The city's underbelly was a complex web of deceit, and I had few allies I could trust. One name, however, stood out in my mind – Lily St. Claire, the singer at the Blue Note who had delivered Tommy's letter. She had been close to Tommy and might hold vital information.

I found myself back at the jazz club, the neon lights flickering a haunting, sapphire blue. Lily was performing on stage, her voice laced with melancholy as she sang a soulful jazz ballad. The audience was spellbound, their attention consumed by her ethereal presence.

After her performance, I waited for her in the dimly lit dressing room. She emerged, her emerald eyes carrying the weight of the world. She'd heard about Smooth Lou, and her voice trembled as she spoke.

"Jack, I can't believe he's gone. What's happening in this city?"

I nodded, understanding that fear had gripped the heart of the city's underworld. "Lily, I need your help. I'm determined to find Tommy and uncover the truth about 'the blue notes.' Do you know anything else that might lead me in the right direction?"

She sighed and lowered her gaze. "There's something else, Jack. Tommy was involved with a group of musicians, a secret society of sorts. They would meet in hidden jazz clubs, playing music that was unlike anything I'd ever heard. They called themselves 'The Midnight Maestros.'"

"The Midnight Maestros?" I repeated, intrigued.

Lily nodded. "Yes, Jack. They believed that music held the power to reveal hidden truths, secrets that were buried deep within the city's underbelly. Tommy was obsessed with their mission, and he said that he had found a melody that could change everything. He never told me more, but he was convinced it was dangerous, that it could put us all in danger."

My curiosity deepened, and I knew I had to track down this enigmatic group, the Midnight Maestros. They could hold the key to unraveling the mysteries Tommy had uncovered. The thought of hidden melodies, secret jazz clubs, and a power hidden within the music itself sent shivers down my spine.

As I left the Blue Note, I felt the weight of the city's shadows pressing down on me, a burden that threatened to consume me. The path ahead was treacherous, and I couldn't help but wonder who had killed Smooth Lou and why they had spared me. Were they toying with me, luring me deeper into the web of deception, or did they have their own hidden motives?

The rain had turned the city's streets into a mirror of fractured neon lights, and as I looked into the reflection, I knew that the melody in the shadows was waiting to be unraveled. The Midnight Maestros were my next lead, and they were the key to finding Tommy and the truth that could change the city forever.

As I walked further into the night, the city of shadows whispered its secrets, promising answers and danger in equal measure. I was determined to uncover the melody that held the city's darkest secrets and unravel the mysteries that threatened to consume us all.

## Chapter 4: The Midnight Maestros

The search for the enigmatic Midnight Maestros led me to a labyrinth of dark alleys, concealed entrances, and hidden speakeasies. It was a treacherous journey into the underbelly of the city, where secrets lurked in every shadow, waiting to be uncovered.

The name of one such establishment, "The Velvet Groove," whispered among the city's jazz enthusiasts, became my first lead. It was said to be the meeting place for the Midnight

Maestros, a secret society of musicians whose quest was to unearth the hidden truths buried deep within the city's soul.

The Velvet Groove was located in a dilapidated building at the end of a deserted alley. Its entrance was marked only by a faded neon sign that cast a dim, crimson glow on the rainy streets. I stepped inside and was immediately enveloped in a world of hushed conversations and the hypnotic rhythm of jazz.

The club's interior was a stark contrast to the outside world. Velvet drapes hung from the walls, their rich, deep burgundy absorbing the whispers of secrets shared within. Candlelight cast a warm, inviting aura, and the jazz band played a haunting melody that sent shivers down my spine.

The clientele was a mix of musicians, artists, and those who had an insatiable thirst for the city's mysteries. Their eyes watched as I entered, assessing my presence. I could sense their collective curiosity and wariness.

A tall man with a well-groomed beard and a fedora that cast a shadow over his eyes approached me. "You're not a regular here, friend," he said with a hint of suspicion.

"I'm looking for the Midnight Maestros," I replied, choosing my words carefully.

The man's eyes softened, and he nodded toward a discreet door at the back of the club. "Through there. But be warned, they don't take kindly to outsiders."

I nodded my thanks and made my way to the door, my heart pounding with a mixture of anticipation and apprehension. I had no idea what to expect but was prepared for whatever lay beyond.

The room beyond the door was cloaked in an otherworldly ambiance. A circle of musicians, their instruments poised, sat in the center of the dimly lit space. Their eyes were closed, lost in a trance as they played music that transcended the ordinary. It was as if the notes themselves held the power to unlock hidden truths.

At the center of the circle was a grand piano, and seated at the keys was a woman, her fingers dancing over the ivory with a grace and fervor that defied description. Her presence commanded attention, and I realized she was the leader of the Midnight Maestros.

The music was haunting, ethereal, and it seemed to tell a story, a story of the city's forgotten secrets. The room pulsed with energy, and I was drawn into the melody's spell.

As the music reached its crescendo, the woman opened her eyes, and they locked onto mine. Her gaze was penetrating, as if she could see deep into my soul. She rose from the piano, and the other musicians fell into a reverent silence.

"You're not one of us," she said, her voice like a whisper on the wind.

"I'm looking for Tommy Davis," I replied, breaking the spell of the music. "He was involved with your group, and he's disappeared."

The woman's expression hardened, and the room's atmosphere grew tense. "Tommy was a passionate soul, drawn to the melody of the city's hidden secrets. He uncovered something, something that could change everything. But he's in danger, Mr. Malone, danger that goes beyond our control."

I was on the verge of a breakthrough, and the stakes had never been higher. "Tell me everything you know. Tommy left a cryptic message, 'the blue notes.' What does it mean, and who is after him?"

The woman's eyes flickered with uncertainty, and she seemed to be weighing her words carefully. "The blue notes, Mr. Malone, represent a melody, a melody that holds the power to reveal the city's darkest truths. It's a tune that has been passed down through generations, a forbidden song that could shatter the balance of power in this city."

She leaned in closer, her voice barely audible. "Moretti, the ruthless gangster, he discovered the existence of the blue notes. He believed they could be the key to consolidating his control over the city, and he will stop at nothing to obtain them. Tommy was getting close to uncovering the melody, and that's why he's in danger."

My mind raced as I absorbed the revelation. The city's destiny was tied to a melody, a song that could change everything. But Moretti's greed and power threatened to consume it, and I couldn't let that happen.

"I need to find Tommy," I said, a steely determination in my voice. "I won't let Moretti get his hands on the blue notes. Tell me where to start."

The woman hesitated, then nodded. "I can point you in the right direction, but you must promise me this, Mr. Malone – protect the blue notes, and ensure they are never used for evil. The city's destiny rests in your hands."

I made the promise and left The Velvet Groove with a sense of purpose burning within me. The city's darkest secrets were within reach, and the elusive melody of the blue notes had drawn me deeper into its spell.

As I ventured back into the rainy streets, I couldn't shake the feeling that Moretti was closing in, that the city's shadows were converging to protect their secrets. The melody of deception was playing, and I was determined to play it to the end, no matter the cost.

But little did I know, the city's shadows held one final secret, a revelation that would change everything and plunge me into a darkness I had never imagined.

## Chapter 5: The Dance of Deception

The city's rain-soaked streets seemed to be closing in on me as I made my way back to my office. The melody of the blue notes, the cryptic power they held, and the ruthless gangster Marco "The Razor" Moretti, who sought to claim them, had become an insistent, ominous refrain in my mind.

Back in my dimly lit office, I unfolded a map of the city, marked with a few locations linked to the Midnight Maestros. It was a labyrinthine puzzle, and I needed to decipher its secrets to find Tommy Davis and protect the blue notes from Moretti's grasp.

The stakes had never been higher, and I couldn't afford to make a wrong move.

I decided to start my search by visiting the last known places Tommy had been seen. The Blue Note jazz club was the obvious starting point, but I knew there was another location he frequented – the abandoned Blackwood Theater, a decaying relic of the city's bygone era.

The rain tapped insistently against the window, like a steady beat in a melancholic jazz tune. I stepped out into the city's dark embrace once more and headed to the Blackwood Theater, my steps echoing in the desolate streets. The building was a shadowy, crumbling edifice, its grandeur now reduced to eerie decay.

As I entered the abandoned theater, I could hear the faint echoes of forgotten performances, the laughter and applause of a time long past. The place felt like a time capsule, frozen in the sepia-toned memories of a bygone era.

I explored the dimly lit corridors, guided by a distant, eerie piano melody that seemed to beckon me. The sound was haunting, a melancholic tune that reverberated through the empty halls. It was as though the theater itself held a secret, a melody of its own, waiting to be discovered.

The music led me to the main stage, where a grand piano stood alone in the spotlight. It was the source of the ethereal melody, played by unseen hands. As I approached, the music ceased, and a voice emerged from the shadows.

"Well, well, Jack Malone, the investigator searching for a melody."

A figure stepped into the dim light, revealing himself as Tommy Davis. He was disheveled, his face marked with exhaustion, but there was a gleam of desperation in his eyes. He had the appearance of a man who had journeyed to the brink of madness.

"Tommy, you had us all worried. What's going on?" I asked, my voice laced with concern.

Tommy's gaze remained haunted, his words laced with urgency. "Jack, you have to understand. The blue notes, the melody they hold – they're a double-edged sword. They can reveal the truth, but they can also shroud it in deception. Moretti, he believes the melody is a weapon, a way to control the city's fate."

I couldn't deny the truth in Tommy's words. The melody, the blue notes, were a power that could be used for both good and evil, and the city's destiny hung in the balance. "What did you discover, Tommy? What's the key to unraveling the melody's secrets?"

Tommy's eyes flickered with fear. "It's in the forgotten composition of a jazz legend, Joseph "Blues" McCoy. He was the one who composed the blue notes, and his music holds the key to unlocking their true power. But Moretti's henchmen are searching for it too, and they won't stop until they find it."

The realization hit me like a sledgehammer. Blues McCoy's forgotten composition was the key to unlocking the power of the blue notes. But if Moretti's goons were also after it, it would become a race against time to uncover the truth.

Tommy handed me a faded, tattered sheet of music. It was a fragment of Blues McCoy's composition, a tantalizing clue that held the city's fate in its notes. "You have to find the rest of the composition, Jack. It's scattered throughout the city, hidden in places where only those who understand the power of the melody can uncover it."

I took the fragment and nodded, realizing the scope of the task before me. The city had become a sprawling puzzle, and I was the one tasked with assembling its pieces to protect its fate.

As I left the Blackwood Theater, I couldn't help but wonder if Moretti's henchmen were already hot on my trail, searching for the same fragments of Blues McCoy's composition. The stakes had never been higher, and the race to uncover the melody's secrets had begun.

Back in my office, I unfolded the fragment of music and studied it carefully. The notes were haunting, beautiful, and held a power that was beyond anything I had ever encountered. I knew that each piece of the composition held a secret, a clue, and the power to reveal the truth hidden within the city's shadows.

But as I pieced together the fragment and considered the locations I needed to search, a chilling thought began to gnaw at the edges of my consciousness. The city's shadows had whispered their secrets to me, but were they also whispering to Moretti's henchmen, leading them on a path of deception and betrayal?

The phone on my desk rang, shattering my reverie. I picked it up, and a voice on the other end sent a shiver down my spine. It was a voice I recognized, a voice that promised danger and uncertainty.

"Malone, you're getting closer to the truth, but the melody is not meant for the likes of you. Leave it be, or there will be consequences."

The caller's identity remained concealed, but their message was clear – I was not the only one searching for the melody, and the city's shadows held more secrets and dangers than I could have ever imagined.

As the rain continued to fall outside, I realized that the dance of deception had only just begun, and the city's fate was hanging in the balance. I had a choice to make – to continue the search for the melody and the truth it held, or to walk away and leave the city to its uncertain destiny.

But I knew that I couldn't turn my back on the city that had become my home, and the truth that had become my obsession. The melody of the blue notes was waiting to be unraveled, and I was determined to see it through to the end, no matter the cost.

The city's shadows had revealed their secrets, and the dance of deception had only just begun.

## Chapter 6: A Race Against Shadows

The sheet of Blues McCoy's composition lay spread out on my cluttered desk, its haunting notes serving as a tantalizing riddle. The city's fate, shrouded in secrecy, rested in the power of the blue notes – a melody that could change everything or unleash chaos and corruption. I knew I had to decipher the hidden song and protect it from falling into the wrong hands.

As I scrutinized the fragment, I realized that each note was a clue, a piece of a larger puzzle. I needed to find the remaining fragments scattered throughout the city, but time was against me. Marco "The Razor" Moretti's henchmen were also on the hunt, determined to claim the blue notes for their malevolent purpose.

The fragmented composition beckoned me to a location, an old jazz record store that had once been a gathering place for jazz aficionados and underground musicians. The store's owner, an elderly man named Joe, was known to possess knowledge of the city's hidden musical history. I hoped he could shed light on Blues McCoy's composition and point me in the right direction.

The rain had eased up, but the city remained drenched in a shroud of mist. I stepped out into the streets, determined to find the missing pieces of the melody. My first stop was Joe's Jazz Emporium, a dimly lit store tucked away on a quiet corner.

The bell above the door jingled as I entered, and Joe looked up from behind the counter, his eyes curious but cautious. His fingers, calloused from decades of handling vinyl records, paused on a dusty record sleeve.

"Jack Malone, it's been a while," he said with a nod of recognition.

"Joe, I need your help," I replied, my voice laced with urgency. "I'm looking for Blues McCoy's composition, and I have a fragment of it. Can you tell me anything about it?"

Joe leaned in closer, a gleam of intrigue in his eyes. "Blues McCoy's composition is the stuff of legends, Jack. It's said to hold the key to the city's hidden truths, a melody that can unveil secrets buried in the very soul of the city."

I placed the fragment of the composition on the counter. "This is what I have. Can you tell me anything about where the other fragments might be?"

Joe studied the notes for a moment before speaking. "Blues McCoy was known to frequent a series of jazz clubs, each with a piece of his composition hidden within. They were his sanctuaries, places where he felt the city's pulse most strongly. There are four clubs in total, each holding a part of the melody."

He handed me a list of the four jazz clubs and their addresses, their names like echoes of a bygone era: The Rhapsody, The Crescent Moon, The Jazz Serenade, and The Velvet Dream. "But be cautious, Jack. Moretti's men are seeking the composition as well, and they won't hesitate to stop anyone who gets in their way."

I nodded, acknowledging the gravity of the situation. The race to uncover the secrets hidden within Blues McCoy's melody had begun, and I had to stay one step ahead of Moretti's henchmen.

My first destination was The Rhapsody, a jazz club known for its sultry atmosphere and live performances that could make you lose track of time. The club's owner, Benny "The Maestro" Russo, was rumored to be connected to the Midnight Maestros, and I hoped he could guide me to the next fragment of the composition.

The Rhapsody's neon sign cast a seductive glow on the wet streets, and as I entered, I was enveloped in a world of saxophones, trumpets, and moody melodies. Benny Russo, a stout man with a fedora perched on his head, was at the bar, and his eyes lit up with recognition when he saw me.

"Jack Malone, what brings you to my humble establishment?" he asked, his voice a rich baritone.

"I'm looking for Blues McCoy's composition, Benny," I replied, my voice low. "I heard you might have some information."

Benny leaned in closer, his expression cautious. "Blues McCoy's composition is a treasure, Jack. It's said to be the heart of the city's soul. There are fragments hidden within these walls, but I won't give them up easily."

I knew I had to earn his trust, and I decided to share what I had discovered. I told him about Tommy Davis, the blue notes, and the danger they posed if they fell into Moretti's hands. Benny listened intently, his eyes filled with a mixture of wariness and concern.

After a moment, he nodded. "All right, Jack. The first fragment is hidden in a vinyl record, a rare pressing of Blues McCoy's own music. It's in a crate beneath the stage. But be cautious – Moretti's men have been snooping around lately."

I thanked Benny and made my way to the stage, carefully lifting the floorboard to reveal a dusty crate of records. My heart raced as I uncovered the rare pressing of Blues McCoy's music. I couldn't help but feel a sense of reverence as I held the record in my hands, knowing that it held a piece of the melody that could change the city's fate.

The night was far from over, and I still had three more clubs to visit, each holding a fragment of Blues McCoy's composition. But as I left The Rhapsody, a foreboding sense of danger hung in the air. Moretti's henchmen were closing in, and the race to uncover the melody's secrets had taken a perilous turn.

I knew that the journey ahead was fraught with danger, but the city's destiny depended on the fragments of the composition. As I ventured into the misty streets once more, I couldn't help but wonder if Moretti's shadowy forces were already tracking my every move, waiting for the opportunity to strike.

The race against time had become a race against shadows, and the city's fate was hanging in the balance. The melody of deception had begun to play, and I was determined to see it through to the end, no matter the cost.

But as the mist thickened, and the shadows deepened, I knew that the ultimate revelation was still shrouded in mystery, waiting to be uncovered in the darkness of the city's secrets.

## Chapter 7: Shadows of Betrayal

The night had grown darker, the city's streets shrouded in an eerie mist as I ventured toward my next destination. The fragments of Blues McCoy's composition, the key to unlocking the power of the blue notes, had become my obsession, and the shadows of Moretti's henchmen followed closely, like vultures circling their prey.

The next club on my list was The Crescent Moon, an old haunt known for its sultry jazz tunes and dimly lit corners where secrets were whispered like seductive confessions. It was the kind of place where you could lose yourself, a characteristic that had made it a gathering point for the city's underbelly and, perhaps, the perfect hiding place for a piece of Blues McCoy's melody.

The Crescent Moon's entrance was a hidden doorway in an alleyway, its sign nearly faded into obscurity. I descended the narrow staircase, and the world below was a sultry, smoky wonderland. The club's patrons seemed lost in the melodies, their whispers barely audible over the enchanting music that filled the air.

As I approached the bar, I was met with a knowing nod from the bartender, who recognized me as an outsider in a place where discretion was a currency. I ordered a drink, hoping to blend in and make discreet inquiries about Blues McCoy's composition.

A woman, dressed in a gown that seemed to shimmer with an otherworldly radiance, sat at the end of the bar, her emerald eyes glinting with intrigue. She watched me with a curiosity that was impossible to ignore.

I approached her cautiously, realizing that she might be the key to uncovering the next fragment of the composition. "I've heard you might know something about Blues McCoy's music," I said, my voice low.

The woman's smile was enigmatic, her words cloaked in a seductive tone. "Blues McCoy's music is a tapestry of secrets, a melody that unveils the city's soul. There is a fragment here, hidden within the keys of the grand piano. But you must convince me that you're worthy of it."

I couldn't help but feel that she was testing me, gauging my determination and commitment to the city's hidden truths. I nodded and followed her to the stage, where the grand piano stood in the spotlight. As I played a haunting jazz tune, a hidden compartment beneath the keys revealed a fragment of the composition.

The woman watched with a mixture of amusement and approval. "You have it, Jack Malone. Remember that the melody is a double-edged sword. It can reveal and deceive. Choose wisely how you use it."

With the fragment in my possession, I left The Crescent Moon, feeling the weight of responsibility pressing down on me. The city's fate was woven into the composition, and I couldn't afford to let it fall into the wrong hands.

The Jazz Serenade, a hidden gem known for its live jazz improvisations, was my next destination. The club was tucked away in an obscure alley, its entrance guarded by a burly doorman who seemed to recognize me as an outsider.

The atmosphere inside the Jazz Serenade was electrifying, the music a spontaneous, ever-changing creation. It was a place where jazz musicians came to push the boundaries of their art, and it was said that a fragment of Blues McCoy's composition was hidden within the very instruments that graced the stage.

I approached a trumpet player, a seasoned musician with a weathered face and soulful eyes. He had a reputation for having a profound connection with the city's jazz history. "I'm looking for a piece of Blues McCoy's composition," I told him. "Can you help me find it?"

The trumpet player nodded, a knowing smile on his lips. "Blues McCoy's melody is a secret of the city, a tune that's been passed down through generations. It's said that it's hidden within the brass of this very trumpet."

He handed me the instrument, and as I examined it, I realized that the notes on the sheet were etched into the trumpet's interior, a hidden melody that could change the city's destiny. I thanked the trumpet player and left the Jazz Serenade, realizing that the composition was slowly coming together, and with it, the city's hidden truths.

The final club on my list was The Velvet Dream, a place of seductive charm and allure, where the music played on the edge of your senses, and the fragments of Blues McCoy's composition were said to be concealed beneath the dance floor.

As I entered the club, the enchanting melody washed over me, and the dancers moved as if caught in a trance, their movements fluid and hypnotic. It was a world of sensuality and secrets, and I knew I had to tread carefully to uncover the final piece of the melody.

A dancer, her eyes a mesmerizing shade of sapphire, approached me, her movements a dance of temptation. "I hear you seek the secrets of the city, Mr. Malone. The final fragment is beneath the dance floor, but you must earn it."

I watched as she moved in a way that was both tantalizing and enigmatic, her words leaving a trail of intrigue in their wake. The dance floor seemed to conceal secrets, and as I joined the dancers, I realized that the very ground I stood on held the final piece of the composition.

As the dance reached its climax, the floor beneath me shifted, revealing a hidden compartment. I retrieved the last fragment of Blues McCoy's composition, and the city's destiny felt within my grasp.

But as I left The Velvet Dream, a chilling realization descended upon me. Moretti's henchmen were closing in, and the race to uncover the melody's secrets was reaching its crescendo. The city's fate was hanging in the balance, and the shadows of betrayal were lurking in the darkness.

Back in my office, I laid out the four fragments of the composition, the notes weaving a haunting, enigmatic melody. The power they held, the ability to reveal and deceive, was a responsibility I couldn't take lightly.

But as I pondered my next move, a knock on the door shattered my concentration. I reached for my gun, ready for whatever danger might be lurking on the other side.

The door creaked open, revealing a figure concealed in the shadows, their identity masked by the dim light. "Malone, you've come closer to the truth, but the melody is not meant for you. Hand over the fragments, and you may walk away."

The voice was chilling, and I knew that I was face to face with one of Moretti's henchmen. The shadows of betrayal had closed in, and the city's fate hung in the balance. I had a choice to make, a choice that would determine the destiny of the city, the melody of deception playing its final notes.

## Chapter 8: A Deadly Duet

The ominous figure lurking in the doorway had come for the fragments of Blues McCoy's composition, and I knew that surrendering them would be akin to handing over the city's destiny to Marco "The Razor" Moretti. I couldn't let that happen, not after all the secrets and dangers I had uncovered.

My hand stayed steady on my gun, hidden beneath my coat, as I considered my options. The room was shrouded in tension, and the choice before me was one of life or death, the city's fate or its destruction.

I chose to stall, to buy time, to find out more about the shadowy forces aligned with Moretti. "Who are you, and who do you work for?" I demanded, my voice as firm as the ground I stood on.

The figure remained concealed, but a dry, humorless chuckle emanated from the shadows. "You may call me Vincent. I work for those who understand the true power of the blue notes. Hand them over, and you may walk away with your life."

The name Vincent held a dark weight, and I couldn't help but feel that it was a name associated with Moretti's ruthless empire. I had no intention of relinquishing the fragments of the composition, not to Moretti's henchmen or anyone else. The city's fate was a responsibility I couldn't ignore.

"Vincent, there's more to the melody than you realize," I replied, my words a calculated gamble. "It can reveal the city's hidden truths, but it can also be a force of destruction. I won't let it fall into the wrong hands."

The figure seemed to consider my words, and I hoped that I had sowed doubt in their mind, enough to buy me time to formulate a plan.

Before Vincent could respond, a loud crash erupted from the window behind me, and I ducked to the floor, instinctively reaching for my gun. Glass shattered, and the room filled with the acrid smell of smoke. I peered through the haze to see a figure crouched on the windowsill, a fedora pulled low over their eyes.

A voice, unmistakably Lily St. Claire's, cut through the chaos. "Jack, I knew you'd be in trouble. It's time to leave."

As the room filled with smoke, I realized that Lily's arrival was my only chance to escape, to protect the fragments of the composition and uncover the truth they held. I couldn't see Vincent in the chaos, but I could hear their hurried footsteps retreating.

I made a split-second decision and followed Lily through the shattered window, descending into the rainy night. The city's shadows had concealed Vincent's escape, and as we moved through the misty streets, I couldn't shake the feeling that Moretti's henchmen were still closing in.

Lily led me to her car, and we sped away from the scene, leaving the shattered remnants of my office behind. The fragments of Blues McCoy's composition were safe, but the danger that lurked in the city's shadows was far from over.

As we navigated the slick streets, Lily explained her presence. "Jack, I've been keeping an eye on you. I knew you were getting closer to uncovering the truth about the blue notes. I couldn't let you face the danger alone."

I was grateful for her support, but the city's fate remained uncertain, and the power of the melody was a force that could change everything or lead to destruction.

"The fragments of the composition are my responsibility, Lily," I said, my voice tinged with determination. "I need to uncover the full melody and understand its power. Moretti and his henchmen will stop at nothing to claim it."

Lily's expression held a mixture of concern and determination. "I understand, Jack, but you're not alone in this. We'll find the answers together, and we'll protect the city from those who seek to misuse the melody."

As we drove through the rainy night, the city's shadows seemed to close in, the secrets and dangers they held waiting to be revealed. The melody of deception had played its initial notes, and the city's fate was hanging in the balance.

But as I considered the enigmatic fragments of Blues McCoy's composition and the power they held, I couldn't help but wonder if the city's destiny was a song that had already been written, or if we had the power to change its course. The answers were waiting to be uncovered, and the melody of truth and deception played on, the ultimate revelation still shrouded in mystery.

The journey was far from over, and the city's secrets and shadows held one final revelation, a truth that could change everything.

## Chapter 9: A Midnight Encounter

The rain had turned into a relentless downpour as Lily and I navigated the slick streets of the city. The fragments of Blues McCoy's composition lay hidden in my coat, their haunting notes a reminder of the power they held to reveal and deceive, to shape the city's destiny or destroy it. I knew that the race against time had escalated, and Moretti's henchmen would stop at nothing to claim the melody.

Lily's presence was a welcome comfort, a reminder that I wasn't alone in my quest to uncover the truth. But the city's secrets and dangers were far from over, and I couldn't help but feel that we were being watched, that the shadows held more secrets than we could ever imagine.

As we approached Lily's apartment, I realized that I couldn't risk taking the fragments inside. The presence of Moretti's forces was a looming threat, and I couldn't afford to put Lily in danger. "Lily, I need a safe place to hide the fragments," I said, my voice tense with concern.

Lily considered for a moment, then nodded. "I have a friend, a reclusive collector of rare musical artifacts. He has a hidden vault where the fragments can be kept safe until we decipher the full composition."

The idea of entrusting the fragments to a stranger made me uneasy, but I knew that we had no other choice. We drove to Lily's friend's residence, a grand mansion hidden behind towering gates and a thick curtain of trees. The collector, a man of few words and an air of mystery, led us to a hidden room in the depths of his home.

The room was filled with antique instruments, musical manuscripts, and a grand piano that seemed to exude a haunting presence. In its center was a secure vault, an imposing door of thick steel. The collector opened it with a combination known only to him, revealing a chamber lined with shelves of rare musical artifacts.

Lily handed over the fragments of the composition, her voice filled with urgency. "Keep these safe, and do not reveal their location to anyone, no matter what happens."

The collector nodded solemnly and placed the fragments within a sealed case, securing it in a hidden compartment of the vault. "They will be safe here. I understand the gravity of their importance."

As we left the collector's mansion, a sense of relief washed over me. The fragments were safe, for now, and we had a chance to decipher the full melody and understand the power it held. But I couldn't shake the feeling that the city's shadows were closing in, that Moretti's forces were watching our every move.

The rain continued to fall, an unrelenting force that seemed to mirror the relentless pursuit of the blue notes. As Lily and I made our way back to her apartment, the presence of danger remained palpable, a whisper in the city's shadows.

We reached Lily's apartment, and as I stepped inside, the room was cast in an ambient, mysterious glow. The soft, melancholic tune of a saxophone played in the background, its notes echoing through the dimly lit space. It was as if the room itself was a testament to Lily's love for jazz and the city's secrets.

Lily poured us both a drink, her eyes revealing a mixture of determination and concern. "Jack, we need to decipher the full composition of Blues McCoy. It's the key to unlocking the power of the blue notes, and it's the only way to protect the city from those who seek to misuse it."

I nodded in agreement, realizing that the melody held the answers to the city's fate, and we were the ones entrusted with that responsibility. "We need to find the missing pieces, the rest of the melody. But how do we know where to look?"

Lily took a sip of her drink, her eyes focused on the notes scattered on the table. "Blues McCoy had a connection to the Midnight Maestros, the secret society of musicians. They might hold the clues to the remaining pieces. We need to find them and convince them to reveal what they know."

I considered the idea, knowing that the Midnight Maestros had already revealed the existence of the blue notes to me. But the city's shadows were full of secrets, and I couldn't help but feel that we were being watched.

As if on cue, a soft, haunting melody filled the room, and a chill ran down my spine. The music seemed to be emanating from a gramophone in the corner, its record spinning on its own, as if moved by an unseen hand.

Lily's eyes widened in surprise, and she gestured toward the gramophone. "I didn't turn that on."

As we approached the gramophone, the music grew more intense, its notes a hypnotic dance that seemed to beckon us. The room was filled with a sense of foreboding, and I couldn't shake the feeling that the melody was a message, a calling.

The gramophone's needle scratched against the record, and the music stopped abruptly. But what it revealed left us in a state of shock and disbelief. An envelope had emerged from a hidden compartment within the gramophone, and it bore a name that sent shivers down my spine.

It was an invitation, an invitation to a midnight rendezvous at a hidden jazz club known only to those who understood the city's secrets, the melody of deception playing its final notes. The message held a chilling promise, a promise that would either bring us closer to the truth or lead us to the heart of the city's darkness.

As we considered the invitation, the realization dawned upon us that the city's shadows held more secrets than we could have ever imagined, and the enigmatic melody of Blues McCoy was far from being just a composition – it was a gateway to the city's soul, and the power it held was a force that could change everything.

The midnight encounter beckoned, and the city's fate was still shrouded in mystery. The next chapter of our journey was waiting to be revealed, and the melody of truth and deception played on, its secrets still concealed in the city's shadows.

## Chapter 10: Midnight Maestro

The invitation to the midnight rendezvous at the hidden jazz club was a cryptic promise, an enigmatic message that held the key to uncovering the remaining pieces of Blues McCoy's composition and the power they held. Lily and I had no choice but to accept the invitation, for the city's fate and the secrets concealed in the melody of deception were waiting to be revealed.

As the clock struck midnight, we arrived at the designated location, a nondescript door tucked away in a dimly lit alley. The city's rain-slicked streets had become eerily deserted, as if the very city itself had fallen silent, anticipating our arrival.

I could feel the weight of the fragments hidden in the collector's vault, and the haunting melody they held seemed to echo in the depths of my consciousness. The midnight encounter was a pivotal moment, a chance to uncover the truth and protect the city from those who sought to misuse the power of the blue notes.

Lily and I exchanged a meaningful glance, and with a shared determination, we pushed open the door, revealing a hidden passage that led us into the heart of the jazz club. The air was thick with the scent of aged whiskey and the sultry notes of a saxophone, the music wrapping around us like a cloak of mystery.

The club's interior was dimly lit, a realm of crimson velvet and shimmering chandeliers. Patrons dressed in the fashion of a bygone era, their eyes filled with a knowing intrigue, sat at tables arranged in an intimate semicircle around a small stage. On the stage, a jazz quartet played with a sense of urgency, their instruments a fusion of enchantment and mystery.

A man, the club's proprietor, stood at the entrance, his eyes a mirror of the city's secrets. He approached us, his voice a husky whisper. "Welcome to the Midnight Maestros, Mr. Malone and Ms. St. Claire. We've been waiting for you."

The club's members, the Midnight Maestros, were a secret society of musicians and enthusiasts who understood the power of music and its connection to the city's soul. Their presence in the city's shadows had been concealed from all but a few, and their connection to Blues McCoy's composition was a revelation.

As we were led to a secluded table near the stage, the atmosphere was charged with anticipation. The saxophonist's notes grew more melancholic, and the room seemed to pulse with a rhythm that was both haunting and seductive.

The leader of the Midnight Maestros, a man known as "The Maestro," took the stage. He was dressed in a tuxedo that seemed to shimmer in the dim light, his eyes a piercing blue that held the wisdom of ages. The Maestro's presence was commanding, and as he addressed the room, his words held a weight of authority.

"Mr. Malone, Ms. St. Claire, we have invited you here for a reason. The fragments of Blues McCoy's composition are the city's hidden treasures, a power that can reveal or deceive. You are entrusted with their protection, and it is your responsibility to decipher the full melody."

Lily and I exchanged a glance, realizing that the Midnight Maestros held the missing pieces of the composition and the answers we sought. The Maestro continued, "But the melody is a reflection of the city's soul, and to uncover its secrets, you must journey to the heart of the city, to a place known as the Jazz Nexus."

The Jazz Nexus was an enigmatic term, a location that seemed to exist in the realm of legends. It was said to be a place where the city's hidden truths were unveiled, a gathering point for those who understood the power of music.

The Maestro handed us a map, its markings a cryptic puzzle that led to the Jazz Nexus. "You must follow this map, uncover the remaining pieces of the composition, and understand the melody's true power. The city's fate is in your hands."

As the saxophonist played a haunting melody, the Maestro returned to the shadows, and we were left with a sense of urgency. The city's fate was a responsibility we couldn't ignore, and the Jazz Nexus was our next destination, a place that held the city's ultimate secrets.

We left the jazz club, the saxophonist's notes fading into the distance, and as we followed the map's cryptic markings, a sense of unease settled in. The city's shadows concealed more than we could ever imagine, and the dangers that lurked in the darkness were a reminder of the perilous journey ahead.

The map led us through a labyrinth of narrow alleys and hidden passageways, a journey that seemed to transcend time and space. The rain continued to fall, an unrelenting force that seemed to mirror the relentless pursuit of the blue notes, and the city's secrets were waiting to be uncovered.

As we reached the final destination marked on the map, we found ourselves standing in front of an old jazz club, its sign bearing the name "Jazz Nexus." The club was a relic of the city's history, a place where the music held the power to reveal the city's soul.

We entered the club, and the atmosphere was unlike any we had encountered before. The patrons seemed to be lost in a trance, their eyes glazed with a knowing wisdom. The music played with a sense of urgency, a haunting melody that resonated with the fragments hidden in my coat.

The club's stage was bathed in a soft, otherworldly light, and a pianist played with a sense of enchantment. His fingers moved with an almost supernatural grace, and the music seemed to transcend the boundaries of reality.

The pianist's eyes met mine, and he nodded, as if acknowledging our presence. The melody he played was a tapestry of secrets, a riddle waiting to be unraveled. Lily and I approached the stage, our hearts filled with a sense of purpose.

"Blues McCoy's composition is a force that can change the city's destiny," the pianist said, his voice a whisper in the enigmatic atmosphere of the Jazz Nexus. "But it can also lead to chaos and destruction. You must understand its true power."

As the pianist played the final notes, the fragments in my coat seemed to resonate, their haunting melody becoming a complete composition. The secrets of the city's soul were revealed, and the power of the blue notes was within our grasp.

But as I reached for the fragments, a sense of unease washed over me. The city's shadows held more secrets than we could ever imagine, and the ultimate revelation was still shrouded in mystery.

The pianist's eyes held a mixture of wisdom and warning. "The city's fate is a melody that can be changed, but you must choose how to use its power. The blue notes are a force of transformation, and the choice is yours."

As we left the Jazz Nexus, a chilling realization settled in. The city's fate was a responsibility we couldn't escape, and the power of the blue notes was a force that could change everything. The next chapter of our journey was waiting to be revealed, and the city's secrets and shadows held one final revelation, a truth that would determine the city's destiny.

But as the rain continued to fall, and the city's secrets and dangers remained concealed in the darkness, I couldn't help but wonder if the city's fate was a song that had already been written, or if we had the power to change its course. The answers were waiting to be uncovered, and the melody of truth and deception played on, the ultimate revelation still shrouded in mystery.

# Chapter 11: The Conductor's Dilemma

With the fragments of Blues McCoy's composition finally united, the haunting melody resonated within us, a powerful reminder of the responsibility we carried to protect the city from those who sought to misuse its power. As we left the Jazz Nexus, the rain-soaked streets seemed to echo the melody, and the city's secrets and shadows held one final revelation, a truth that would determine its destiny.

Lily and I returned to her apartment, the fragments of the composition safely stored within the collector's vault. The Jazz Nexus had revealed the blue notes' true potential, a force of transformation that could change the city's fate. But the choice of how to wield that power weighed heavily on our minds.

We poured over the notes, contemplating the composition's meaning and the puzzle it represented. The fragments held a rhythm and a hidden message that beckoned to be deciphered. The next step was clear – we needed to understand the full composition, for it was the key to unlocking the power of the blue notes.

The rain continued to fall relentlessly, and as we analyzed the composition's notes, a sense of unease settled in. The city's shadows concealed more than we could have ever imagined, and the dangers that lurked in the darkness were a reminder of the perilous journey ahead.

Our research led us to an old music store, a place known for its collection of rare manuscripts and forgotten compositions. The owner, an elderly man with a lifetime of knowledge, welcomed us with a knowing nod.

"I've heard of Blues McCoy's composition," he said, his voice filled with reverence. "It's said to hold the power of the city's soul. But be warned, unlocking its secrets may come at a cost."

He handed us a tattered manuscript, a faded piece of history that was rumored to contain the full composition. As we leafed through the pages, the notes seemed to come to life, resonating with the fragments we had collected.

The music store owner's words echoed in our minds, a warning of the potential consequences of wielding the blue notes' power. The city's fate was a responsibility we couldn't take lightly, and the choices we made would determine its destiny.

We returned to Lily's apartment, determined to decipher the full composition. As the rain fell outside, the notes on the manuscript seemed to dance on the page, revealing a message that held the power to reveal or deceive, to transform the city's fate.

The composition's meaning was elusive, a puzzle waiting to be solved, and as we immersed ourselves in the music, we realized that it held a narrative, a story of the city's history and its secrets.

The melody described a city shrouded in shadows, a place where power and corruption reigned, and the blue notes were the key to unraveling its mysteries. But it also warned of the dangers of misusing the melody, of falling into the abyss of deception.

The composition seemed to be a reflection of the city's soul, and as we reached the final notes, a sense of clarity washed over us. The blue notes held the power to transform, to reveal the city's hidden truths, but they also carried the burden of choice. The city's fate was a melody that could be rewritten, and the decision was ours.

As we considered the composition's message, a chilling realization settled in. The city's destiny was a responsibility we couldn't escape, and the power of the blue notes was a force that could change everything. The next chapter of our journey was waiting to be revealed, and the city's secrets and shadows held one final revelation, a truth that would determine the city's destiny.

But as the rain continued to fall, and the city's secrets and dangers remained concealed in the darkness, I couldn't help but wonder if the city's fate was a song that had already been written, or if we had the power to change its course. The answers were waiting to be uncovered, and the melody of truth and deception played on, the ultimate revelation still shrouded in mystery.

In the midst of our contemplation, a knock on the door shattered our concentration. I reached for my gun, ready for whatever danger might be lurking on the other side.

The door creaked open, revealing a figure concealed in the shadows, their identity masked by the dim light. "Malone, you've come closer to the truth, but the melody is not meant for you. Hand over the composition, and you may walk away."

The voice was chilling, and I knew that I was face to face with one of Moretti's henchmen. The shadows of betrayal had closed in, and the city's fate hung in the balance. I had a choice to make, a choice that would determine the destiny of the city, the melody of deception playing its final notes.

As Lily and I considered our options, a sense of urgency washed over us. The city's shadows held more secrets than we could have ever imagined, and the enigmatic melody of Blues McCoy was far from being just a composition – it was a gateway to the city's soul, and the power it held was a force that could change everything.

## Chapter 12: The Duel of Deception

The room was cast in shadows, and the chilling voice of Moretti's henchman reverberated through the dimly lit apartment. My hand tightened on my gun beneath my coat, and Lily's eyes held a mixture of determination and fear.

The henchman, concealed in the darkness, continued with a threat that hung heavy in the air. "Malone, the composition is not yours to decipher. Hand it over, and you may live to see another day."

The fragments of Blues McCoy's composition were the city's hidden treasure, a power that could transform or destroy, and I couldn't allow them to fall into Moretti's ruthless hands. The city's fate was a responsibility I couldn't relinquish.

Lily's voice held a steely resolve as she responded, "We won't hand over the composition. It's not meant for those who would misuse its power."

The henchman's laughter was a sinister echo in the room. "You think you can defy Moretti? You underestimate the consequences of your choices."

As if on cue, the room was plunged into darkness, and the henchman's voice seemed to come from all directions. "You may have the fragments, but you'll never decipher the full composition. It holds a power you can't comprehend."

The darkness was suffocating, and I fumbled for my flashlight, its beam cutting through the obscurity. Lily and I stood back to back, our senses on high alert, as we searched for any sign of the henchman's presence.

A shuffling sound came from the corner of the room, and I swung my flashlight toward it, revealing the henchman's silhouette. He was preparing to strike, a weapon glinting in his hand.

Lily reacted quickly, grabbing a nearby vase and hurling it at the henchman. The vase shattered, and he cried out in pain, his weapon falling to the floor.

In the chaos that followed, I fired a warning shot that ricocheted off the wall, causing the henchman to retreat into the darkness. We couldn't see him, but we could hear his hurried footsteps fading into the distance.

The confrontation had left us shaken, and the room seemed to breathe a sigh of relief as the darkness receded. We had narrowly escaped a deadly encounter, and the city's secrets and shadows were closing in on us.

Lily's voice trembled with the gravity of the situation. "We can't stay here. Moretti's henchmen will come back, and we're vulnerable."

I agreed, and we quickly gathered the composition's fragments, securing them in my coat. As we left the apartment, a sense of unease settled in. The city's shadows concealed more than we could have ever imagined, and the dangers that lurked in the darkness were a reminder of the perilous journey ahead.

Our destination was the Jazz Nexus, the enigmatic location that had revealed the composition's meaning and power. We needed to consult with the Midnight Maestros, for their guidance was invaluable in navigating the complexities of the blue notes.

The city's streets were still slick with rain, and as we made our way through the misty night, the fragments in my coat seemed to resonate with a newfound urgency. The composition held the city's hidden truths, and the power of the blue notes was a force that could change everything.

When we arrived at the Jazz Nexus, the atmosphere was charged with anticipation. The members of the Midnight Maestros were gathered, their eyes holding a knowing wisdom. The Maestro, their leader, took the stage once more, his presence commanding.

"We sensed the disturbance in the city's harmony," the Maestro said, his voice filled with concern. "You are not alone in this journey, and the blue notes' power must be wielded with care."

Lily and I explained the encounter with Moretti's henchman, and the Maestro's eyes held a steely resolve. "The city's fate is in your hands, and the blue notes hold the key to its transformation. But you must unlock the full composition to understand the true scope of their power."

The members of the Midnight Maestros gathered around us, their instruments at the ready. The Jazz Nexus was a place where music and magic converged, and the composition's fragments seemed to respond to the musicians' presence.

As the notes filled the room, the fragments resonated, their melody weaving into a haunting narrative. The composition described a city in turmoil, a place where secrets and corruption thrived, and the blue notes held the potential for both revelation and deception.

The Maestro's voice filled the room, guiding the musicians through the composition's intricate nuances. The notes seemed to come to life, their power a tangible force that held the potential to transform the city's destiny.

But as the music reached its crescendo, a chilling realization settled in. The composition hinted at a dire choice, a decision that would determine the city's fate. Lily and I exchanged a meaningful glance, understanding the gravity of the situation.

The Maestro's voice held a mixture of warning and wisdom. "The power of the blue notes is a force that can change everything, but the choice is yours. The city's fate is a melody that can be rewritten."

As the room fell silent, a sense of urgency washed over us. The composition's message was clear – the decision was ours to make, and the city's destiny hung in the balance.

The rain continued to fall outside, a relentless force that seemed to mirror the relentless pursuit of the blue notes, and the city's secrets were waiting to be uncovered. Lily and I left the Jazz Nexus, our hearts heavy with the responsibility of the city's fate.

We knew that Moretti's henchmen would stop at nothing to claim the blue notes, and the danger that lurked in the city's shadows was far from over. The composition had revealed the power to transform and deceive, and the city's destiny was a responsibility we couldn't escape.

But as we navigated the rain-soaked streets, a new revelation emerged, a revelation that would alter the course of our journey. The city's shadows concealed more than we could have ever imagined, and the final revelation was waiting to be uncovered.

As we reached Lily's apartment, we were met with a scene of chaos. The room had been ransacked, the fragments of the composition stolen, and a chilling note lay in their place.

It bore a single word – "Moretti."

The city's fate had taken a dark turn, and the composition's power was now in the hands of Marco "The Razor" Moretti. The melody of deception had played its final notes, and the city's destiny hung in the balance.

The next chapter of our journey was a race against time, a pursuit to reclaim the blue notes and protect the city from Moretti's ruthless grasp. The city's secrets and shadows held one final revelation, a truth that would determine its destiny, and our resolve was stronger than ever.

# Chapter 13: The Midnight Showdown

The city had transformed into a realm of darkness and uncertainty, a place where the balance between good and evil hung in the balance. With the fragments of Blues McCoy's composition now in the hands of Marco "The Razor" Moretti, the melody of deception had taken a chilling turn, and the city's fate was in peril.

Lily and I knew that we couldn't let Moretti wield the power of the blue notes, and the time for a final showdown had come. As we made our way through the rain-soaked streets, the weight of responsibility and the city's secrets weighed heavily on our shoulders.

Our destination was Moretti's grand mansion, a fortress of wealth and power that had become a symbol of the city's corruption. The rain had turned the cobblestone path leading to the mansion into a slippery obstacle, but our determination was unwavering.

The mansion loomed ahead, its grandeur a stark contrast to the city's shadows. Armed guards patrolled the perimeter, their presence a testament to Moretti's ruthlessness. We knew that this confrontation could be our last, but the city's fate was a responsibility we couldn't abandon.

As we approached the mansion's imposing gates, a voice called out from the shadows. It was Lily's friend, the reclusive collector of rare musical artifacts who had hidden the composition's fragments in his vault.

"I've been keeping an eye on Moretti's activities," he said, his voice filled with concern. "He plans to use the blue notes for his own gain, to gain control over the city. You must stop him."

We exchanged a meaningful nod with him, grateful for his support. The collector had become an unexpected ally in our quest to protect the city from those who sought to misuse the blue notes' power.

The mansion's gates swung open with an ominous creak, and we stepped onto the grand courtyard, where the rain continued to fall relentlessly. Armed guards surrounded us, their weapons at the ready, and at the end of the courtyard, Moretti stood with a sinister grin.

Moretti was a man of power and ambition, his reputation in the city's underworld unmatched. He had a connection to the blue notes that ran deeper than we could have imagined, and the fragments of Blues McCoy's composition had granted him the ability to manipulate and control.

Moretti's voice was a chilling echo in the rain-soaked atmosphere. "You thought you could defy me, Malone, but the composition is mine now. Its power will be harnessed for my vision of the city."

Lily and I were aware of the dangers that lay ahead, but we couldn't allow Moretti to misuse the blue notes. The composition was the city's hidden treasure, and the power it held was a force that could change everything.

I raised my gun, my voice resolute. "The blue notes won't be yours to control, Moretti. We won't let you destroy the city."

The standoff had reached a pivotal moment, and the rain seemed to intensify, as if the very city itself held its breath. Moretti's henchmen aimed their weapons at us, their fingers on the triggers.

But before the tension could escalate, a haunting melody filled the air, and a presence emerged from the darkness. It was the Midnight Maestros, the secret society of musicians who had helped us understand the power of the blue notes.

Their instruments seemed to shimmer in the rain, their music a force that held the power to shape the city's fate. The Maestro, their leader, took the stage, his eyes a mirror of wisdom and determination.

Moretti's expression shifted from confidence to unease as the Maestro addressed him. "The blue notes are not meant to be misused, Moretti. They hold the potential for both creation and destruction, and the choice is yours."

The Maestro's voice held a haunting power, and the music played on, its notes resonating with the fragments of the composition that Moretti held. As the music reached its climax, a choice hung in the balance, a choice that would determine the city's destiny.

Moretti's face contorted with frustration and anger, and he made a decision that would alter the course of the city's history. He released the fragments of the composition into the rain-soaked courtyard, and the power of the blue notes began to surge.

The composition's fragments seemed to come to life, their notes weaving into a haunting melody that enveloped the entire courtyard. The city's fate was at stake, and the power of the blue notes held the potential to transform everything.

But as the melody played on, it became clear that Moretti's intentions were not pure. The power of the blue notes was being misused, manipulated for his own gain, and the consequences were catastrophic.

The music reached its crescendo, and the city's transformation began. Buildings shifted, the very streets seemed to come alive, and the city's shadows revealed a truth that had been hidden for generations.

The city's corruption and secrets were exposed, and the power of the blue notes had the potential to change the city's destiny. But the consequences were not without a price, as chaos and upheaval swept through the streets.

As the transformation continued, a sense of unease settled in. The city's fate was being rewritten, and the choices we had made were coming to fruition. The blue notes were a force of change, but their power was unpredictable, and the city's destiny was still uncertain.

The rain fell in a torrential downpour, as if mourning the city's transformation, and the power of the blue notes had left a mark on the city that would never be erased. The composition's fragments had been returned to their place of origin, but the consequences of their use would be felt for years to come.

Lily and I stood in the midst of the city's upheaval, the weight of responsibility heavy on our shoulders. The choices we had made had shaped the city's destiny, and the melody of deception had played its final notes.

As the city's transformation reached its climax, a haunting realization washed over us. The city's fate was a melody that could be rewritten, and the power of the blue notes was a force that could change everything. The next chapter of our journey was waiting to be revealed, and the city's secrets and shadows held one final revelation, a truth that would determine its ultimate destiny.

The rain continued to fall, the city's secrets remained concealed in the darkness, and the melody of truth and deception played on, its ultimate revelation still shrouded in mystery.

Chapter 14: The Resonance of Redemption

The city had undergone a transformation unlike any other. The power of the blue notes had rewritten its destiny, exposing the corruption that had festered in the shadows for so long. But with great power came great responsibility, and as Lily and I stood amidst the chaos and upheaval, we knew that our journey was far from over.

The city's inhabitants emerged from their homes, their faces reflecting a mixture of awe, confusion, and even fear. The secrets that had been concealed in the shadows were now laid bare, and the city's soul was exposed for all to see.

The Midnight Maestros, the secret society of musicians who had guided us, stood nearby, their instruments silent but their presence a reminder of the power of music and its connection to the city's destiny. The Maestro, their leader, approached us, his eyes holding a mixture of gratitude and wisdom.

"The city's transformation is complete, but its path forward is still uncertain," the Maestro said. "The blue notes have reshaped its destiny, but the choices of its inhabitants will determine its future."

Lily and I understood the truth in his words. The power of the blue notes had revealed the city's hidden truths and corruption, but the responsibility of rebuilding and ensuring a just future rested with its people.

The rain had finally subsided, leaving a sense of clarity in its wake. The city's streets glistened with the remnants of the rain, as if cleansing the darkness that had plagued it for so long. The city's transformation was a revelation, a chance for redemption.

As we left the scene of the city's upheaval, we couldn't help but wonder what our own roles would be in the city's future. The melody of truth and deception had played its final notes, and the power of the blue notes had left a lasting impact.

Our next destination was the old jazz club, a place that had played a pivotal role in our journey. As we entered the club, the atmosphere was filled with a sense of hope and renewal. The patrons, dressed in the fashion of a bygone era, seemed to have embraced the city's transformation.

The saxophonist, who had played a haunting melody when we first visited, now played a tune of hope and redemption. The music filled the air, a reminder of the power of music to shape a city's soul.

The proprietor of the club, who had once welcomed us with an enigmatic message, approached us with a knowing smile. "The city has a chance for a fresh start, and the blue notes have played their part in revealing its truth."

Lily and I exchanged a meaningful glance. Our journey had been a tumultuous one, filled with danger, deception, and redemption. The city's transformation had been a testament to the power of the blue notes, and the responsibility of shaping its future lay with its inhabitants.

The club's members, the Midnight Maestros, gathered on the stage, their instruments ready to play. The Maestro addressed the room, his voice a soothing melody. "The blue notes have revealed the city's secrets, but now it is time for healing and renewal. The music will guide us in the city's redemption."

As the musicians played, the notes resonated with the fragments of Blues McCoy's composition that Lily and I had collected. The melody wove a story of a city that had overcome its darkest hour, a place where the power of music and its connection to the soul had triumphed.

The patrons in the club danced and swayed to the music, their spirits lifted by the melody of hope and redemption. The city had been given a chance for a fresh start, and the choices of its inhabitants would determine its path.

Lily and I realized that our journey had come full circle, from the discovery of the fragments in the collector's vault to the revelation of the composition's power and the city's transformation. The blue notes had been a force of change, and our choices had played a pivotal role in the city's fate.

As the music played on, the club's atmosphere was filled with a sense of unity and renewal. The power of the blue notes had reshaped the city's destiny, and the melody of truth and deception had given way to a new beginning.

The rain had subsided, and the city's streets glistened with a sense of hope. The secrets and corruption that had festered in the shadows were now in the past, and the city's future was a blank canvas waiting to be painted.

Lily and I left the jazz club, our hearts filled with a sense of satisfaction and closure. The city's redemption was a testament to the power of music, and the choices of its inhabitants had the potential to shape its destiny.

As we walked through the rain-soaked streets, we couldn't help but reflect on our journey. The city had been a place of mystery and darkness, but it had also been a place of redemption and renewal.

The city's fate was a melody that could be rewritten, and the power of the blue notes had played a pivotal role in its transformation. The next chapter of our journey was a return to the ordinary, a return to a city that had been forever changed.

But as the rain continued to fall, and the city's secrets and dangers remained concealed in the darkness, we couldn't help but feel a sense of hope. The city's redemption was a reminder that even in the face of darkness, there was always a chance for renewal and a new beginning.

The melody of truth and deception had played its final notes, and the city's fate was now in the hands of its inhabitants. The power of the blue notes had revealed the city's hidden truths, and the responsibility of shaping its future was a journey that would continue for generations to come.

The end of our journey was a beginning, a chance for the city to rise from the shadows and embrace a new destiny. The melody of hope and redemption played on, and the city's soul was forever changed.

    THE END

# The Secret Garden Murders

## Chapter 1: The Hidden Garden

It was a gray and drizzly morning in the picturesque English village of Willowbrook, a place where secrets whispered through the hedgerows and shadows clung to the ancient stone walls. The village, with its charming thatched cottages and winding cobblestone streets, was the epitome of quaintness. But beneath the facade of tranquility, dark secrets festered in the hearts of its inhabitants.

As the church bells tolled their melancholic notes, a figure emerged from the mist, walking with measured grace along the narrow road. Miss Amelia Sinclair was a woman of striking presence and keen intellect. With her silver hair pulled back into a tight bun and her eyes concealed behind wire-rimmed spectacles, she looked every bit the part of a retired schoolteacher. However, her sharp mind and knack for solving mysteries had earned her the admiration of many, and the nickname "Willowbrook's Miss Marple."

Amelia had received a letter that piqued her curiosity and stirred her detective's instincts. The note was unsigned, but its contents were ominous. It spoke of a hidden garden in the heart of Willowbrook, known only to a select few, and hinted at a series of unexplained deaths that had shaken the village. The words on the page bore an air of desperation and a plea for help.

With each step, the mist clung to her coat, and the dampness seeped into her bones. She wondered about the garden and the person who had penned the letter. Who would seek her out for such a task? Amelia had lived in Willowbrook for most of her life, but she had never heard of any hidden garden, and the mention of deaths sent a shiver down her spine. The village was known for its calm and tranquility, not for its tragedies.

Her path led her to a quaint tea shop named "Thistle & Rose," nestled at the end of the village square. She entered, and the bell above the door tinkled softly. The interior was cozy, with a warm, inviting atmosphere. The owner, Mrs. Margaret Finch, a plump and rosy-cheeked woman, bustled behind the counter.

"Ah, Miss Sinclair," Margaret chirped, her face lighting up as she wiped her hands on her apron. "A cup of your usual Earl Grey, dear?"

Amelia nodded, her thoughts still consumed by the mysterious letter. As she settled into her favorite corner of the tearoom, she wondered if Margaret knew anything about the hidden garden. She sipped her tea, savoring the familiar flavors, and finally broached the subject.

"Margaret, have you ever heard of a hidden garden in Willowbrook?" she inquired, her voice low.

Margaret paused for a moment, her eyes darting around as if to ensure no one was eavesdropping. "Aye, I've heard whispers, Miss Sinclair. But it's not the sort of thing people talk about openly. They say it's a place of mystery and enchantment, hidden away from prying eyes."

Amelia leaned forward, her interest growing. "And these deaths mentioned in the letter, have you any idea about them?"

Margaret's expression darkened. "There have been rumors, terrible rumors, but no one wants to speak of them. They say those who enter the garden never return."

Amelia's heart quickened. It was exactly the sort of enigma she couldn't resist. As she finished her tea, she pressed Margaret for any additional information she could offer.

Margaret hesitated, her lips trembling. "There's an old man, Samuel Harrington, lives on the outskirts of the village. He's been known to babble about the garden. They say he's seen things, things no one else has. But he's a recluse, and the villagers avoid him."

Amelia knew she needed to speak with Samuel Harrington, despite the village's reluctance to engage with him. She paid for her tea and headed out into the drizzly afternoon. The winding road led her to the edge of Willowbrook, where she found the cottage that had been described to her.

The cottage, much like its owner, seemed to have weathered the passage of time. Ivy clung to the walls, and the garden was overgrown with wildflowers and weeds. She approached the door and knocked gently. After a long moment, it creaked open, revealing an elderly man with thinning white hair, stooped shoulders, and a haggard look in his eyes.

"Are you Mr. Harrington?" Amelia asked.

He regarded her with a mixture of suspicion and fear. "Aye, that's me. What do you want, Miss?"

Amelia introduced herself and explained the purpose of her visit. She mentioned the letter, the hidden garden, and the strange deaths that had plagued the village. Samuel Harrington's eyes widened, and for a moment, the fog of his mind seemed to clear.

"Come inside," he said, his voice trembling. "I'll tell you what I know, but you must promise to help me."

Amelia entered the cottage, and as the door closed behind her, the mysteries of Willowbrook began to unravel. Samuel Harrington's tale was a tapestry of dark secrets, hidden intrigues, and the ominous garden that concealed horrors beyond imagination.

As he spoke, the shadows deepened in the room, and Amelia's resolve to uncover the truth only grew stronger. The sinister web of deceit woven around the garden and its enigmatic owner, combined with the tragic deaths that had befallen the villagers, filled the room with an air of dread.

With each word, Samuel Harrington led Amelia further into the heart of the mystery, deeper into the hidden garden's secrets, and closer to the edge of danger. It was a puzzle that begged to be solved, and Amelia Sinclair was determined to unravel it, no matter the cost.

As the last rays of daylight vanished outside, and the room was shrouded in darkness, Samuel Harrington's voice reached a crescendo, leaving Amelia with a cliffhanger that sent shivers down her spine.

"To know the truth, Miss Sinclair, you must visit the garden," he said, his voice quivering with a mixture of fear and anticipation.

"But beware, for it holds secrets that should never see the light of day."

## Chapter 2: The Forbidden Garden

The night had descended upon Willowbrook, casting the village into an eerie stillness, and Amelia Sinclair found herself on the threshold of an enigma. She had been drawn deeper into the mystery of the hidden garden by Samuel Harrington's harrowing account of what lay within. The chilling tales of deaths and secrets had left her both unsettled and resolute. As she stood on the threshold of Samuel's cottage, her determination to uncover the truth blazed like a beacon.

"Tell me more about this garden, Mr. Harrington," she implored, her voice resolute but tinged with concern.

Samuel Harrington's gnarled hands trembled as he recounted the legends of the garden. He spoke of the whispers that permeated the village, the vanished souls, and the dark enchantment that cloaked it. He claimed that those who ventured into the garden never returned, and the flowers that bloomed within were said to be a dark, unnatural shade of crimson.

"I heard tales, Miss Sinclair, that the garden is cursed, that it hungers for the living," he whispered, his eyes filled with dread. "But that ain't the worst of it. There's something else, something that nobody dares speak of."

Amelia leaned closer, captivated by the old man's words. "What is it, Mr. Harrington? What else have you heard?"

Samuel hesitated for a moment, as if gathering his last reserves of courage. "They say that the garden has a keeper, a woman named Elowen, who guards its secrets fiercely. She is said to be the source of its power, and her will is unyielding. Some even believe she can control the very elements, bending them to her whims."

The name "Elowen" struck a chord with Amelia. It was whispered in hushed tones around the village, but no one would speak of her openly. Elowen was a figure of both fear and fascination, and her connection to the hidden garden was an intricate piece of the puzzle.

Determined to uncover the truth, Amelia pressed further. "Do you know where this garden is, Mr. Harrington?"

He nodded, his eyes clouded with sorrow. "I can take you there, Miss Sinclair. I've been there once, only once, and I can show you the way. But you must promise me, promise me that you'll find out what happened to my daughter, Eleanor, who went into that cursed garden and never returned."

Amelia's heart ached for the old man, and she made the solemn promise. She was committed to uncovering the secrets of the garden, and if that meant finding answers about Eleanor's fate, she would do it.

The moon was high in the sky as they set out on their journey. Samuel Harrington led Amelia through a winding forest path, the thick canopy of trees casting eerie shadows on the ground. The air was thick with anticipation, and the ominous feeling of being watched pervaded every step.

As they reached a clearing, Samuel halted, and his voice quivered. "This is it, Miss Sinclair. The garden is just beyond this clearing."

Amelia's pulse quickened, and she held her breath. They stepped into the clearing, and there, before her, lay a garden unlike any other she had seen. It was shrouded in mist, the petals of its flowers a deep, unnatural shade of crimson. The garden exuded an aura of malevolence, as if it were a living entity, a sinister force that defied the laws of nature.

But it was the figure standing at the center of the garden that sent a shiver down Amelia's spine. A woman, her long, raven-black hair cascading like a waterfall, stood there, her eyes fixed on them. She was dressed in a flowing gown of emerald green, and her presence seemed to command the very elements, for the mist swirled around her, and the flowers seemed to bend to her will.

Elowen.

Amelia's heart raced, her detective's instincts kicking into high gear. Who was this enigmatic woman, and what secrets did she hold? What had drawn her to the garden, and why did she seem so connected to its dark power?

As they approached, Elowen's eyes bore into Amelia's, a mix of curiosity and something more sinister. She spoke in a voice that seemed to echo through the garden like a haunting melody. "Welcome, Miss Sinclair. You've come seeking answers, have you not?"

Amelia nodded, her voice unwavering. "I have, Elowen. I want to know the truth about this garden and the deaths that are tied to it."

Elowen's lips curled into a sinister smile, and her eyes danced with an otherworldly light. "The truth is not easily obtained, Miss Sinclair. It requires sacrifice, determination, and an unwavering resolve. Are you prepared to pay the price for the truth?"

The garden seemed to close in around them, the mist thickening and the flowers' crimson hues intensifying. Amelia's mind raced with possibilities, her detective's instincts warning her of the danger ahead. The mysteries of Willowbrook were unraveling, but they led her further into the heart of darkness.

## Chapter 3: The Garden's Enchantment

Amelia Sinclair stood at the precipice of a decision, her gaze locked with the mysterious figure known as Elowen. The air grew heavier as the garden's enchantment threatened to overwhelm her, yet her resolve remained unwavering. She had come this far in her quest for the truth, and she was not one to back down in the face of uncertainty.

"I am prepared to pay the price, Elowen," she replied, her voice steady. "But first, you must tell me about the deaths that have plagued Willowbrook and the secrets of this garden."

Elowen's laughter was as haunting as the garden itself. "The deaths, Miss Sinclair, are but the echoes of a price unpaid. This garden hungers for souls, and its dark power demands a life for a life. As for its secrets, they are bound by ancient spells, hidden beneath layers of enigma."

Amelia's curiosity burned brighter as she realized the magnitude of the challenge she faced. She was entangled in a web of folklore, mysticism, and unexplained deaths, and she could not escape without uncovering the truth.

"Then let us begin," she said, her determination unyielding. "I am here to break through those layers and reveal the secrets of this garden, no matter the cost."

Elowen nodded, her emerald eyes glittering with an eerie satisfaction. "Very well, Miss Sinclair. To delve into the garden's mysteries, we shall begin with a journey into the past, a journey of visions."

With a wave of her hand, the garden seemed to come alive. The flowers swayed and parted, revealing an ancient stone path that led deeper into the heart of the garden. Amelia followed Elowen along the path, her senses heightened, and her heart racing. She had entered a realm where the boundaries between reality and illusion blurred, and the past began to unravel before her eyes.

As they walked, the garden transformed, becoming an intricate tapestry of memory. The whispers of the past echoed in the rustling leaves, and the crimson flowers seemed to pulse with life. Amelia felt herself drawn into a vision, a scene that unfolded as if she were a silent spectator.

Before her, a young woman with auburn hair and a white summer dress appeared. It was Eleanor, Samuel Harrington's daughter. She seemed to move through the garden with a dreamy, distant expression, her eyes vacant as if under a spell.

"What is this, Elowen?" Amelia whispered, her voice filled with both fascination and dread.

Elowen's voice accompanied the vision. "This is the past, Miss Sinclair. The garden's memories are a reflection of the lives it has claimed. Eleanor Harrington was the garden's last victim, and she paid the ultimate price for her curiosity."

The vision unfolded, and Eleanor reached the center of the garden, where an ancient, gnarled tree stood. The tree's roots seemed to pulse like veins, and the air grew heavy with foreboding. Eleanor reached out to touch the tree, and as her fingers made contact, her eyes filled with terror.

Amelia could sense Eleanor's fear, her desperation, and the realization that she was trapped within the garden's insidious grasp. The vision played out like a tragedy, as Eleanor's body seemed to wither and fade away, her essence absorbed by the tree.

"Elowen, this is... this is horrifying," Amelia stammered, her heart aching for the young woman who had met such a gruesome fate.

Elowen's eyes remained fixed on the vision, her expression unreadable. "The garden hungers, Miss Sinclair, and it devours those who dare to enter. It is a curse that has plagued Willowbrook for centuries, and it is a curse that cannot be broken easily."

As the vision of Eleanor's tragic end faded, Amelia was left with a sense of helplessness and a newfound determination. The garden was a malevolent force that needed to be confronted, but she could not do it alone. She turned to Elowen with a burning question.

"Elowen, how can this curse be broken? How can we release the souls trapped within this garden?"

Elowen's gaze shifted to Amelia, and for a moment, her eyes held a glimmer of uncertainty. "The curse can only be broken through a sacrifice of pure intent, an act of selflessness that defies the garden's insatiable hunger. But that, Miss Sinclair, is a choice you must make for yourself."

Amelia's mind raced as she grappled with the weight of Elowen's words. Breaking the curse would require a sacrifice, but the nature of that sacrifice remained shrouded in ambiguity. What could she offer that would satisfy the garden's dark appetite and release the trapped souls?

As she pondered her next steps, Elowen beckoned her deeper into the garden, where more secrets awaited. Amelia knew that uncovering the truth would demand her courage, resourcefulness, and the ability to decipher the enigmatic puzzles that lay before her. The mysteries of Willowbrook were entwined with an ancient malevolence, and as she ventured further into the heart of the garden, the shadows of her own past merged with the ominous tapestry of the present.

The cliffhanger loomed ever closer, as the garden's secrets beckoned, and the price of the truth remained shrouded in uncertainty. Amelia Sinclair had embarked on a treacherous journey, and the darkness that enveloped her only grew deeper.

As she delved further into the enigma of Willowbrook's hidden garden, the final revelation remained tantalizingly out of reach, and the reader's curiosity and anticipation were left hanging in the balance.

## Chapter 4: Unveiling the Past

Amelia Sinclair followed Elowen deeper into the hidden garden, her heart heavy with the weight of the curse that had ensnared this place for centuries. The garden seemed to shift and change as they walked, a living memory of tragedies and secrets long buried. The air was filled with an eerie hush, and the path ahead beckoned with both foreboding and fascination.

As they moved further into the garden, Amelia noticed that the colors of the flowers shifted, transitioning from crimson to a deep, mournful violet. The path they followed seemed to narrow, with the towering trees pressing in on both sides, creating a tunnel-like atmosphere. The very essence of the place felt as if it were closing in around her, drawing her deeper into its spell.

"Elowen," Amelia began, her voice almost lost in the stillness of the garden. "What more can you tell me about this place? Its history, its purpose..."

Elowen's voice was a soft whisper, as if carried by the breeze. "This garden, Miss Sinclair, has existed for longer than memory can reach. It is a place where the boundaries between the living and the dead blur. Its origins are lost to time, but it was said to have been created to serve as a gateway between our world and the realms beyond. A portal to the afterlife."

Amelia felt a chill run down her spine. A portal to the afterlife? It was a notion that defied rationality, and yet the garden seemed to defy the very laws of nature.

As they continued along the path, the garden's memory began to unfold before them once more. This time, it revealed a scene from the past, one that seemed to resonate with the tales Amelia had heard from the villagers. It was a dark and stormy night, with rain pouring from the heavens and the garden shrouded in mist.

A group of villagers, carrying torches and lanterns, had gathered at the entrance to the garden. Among them was Samuel Harrington, much younger and less worn by life. They were determined to confront the malevolent force that had claimed the lives of their loved ones.

Elowen explained, "This is the night they attempted to break the curse, to put an end to the garden's hunger for souls."

The villagers began to chant incantations, attempting to ward off the garden's influence. Their torches cast eerie shadows, and the tension in the air was palpable. But as they ventured deeper into the garden, a sense of despair and futility overcame them.

Amelia watched as the villagers grew increasingly disoriented, their movements sluggish, and their voices filled with fear. It was as if the garden itself were resisting their efforts, sapping their willpower and leaving them vulnerable to its dark allure.

Then, a figure emerged from the shadows. It was Elowen, but she appeared different, younger and less ethereal, as if she were a part of the village rather than an otherworldly presence.

Elowen approached the villagers with a sense of purpose, her voice filled with a strange, mesmerizing power. She urged them to abandon their efforts, to embrace the garden's enchantment, and to submit to its dark desires.

The villagers began to waver, their determination giving way to a haunting submission. One by one, they succumbed to the garden's influence, losing themselves in its dark allure. It was a night of betrayal, not just of the villagers by Elowen, but of the very essence of their humanity.

As the vision came to an end, Amelia was left with a profound sense of unease. Elowen had once been part of the village, but she had chosen to serve the garden, to become its guardian and enforcer. The betrayal ran deep, and the echoes of that fateful night continued to resonate in the present.

"Elowen," Amelia asked, her voice laced with determination. "What happened to the villagers that night? What did the garden do to them?"

Elowen's eyes bore into her, a mixture of regret and guilt haunting their depths. "The garden claimed their souls, Miss Sinclair. They became one with its malevolence, and their humanity was extinguished. They became its guardians, forever bound to protect the garden and ensure its secrets remained hidden."

Amelia's heart sank. The villagers had paid a terrible price for their attempt to break the curse, and their souls were now trapped within the very entity they had sought to confront. The enigma of the garden had only grown deeper and more sinister.

As they moved deeper into the garden, Amelia couldn't help but wonder about her own role in this unfolding tragedy. Elowen had hinted at the need for a sacrifice to break the curse, and the notion of giving up something of herself lingered in the back of her mind.

The garden's enchantment seemed to intensify as they walked, and the path ahead led to a place of darkness and uncertainty. Amelia knew that to uncover the final truth and free the souls trapped within, she would have to make a decision, one that would test the very essence of her being.

The cliffhanger awaited, as Amelia stood at the precipice of revelation and sacrifice. The mysteries of Willowbrook were drawing closer to their resolution, but the final pieces of the puzzle remained just out of reach, leaving both the protagonist and the reader in a state of tantalizing uncertainty.

## Chapter 5: A Haunting Dilemma

Amelia Sinclair continued to follow Elowen deeper into the heart of the hidden garden, the weight of its history and malevolence pressing in on her from all sides. The enigma that had shrouded Willowbrook for centuries was unraveling, but it left her with a chilling awareness of the cost that must be paid to break the curse.

The garden's enchantment seemed to intensify with each step, the air heavy with the whispers of the trapped souls and the echoes of past tragedies. As they ventured further, the path became narrower, winding through a grove of twisted trees, their branches reaching out like skeletal fingers, as if they, too, sought to ensnare any intruder.

Amelia could feel the presence of the garden closing in around her, its influence growing more potent. She couldn't help but recall Elowen's words about the necessity of a sacrifice, a selfless act to break the curse. The garden demanded a price, and the nature of that price was still veiled in uncertainty.

"Elowen," Amelia finally spoke, her voice barely above a whisper, "what must I offer to the garden? What can satisfy its hunger for a soul, for a sacrifice?"

Elowen turned to her, her eyes reflecting the turmoil within. "To break the curse, Miss Sinclair, you must offer your own essence, a piece of your own soul. The garden hungers for a life, and it must be a life freely given, an act of pure selflessness."

Amelia's heart sank at the gravity of the choice she faced. The very essence of her being, her soul, was on the line. But the lives that had been claimed by the garden, the trapped souls crying out in the echoes of the past, demanded justice and freedom. She couldn't turn away from their plight, no matter the personal cost.

With each step along the path, the garden seemed to respond to her internal struggle. The flowers shifted from deep violet to an even darker shade, a mournful black that exuded an eerie allure. It was as if the garden itself was urging her to make a decision, to fulfill the unspoken pact.

Elowen led her to a clearing, where the ancient, gnarled tree stood—the very same tree where Eleanor Harrington had met her tragic end. The tree's roots writhed like serpents, and its presence felt malevolent. Amelia knew that this was the place where the ultimate decision had to be made.

"Miss Sinclair," Elowen said, her voice low and filled with sorrow, "the time has come. You must decide whether to offer a piece of your soul to the garden, to break the curse and release the trapped souls, or to turn away and leave this place, its mysteries forever hidden."

Amelia stood in silence, her thoughts in turmoil. She thought of the villagers who had attempted to confront the garden, of Eleanor Harrington, and of the generations of souls that had been claimed by its malevolence. She knew that her choice would shape the destiny of Willowbrook and determine whether the curse would persist.

But as she contemplated the haunting dilemma, a question gnawed at her. Why had Elowen brought her here in the first place? What was her role in the unfolding of this ancient curse? The answers seemed just out of reach, hidden behind layers of enigma.

Finally, Amelia made her decision. With a resolute breath, she spoke to Elowen, her voice unwavering. "I choose to make the sacrifice, to offer a piece of my own soul to break the curse. The trapped souls must be freed, and the secrets of this garden must be unveiled."

Elowen nodded, her eyes filled with both gratitude and sorrow. "Your choice is a selfless one, Miss Sinclair, and it is a path that few would willingly tread. But you must understand that this act will forever bind you to the garden, and it will come at a great cost."

As Amelia stepped closer to the ancient tree, she extended her hand to touch its gnarled bark. The roots of the tree seemed to respond, shifting and pulsating, as if they were preparing to accept the offering.

But just as she was about to complete the act of sacrifice, a sudden realization struck her. Elowen's eyes held a glint of something other than gratitude—guilt. She couldn't ignore the nagging doubt that had taken root in her mind. Why had Elowen led her to this choice, and what role did she play in the perpetuation of the curse?

Before she could proceed, a voice filled with sorrow echoed in her mind, a voice that seemed to emanate from the very tree itself. "Wait, Miss Sinclair, before you make your sacrifice, there is a truth that must be revealed."

Amelia withdrew her hand from the tree, her instincts on high alert. "What truth, and who are you?"

The voice continued, a blend of longing and regret. "I am Eleanor Harrington, the last to be claimed by the garden. There is more to this curse than you know, and Elowen's role in it is not what it seems."

Elowen's eyes widened, a mixture of fear and desperation in her expression. "Eleanor, you must not reveal—"

But it was too late. The truth was out, and the garden itself seemed to respond, the air growing thick with tension. Amelia had unwittingly stumbled upon a web of secrets that went beyond the curse, and she now had to confront a haunting dilemma: who could she trust, and what was the true nature of the enigmatic force that held Willowbrook in its grasp?

The cliffhanger loomed, as the revelation of Eleanor's presence and her cryptic words opened a new chapter of uncertainty and danger. The mysteries of the garden were deeper than anyone had imagined, and Amelia Sinclair was now entangled in a treacherous web of deception and intrigue.

## Chapter 6: Echoes of Betrayal

Amelia stood in the midst of the hidden garden, her hand withdrawn from the gnarled tree. The revelation that Eleanor Harrington's spirit still lingered within the garden had sent shockwaves through her, casting doubt upon the very nature of the curse and Elowen's true role in it. The enigma of Willowbrook had taken a new, bewildering turn.

"Is it truly you, Eleanor?" Amelia inquired, her voice a mixture of astonishment and trepidation.

Eleanor's presence resonated within Amelia's mind, a voice filled with sorrow and longing. "Yes, Miss Sinclair, it is I. I am bound to the garden, a guardian like the others, but I possess the ability to reach out, to share the truth that has been hidden for so long."

Elowen, her eyes wide with apprehension, implored Eleanor to remain silent. "Eleanor, you mustn't reveal our secrets. The curse must be preserved."

Amelia's eyes darted between Elowen and Eleanor, a sense of urgency propelling her forward. "Tell me, Eleanor, what is this hidden truth? What is the nature of the curse, and what role does Elowen play in it?"

Eleanor's voice grew clearer, her spectral presence seeking to shed light on the mystery that had plagued Willowbrook for centuries. "The curse, Miss Sinclair, is not what it appears. The garden was created not as a malevolent force, but as a means to protect a forbidden secret, a secret that could have had devastating consequences for the world if it were unleashed."

The revelation sent shockwaves through Amelia. The garden, once seen as a sinister entity, had been conceived to safeguard something of immense importance. She demanded further clarification. "What secret, Eleanor? What is it that must be protected at all costs?"

Elowen's voice wavered, her desperation palpable. "Eleanor, you must not—"

Eleanor's response was resolute. "It is time for the truth to be known, even if it means my own release. The garden was created to guard the entrance to a realm, a realm where an ancient evil sleeps, a force that could unleash chaos and destruction upon the world. Elowen's role is not to perpetuate a curse but to ensure that the secret remains hidden, to prevent anyone from gaining access to that realm."

Amelia's mind reeled as she tried to absorb the weight of the revelation. The curse was a safeguard, not a malevolent force, and Elowen had been tasked with preventing access to a realm that held an ancient evil. The very essence of Willowbrook's enigma had shifted, and the moral and ethical dilemmas now loomed larger than ever.

"But at what cost, Eleanor?" Amelia asked, her voice heavy with sorrow. "The villagers, their souls, the lives lost—were they all sacrificed to maintain this secret?"

Eleanor's voice trembled with remorse. "Yes, Miss Sinclair. It is a haunting burden that we, the guardians, have carried. We must protect the world from the ancient evil that stirs within that realm, even if it means condemning ourselves to an eternity of servitude."

Elowen, her resolve shaken, added, "Eleanor speaks the truth, but the consequences of the curse are not without their own torment. To maintain the secret, we must claim the lives of those who venture into the garden, and their souls become intertwined with the curse."

Amelia was faced with an agonizing dilemma. The garden was both protector and tormentor, and the choices she now had to make would shape the fate of Willowbrook and the world beyond. The secrets of the realm, the ancient evil, and the souls of the trapped guardians demanded a resolution.

As she contemplated her next steps, the garden itself seemed to respond, the very earth beneath her feet quaking. The trees twisted and groaned, and the flowers shifted from black to a deep, sinister crimson. It was as if the garden itself were an entity torn between its role as a guardian and the price it exacted.

Eleanor's voice grew urgent. "Miss Sinclair, you must decide whether to continue with the sacrifice and release the souls, or to protect the world from the ancient evil. The choice is yours, but it comes with an unfathomable cost."

Amelia felt the weight of the world pressing down upon her. The revelation had raised more questions than answers, and the choices she faced were not just moral but also profound in their consequences. She couldn't turn away from the duty that had been thrust upon her, to make a decision that would determine the fate of the garden, the souls of the villagers, and the realm beyond.

## Chapter 7: The Unveiling

Amelia Sinclair stood at the crossroads of destiny within the heart of the hidden garden. The revelations that had shaken the foundations of Willowbrook's enigma weighed heavily on her, and the choices she faced were neither clear nor easy. The garden, once seen as a malevolent force, now stood as the guardian of a realm harboring an ancient evil.

Eleanor Harrington's voice continued to echo in her mind, a plea for the truth to be known, for the ancient secret to be preserved, and for the curse to be broken. Elowen's conflicted presence added to the complexity of the dilemma, as the enigmatic guardian seemed torn between her duty and the toll it exacted.

Amelia gazed at the ancient, gnarled tree, her thoughts a whirlwind of turmoil and determination. The very essence of her being, her soul, was the price demanded to break the curse and release the souls of the villagers who had been trapped for centuries. She knew that her choice would not only impact the fate of Willowbrook but could also unleash the ancient evil within the guarded realm.

With the weight of centuries upon her, Amelia whispered to herself, "To preserve the secret or to release the souls... I must decide."

Eleanor's voice, still resolute, resonated within her thoughts. "The choice is yours, Miss Sinclair. I am bound to the garden, but I long for release. The souls of the villagers have suffered for far too long."

Amelia reached a decision. She couldn't condemn the trapped souls to an eternity of torment, and she couldn't bear the weight of further suffering. With a deep breath and a heavy heart, she extended her hand once more to the gnarled tree, ready to offer a piece of her own soul to break the curse.

As her fingers touched the bark, the garden itself seemed to come alive, the air crackling with energy. The roots of the tree writhed and pulsed, responding to her sacrifice. A mournful cry echoed through the garden, and the flowers changed from crimson to a brilliant, ethereal white, a symbol of hope and release.

Eleanor's voice grew more distant, tinged with gratitude. "Thank you, Miss Sinclair, for your selflessness. The curse is broken, and the souls are free."

Elowen's presence seemed to waver, as if a weight had been lifted from her shoulders. "I, too, thank you for your choice, Miss Sinclair. The ancient evil remains sealed, and the realm is safeguarded."

Amelia felt a profound sense of relief and accomplishment. The torment of the trapped souls had ended, and the world beyond remained protected from the ancient evil. She had fulfilled her duty as a detective and protector, but she couldn't help but wonder about the cost to her own soul.

As the garden settled into a tranquil stillness, a sense of closure washed over her. The centuries-old curse had been broken, and the enigma of Willowbrook had been unveiled. But her journey was far from over, and the mysteries that had plagued the village were far more complex than she had ever imagined.

Before she could contemplate her next steps, a voice filled with malevolence and ancient power echoed through the garden. "You have broken the curse, detective, but you have also set me free."

Amelia turned to see a rift opening within the garden, a portal to the realm that had been guarded for centuries. A dark, looming figure emerged from the rift, a being of shadow and dread. It was the ancient evil, the very force the garden had been created to protect against.

Elowen's eyes filled with terror as she realized the magnitude of the threat. "No, it cannot be... You were supposed to remain sealed!"

The ancient evil, now free, turned its gaze upon Amelia, its voice dripping with malice. "You have released me, and now I shall have my vengeance, beginning with you, detective."

## Chapter 8: The Malevolent Force Unleashed

Amelia Sinclair stood at the precipice of a cataclysmic revelation. The ancient evil, once sealed away within the guarded realm, had been set free, and its malevolence now bore down upon the hidden garden. The air grew heavy with darkness as the being of shadow and dread advanced towards her, its power palpable, its intentions sinister.

Elowen, her voice trembling, attempted to explain. "This was not meant to happen, detective. The curse was created to safeguard the realm and to prevent the ancient evil from escaping."

The being of darkness, its presence growing more ominous, spoke with a chilling assurance. "Your actions have shattered the seal, and now I shall exact my revenge upon the world. You are my first victim, detective, and you will witness the consequences of your choice."

Amelia knew that she had inadvertently unleashed a force that threatened not only her life but also the entire village of Willowbrook. The ancient evil possessed a power that defied comprehension, and its malevolence sought to engulf all in its path.

As the being of darkness reached out, Amelia's instincts kicked in, and she turned to flee. But the very fabric of the garden seemed to warp and shift, as if conspiring with the ancient evil.

The path she had entered through had vanished, leaving her surrounded by an eerie, shifting labyrinth of darkness.

Desperation seized her, and she had no choice but to press forward, seeking an escape from the garden's ever-changing terrain. The malevolent force pursued her with relentless determination, its shadowy presence encroaching from all sides.

In the midst of the maze, the garden's flora had transformed into grotesque, sentient forms, with thorny tendrils and wicked, tooth-like petals. They seemed to be extensions of the ancient evil's power, reaching out to ensnare and entangle.

Amelia fought through the labyrinth, her heart racing, her determination unwavering. She couldn't allow the malevolent force to escape into the world, and she knew that the only way to prevent it was to find a means of resealing the realm. But in the heart of the garden, with its shifting pathways and ominous flora, the task seemed insurmountable.

Elowen, who had accompanied her, spoke with a sense of urgency. "We must find the guardian's relic, Miss Sinclair. It is the key to resealing the realm and preventing the ancient evil from escaping."

Amelia nodded, her focus clear. The relic was a thread of hope amidst the encroaching darkness, and she was determined to retrieve it. As they ventured deeper into the labyrinth, the malevolent force pursued relentlessly, its presence casting a long shadow.

The garden's shifting pathways seemed to lead them in circles, as if mocking their efforts. Amelia couldn't help but wonder if the malevolent force itself was influencing the garden's terrain, seeking to thwart their progress.

But with each step, they uncovered clues—strange markings on the flora, symbols etched into the ground, and a faint, haunting melody that seemed to guide them. The clues hinted at the relic's location and the means to reseal the realm.

As they followed the trail of clues, the ancient evil's presence grew more tangible, its power threatening to overwhelm them. Amelia could feel its malevolence, a force born of eons of captivity and fury. The stakes had never been higher, and the fate of Willowbrook and the world beyond hung in the balance.

Finally, they reached a clearing within the labyrinth, where an ancient stone pedestal stood. Atop the pedestal, bathed in a faint, ethereal light, rested the guardian's relic—a small, intricately carved amulet. It pulsed with an otherworldly energy, its significance undeniable.

Elowen urged Amelia to take the relic. "This is the key, Miss Sinclair. With it, we can reseal the realm and prevent the ancient evil from escaping."

Amelia reached for the amulet, her fingers trembling. The very fate of Willowbrook and the world beyond rested in her hands, and the malevolent force closed in, its presence now a looming, suffocating darkness.

But just as she was about to grasp the amulet, a sinister laughter echoed through the clearing. The malevolent force had caught up to them, its shadowy form twisting and undulating. It was almost upon them, its intent clear—to prevent the resealing of the realm at all costs.

## Chapter 9: The Battle Within

Amelia Sinclair, standing in the heart of the hidden garden, reached for the guardian's relic—an intricately carved amulet that pulsed with otherworldly energy. Her fingers brushed against it just as the malevolent force, the ancient evil once sealed within the guarded realm, closed in on her and Elowen. Its shadowy form twisted and undulated, a presence of darkness and dread.

Sinister laughter echoed through the clearing as the malevolent force sought to prevent the resealing of the realm. It had been set free by Amelia's choice, and now, it would stop at nothing to exact its revenge upon the world and all those who had confined it for centuries.

Amelia's determination flared as she clutched the guardian's relic. The amulet radiated power and purpose, and she knew that it was the key to resealing the realm, a means to prevent the ancient evil from escaping and wreaking havoc upon the world. But the malevolent force stood between her and that crucial task.

Elowen, her voice tinged with fear and resolve, spoke urgently, "Miss Sinclair, we must act quickly. The ancient evil will not relent. We must use the amulet to reseal the realm and protect the world from its vengeance."

As the malevolent force closed in, Amelia realized that the battle ahead was not just a physical one but a contest of wills, a test of the strength of the guardian's relic against the ancient evil's malevolence. The amulet's energy had to be harnessed, its purpose fulfilled.

With a surge of determination, Amelia channeled the amulet's power, a brilliant light emanating from the intricate carvings. The light clashed with the malevolent force's darkness, a tumultuous struggle of opposing energies.

The ground beneath them shook as the battle raged on, the very fabric of the garden quaking in response. The ancient evil's laughter turned to a furious howl, and its shadowy form recoiled from the radiant energy of the amulet.

But it was a battle of near-equals, and the malevolent force would not be vanquished easily. Its shadows snaked and twisted, seeking to ensnare and smother the amulet's light.

Elowen's voice resonated with encouragement. "We can do this, Miss Sinclair. We have the power of the amulet on our side. Channel it, focus your will, and let it overcome the ancient evil's malevolence."

Amelia concentrated, the struggle within her mind and spirit mirroring the physical battle taking place. The amulet's light surged, pushing back against the encroaching darkness. With every ounce of her resolve, she channeled the power of the relic.

The very air seemed to crackle with tension as the balance teetered on a precipice. The malevolent force's howls grew desperate, and its form wavered, as if the amulet's light were slowly gaining the upper hand.

But just as it seemed that victory was within reach, the malevolent force unleashed a final surge of power, a tremendous burst of darkness that threatened to overwhelm the amulet's light. The battle reached its climax, the fate of Willowbrook and the world beyond hanging in the balance.

With a tremendous effort, Amelia pushed back against the darkness, her will fortified by the knowledge that the guardian's relic was the key to preserving the world. The amulet's light shone brilliantly, and the malevolent force let out one final, anguished cry.

The darkness receded, vanquished, and the amulet's light remained triumphant. The ancient evil had been repelled, and the realm was resealed, its malevolence contained once more. A profound silence settled over the garden, the battle having come to its awe-inspiring conclusion.

Elowen, her voice filled with relief and gratitude, spoke softly, "You have done it, Miss Sinclair. The world is safe once more, and the realm is sealed."

Amelia lowered the amulet, her breath heavy with the aftermath of the battle. She had faced the ancient evil and emerged victorious, and the weight of her responsibility as Willowbrook's protector was more apparent than ever.

But as they stood in the clearing, the malevolent force's final words echoed through the garden, a chilling reminder of the darkness that had been set free. "You may have won this battle, detective, but the war has just begun. I shall return, and when I do, the world will know true despair."

# Chapter 10: The Shifting Shadows

Amelia Sinclair, having repelled the malevolent force and resealed the guarded realm within the hidden garden, stood in the clearing alongside Elowen. The aftermath of the battle had left an air of uncertainty and foreboding, as the ancient evil's haunting promise of return weighed heavily upon them.

Elowen's voice quivered as she spoke, "Miss Sinclair, we have faced the ancient evil, but its threat remains. We must be vigilant, for it is a malevolence that knows no bounds."

Amelia nodded, her gaze focused on the guardian's relic—an intricately carved amulet that had been the key to resealing the realm. The amulet still pulsed with otherworldly energy, a reminder of the power they had harnessed to protect the world.

"The threat is not over," Amelia acknowledged, her voice filled with determination. "We must find a way to ensure that the ancient evil remains sealed, to prevent its return and the havoc it could unleash."

Elowen's eyes held a glint of hope, despite the lingering fear. "There is a way, Miss Sinclair, but it is a path filled with challenges and mysteries. We must unravel the secrets of the garden and uncover the full extent of the curse."

The enigma of the garden had deepened, and the mysteries that had plagued Willowbrook were far more complex than anyone had ever imagined. Amelia knew that they had to delve deeper into the garden's history, uncover its secrets, and find a means to protect the village and the world beyond from the ancient evil's return.

As they ventured deeper into the garden, the very terrain seemed to respond to the presence of the malevolent force, its darkness still lingering. The flora, once grotesque and sentient, now bore an even more sinister aspect, as if tainted by the evil that had been set free.

The path led them to a tranquil glade, a place that had once been untouched by the curse's malevolence. But even here, a sense of unease settled upon them, as if the shadows of the ancient evil's presence still lingered.

Elowen pointed to a magnificent fountain at the center of the glade, its waters crystal clear and inviting. "This is the Fountain of Echoes, Miss Sinclair. It holds the key to uncovering the garden's secrets and protecting the village."

Amelia approached the fountain, its waters reflecting the sky above. As she gazed into its depths, she could sense a powerful, ancient energy, a source of knowledge that could shed light on the mysteries of Willowbrook.

Elowen urged her to focus on the waters, to seek the knowledge that the Fountain of Echoes could provide. "The garden has witnessed the passage of centuries, Miss Sinclair. It holds the echoes of the past, the memories of those who have been trapped and the secrets of the realm. It is a font of both knowledge and peril."

Amelia complied, concentrating on the fountain's waters, her mind open to the revelations that might come. As she delved into the depths of the Fountain of Echoes, a torrent of images and voices flooded her senses.

She saw the faces of villagers from centuries past, their lives and tragedies etched in the waters. She heard the echoes of their conversations, their fears and hopes. The garden's history unfolded before her, revealing the creation of the curse, the sacrifice that had been demanded, and the sealing of the realm.

But as the memories coalesced, Amelia felt a presence—a voice from the past, a guardian who had served as a protector of the realm. The guardian's voice whispered to her, a plea for help and a revelation of a hidden chamber that held the ultimate means of safeguarding the garden.

Elowen watched as Amelia's eyes glazed over, her connection with the Fountain of Echoes deepening. She knew that the revelations were of paramount importance, a way to secure the garden's future and prevent the malevolent force from returning.

But just as the guardian's voice reached its climax, a sinister shadow fell over the glade, casting a pall over the waters of the fountain. The ancient evil had returned, its presence a looming threat.

Amelia, torn between the need for knowledge and the imminent danger, felt the connection with the Fountain of Echoes break. The malevolent force's laughter echoed through the glade, a chilling reminder of the darkness that had been set free.

Elowen urged her to act swiftly, her voice filled with urgency. "We have the knowledge we need, Miss Sinclair, but the ancient evil is upon us. We must find the hidden chamber and secure the garden's protection."

Amelia nodded, her heart racing as they hurriedly left the glade and followed the guardian's voice, which had revealed the location of the chamber. The shadows cast by the malevolent force grew longer and more sinister, as if it sought to thwart their every step.

As they ventured deeper into the garden, the very terrain seemed to shift and change, as if the malevolent force were warping the path ahead. The mysteries of Willowbrook's enigma had given way to a treacherous journey, a race against time to secure the garden's protection and prevent the ancient evil's return.

## Chapter 11: The Chamber of Shadows

Amelia Sinclair and Elowen ventured deeper into the hidden garden, their footsteps guided by the whispered voice of the guardian from the past. The revelations of the Fountain of Echoes had offered a path forward, a way to secure the garden's protection and prevent the return of the malevolent force.

The ancient evil's presence, like a shadowy noose, still encircled them, its malevolence a looming threat. As they navigated the shifting terrain of the garden, the very earth seemed to respond to the malevolent force's proximity, twisting and contorting, as if conspiring against them.

The guardian's voice led them to a remote corner of the garden, where the flora appeared untouched by the curse's malevolence. Here, amidst a grove of ancient, gnarled trees, stood a weathered stone door, its surface adorned with enigmatic carvings.

Elowen approached the door, her fingers tracing the carvings, as if seeking a connection with the past. "This is the entrance to the Chamber of Shadows, Miss Sinclair. Within lies the means to secure the garden's protection."

Amelia nodded, her gaze focused on the stone door. She knew that the revelations of the guardian held the key to their quest, a way to ensure the safety of Willowbrook and the world beyond. The malevolent force, its presence still looming, demanded their haste.

As they pushed open the stone door, the chamber beyond was bathed in a dim, ethereal light. The walls were adorned with ancient inscriptions and carvings, each telling a part of the garden's history and the secrets that had been hidden for centuries.

Amelia approached a central pedestal, where an ornate, jeweled amulet rested. The amulet pulsed with an inner light, as if aware of their presence. It was the Chamber of Shadows' guardian relic—a key to securing the garden's protection.

Elowen's voice was filled with hope and determination. "This is the amulet that will safeguard the garden, Miss Sinclair. It holds the power to ward off the malevolent force and prevent its return."

Amelia reached for the amulet, her fingers trembling with anticipation. As she grasped it, a surge of power coursed through her, a connection to the amulet's energy. She knew that their quest was nearing its climax, but the malevolent force, a shadowy presence, still cast its influence over them.

With the guardian relic in hand, Amelia and Elowen retraced their steps, making their way back through the Chamber of Shadows and towards the stone door. But as they stepped into the grove of ancient trees, the malevolent force's presence grew more tangible, as if it sought to thwart their progress.

The very flora of the garden, once untouched by the curse's malevolence, now seemed to wither and contort, its grotesque forms reaching out to ensnare and entangle. It was as if the malevolent force was attempting to prevent their escape.

Elowen spoke with urgency, her eyes darting between the guardian relic and the encroaching darkness. "We must use the amulet's power, Miss Sinclair. It is the only way to ward off the malevolent force and ensure our safe return."

Amelia nodded, focusing her will on the guardian relic. As the malevolent force's shadowy tendrils closed in, she channeled the amulet's energy, releasing a brilliant burst of light that pushed back the darkness.

The malevolent force recoiled, its presence diminished by the amulet's power. It howled in frustration, its anguished cries echoing through the garden. But the guardian relic's light remained triumphant, allowing Amelia and Elowen to press forward.

As they reached the stone door that led out of the Chamber of Shadows, a sinister laughter echoed through the grove of ancient trees. The malevolent force had not been defeated, and its malevolence still cast a long shadow.

Elowen's voice trembled as she spoke, "We have the amulet, Miss Sinclair, but the malevolent force will not be vanquished so easily. It seeks to prevent our escape and return."

Amelia knew that their quest was far from over, and the malevolent force's promise of return weighed heavily upon them. They had secured the means to protect the garden, but the ancient evil's shadow still loomed over Willowbrook, casting a pall of uncertainty.

As they pushed open the stone door and stepped back into the garden, they could feel the malevolent force's presence still lurking in the shadows. The mysteries of Willowbrook had taken a new, ominous turn, and the resolution seemed more elusive than ever.

## Chapter 12: The Ancient Evil's Reckoning

Amelia Sinclair and Elowen emerged from the Chamber of Shadows, guardian relic in hand, and returned to the heart of the hidden garden. They knew that the amulet held the power to protect the garden and prevent the return of the malevolent force, but the ancient evil's shadow still cast a long and ominous presence.

As they ventured deeper into the garden, the very terrain seemed to respond to the malevolent force's proximity. The flora twisted and contorted, as if influenced by the darkness that had been set free. Amelia knew that they were in a race against time to secure the garden's protection.

Elowen's voice held a note of urgency. "Miss Sinclair, we must use the amulet to ward off the malevolent force. Its power is the only way to ensure our safety and prevent the ancient evil from returning."

Amelia nodded, her fingers clutching the guardian relic tightly. She knew that the malevolent force would not give up easily, and their quest was far from over. With each step, they drew closer to the heart of the garden, where the malevolent force's presence was most palpable.

As they approached a secluded clearing, a sense of foreboding settled upon them. The flora here had taken on an even more grotesque aspect, their thorny tendrils and tooth-like petals reaching out menacingly. The malevolent force's laughter echoed through the clearing, a chilling reminder of the darkness that had been set free.

Elowen urged Amelia to use the amulet's power, her voice filled with resolve. "We must hold our ground, Miss Sinclair. The amulet's light can ward off the malevolent force and protect us from its malevolence."

Amelia focused her will, channeling the amulet's energy to create a protective barrier of light. As the malevolent force's shadowy tendrils closed in, the guardian relic's brilliance held them at bay. The ancient evil recoiled, its howls of frustration filling the clearing.

But the malevolent force was not so easily defeated. It launched a final, desperate assault, a surge of darkness that sought to overwhelm the amulet's light. The battle raged on, the fate of Willowbrook and the world beyond hanging in the balance.

With every ounce of her resolve, Amelia pushed back against the darkness, her determination unwavering. The guardian relic's light shone brilliantly, and the malevolent force's power began to wane.

As the ancient evil's presence receded, its anguished cries grew more distant, and the guardian relic's light remained triumphant. Amelia had held her ground, protecting herself and Elowen from the malevolent force's onslaught.

But the malevolent force was not defeated. It vowed to return, its haunting promise echoing through the clearing. "You may have won this battle, detective, but the war is far from over. I shall return, and when I do, the world will know true despair."

Elowen's voice trembled as she spoke. "The ancient evil will not rest, Miss Sinclair. It will continue to seek its vengeance, and we must be prepared."

Amelia knew that their quest was far from over, and the malevolent force's promise of return weighed heavily upon them. The mysteries of Willowbrook had taken a new, ominous turn, and the resolution seemed more elusive than ever.

As they continued through the garden, the malevolent force's presence still loomed in the shadows, a constant reminder of the threat that persisted. They were poised on the brink of a new challenge, a quest to protect the garden and the world from the ancient evil's return, while the mysteries of the enigmatic village remained tantalizingly unresolved.

## Chapter 13: A New Dawn

Amelia Sinclair and Elowen had faced the malevolent force within the hidden garden, repelling its darkness and securing the guardian relic that held the power to protect Willowbrook and the world beyond. The ancient evil had been set free, but its return had been thwarted, at least for the time being.

As they ventured deeper into the garden, the malevolent force's presence continued to linger in the shadows, a constant reminder of the threat that persisted. Amelia knew that their quest was not yet complete, and the mysteries of Willowbrook had left her with a sense of unease.

They arrived at the heart of the garden, where the ancient, gnarled tree stood—the very tree that had been the source of the curse and the guardian of the hidden realm. The tree's roots twisted and turned, a testament to the centuries of history it had witnessed.

Elowen's voice was filled with determination. "This is where we must use the guardian relic, Miss Sinclair. With its power, we can protect the garden and prevent the ancient evil from returning."

Amelia nodded, her fingers clutching the amulet tightly. She knew that they had come to a pivotal moment in their journey, a moment that would determine the garden's fate and the safety of the world.

With the guardian relic in hand, Amelia channeled its power, allowing the amulet's light to envelop the ancient tree. The light spread, infusing the tree's roots and branches with an ethereal energy.

The very ground trembled as the guardian relic's power mingled with the tree's ancient essence. The air crackled with a sense of renewal, as if the very heart of the garden was being reborn.

As the transformation took place, Elowen's eyes shone with a glint of hope. "We have done it, Miss Sinclair. The garden is protected once more, and the ancient evil remains sealed."

Amelia felt a profound sense of relief and accomplishment. The centuries-old curse had been broken, the ancient evil's return thwarted, and the garden was safeguarded. The enigma of Willowbrook had unraveled, and its mysteries had been laid to rest.

But the village still held its secrets, and Amelia couldn't help but wonder about the residents of Willowbrook. As the protector of the garden, she had played her part, but there were unanswered questions, unresolved mysteries, and a community that had suffered in silence.

Elowen's voice was tinged with gratitude. "Miss Sinclair, you have brought peace to Willowbrook and to the souls of those who were trapped by the curse. You have fulfilled your duty as the guardian of the garden."

Amelia glanced at the ancient tree, its branches now adorned with radiant blossoms. The transformation was a symbol of hope and renewal, a new beginning for Willowbrook.

But there was one more piece of the puzzle that needed to be addressed. The guardian relic had offered protection, but it also held the power to reveal the ancient evil's origins and the history of the garden. With a determined expression, Amelia turned to Elowen.

"We have safeguarded the garden, but there is one last piece of the puzzle to unravel. I must use the amulet's power to reveal the history and origins of the ancient evil."

Elowen nodded in agreement, knowing that the amulet held the knowledge they needed to fully understand the enigma of the garden and the curse that had plagued Willowbrook.

Amelia focused her will, the amulet's energy guiding her to the revelations hidden within the garden's history. The guardian relic's light spread, illuminating the ancient tree's branches and the surrounding area.

As the amulet's power reached its zenith, the air seemed to shimmer with memories and echoes of the past. Images and voices filled Amelia's mind, revealing the truth about the ancient evil and the creation of the curse.

She saw a group of villagers from centuries past, gathered beneath the ancient tree, their faces etched with fear and determination. They had created the curse as a desperate means to contain the ancient evil, a force born of ancient magic and malevolence.

Amelia heard their voices, their pleas for protection, and their sacrifices. The curse had demanded a great toll, but it had served as a guardian of the realm and a protector of the world beyond.

As the revelations unfolded, Elowen's eyes filled with understanding. "The curse was born out of necessity, Miss

Sinclair. It was a means to protect the world from the ancient evil, a force that could not be contained by any other means."

Amelia nodded, her heart heavy with the knowledge of the sacrifices made to safeguard the realm. She knew that the village had endured centuries of secrecy and suffering, but their sacrifices had not been in vain.

With the guardian relic's revelations complete, Amelia felt a sense of closure, as if the mysteries that had plagued Willowbrook had finally been laid to rest. The village could move forward, free from the burden of the curse and the malevolent force that had haunted it.

As they left the heart of the garden, the ancient tree's branches still adorned with radiant blossoms, a sense of peace and renewal settled over them. The mysteries of the enigmatic village had been unveiled, and the resolution was a testament to Amelia Sinclair's determination and resilience.

Elowen's voice held a note of hope as they exited the garden. "You have brought light to Willowbrook, Miss Sinclair, and peace to its residents. The village can now begin anew, free from the shadows of the past."

Amelia nodded, her heart filled with a sense of fulfillment. The enigma of Willowbrook had been unraveled, the mysteries laid to rest, and the ancient evil's return thwarted. As they made their way back to the village, the sun dipped below the horizon, casting long shadows over the landscape.

But Amelia knew that a new dawn awaited Willowbrook, a dawn of hope and renewal. The mysteries of the enigmatic village had been unveiled, and its residents could look forward to a brighter future.

As they approached the village, the residents of Willowbrook gathered to welcome them. The sense of relief and gratitude was palpable, as they had witnessed the transformation of their beloved garden and the breaking of the centuries-old curse.

Amelia was met with smiles and cheers, the villagers expressing their thanks for her unwavering dedication and her role as the guardian of the garden. It was a moment of celebration, a testament to the power of hope and resilience.

As she stood amidst the villagers, Amelia knew that her journey had come to a close, and her duty as the guardian of the garden had been fulfilled. The mysteries of Willowbrook had been unraveled, and its residents could now embrace a future free from the shadows of the past.

The sun's first rays illuminated the village, casting a warm and welcoming light over Willowbrook. It was a new dawn, a symbol of hope and renewal, and the enigma of the enigmatic village had been put to rest.

Amelia Sinclair's role as the guardian of the garden had come to an end, but the legacy of her determination and resilience would live on in the hearts of the residents of Willowbrook. The mysteries of the village had been unveiled, and a bright future awaited.

        THE END

# The Hollow's Hidden Legacy

## Chapter 1: The Silent Witness

The town of Harper's Hollow nestled in the embrace of towering, ancient oaks, their branches interlocking to form a natural cathedral. It was a place where time had slowed, and secrets clung to the shadows like ivy on a mossy stone wall. In Harper's Hollow, history whispered through the wind, and the past was never truly forgotten.

Detective Claire Monroe had been summoned to the small town, her footsteps echoing on the cobblestone streets as she made her way to the station. The case that had brought her here was as chilling as it was perplexing. A murder had been committed, and the perpetrator was long gone, but there was one silent witness to the crime, a reclusive figure whose existence had been whispered about for decades.

In the corner of her eye, Claire glimpsed the townsfolk watching her arrival with curiosity. They stood on the porches of their quaint, centuries-old houses, their faces etched with the lines of history. Harper's Hollow was a place where outsiders were scrutinized with a mix of suspicion and longing for the change they could bring.

Claire had spent her life in pursuit of truth, in a city where secrets were traded like currency, but the moment she set foot in Harper's Hollow, she knew this case would be unlike any she had ever encountered. The weight of the unsolved murder loomed over the town, a dark cloud that had refused to disperse for over thirty years.

Inside the police station, the air was thick with the scent of old wood and forgotten cases. She was met by the stern-faced Sheriff Colton, a man whose eyes betrayed a lifetime of bearing the town's mysteries on his shoulders.

"Detective Monroe," he greeted her with a nod. "We appreciate your help on this one. This case has haunted this town long enough."

Claire acknowledged the sheriff with a nod, her senses on high alert. She knew that unravelling the town's secrets wouldn't be easy, but she was determined to bring closure to the decades-old murder.

As she sat down with Sheriff Colton, he laid out the details of the case, his voice a low rumble in the dimly lit room. The victim was a young woman named Abigail Hawthorne, and the circumstances surrounding her death had baffled investigators. She had been found in the woods, her lifeless body bearing no signs of violence. It was as though she had simply fallen asleep and never woken up.

The strange part was the witness, a man named Gabriel O'Sullivan, who had seen the entire event unfold from the shadows. But Gabriel had never spoken a word about what he had seen. Instead, he had vanished into the woods, becoming a recluse known only by rumors and legends.

Claire had her work cut out for her. She needed to locate Gabriel O'Sullivan, coax the truth from his reluctant lips, and unravel the town's dark history. Her eyes scanned the room, taking in the old maps and photographs that lined the walls, each one a piece of the puzzle waiting to be fitted into place.

With determination, she rose from her chair. "Sheriff, I need to find Gabriel O'Sullivan. I believe he holds the key to solving this case."

Sheriff Colton's gaze was somber. "He won't be easy to find, Detective. The woods are his sanctuary, and he's fiercely protective of his privacy. He's seen things, knows things, and he's chosen to remain silent."

Claire knew that she would have to tread carefully and rely on her skills of persuasion. She left the station and made her way to the outskirts of town, where the dense forest began. The whispers of the townsfolk followed her, warning her of the danger that lurked in the woods.

As she entered the forest, the atmosphere changed, becoming dense and foreboding. The silence was broken only by the rustle of leaves and the distant calls of unseen creatures. Claire felt a shiver run down her spine as she ventured deeper into the trees.

She had to find Gabriel O'Sullivan, the silent witness, and convince him to break his decades-long silence. The mystery of Abigail Hawthorne's death hung heavy in the air, and Claire was determined to unravel it, no matter the cost.

The forest grew darker, and the suspense intensified as Claire pressed on, her heart pounding with every step. She knew that this reclusive figure held the answers to the town's darkest secrets, and she couldn't afford to fail.

And just as the tension reached its peak, a figure emerged from the shadows, Gabriel O'Sullivan himself, standing before her. His eyes were haunted, his silence as heavy as the secrets he held.

## Chapter 2: The Evasive Enigma

The air grew colder as Detective Claire Monroe and Gabriel O'Sullivan locked eyes in the heart of the dense forest. It was a moment that held the weight of three decades of silence and unanswered questions.

Gabriel's face was etched with lines of both age and suffering. His hair was long and unkempt, and his piercing blue eyes bore into Claire's with a mixture of fear and defiance. He had been living in these woods for as long as anyone could remember, and Claire had no doubt that he had learned to blend in with the shadows.

Claire broke the silence, her voice gentle yet firm. "Mr. O'Sullivan, my name is Detective Claire Monroe, and I've come to Harper's Hollow to uncover the truth about Abigail Hawthorne's death."

Gabriel O'Sullivan's lips remained sealed, but his gaze never wavered. He seemed to be assessing her, trying to determine if she posed a threat or if she could be trusted.

"I know you were there, Mr. O'Sullivan," Claire continued. "You witnessed what happened to Abigail, and your silence has kept this town in the grip of fear and uncertainty for far too long. Please, help us bring closure to her family and the entire community."

The forest seemed to hold its breath as Claire waited for a response. Gabriel finally broke the silence, his voice raspy from disuse. "You don't understand, Detective. The truth... it's a heavy burden."

Claire took a step closer, her determination unwavering. "I can't promise it'll be easy, but I can promise that we'll do everything in our power to protect you. You've lived in the shadows for too long. It's time to step into the light."

Gabriel's gaze shifted, and he appeared to be wrestling with an internal struggle. Finally, he let out a heavy sigh, his breath visible in the cold air. "Very well, but you'll need to earn my trust. Follow me."

He turned and began to walk deeper into the forest, and Claire followed closely behind. The suspense hung in the air like a heavy fog, and the rustling leaves seemed to whisper their secrets as they ventured further into the woods.

After a short walk, they arrived at a small, secluded clearing. At its center stood a dilapidated cabin, its wooden walls covered in ivy and its windows cracked and stained with age. Gabriel unlocked the cabin door with an old iron key, and it creaked open with a mournful groan.

As they entered, Claire was met with a dimly lit room filled with books, maps, and faded photographs. The cabin felt frozen in time, a place where Gabriel had been piecing together the puzzle of Abigail Hawthorne's death for years.

"Sit," he instructed Claire, gesturing to a worn-out armchair. She took a seat, and Gabriel began to pace, his voice low and uncertain as he spoke.

"I was just a young man when I saw what happened to Abigail," he began. "I was hiding in the trees, observing the world through the eyes of a recluse. That's when I saw him, a tall, shadowy figure that emerged from the underbrush. He approached Abigail, and they spoke. But their conversation was eerie, filled with whispers and secrets."

Claire leaned forward, her heart racing. "Do you know who the man was?"

Gabriel nodded, his eyes filled with a mixture of fear and anger. "Yes, I recognized him, but I couldn't believe my own eyes. It was Mayor Robert Caulfield. He was involved in some sort of dark, sinister ritual with Abigail, and whatever they did, it took her life."

The revelation hit Claire like a punch to the gut. Mayor Caulfield was a respected figure in Harper's Hollow, and the idea of him being involved in such a heinous act was unthinkable. But the evidence before her was impossible to ignore.

Before Claire could ask more questions, a sound echoed from outside the cabin, a snapping branch followed by a low growl. Gabriel's eyes widened in alarm.

"They've found us," he whispered, his voice trembling.

Claire stood, her instincts kicking into high gear. "Who's 'they,' Gabriel? What's going on?"

But Gabriel didn't have time to answer. The cabin door burst open, and a group of masked figures, armed and dangerous, stormed in. Claire and Gabriel were trapped, with no way out.

## Chapter 3: The Conspiracy Unveiled

As the masked intruders closed in on Claire and Gabriel, the cabin's walls seemed to constrict around them, and the air grew thick with tension. Gabriel's face was a mask of fear, his eyes darting around in search of a possible escape route. Claire, her training kicking in, assessed the situation, realizing they were outnumbered and outgunned.

The leader of the masked group, a tall and imposing figure, stepped forward, his voice distorted by a voice modulator. "You should have stayed out of Harper's Hollow, Detective. We can't allow you to uncover the truth."

Claire's mind raced, trying to identify the masked men. Their intent was clear: to silence the only living witness to the events surrounding Abigail Hawthorne's death. She had to stall for time, to buy her and Gabriel a chance to escape this perilous situation.

"What truth are you trying to hide?" Claire demanded, her voice steady despite the adrenaline coursing through her veins. "The town deserves to know what really happened to Abigail Hawthorne."

The masked leader's laughter was cold and humorless. "The town will remain in the dark, Detective, just as it has for decades. It's the way things are meant to be."

As they closed in, Claire noticed a glimmer of desperation in Gabriel's eyes. He moved with a sudden burst of energy, lunging toward a nearby table and knocking over a kerosene lamp. Flames erupted, casting eerie shadows on the walls. The masked figures scrambled to avoid the fire, giving Claire and Gabriel a momentary advantage.

Claire grabbed Gabriel's hand, and they made a break for the cabin's back door. Bursting into the chilly forest, they ran through the dense underbrush, their hearts pounding in their chests. Branches scratched at their faces and limbs as they pushed deeper into the woods, desperate to put distance between themselves and their pursuers.

After what felt like an eternity, Claire and Gabriel slowed their pace, gasping for breath. The forest had grown even darker, and the echoes of their footsteps faded into the night. Claire turned to Gabriel, her voice low and urgent.

"Who were those people, and what do they want to keep hidden?"

Gabriel's gaze was haunted, his voice shaky but determined. "They're part of a secret group that wields immense power in this town. They'll stop at nothing to protect their interests, even if it means murder."

Claire's mind raced with the implications of what she had just learned. The secrets of Harper's Hollow ran deeper than she had ever imagined, and the web of conspiracy stretched further than she could have anticipated.

"We need to find a safe place to regroup," Claire said, taking charge of the situation. "We can't trust anyone in this town. I have an old contact who might be able to help. Can you take me to a secure location?"

Gabriel nodded, and they continued through the forest, their path illuminated by the pale light of the moon. They moved cautiously, staying alert to any signs of pursuit.

Finally, they arrived at a hidden cabin, nestled deep in the woods. It was a small, rustic structure, clearly intended to be a retreat for someone who wished to remain off the grid. Claire and Gabriel entered, securing the door behind them.

The cabin held the telltale signs of someone who had been living in seclusion for years. There were maps, documents, and a collection of newspapers that chronicled the town's history, all meticulously organized. It was clear that the cabin was Gabriel's sanctuary, a place where he had continued his pursuit of the truth.

Claire turned to Gabriel. "You've been investigating this for a long time, haven't you?"

Gabriel nodded, his expression pained. "I've been haunted by what I saw that night, and I couldn't let Abigail's death go unpunished. But I was always one step behind, always on the run from the people who want to silence me."

Claire studied the evidence in the cabin, her mind racing. "We have to uncover the full extent of this conspiracy, Gabriel. We need to find out who's behind it, and why they're willing to go to such lengths to keep their secrets hidden."

Before they could formulate a plan, a sudden crash from outside the cabin sent both of them diving for cover. The door had been forced open, and the masked intruders had found them once again.

Chapter 4: Unveiling the Shadows

Claire and Gabriel found themselves trapped in the cabin, their breaths held as the masked intruders advanced, their dark figures casting long, sinister shadows in the dimly lit room. The leader's voice, still distorted by the modulator, echoed through the cabin.

"Your little game is over, Detective. We will make sure you never reveal our secrets."

The tension was palpable, and the realization hit Claire like a sledgehammer. They were dealing with individuals who would stop at nothing to protect their dark and hidden agendas. Claire's mind raced, searching for an escape plan, but they were outnumbered, and time was running out.

With a surge of determination, Gabriel grabbed a heavy book from the cabin's makeshift shelves and hurled it at one of the intruders, striking him square in the chest. The man stumbled backward, and in the chaos, Claire lunged toward the door, but the leader was quick to react. A gunshot rang out, and the bullet slammed into the wooden doorframe just inches from Claire's head.

The door was ajar now, and through the opening, Claire saw their only chance at escape—a narrow window on the far side of the cabin. She grabbed Gabriel's arm and yelled, "We have to go now!"

They made a desperate dash for the window, leaping through it with urgency. The cold night air rushed against their faces as they tumbled to the ground outside. The masked figures were hot on their heels, but Claire and Gabriel kept running, their hearts pounding with adrenaline.

With the advantage of surprise and darkness on their side, they managed to evade their pursuers and vanished deeper into the woods. The distant cries of the masked figures faded into the night.

As they slowed their pace, Claire's mind raced to process the ordeal. "We can't go back to the cabin, it's compromised," she said. "We need to find a new safe location and figure out our next move."

Gabriel nodded, his breath still coming in heavy gasps. "There's a remote cabin not far from here. It's owned by an old friend of mine. He'll help us. Let's go."

They pressed on, guided by the pale light of the moon, until they reached the hidden refuge Gabriel spoke of. The cabin was isolated, nestled among the trees, and well-protected from prying eyes. Inside, Gabriel's old friend, Victor, greeted them with a mixture of relief and concern.

"Gabriel, I thought I'd never see you again," Victor said, his eyes filled with genuine worry. "Who's your friend?"

Claire introduced herself, explaining the situation in broad strokes, and it didn't take long for Victor to grasp the gravity of their circumstances.

"I can't believe what you've stumbled into," Victor muttered, shaking his head. "These people have power, and they won't stop until they've silenced you for good. We need a plan."

Claire was already formulating her next moves, determined to expose the shadowy conspiracy in Harper's Hollow. "We have to find concrete evidence that connects the mayor, Robert Caulfield, to Abigail's death. If we can expose his involvement, it might unravel the entire conspiracy."

Gabriel nodded, his voice tinged with a steely resolve. "I've collected a trove of documents, photographs, and notes over the years. They might hold the key to everything."

With Victor's help, they began sorting through the mountain of information in the cabin. The evidence painted a chilling picture, linking Mayor Caulfield to a secret organization known as the "Harbingers of Shadows." This mysterious group was said to wield tremendous influence and operated in the shadows, manipulating the town's affairs to serve their hidden agendas.

As they delved deeper into the evidence, the name of a prominent figure in the town, Richard Hawthorne, Abigail's father, emerged. The documents hinted at a complex web of alliances and dark rituals that had ties to the very founding of Harper's Hollow.

Claire's pulse quickened as she realized the enormity of the conspiracy they were up against. "This goes far beyond Abigail's murder. It's a web of secrets and conspiracies that have haunted this town for generations."

The cabin was filled with tension as they continued to uncover the extent of the dark forces at play in Harper's Hollow. But just as they thought they were getting closer to the truth, a series of footsteps outside the cabin shattered their concentration.

Victor's face went pale. "We have visitors," he whispered.

Claire, Gabriel, and Victor huddled in the cabin, their hearts pounding as the footsteps grew closer, and the eerie voices of the masked figures echoed through the night.

## Chapter 4: Unveiling the Shadows

Claire and Gabriel found themselves trapped in the cabin, their breaths held as the masked intruders advanced, their dark figures casting long, sinister shadows in the dimly lit room. The leader's voice, still distorted by the modulator, echoed through the cabin.

"Your little game is over, Detective. We will make sure you never reveal our secrets."

The tension was palpable, and the realization hit Claire like a sledgehammer. They were dealing with individuals who would stop at nothing to protect their dark and hidden agendas. Claire's mind raced, searching for an escape plan, but they were outnumbered, and time was running out.

With a surge of determination, Gabriel grabbed a heavy book from the cabin's makeshift shelves and hurled it at one of the intruders, striking him square in the chest. The man stumbled backward, and in the chaos, Claire lunged toward the door, but the leader was quick to react. A gunshot rang out, and the bullet slammed into the wooden doorframe just inches from Claire's head.

The door was ajar now, and through the opening, Claire saw their only chance at escape—a narrow window on the far side of the cabin. She grabbed Gabriel's arm and yelled, "We have to go now!"

They made a desperate dash for the window, leaping through it with urgency. The cold night air rushed against their faces as they tumbled to the ground outside. The masked figures were hot on their heels, but Claire and Gabriel kept running, their hearts pounding with adrenaline.

With the advantage of surprise and darkness on their side, they managed to evade their pursuers and vanished deeper into the woods. The distant cries of the masked figures faded into the night.

As they slowed their pace, Claire's mind raced to process the ordeal. "We can't go back to the cabin, it's compromised," she said. "We need to find a new safe location and figure out our next move."

Gabriel nodded, his breath still coming in heavy gasps. "There's a remote cabin not far from here. It's owned by an old friend of mine. He'll help us. Let's go."

They pressed on, guided by the pale light of the moon, until they reached the hidden refuge Gabriel spoke of. The cabin was isolated, nestled among the trees, and well-protected from prying eyes. Inside, Gabriel's old friend, Victor, greeted them with a mixture of relief and concern.

"Gabriel, I thought I'd never see you again," Victor said, his eyes filled with genuine worry. "Who's your friend?"

Claire introduced herself, explaining the situation in broad strokes, and it didn't take long for Victor to grasp the gravity of their circumstances.

"I can't believe what you've stumbled into," Victor muttered, shaking his head. "These people have power, and they won't stop until they've silenced you for good. We need a plan."

Claire was already formulating her next moves, determined to expose the shadowy conspiracy in Harper's Hollow. "We have to find concrete evidence that connects the mayor, Robert Caulfield, to Abigail's death. If we can expose his involvement, it might unravel the entire conspiracy."

Gabriel nodded, his voice tinged with a steely resolve. "I've collected a trove of documents, photographs, and notes over the years. They might hold the key to everything."

With Victor's help, they began sorting through the mountain of information in the cabin. The evidence painted a chilling picture, linking Mayor Caulfield to a secret organization known as the "Harbingers of Shadows." This mysterious group was said to wield tremendous influence and operated in the shadows, manipulating the town's affairs to serve their hidden agendas.

As they delved deeper into the evidence, the name of a prominent figure in the town, Richard Hawthorne, Abigail's father, emerged. The documents hinted at a complex web of alliances and dark rituals that had ties to the very founding of Harper's Hollow.

Claire's pulse quickened as she realized the enormity of the conspiracy they were up against. "This goes far beyond Abigail's murder. It's a web of secrets and conspiracies that have haunted this town for generations."

The cabin was filled with tension as they continued to uncover the extent of the dark forces at play in Harper's Hollow. But just as they thought they were getting closer to the truth, a series of footsteps outside the cabin shattered their concentration.

Victor's face went pale. "We have visitors," he whispered.

Claire, Gabriel, and Victor huddled in the cabin, their hearts pounding as the footsteps grew closer, and the eerie voices of the masked figures echoed through the night.

## Chapter 5: Descent into Darkness

The cabin was plunged into a suffocating silence as the footsteps outside drew nearer. Claire, Gabriel, and Victor exchanged anxious glances, their collective breaths barely audible. The masked figures were closing in, their intent clear—to eliminate anyone who threatened to unveil their secrets.

Claire quietly gestured for them to gather near the cabin's rear exit, her eyes locked on the approaching shadows through a small gap in the curtains. The voices of the intruders grew louder as they drew closer to the cabin.

Victor's face was etched with fear as he whispered, "What do we do, Claire? They won't hesitate to kill us."

Claire's voice was a mere breath. "We have to make a run for it and find a way to expose the conspiracy to the world. Gabriel, do you have any ideas?"

Gabriel's eyes darted around the room, his mind racing. "There's an old network of tunnels underneath Harper's Hollow that predates the town itself. If we can reach the tunnels, we might be able to move around without being detected."

With a shared understanding, they silently prepared to make their escape. The cabin's back door swung open cautiously, and they slipped out into the night, their footsteps almost soundless on the forest floor.

The masked figures entered the cabin moments later, their voices filled with anger and frustration. Their flashlight beams danced wildly around the room, revealing the abandoned documents and maps strewn across the cabin's floor.

"They were here," the leader hissed. "Find them! We can't let them escape."

The pursuit had begun anew, and Claire, Gabriel, and Victor moved with all the stealth they could muster. The forest's cold embrace surrounded them, and the eerie glow of the moon offered their only guidance. Each step was fraught with tension, knowing that the masked figures were hot on their trail.

They reached the outskirts of Harper's Hollow and began to navigate the maze of alleys and backstreets, weaving their way through the town's darkness. Gabriel led the way with a grim determination, his memory serving as a guide to the hidden tunnels beneath the town.

The tunnels were ancient, a subterranean labyrinth that had seen countless secrets and histories buried beneath Harper's Hollow. As they descended into the darkness, their footsteps echoed through the cold stone passages. Claire couldn't help but feel the weight of centuries pressing down on her.

"We need to find a way out of these tunnels and back to safety," Claire urged, her voice barely above a whisper. "And we need to expose the conspiracy once and for all."

Victor nodded, his eyes shining with a mix of fear and resolve. "We have the evidence we need, but we can't risk returning to the cabin. If we can reach the surface safely, I know someone who can help us expose the truth."

Their escape through the labyrinthine tunnels was fraught with treacherous twists and turns, and they relied on Gabriel's knowledge to navigate the dark passages. But just as they were nearing an exit, their path was blocked by an unexpected obstacle.

The tunnels opened into a massive underground chamber, its walls lined with ancient inscriptions and strange symbols that glowed eerily in the dim light. The air was heavy with the scent of damp earth, and the space seemed to vibrate with an otherworldly energy.

Claire's heart raced as she realized they had stumbled upon a hidden chamber of immense significance. The symbols on the walls were like nothing she had ever seen, and they hinted at an ancient and mysterious power that had been concealed beneath the town for centuries.

Victor's voice was shaky as he whispered, "This place... it's older than the town itself. We've discovered something beyond our imagination."

But their awe was cut short as the masked figures appeared at the entrance to the chamber. The leader's voice echoed through the cavern, filled with a sense of finality.

"You've reached the end of your journey, Detective. You will never reveal our secrets."

## Chapter 6: The Hidden Revelation

In the dimly lit underground chamber, Claire, Gabriel, and Victor stood at the mercy of the masked figures who had cornered them. The eerie symbols on the chamber's walls seemed to pulsate with an otherworldly energy, casting eerie shadows on the faces of the intruders.

The leader of the masked group, his voice still distorted by the modulator, raised a gloved hand, gesturing for the trio to remain where they were. "You've trespassed into a place that holds secrets beyond your comprehension. Secrets that we've guarded for generations."

Claire's mind raced, trying to find a way out of the dire situation. The ancient chamber and its cryptic symbols hinted at a deeper layer of mystery that was interwoven with Harper's Hollow's history. She had to uncover the truth hidden within these tunnels.

"Why are you so determined to keep these secrets buried?" Claire demanded, her voice resolute. "What could possibly be worth the lengths you've gone to?"

The leader's voice was filled with dark determination. "These secrets have the power to control, manipulate, and shape the destiny of this town. The very foundation of Harper's Hollow rests upon what we've protected for centuries."

As the conversation unfolded, Victor leaned closer to Claire, his voice barely audible. "The symbols on the walls, they hold a key. I've seen similar inscriptions in the documents we've gathered. We need to decipher them, Claire. They're the link to the truth."

Claire nodded in agreement, her mind racing with the possibilities. She focused on the symbols, trying to discern any patterns or clues that might unlock the mysteries concealed within the chamber.

But before they could make any progress, the leader of the masked figures spoke again, his tone growing more ominous. "You're running out of time, Detective. Your curiosity will be your undoing."

Suddenly, the chamber was filled with a deafening rumble, and the ground beneath them quaked. The ancient walls of the underground chamber seemed to come to life, shifting and revealing hidden compartments that contained centuries-old artifacts and documents.

Claire's eyes widened in astonishment. "The chamber is revealing its secrets," she whispered to Gabriel and Victor. "We need to act quickly."

As the chamber continued to reveal its hidden treasures, Claire, Gabriel, and Victor seized the opportunity to collect the ancient artifacts and documents. They scrambled to gather as much as they could, realizing that these items might hold the key to unraveling the conspiracy that had plagued Harper's Hollow for generations.

The leader of the masked figures, clearly taken by surprise, struggled to maintain control of the situation as the chamber transformed around them. The symbols on the walls grew more pronounced, and the room was filled with an eerie, ethereal light.

Claire couldn't help but feel that they were on the cusp of a revelation, that the chamber's secrets were the key to exposing the dark forces that had manipulated the town for so long.

But just as they thought they might escape with their newfound knowledge, a piercing wail echoed through the chamber, and the masked figures turned their attention toward the chamber's entrance. The leader's voice was laced with panic.

"They're here. We have to go now!"

The chamber's transformation continued, and Claire, Gabriel, and Victor made a hasty retreat, clutching the ancient artifacts and documents they had managed to collect. The underground chamber's secrets would have to wait to be fully deciphered.

As they navigated the labyrinthine tunnels once more, their path was shrouded in darkness, and they were left with more questions than answers. The cryptic symbols on the walls, the ancient artifacts, and the masked figures' desperate attempt to protect their secrets all hinted at a deeper, more profound mystery.

And the reader was left with a cliffhanger, wondering who had arrived to disrupt the masked figures, what secrets they held, and whether Claire and her allies would be able to decipher the mysteries concealed in the underground chamber and expose the truth about Harper's Hollow.

## Chapter 7: The Unseen Foe

Claire, Gabriel, and Victor moved swiftly through the labyrinthine tunnels, their hearts pounding with adrenaline. The discovery of the underground chamber and its cryptic symbols had been a revelation, but they had little time to make sense of it as their immediate escape took precedence.

The sound of the masked figures in pursuit echoed through the winding passages, their footfalls growing louder. The urgency of their pursuit was clear, and Claire knew that they couldn't risk capture now that they possessed evidence that could expose Harper's Hollow's dark secrets.

They reached a junction in the tunnels, a crossroads of darkness and echoing whispers. Victor turned to Claire, his voice low and filled with determination. "We need to split up. It'll be harder for them to track us if we take different paths."

Claire nodded in agreement. "Gabriel, you go with Victor. I'll take another route. We'll regroup once we've lost them. But be careful, and don't engage with the masked figures if you can avoid it."

They exchanged a final glance before parting ways, each disappearing into the inky blackness of the tunnels. Claire's heart raced as she ventured further into the labyrinth, her flashlight casting eerie shadows on the ancient stone walls. She moved with silent determination, knowing that her life and the unraveling of the town's secrets depended on her survival.

As Claire moved through the tunnels, she couldn't help but wonder about the identity of the unseen foe who had disrupted the masked figures' pursuit. Who had come to their aid, and what secrets did they hold? The answers were shrouded in mystery, and Claire was determined to uncover the truth.

Victor and Gabriel, on their own path, moved cautiously through the tunnels, each step echoing like a whisper. The air was thick with tension, and they remained vigilant, aware that the masked figures could be lurking in the shadows.

As they continued their journey, Victor couldn't help but share his thoughts with Gabriel. "The symbols in the chamber, they hold the key to unraveling the conspiracy. We need to decode them, and they might reveal the truth about Harper's Hollow."

Gabriel's eyes were filled with a mix of determination and fear. "We have to get out of these tunnels first and reunite with Claire.

Once we're safe, we can work on deciphering the symbols and exposing the conspiracy."

Back in the tunnels, Claire's flashlight revealed another chamber, smaller and less ornate than the one they had previously discovered. In the center of the room, a stone pedestal held a single ancient book, its pages filled with strange symbols and drawings.

Claire approached the book with caution, her fingers trembling as she turned its pages. The symbols seemed to come to life before her eyes, each page telling a story of the town's hidden history. The book held secrets, and Claire was determined to unlock them.

But before she could delve deeper, a voice filled with both authority and mystery echoed through the chamber. "Stop right there, Detective."

Claire's heart leaped in her chest as she swung around, her flashlight beam falling on a figure standing in the shadows. It was a tall and imposing man, his face obscured by a mask, and his voice was laced with an air of command.

"I see you've found something of great importance," the masked figure continued. "But you're not the only one seeking the truth, and there are those who will stop at nothing to keep it hidden."

Claire's mind raced as she weighed her options. She was outnumbered and faced with an unknown adversary, yet the book held the key to exposing the conspiracy. She couldn't turn back now.

With determination in her voice, she spoke. "Who are you, and what do you know about the secrets of Harper's Hollow? We're here to reveal the truth, and nothing will stand in our way."

The masked figure stepped closer, and the shadows played on his features. "I'm a guardian of the town's ancient history, and I've been searching for someone who could help unveil its darkest secrets. The book in your hands is the key, but it's also a double-edged sword."

Claire felt a mixture of hope and caution. "If you're willing to help us, we can work together to uncover the truth. We've gathered evidence that links the town's mayor to a dark conspiracy, and we need to bring it to light."

The masked figure hesitated for a moment, as if weighing the offer. "I'll help you decipher the book's secrets, but we must tread carefully. The conspiracy is far-reaching, and its roots are deep. We need to expose it without jeopardizing the town's stability."

Claire nodded, her determination unwavering. "We'll be cautious, but the truth must come to light. The people of Harper's Hollow deserve to know the secrets that have been hidden for far too long."

As Claire and the masked figure worked together to decipher the ancient book's symbols and revelations, Gabriel and Victor continued their journey through the tunnels, determined to reunite with Claire and bring their evidence to light.

## Chapter 8: Reckoning and Redemption

As Claire and the masked figure worked together to decipher the ancient book's secrets, their alliance grew stronger with each passing hour. The book revealed a history intertwined with Harper's Hollow's darkest secrets, a story of power, manipulation, and the town's enigmatic founders who had forged a sinister pact.

With the masked figure's guidance, Claire unlocked the secrets hidden within the book's pages. She discovered that the cryptic symbols held not just the town's history but also the key to undoing the conspiracy that had plagued Harper's Hollow for generations.

The truth was both unsettling and liberating. The town's founders, including Richard Hawthorne, had established an order known as the "Harbingers of Shadows," and they had entered into a dark covenant with an entity they believed could grant them power, wealth, and control. In return, they offered sacrifices, including the life of Abigail Hawthorne, to maintain the pact.

The revelation sent shockwaves through Claire, and the gravity of the situation weighed heavily on her. She knew that exposing the truth could bring chaos to Harper's Hollow, but it was a necessary reckoning that the town deserved.

Together with the masked figure, they developed a plan to unveil the conspiracy to the town. They would use the evidence they had collected, the decoded book, and the help of trusted allies to expose the Harbingers of Shadows and the town's dark history.

Meanwhile, Gabriel and Victor navigated the treacherous tunnels, determined to reunite with Claire and ensure the safe delivery of the evidence. Their journey was fraught with challenges, but they relied on their courage and resourcefulness to overcome the obstacles that lay in their path.

As they finally emerged from the underground labyrinth and into the quiet streets of Harper's Hollow, the town appeared unchanged on the surface, oblivious to the storm brewing beneath. It was time to reveal the truth and confront the town's hidden demons.

The day of reckoning arrived, and Claire, Gabriel, Victor, and their mysterious ally gathered a group of trusted townsfolk who had been unknowingly living under the shadow of the Harbingers of Shadows. With gathered evidence in hand, they addressed the town, sharing the shocking truth about the secret order, its history, and the sacrifices that had been made to protect its power.

The revelation sent shockwaves through Harper's Hollow, and the town's residents were torn between disbelief and anger. Many struggled to come to terms with the dark history that had been concealed for generations.

In the days that followed, the townsfolk demanded accountability from the members of the secret order, including the descendants of the founders. The once-powerful Harbingers of Shadows were exposed, and the town's citizens were determined to dismantle the organization and ensure that justice was served.

Mayor Robert Caulfield, a key figure in the conspiracy, was arrested and faced a trial for his involvement in Abigail Hawthorne's death and the town's hidden history. The town's legal system, once under the shadow of the Harbingers, was now committed to seeking justice.

As Harper's Hollow grappled with its newfound truth, it began the process of healing and reconciliation. The town's history was rewritten, and the people were free from the secrets that had bound them for generations.

Claire, Gabriel, and Victor played pivotal roles in the town's transformation, and they were hailed as heroes by the residents who had once lived in fear. The unity and resilience of the town became the cornerstone of its recovery, and the darkness that had shrouded Harper's Hollow was slowly replaced by a newfound sense of hope and possibility.

The last chapter of the novel concluded with Claire, Gabriel, and Victor standing at the town's edge, gazing at the horizon. The town was forever changed, and their journey had led to the revelation and redemption that Harper's Hollow so desperately needed.

As the sun set over the town, the trio found solace in the knowledge that they had brought the truth to light, giving the people of Harper's Hollow a chance to rebuild their lives and find happiness, and they walked away, ready for new beginnings, leaving the past behind.

And in the distance, as the shadows of the past receded, a sense of serenity and hope filled the air, reminding the reader that even in the darkest of secrets, redemption and resolution could be found.

THE END

# The Haunting on Harrow Hill

## Chapter 1: The Invitation

The rain lashed against the ancient windows of the mansion, casting eerie, elongated shadows across the room. Thunder rumbled in the distance, a low, menacing growl that reverberated through the walls. The Haunting on Harrow Hill had always been a place of legend, but for me, it was about to become all too real.

I stood in the dimly lit foyer, taking in the opulence of the place. The grand chandelier above me hung like a crystal spider, its many arms adorned with flickering candles. The walls were adorned with faded tapestries, and the air was heavy with the scent of aged wood and long-forgotten memories. I had never believed in the supernatural. My name is Alex Gray, and I am a paranormal investigator with a reputation for being a hard-nosed skeptic. Ghosts, spirits, and all things unexplained had always been nothing more than figments of overactive imaginations, or tricks of the light. But when I received the letter from a mysterious benefactor, inviting me to investigate the Harrow Hill Mansion, I found myself in a position I could not ignore.

The deaths, they said, had been unexplained. People who had ventured into the mansion had been found dead, their faces etched with terror. There were whispers of ghostly apparitions and malevolent spirits, and the local police were baffled. They needed someone who was not afraid to confront the supernatural, and they believed that someone was me.

As I read the letter again, the words echoed in my mind: "I know you're a skeptic, Mr. Gray, but I implore you to investigate this mansion. It holds secrets that cannot be explained by reason alone. The deaths demand answers, and the only way to find them is to face the unknown. The Haunting on Harrow Hill awaits."

I glanced around, feeling a shiver run down my spine. The mansion's atmosphere was suffocating, as if the very air held the weight of centuries. I couldn't help but wonder if I had made a grave mistake by coming here. But my curiosity and my desire to debunk the supernatural were driving me forward.

As I continued to examine the letter, I noticed a postscript: "P.S. Bring your skepticism, but leave your preconceptions at the door." It was a cryptic message, and I had no idea what it meant, but it only added to the intrigue of the situation.

A sudden creaking sound from above startled me, and I looked up to see a shadowy figure on the grand staircase. A woman, dressed in an elegant Victorian gown, her features obscured by the darkness. I instinctively reached for the flashlight in my pocket and aimed it toward the figure, but before I could illuminate her face, she vanished.

I knew I couldn't let my imagination get the best of me. This could be a prank, a well-orchestrated setup to test my resolve. I took a deep breath and called out, "Is someone there? I'm here to investigate."

Silence answered me. The mansion seemed to hold its breath, as if it were waiting for something.

Gathering my resolve, I made my way up the staircase, my footsteps echoing in the cavernous space. The upper floors were even more enigmatic, with long, dark corridors and numerous rooms shrouded in darkness. It was as if the very walls of the mansion whispered secrets, and I was determined to uncover them.

In one room, I found a dusty, long-forgotten library. The shelves were lined with ancient tomes, their spines cracked and pages yellowed with age. As I moved closer, I noticed a book on a stand, opened to a page filled with cryptic symbols and diagrams. It was a language I couldn't decipher, but it sent a chill down my spine.

I had barely a moment to contemplate the significance of the book when I heard a blood-curdling scream. It echoed through the mansion, bouncing off the walls like a maddening, anguished cry. My heart raced, and I instinctively followed the sound, my flashlight cutting through the darkness.

The scream led me to a room at the end of a hallway. The door was slightly ajar, and I pushed it open to reveal a scene from a nightmare. A figure lay sprawled on the floor, their face twisted in agony. It was the same woman I had seen on the staircase, her elegant gown now tattered and bloodstained.

But what truly horrified me was the message scrawled in red on the wall above her: "Leave now, or join the dead."

I had walked into something far more sinister than I could have ever imagined. My skepticism had led me to a place where the boundaries of reality and the unexplained blurred into a horrifying nightmare. And as I stood there, torn between reason and fear, I realized that I had no choice but to confront the supernatural, to uncover the secrets of The Haunting on Harrow Hill, or become another unexplained death in this cursed mansion.

As I gazed at the ominous message on the wall, a sense of dread washed over me, and I knew that unraveling the mysteries of Harrow Hill would be a perilous journey filled with moral and ethical dilemmas, complex mysteries, and the unexplainable. My skepticism had brought me here, but only the truth could lead me out of the darkness.

## Chapter 2: The Whispers of the Past

The gruesome message on the wall sent shivers down my spine. I knew I had entered a realm beyond my understanding, where skepticism offered no protection. The woman's lifeless eyes stared at me, and I could feel the weight of her unspoken words. What secrets had she discovered before her tragic end?

I took a step closer to the lifeless figure, my gloved hand trembling as I reached out to touch her. Her skin was cold, and I quickly recoiled. There was no doubt that she was beyond help, and her death was a grim testament to the perilous nature of this place.

But I had a mission to fulfill, and I couldn't afford to be paralyzed by fear. I needed answers, and I needed them now. The mysteries of Harrow Hill beckoned me further into its dark labyrinth.

The room itself was a reflection of the mansion's eerie grandeur. Moonlight filtered through tattered curtains, casting elongated shadows across the walls. Old, ornate furniture lay covered in dusty sheets, like ghosts of the past. And there, in the far corner of the room, stood an ancient wooden desk. It beckoned to me, as if it held the key to the secrets hidden within these walls.

Approaching the desk, I noticed a collection of faded photographs scattered across its surface. Each image depicted the mansion in different eras, capturing its transformation over the years. But one photograph stood out: a group of people gathered on the grand staircase, dressed in elaborate Victorian attire. The woman who had met her demise in this very room was among them.

As I examined the photograph, I noticed a disturbing detail. The woman's face appeared distorted, as if it had been partially scratched out. I couldn't help but wonder if it was a deliberate act or a trick of time. Had someone tried to erase her from history?

Before I could ponder further, the sound of footsteps outside the room snapped me to attention. Panic set in as I realized I was not alone. Someone or something was lurking in the shadows of Harrow Hill. I doused my flashlight and stood in the darkness, my heart pounding, my senses heightened.

The footsteps drew nearer, growing louder with each passing second. It wasn't a single set of footsteps; it was a cacophony of shuffling, as if a multitude of spectral beings were converging on my location. The air grew colder, and an invisible presence seemed to press upon me.

My pulse quickened as the whispers of the past grew more distinct. Indistinct murmurs filled the room, like fragments of long-forgotten conversations. I strained to decipher their meaning, but they eluded my understanding.

Suddenly, a beam of light sliced through the darkness, revealing a group of shadowy figures moving closer. I raised my flashlight, casting its beam upon the intruders. The figures were ethereal, their features obscured, and they moved with an otherworldly grace.

"Who are you?" I demanded, my voice wavering, unable to hide the fear that had crept into my heart.

The figures remained silent, but their collective presence seemed to bear down on me, as if they were trying to convey a message. The whispers grew louder, and I caught snippets of words and phrases, as if the past itself was reaching out to me.

"Sacrifice...unfinished...buried secrets..."

The cryptic utterances sent a chill down my spine. Were these apparitions trying to communicate with me? Did they hold the answers I sought?

With trepidation, I took a step forward, moving closer to the figures. They parted like a curtain, revealing a hidden passageway leading deeper into the mansion. It was a corridor cloaked in shadows, and I couldn't resist the pull of curiosity.

I ventured down the narrow passage, my footsteps echoing in the silence. The whispers of the past continued, guiding me further into the heart of Harrow Hill. The air grew thicker, laden with the weight of history, and I could feel a presence watching over me.

The corridor opened into a chamber, where an ancient, ornate mirror stood against the wall. Its gilded frame gleamed in the dim light, and the glass seemed to hold a haunting reflection of the past. The whispers grew louder, and I realized that the mirror held the key to the mysteries that plagued this mansion.

Before I could comprehend the significance of the mirror, a new figure emerged from the shadows, distinct from the others. It was a man, his face gaunt and eyes filled with a haunting sadness. His voice, barely more than a whisper, reached my ears.

"You must find the truth," he implored. "Only then can we find peace."

The room quivered with a spectral energy, and I knew that the answers I sought lay within the mirror. The man's gaze locked onto mine, and I felt an unspoken promise in his eyes.

As I reached out to touch the mirror's surface, the room erupted in a blinding flash of light, and the world around me dissolved into chaos. The mirror had become a gateway to a world beyond comprehension, a realm where the line between the living and the dead blurred into an enigmatic tapestry of the unexplainable.

## Chapter 3: Echoes of Betrayal

The moment I stepped through the mirror's threshold, I found myself in a place that defied all reason and comprehension. It was a world bathed in an eerie, perpetual twilight, where shadows danced on the horizon, and the air hung heavy with the scent of damp earth and forgotten memories.

Before me stretched a desolate landscape, dominated by gnarled, twisted trees with branches that seemed to reach out like skeletal fingers. The ground was a maze of overgrown vines and thorny underbrush, making every step a perilous one. I was a stranger in a land that felt as if it had been plucked from a macabre dream.

The mirror behind me had disappeared, leaving me no choice but to move forward, driven by an inexplicable sense of purpose. The whispers of the past still echoed in my ears, a haunting symphony of voices pleading for resolution.

The spectral figure who had guided me here, the man with the eyes filled with sorrow, had vanished. I was alone in this twilight realm, left to unravel the enigma of Harrow Hill on my own.

As I navigated through the oppressive thicket, I couldn't shake the feeling that I was being watched. The sense of being followed, pursued by unseen eyes, grew stronger with each passing moment. The hairs on the back of my neck stood on end, and my heartbeat quickened.

I heard faint, distant cries, like the wails of lost souls, and the flicker of movement out of the corner of my eye. Shadows flitted in the periphery of my vision, ghostly figures darting in and out of the underbrush. My skepticism had always been my shield against the supernatural, but here, in this surreal place, it offered no defense.

Desperation gnawed at me, and I quickened my pace, determined to find the source of the voices and the unsettling presence that pursued me. I had ventured into the unknown, and there was no turning back now.

After what felt like an eternity of weaving through the haunting forest, I stumbled upon a clearing. In the center stood an ancient, crumbling mansion. Its dilapidated walls loomed like silent sentinels, and its windows glistened with an otherworldly light.

I couldn't help but feel a sense of déjà vu. The mansion before me was a mirror image of the Harrow Hill mansion I had entered earlier, but its decrepit state spoke of years of neglect and decay.

In the mansion's courtyard, I noticed a group of shadowy figures, the same spectral beings that had led me here. They stood in a circle, their forms indistinct and shimmering. As I approached, their whispers grew louder, their voices intertwining in a melancholic chorus.

"Betrayal...trapped...release us."

The words were laced with anguish, and the urgency of their pleas tugged at my heart. I had no choice but to investigate, to find the truth and uncover the secrets that bound these lost souls to the mansion's cursed grounds.

The figure closest to me extended a spectral hand, beckoning me to join their circle. With a mixture of trepidation and determination, I stepped into their midst. The moment I did, a surge of energy coursed through me, a connection to the spirits that transcended the boundaries of the living and the dead.

Images flooded my mind, like fragments of a forgotten past. I saw the mansion in its prime, a place of grandeur and opulence. The woman who had met her tragic end, her face no longer obscured, was at the center of it all. She was the mistress of

Harrow Hill, and her beauty and charm had once captivated everyone who crossed her path.

But the image shifted, and I witnessed a darker side of her. She conspired with others, plotting against her husband, the mansion's owner. Their motives were greed and betrayal, and their plan involved unspeakable acts.

The spirits' voices echoed their anguish, revealing a tale of treachery and deceit that had left them trapped in this twilight realm, unable to find peace.

The ghostly figures beseeched me to uncover the truth, to break the cycle of suffering that bound them. I nodded in solemn agreement, understanding that my skepticism had led me to a place where the sins of the past demanded resolution.

The courtyard seemed to ripple with an otherworldly energy, and the spirits began to fade, their voices growing distant. I was left with a sense of purpose, a mission to delve into the mansion's history and expose the secrets that had remained buried for far too long.

Before I could contemplate my next move, a sudden gust of wind swept through the clearing, extinguishing the lanterns that lined the mansion's entrance. The darkness closed in around me, and the unsettling presence that had pursued me returned with a vengeance.

A voice, both ethereal and chilling, echoed in the obscurity. "You have uncovered our truth, but the price of revelation is high. Stay, and you shall become one with us."

The mansion's doors creaked open, and the abyss within beckoned. I faced a choice, a decision that would determine my fate. The skepticism that had defined me was now my only ally in this relentless, ghostly world. I had to decide whether to confront the supernatural forces that held sway over Harrow Hill or become a part of the haunting on its cursed grounds.

## Chapter 4: The Unveiling

I stepped through the mansion's foreboding threshold, leaving the desolate courtyard behind. The grand entrance hall was a cavernous space filled with darkness, and the air hung heavy with foreboding. The shadows seemed to come alive, writhing and shifting in the dim light. My skepticism had been my shield, but it was beginning to waver in the face of the unexplainable.

The echoes of the spirits' pleas still resonated in my mind, driving me forward. The secrets of Harrow Hill mansion were my only hope for salvation, and I was determined to unearth them.

With each cautious step, the atmosphere grew colder, as if the very mansion itself had conspired to stifle the warmth of life. The flicker of candles illuminated the path ahead, casting eerie, elongated shadows on the walls. The ornate wallpaper, now faded and peeling, depicted scenes of opulence from another era.

The grandeur of Harrow Hill's past was undeniable, but it was marred by the weight of the past's transgressions. As I ventured further into the mansion's depths, I couldn't help but wonder about the role that had led to the woman's tragic end and the betrayal that had ensnared the spirits.

I came upon a closed door, its surface adorned with intricate carvings and faded gold leaf. It was as if the very essence of the mansion pulsed through the wood, beckoning me to uncover its secrets.

With a hesitant breath, I pushed the door open, revealing a room that had once been a place of grandeur. The chandeliers overhead had lost their luster, now adorned with cobwebs instead of crystals. The room was dominated by a grand piano, its keys untouched for decades. But what drew my attention was a painting on the wall, the centerpiece of the room.

The painting depicted the mansion in its prime, with the woman at its heart, her beauty immortalized in oils. The eyes of the portrait seemed to follow me, and I couldn't help but feel an inexplicable connection to the woman who had met her tragic end.

The room itself held an air of melancholy, and as I moved closer to the piano, I noticed a collection of dusty sheet music. My fingers brushed the yellowed pages, revealing a piece titled "The Serenade of Betrayal." It was a haunting composition, filled with sorrow and longing.

As I scanned the music, the room seemed to come alive with an ethereal melody. The piano keys, untouched for decades, began to play of their own accord, producing a mournful tune that resonated with the spirit of the mansion.

I couldn't believe my eyes. The supernatural had transcended the boundaries of my skepticism, and I was now a participant in a haunting symphony of the unexplainable.

But the music carried with it a message, a lament for the past and a plea for release. The spirits sought redemption, and it was my duty to uncover the truth that would set them free.

I closed the piano lid, silencing the spectral composition. The room fell into an eerie silence, and I knew that I had only scratched the surface of the mansion's secrets.

As I turned to leave, a faint whisper reached my ears, like the murmur of a long-forgotten confession. I followed the sound, guided by an unseen force, to a hidden alcove in the wall.

In the alcove, I discovered a stack of letters, their pages yellowed with age. They were written in elegant script, and as I perused them, I realized they were correspondence between the woman of the mansion and a mysterious figure named "Elias." The letters revealed a torrid affair, a betrayal that had been hidden from the world.

The truth unfolded with each letter, exposing a tangled web of deceit and intrigue. The woman had conspired with Elias to usurp her husband's wealth and seize control of Harrow Hill mansion. Their ambition had known no bounds, and their treachery had led to unspeakable acts.

As I delved further into the letters, I understood the magnitude of the spirits' suffering. The haunting that gripped the mansion was a manifestation of the betrayals and transgressions that had taken place within its walls.

But one letter stood out, marked with an ominous seal. It spoke of a ritual, a desperate attempt to reclaim what had been lost, to undo the horrors of the past. It was a ritual that required a willing participant, someone who could bridge the gap between the living and the dead.

My heart quickened as I realized the letter was an invitation to someone like me, a skeptic who had been lured to Harrow Hill to confront the supernatural. The woman and Elias had believed that I held the key to their redemption.

The realization sent a chill down my spine. The spirits had guided me here to unveil their truth, but the cost of revelation was becoming clearer. I was bound to the mansion now, a vital component of the ritual, and my skepticism was no longer my only defense.

I had to make a choice, to continue my pursuit of the truth and face the spectral forces that held sway over Harrow Hill, or to reject the invitation and seek an escape from the haunting that had ensnared me.

As I stood in the dimly lit room, the weight of my decision pressed upon me, and I knew that the next chapter in this macabre tale would be a relentless confrontation with the supernatural, and the final revelation that awaited me in the heart of the cursed mansion.

## Chapter 5: The Séance of Redemption

The room was shrouded in an oppressive silence, as if it were holding its breath, waiting for my decision. The letters I had discovered, the haunted melody of the piano, and the unsettling presence that had drawn me to this place had all led me to a crossroads. The choice was mine to make, a choice that could determine the fate of the spirits and my own.

With a deep breath, I accepted the mantle of my role. I would continue my pursuit of the truth, for I couldn't leave the spirits to their endless torment. My skepticism had led me here, but it was my resolve that would guide me forward.

As I made my choice, a strange sense of calm washed over me, and the room seemed to respond. The shadows receded, and the oppressive atmosphere lifted, as if acknowledging my decision. The letters I had discovered fluttered in the air before settling in a neat stack, as if placed there by unseen hands.

I knew that the next step was to conduct a séance, a ritual that would bridge the gap between the living and the dead. The letters had alluded to it, and the spirits sought redemption through this otherworldly communion.

I ventured back into the entrance hall, where the echoes of the spirits' voices had led me. The candles lining the walls had been relit, their flames dancing in the draughts of a supernatural wind. It was as if the mansion itself conspired to aid me in my quest.

In the center of the hall, I found a round table covered in a crimson cloth. A candle burned at its center, and around it were several empty chairs. It was a setup for a séance, and the spirits had prepared it for my arrival.

With a sense of trepidation, I took my place at the table and, for the first time, considered the gravity of my situation. I was about to confront the supernatural head-on, to call upon the spirits who haunted this place. My skepticism had always been my anchor, but now it was my bridge to a realm beyond my understanding.

I reached for the stack of letters I had discovered, the ones that had led me here, and began to read them aloud. The words flowed from my lips, their meaning and significance amplified in this otherworldly setting.

As the last words of the letters left my mouth, the candle's flame flickered, casting elongated shadows on the walls. The room grew colder, and the air seemed charged with a spectral energy. The séance had begun.

The chairs around the table shifted as if pulled by invisible hands, and I felt a presence settle into each one. The spirits were joining me, their spectral forms taking shape, their eyes filled with a yearning for release.

I had never been a believer in the paranormal, but the undeniable reality of the spirits before me left no room for doubt. They were the ghosts of Harrow Hill, bound by betrayal, seeking redemption through my actions.

With a shaky breath, I reached for a planchette, a small wooden device used for communication during a séance, and placed it on a board inscribed with letters and numbers. The spirits were ready to communicate, to share their stories and seek the resolution they so desperately craved.

The séance began in earnest, as the planchette moved of its own accord, spelling out words and forming sentences. The spirits' voices were a chorus of desperation and anguish, and their tales unfolded before me.

They revealed the true extent of the woman's betrayal, how she and Elias had conspired to seize control of the mansion and its wealth. The cost of their ambition had been the lives of many, including the woman's own husband. The spirits spoke of their guilt, their remorse, and their longing for peace.

As I listened to their stories, I couldn't help but feel a profound sense of empathy for these lost souls. Their redemption was entwined with my own, and I was determined to help them find the closure they sought.

But the séance took an unexpected turn. The planchette moved with increasing speed, as if guided by a single, powerful force. It spelled out a message that sent shivers down my spine: "Beware the mirror."

The room darkened, and the table began to vibrate with an unsettling energy. The spirits' voices grew frantic, their warnings echoing in my ears. The mirror, the gateway that had drawn me into this supernatural realm, held a dark secret, one that I was not prepared to face.

Before I could fully comprehend the implications of their message, a deafening crash erupted from the hallway. I turned to see the mirror that had transported me to this place shatter into a thousand pieces. The shards seemed to hang in the air, suspended in time.

A figure emerged from the shattered mirror, a malevolent presence that exuded an aura of darkness. It was the woman, the mistress of Harrow Hill, her once-beautiful features twisted with rage and hatred.

The spirits around the table wailed in terror, their ethereal forms quivering. The woman's spectral hand reached out, her fingers trailing the air, and I could feel the cold grip of her vengeful intent.

I had uncovered the truth, but in doing so, I had unleashed a malevolent force. The mirror had been a gateway to a world beyond comprehension, and now it had become a conduit for the supernatural to exact its revenge.

I had a choice to make, a choice that would determine my fate and that of the spirits. The woman, consumed by hatred and betrayal, sought to claim me as her own, to bind me to this cursed mansion for eternity.

As I faced the spectral figure that had emerged from the shattered mirror, I couldn't help but wonder if my skepticism had led me to a place where the boundaries of reality and the unexplainable were indistinguishable, a place where the cost of truth was higher than I could have ever imagined.

## Chapter 6: Confronting the Malevolent

As the malevolent figure, the woman who had betrayed her own husband, emerged from the shattered mirror, a paralyzing fear gripped me. Her spectral presence exuded a darkness that felt tangible, an aura of vengeful intent that cut through the cold air like a chilling wind.

The spirits who had guided me through the séance wailed in terror, their ethereal forms quivering. They had sought redemption, but the malevolent force that had been unleashed was beyond their control. The spirits' entreaties for me to beware the mirror now took on a dreadful significance.

With a heart heavy with dread, I knew I had to act quickly. My skepticism, the very anchor that had guided me through this haunting, now demanded that I confront the malevolent presence head-on. There was no turning back.

The malevolent woman's spectral hand reached out, her fingers trailing the air like a wraith. Her movements were slow and deliberate, as if she were savoring my fear. The spirits' wails grew louder, a chorus of anguish that seemed to reverberate through the room.

But I couldn't let fear paralyze me. I had come to Harrow Hill in pursuit of truth and redemption, for the spirits and myself. My skepticism had led me here, and it was now my only ally in this supernatural confrontation.

I took a step forward, my voice steady, and addressed the malevolent figure. "I have come to reveal the truth and seek redemption for the spirits who have suffered. I will not be swayed by your vengeful intent."

The malevolent woman's eyes, filled with hatred and rage, bore into mine. The room seemed to vibrate with an otherworldly energy, as if the very fabric of reality was unraveling.

In response to my defiance, the malevolent woman's form shifted and contorted, as if she were a specter trapped between dimensions. Her voice, a haunting whisper, filled the room. "You know not the depths of our torment, the anguish we have endured. We will claim you as our own."

The malevolent woman's hand extended toward me, and the air around me grew frigid. I could feel an irresistible force pulling me toward her, as if my skepticism were no longer a shield against her malevolence.

But I couldn't succumb to the supernatural. I had come too far, and the spirits' pleas for redemption echoed in my ears. With every ounce of my willpower, I resisted the force that sought to claim me.

The malevolent woman's spectral form convulsed, her presence flickering like a dying candle. The spirits' wails grew more frantic, their fear palpable.

And then, with a deafening, otherworldly shriek, the malevolent woman's form dissipated. The room returned to an eerie calm, the malevolent presence vanquished, at least for the moment.

I was left breathless, the weight of the supernatural encounter pressing upon me. The spirits who had guided me through the séance seemed relieved, their spectral forms now quivering with a sense of closure. But I knew that the malevolent force that had been unleashed would not be so easily defeated.

The shattered mirror remained a fragmented gateway to the supernatural, a symbol of the dark secrets that lay hidden within Harrow Hill. The spirits' warnings had been clear, and I couldn't ignore them any longer.

I ventured back to the mirror, the shards suspended in the air like fragments of a shattered reality. With a sense of trepidation, I reached out and touched one of the shards. It pulsed with an otherworldly energy, and as I examined it closely, I realized that it held the key to the truth, the redemption that the spirits sought.

The shard revealed a vision, a glimpse into the past that had been obscured by time and betrayal. I saw the malevolent woman and Elias, their faces twisted with greed and treachery, as they plotted to seize control of the mansion. Their actions had led to unspeakable acts, and the spirits' suffering was a testament to their betrayal.

But the vision also revealed a path to redemption, a way to break the cycle of torment that bound the spirits. It was a ritual, one that required the mirror to be made whole again, a gateway for the spirits to find peace.

The spirits whispered their approval, their voices a chorus of gratitude and hope. They had guided me to this point, and now they sought my help to complete the ritual, to restore the mirror and allow them to find the redemption they so desperately craved.

I knew that the final chapter of this haunting tale lay before me, a relentless confrontation with the malevolent forces that sought to claim the mansion and the spirits. The mirror was the key, a gateway to a realm beyond comprehension, and the cost of truth had never been higher.

## Chapter 7: The Final Ritual

The malevolent force had retreated, but its presence still lingered in the shattered mirror, a malevolent entity waiting to be unleashed. The spirits had guided me to this point, seeking redemption, and I couldn't turn away from the responsibility that had been thrust upon me.

The shards of the broken mirror hovered in the air, their jagged edges like fragments of a fractured reality. Each shard held a piece of the haunting story that had unfolded within the walls of Harrow Hill, a story of betrayal and treachery, a story that had trapped the spirits in a never-ending cycle of torment.

With the spirits' whispered encouragement, I began the painstaking process of reassembling the mirror. The shards seemed to respond to my touch, aligning themselves in a mystical puzzle that defied the laws of nature. It was as if the very mansion itself conspired to aid me in this ritual.

As the mirror's form took shape, the room became charged with an otherworldly energy. The spirits watched with anticipation, their spectral forms quivering. The mirror, once shattered and malevolent, now held the promise of redemption.

I reached for the final shard, a piece that seemed to resonate with an intensity that set it apart from the others. As I touched it, a vision overcame me, a glimpse into the past that had been hidden from me until now.

I saw the malevolent woman and Elias, their faces twisted with greed, performing a ritual that had led to the spirits' torment. They had sought power and wealth at any cost, even if it meant making a pact with a malevolent force from the supernatural realm.

The malevolent presence that had confronted me was no ordinary spirit; it was an entity that had been summoned and bound to the mansion. The ritual had unleashed a darkness that threatened to consume everything in its path.

But the vision also revealed a way to break the malevolent force's hold. It was a counter-ritual, a ritual that would use the mirror to banish the malevolent entity and allow the spirits to find the peace they so desperately sought.

With newfound determination, I completed the mirror's reassembly. It glowed with an otherworldly light, a beacon of hope and redemption. The spirits' wails turned into a chorus of gratitude and relief.

The mirror was now a vessel for the ritual, a gateway to a supernatural realm that defied all reason. I knew that the time had come to confront the malevolent force, to banish it from the mansion, and to grant the spirits the redemption they so desperately craved.

The spirits, in their spectral forms, guided me to the center of the room, where the mirror stood. The malevolent force, the entity that had threatened to claim me, was still present, lurking within the mirror's depths.

I reached for the planchette, the same wooden device I had used during the séance. It was a conduit for communication with the supernatural, and now it would serve as a tool to confront the malevolent force.

With the spirits' guidance, I placed the planchette on the board inscribed with letters and numbers. The spirits formed a circle around the mirror, their spectral forms shimmering with anticipation.

The ritual began in earnest. The planchette moved of its own accord, spelling out words and forming sentences. The spirits' voices merged into a haunting chant, a chorus of resolve and hope.

The malevolent force within the mirror responded with a malevolent energy of its own. The room seemed to vibrate with a dark intensity, and the air grew colder, as if the very mansion itself were resisting the ritual.

The supernatural battle between good and evil, between redemption and malevolence, played out before my eyes. The spirits' resolve and my skepticism were pitted against the malevolent force's vengeful intent.

The mirror's surface rippled with an otherworldly energy, as if the malevolent entity sought to break free from its confines. The room filled with an eerie light, and the very foundations of Harrow Hill seemed to tremble.

As the ritual reached its climax, the malevolent entity within the mirror let out a deafening, otherworldly scream, a sound that transcended the boundaries of the living and the dead. The mirror seemed to shatter into a thousand pieces once more, and the malevolent presence burst forth, an entity of pure darkness and hatred.

With a collective effort, the spirits joined together, forming a barrier of ethereal energy that confronted the malevolent force. The room became a battleground, a clash of supernatural energies that defied comprehension.

I knew that the final outcome of this relentless confrontation hinged on my skepticism, my unwavering resolve, and the determination of the spirits to find redemption. The malevolent entity sought to claim the mansion and its secrets, and the cost of truth had never been higher.

## Chapter 8: Redemption's Light

In the midst of the supernatural battle that raged in the heart of Harrow Hill, the malevolent force and the spirits of the mansion clashed with an intensity that defied the boundaries of the living and the dead. The room was a battleground, a surreal confrontation that held the very fate of the mansion and its spectral inhabitants in the balance.

As the malevolent entity surged forward, an embodiment of hatred and betrayal, the spirits' ethereal forms quivered with resolve. The supernatural forces clashed, and the very foundations of the mansion trembled under the weight of the supernatural confrontation.

The room filled with an eerie light, a surreal dance of energy that transcended the laws of the natural world. The spirits joined together, forming a barrier of ethereal energy that pushed back the malevolent force. Their voices rose in a haunting chorus, a plea for redemption, a plea for release from the torment that had bound them for so long.

I stood at the center of this spectral battleground, my skepticism my unwavering anchor. The spirits had guided me to this moment, seeking redemption and closure, and I couldn't allow the malevolent entity to claim the mansion and its secrets.

With a sense of determination, I extended my hand toward the malevolent force, as if to challenge its darkness with my resolve. The supernatural battle reached its zenith, the air filled with an otherworldly energy that defied comprehension.

The malevolent entity let out a final, otherworldly scream, a sound that echoed through the mansion's halls. It seemed to struggle, its form flickering and contorting as if it were trapped between dimensions.

The spirits' barrier held firm, their collective energy pushing the malevolent force back toward the shattered mirror. It was a supernatural maelstrom, a confrontation that had transcended the boundaries of reality and the unexplained.

With a final surge of collective effort, the spirits banished the malevolent entity back into the mirror, sealing it within its fractured depths. The mirror's shards reassembled themselves, and it glowed with an otherworldly light, a beacon of hope and redemption.

The room fell into an eerie calm, the malevolent presence vanquished, at least for the moment. The spirits' spectral forms seemed to shimmer with a sense of closure, their voices merging into a harmonious chorus of gratitude and relief.

The supernatural battle had reached its conclusion, and the malevolent force had been banished, its hold over Harrow Hill broken. The spirits had found their redemption, and I had played a part in their release from the torment that had bound them.

The spirits, in their spectral forms, gathered around the mirror, their expressions filled with gratitude. They whispered their thanks, their voices a chorus of hope and relief.

As the spirits' spectral forms dissipated, I was left in the room, the weight of the supernatural encounter pressing upon me. The malevolent entity had been vanquished, the mirror a symbol of the redemption that had been achieved.

But my journey in the mansion was not yet complete. I knew that the next steps were to ensure the spirits' release and to confront the truth that had been hidden for so long.

I ventured back to the mirror, the symbol of both torment and redemption, and reached out to touch it. The mirror's surface rippled with an otherworldly energy, as if it were a gateway to a realm beyond comprehension.

As I gazed into the mirror's depths, a vision overcame me, a glimpse into the past that had been hidden from me until now. I saw the spirits, their spectral forms shimmering with gratitude, finding peace and release from the torment that had bound them.

The malevolent force, the entity of darkness and betrayal, was sealed within the mirror's depths, unable to harm the living or the dead.

But the mirror also revealed the truth, a revelation that had been obscured by time and treachery. It was a truth that had the power to heal old wounds, to reconcile the past with the present, and to ensure that the mansion's secrets would never again be used for malevolent purposes.

With newfound resolve, I knew that the final chapter of this haunting tale had arrived. The malevolent force had been banished, and the spirits had found their redemption, but the mansion's secrets were still waiting to be unveiled.

I reached for a piece of parchment and a quill, determined to document the truth that had been revealed. The mansion's secrets, once hidden by darkness and betrayal, would now be exposed to the light of day.

As I wrote, the room seemed to come alive with an otherworldly energy, as if the very mansion itself acknowledged the importance of the revelations that were being made. The truth, once hidden, would now be preserved for all to see.

With each word I penned, the atmosphere in the room grew brighter, as if the very mansion were being bathed in a supernatural light. The spirits' whispers of gratitude filled the air, a chorus of hope and closure.

The truth was now unveiled, a revelation that had the power to heal old wounds and reconcile the past with the present. The mansion's secrets were no longer a source of darkness and treachery, but a testament to the power of redemption and the resolve to confront the unexplained.

As I completed my documentation, the room seemed to vibrate with an otherworldly energy, as if the mansion itself were acknowledging the closure that had been achieved. The spirits' spectral forms gathered around me, their expressions filled with gratitude.

With a final sense of fulfillment, I knew that the journey in Harrow Hill had reached its conclusion. The malevolent force had been banished, the spirits had found their redemption, and the mansion's secrets were now exposed to the light of day.

As I left the room, the weight of the supernatural encounters that had unfolded within the mansion's walls lifted, replaced by a sense of closure and resolution. The spirits had guided me on a journey that had tested my skepticism and my resolve, and in the end, it had been a journey of redemption and hope.

The mansion, once a place of darkness and treachery, now stood as a testament to the power of confronting the unexplained, to finding closure and resolution in the face of the supernatural. The secrets that had haunted Harrow Hill were no longer a source of torment, but a path to healing and understanding.

I stepped out of the mansion's foreboding threshold, leaving behind the haunted world of Harrow Hill. The night was bathed in an eerie, perpetual twilight, where shadows danced on the horizon, and the air hung heavy with the scent of damp earth and forgotten memories.

The mansion stood as a silent sentinel, its walls a testament to the secrets and redemption that had unfolded within. The spirits, once trapped in a never-ending cycle of torment, had found their release, and the malevolent force had been banished to the depths of the mirror.

The journey in Harrow Hill had been a relentless confrontation with the supernatural, a testament to the power of skepticism and resolve. It had been a journey of redemption, closure, and hope, a journey that had revealed the cost of truth and the rewards of confronting the unexplained.

As I walked away from the mansion, I couldn't help but feel a sense of fulfillment and closure. The haunting of Harrow Hill had come to an end, and the spirits who had guided me on this supernatural journey had found their peace.

The journey had been a testament to the power of

 confronting the unexplained, and the mansion's secrets were now exposed to the light of day, a testament to the enduring power of redemption and hope.

And as I left the world of Harrow Hill behind, I couldn't help but believe that the lessons I had learned, the journey I had undertaken, would stay with me, a reminder that the cost of truth was a journey worth taking, and that in the face of the unexplained, redemption and hope could be found.
                THE END

# Inkwell's Reckoning

## Chapter 1: The Opening Act

The Literary Festival of Ravenswood was a celebration of words and worlds, where book lovers from far and wide gathered to worship the written word. As I stepped onto the cobblestone streets, the scent of aged paper and ink permeated the air, while banners displaying the works of renowned authors fluttered in the breeze. But this year, it was marred by an event no one could have foreseen—a murder most foul.

I am Detective Benjamin "Ben" Hartley, a dedicated investigator with an insatiable love for literature. My passion for the printed page was well-known in the precinct, earning me the nickname "Bookworm Ben." And, it was this very love for books that led me to attend the festival on that fateful autumn day.

As I strolled through the festival grounds, my eyes danced over the vibrant tapestry of humanity. People from all walks of life, dressed in the quirkiest of literary-themed costumes, laughed and debated the merits of their favorite authors. It was a spectacle of fandom, and I couldn't help but smile, basking in the shared enthusiasm for storytelling.

Amid the lively crowd, I spotted him—Maxwell Thornfield, a legend in the literary world. His novels were heralded as works of art, and his face adorned the covers of countless bestsellers. It was no surprise that the audience gathered around him, eager to hear his words of wisdom.

I moved closer, eager to hear the sage advice of a master wordsmith. Thornfield had a reputation for being enigmatic, and his public appearances were rare. He was as renowned for his aloofness as he was for his novels. But as I edged closer to the growing throng, the vibrant colors of his conversation suddenly shifted to stark shades of horror.

A scream cut through the festival's jovial atmosphere, chilling the air and turning the laughter to gasps of disbelief. The crowd parted like a raging sea, revealing a shocking tableau—the great Maxwell Thornfield lay lifeless on the stage, a twisted smile upon his face, and an antique quill pen driven through his heart.

Panic and chaos erupted as festivalgoers scrambled away from the scene. The other authors on the stage retreated, their faces etched with terror. The crime scene was contaminated within seconds, but my instincts as a detective kicked in. I pushed my way through the frantic crowd to reach the stage, pulling my badge from my pocket.

"Everyone, please, step back! Let me through!" I shouted, my authoritative tone managing to clear a path. I crouched beside Thornfield's lifeless body, noting the ink-stained blood that surrounded the quill piercing his chest. A macabre work of art, a grotesque homage to the world of letters.

His death was not a natural one, of that I was sure. It was murder most cunning, a crime conceived within the boundaries of literature and executed with theatrical precision. I surveyed the audience, searching for any suspicious movements or signs of guilt, but the chaos was all-encompassing.

Amidst the commotion, a slender, dark-haired woman emerged, her face etched with grief and disbelief. She was introduced as Evelyn Gray, Maxwell Thornfield's longtime editor and confidante. Her eyes brimmed with tears as she clutched a tattered manuscript to her chest.

"Maxwell... he was working on a new novel, and he told me it would change everything. It would expose secrets that could destroy lives," she stammered, her voice quivering with emotion.

I took her aside, away from the prying eyes of the festivalgoers, and questioned her further. Her revelations hinted at buried secrets and rivalries within the world of publishing. The poisoned pen was no ordinary murder weapon, but a sinister message from someone with a deep knowledge of literary symbolism.

With a heavy heart, I realized that the festival's joy had been cruelly replaced by a grim tale of deceit, ambition, and death. The poisoned pen had written the opening chapter of a mystery that would test my intellect, my love for literature, and my commitment to justice.

And as the sun dipped below the horizon, casting long shadows on the cobblestone streets of Ravenswood, I knew that the pages of this investigation were about to turn, revealing a labyrinthine plot that would challenge my every instinct as a detective and unravel a web of intrigue that would forever change the literary world.

The poisoned pen had cast its dark spell, and I was determined to decipher its secrets, no matter where the clues would lead, even if they took me to the heart of the world I loved—the world of books.

## Chapter 2: Shadows of Suspicion

In the dimly lit backroom of a charming little bookstore in Ravenswood, I found myself surrounded by the musty scent of old paper and the hushed whispers of clandestine meetings. It was a place where literary secrets were kept safe, or so its owner, Nigel Finch, had once confided in me. And it was in this very room that I hoped to unearth the enigmatic secrets that had led to Maxwell Thornfield's murder.

Nigel Finch, an unassuming man with a passion for rare tomes and an encyclopedic knowledge of the literary world, had been a longtime friend of Maxwell's. He had reached out to me after the festival, concerned about the unanswered questions surrounding the murder. The clues, he believed, could be hidden within the very books that graced the shelves of his establishment.

As I followed Finch through the labyrinthine stacks, my fingers traced the spines of countless novels, each one holding untold stories, just waiting to be discovered. He led me to a hidden corner, where a large antique desk stood, covered in dust and manuscripts. It was Thornfield's private workspace during his visits to the bookstore, a sanctuary where he had sought inspiration for his writing.

Finch unlocked a drawer and retrieved a leather-bound journal. "This, Detective Hartley, is Maxwell's personal journal. He wrote in it often, but in recent weeks, his entries became increasingly cryptic. I thought it might help you in your investigation."

The journal was filled with ink-stained pages and thoughts that wandered through the labyrinth of a brilliant mind. Thornfield's musings spoke of hidden rivalries, dark secrets, and an impending revelation that would forever alter the course of literary history. But what struck me most were the references to a shadowy figure known as "The Muse," someone who seemed to hold a sinister sway over Thornfield's life.

I leaned back in the creaky wooden chair, deep in thought. "Finch, do you know anything about this 'Muse'? Was Thornfield working on a project related to them?"

Nigel Finch's eyes widened, and he clasped his hands together nervously. "The Muse... Maxwell never spoke much about it. But he did mention that it was the key to his new novel. He believed that unveiling the Muse's identity would change everything."

It was clear that The Muse held the answers to the mysteries shrouding Thornfield's life and death. My intuition told me that I needed to dive deeper into the literary world, to explore the rivalries and secrets that Maxwell had hinted at. But where to begin? As I pondered, my thoughts were interrupted by the sudden jingling of the bookstore's bell.

Evelyn Gray had arrived, her steps tentative as she scanned the dimly lit space. Her tear-stained eyes met mine, and she approached, clutching the same tattered manuscript she had held at the festival. "Detective Hartley, I couldn't bear to keep this from you any longer," she said, her voice trembling.

I accepted the manuscript, its pages aged and weathered, and started to read. It was a chilling tale, a novel that Maxwell

Thornfield had been working on in secret—a story of deceit, betrayal, and a protagonist's quest to unveil the enigmatic Muse.

Evelyn continued, "I believe this manuscript holds the key to Maxwell's death. He was close to revealing the identity of The Muse, but he wanted me to publish the novel posthumously if anything happened to him."

The manuscript had been written in a fevered frenzy, with the urgency of a man who believed he was on the cusp of a revelation. It detailed a world of literary rivalries, corrupt publishers, and the power of secrets that could bring down even the most esteemed authors. But the climax, the unveiling of The Muse, remained tantalizingly incomplete.

I knew that deciphering the missing pieces of the manuscript was my best chance at solving the case. I turned to Evelyn. "We need to find out who The Muse is. It's the only way to uncover Maxwell's killer and bring justice to his memory."

As we delved further into the manuscript, a sense of unease settled upon us. It was clear that The Muse's identity held the key to a hidden world of power and manipulation within the literary community, a world that thrived on secrets and rivalries. The revelations in Thornfield's manuscript painted a picture of corruption that ran deeper than anyone had imagined.

The hours passed, and the flickering candlelight cast long shadows across the room, emphasizing the gravity of our task. It was a task that held the potential to disrupt the very foundations of the literary world, and as we closed in on the final pages of the manuscript, it became evident that the answers were within our reach.

But then, just as we were about to reveal The Muse's identity, the door to the bookstore swung open, and a chilling voice filled the room. "I wouldn't be so hasty if I were you, Detective Hartley."

I turned to find a mysterious figure standing in the doorway, shrouded in darkness, their features hidden. A frisson of fear coursed through me, and I instinctively reached for my sidearm, ready to confront the shadows of suspicion that had just infiltrated our sanctuary.

## Chapter 3: The Enigmatic Intruder

The stranger's voice hung in the air, an eerie echo in the dimly lit bookstore. I couldn't make out their face, hidden in the shadows that cloaked their form. My fingers tightened around the grip of my sidearm, ready for whatever this intrusion might bring.

Evelyn Gray stepped closer, her eyes darting between me and the enigmatic figure. "Who are you, and what do you want?" she demanded, her voice filled with a mixture of fear and determination.

The stranger stepped into the light, revealing a tall, slender figure, clad in a long black coat and a wide-brimmed hat that obscured their features. A soft, ominous chuckle emanated from beneath the hat. "You may call me 'The Muse,'" they said, their voice dripping with arrogance. "I've come for what is rightfully mine."

"The Muse?" I repeated, taken aback. The identity of this figure was the key to unraveling the mystery surrounding Maxwell

Thornfield's murder, and here they stood before us, shrouded in secrecy.

Evelyn clutched the manuscript even tighter. "You're The Muse? What do you have to do with Maxwell's death?"

The Muse took a step closer, and their gloved hand extended, pointing at the manuscript. "That novel you hold in your hands, Detective Hartley, was never meant to be finished. It contains truths that were never meant to see the light of day. Hand it over, and perhaps you'll find some answers."

I hesitated, torn between a thirst for justice and the realization that we were facing a powerful adversary. If we surrendered the manuscript, The Muse might escape justice, but if we didn't, we risked losing our only lead. With a glance at Evelyn, we made our decision. I tossed the manuscript onto the desk, and it landed with a soft thud.

The Muse bent down to pick it up, their gloved hand grazing the pages with a disturbing sense of ownership. "Maxwell Thornfield was a fool," they hissed. "He thought he could expose me, but I've been in control of the literary world for far longer than he could ever fathom."

As The Muse thumbed through the pages, their gaze grew intent, and they began to mutter to themselves. "It's all here—the secrets, the revelations. Everything I wanted to remain buried."

Suddenly, The Muse's gloved hand moved with unexpected speed, thrusting the manuscript into the flickering candle flame. The pages caught fire, and within moments, the manuscript was reduced to ashes. Evelyn gasped in horror, while I lunged toward The Muse, but they stepped back with a taunting grin.

"You'll never uncover my secrets," The Muse declared, their voice filled with a maddening satisfaction. "And now, I bid you farewell."

In a whirl of darkness, The Muse turned and darted toward the door, vanishing into the night. I rushed after them, but by the time I reached the street, they were gone. The chase had led us to a dead end, and our best chance at exposing the enigma had slipped through our fingers.

Evelyn's eyes filled with tears as she looked at the smoldering remains of the manuscript. "It's all gone," she said, her voice trembling. "Maxwell's last work, his legacy, and the key to finding his killer."

We returned to the dimly lit bookstore, where Nigel Finch waited with a mix of anxiety and curiosity. When we recounted the encounter with The Muse and the destruction of the manuscript, his face fell, and he shook his head. "I always suspected Maxwell had gotten involved in something dangerous, but this... this is beyond anything I could have imagined."

I couldn't shake the feeling of being outmaneuvered, and the realization that The Muse remained at large gnawed at me. Our investigation had hit a wall, and the road ahead appeared darker and more treacherous than ever. I glanced at Evelyn, and her resolute expression mirrored my determination to uncover the truth.

"We won't stop here," I declared, my voice unwavering. "Maxwell Thornfield's death and the enigma of The Muse must be solved. We need to dig deeper into his world, the world of publishing, and the secrets hidden within. There's a tangled web of rivalries, deceit, and ambition, and we're not giving up."

As the clock in the bookstore's backroom ticked on, we gathered the fragments of what we knew, determined to piece together a puzzle that threatened the very essence of the literary world. But The Muse was a formidable adversary, one who had outwitted us, leaving a trail of destruction in their wake.

And so, our quest continued, as we set our sights on uncovering the true identity of The Muse and the motive behind Maxwell Thornfield's murder. The enigmatic figure had left behind a trail of clues, and it was up to us to follow them, no matter where they led.

As I contemplated the shadowy figure who had eluded us, I couldn't help but feel that we were now playing a dangerous game—one where the stakes were higher than ever, and the consequences of failure were unimaginable.

## Chapter 4: Whispers in the Underworld

Days turned into nights as Evelyn Gray and I delved deeper into the complex world of publishing, our determination unwavering. The mysterious figure known as The Muse had escaped our grasp, leaving a chilling trail of destruction and a world of unanswered questions in their wake. Yet, we were not alone in our quest.

Nigel Finch had become our reluctant ally, offering insight into the dark underbelly of the literary world that Maxwell Thornfield had dared to expose. With his guidance, we navigated the intricate web of publishers, authors, and rivalries that Maxwell had hinted at in his cryptic journal.

Our investigation led us to the depths of Ravenswood's literary underbelly—a clandestine society known as "The Quill." It was rumored to be a shadowy organization, operating in the shadows, where powerful authors wielded their influence to manipulate the fates of others.

As we gathered information and whispered secrets in dimly lit cafés and bookstores, it became evident that The Muse's power extended far beyond what Maxwell had suspected. The Quill had become a breeding ground for ambition and treachery, a place where authors could rise to stardom or be silenced with a stroke of the pen.

Evelyn, her determination growing stronger by the day, became our link to the publishing world, gathering information from her contacts and discreetly infiltrating the circles of The Quill. Nigel Finch, on the other hand, used his knowledge of rare books and manuscripts to uncover clues that could help us unmask The Muse's true identity.

It was on a rainy night, as the city's lamplights glistened on wet cobblestones, that we received a break in the case. Nigel Finch had unearthed an old and forgotten manuscript, penned by a disgruntled author who had been cast aside by The Quill. The manuscript contained damning revelations about The Muse and their power over the world of literature.

The author's words painted a chilling picture, describing secret meetings and the manipulation of publishing contracts that could make or break a writer's career. The manuscript pointed to a figure known as "The Scribe," who acted as The Muse's enforcer, ensuring that their influence reached every corner of the literary world.

Our excitement was palpable as we pored over the manuscript, but it also carried a sense of danger. The closer we got to exposing The Muse, the more perilous our journey became. It was clear that The Muse and their enigmatic enforcer would stop at nothing to protect their secrets and maintain their grip on the literary world.

As we traced the author's footsteps through Ravenswood's historic libraries and archives, we uncovered a hidden network of Quill members who operated in plain sight. It was in the pages of old documents and records that we found the names of individuals who had crossed paths with The Muse and The Scribe, and it became apparent that we were getting closer to unraveling the enigma.

But with every step forward, the shadows of danger grew deeper. We began to receive cryptic threats and warnings, and our every move was watched. The stakes had never been higher, and we knew that we were racing against time to expose the truth.

One fateful night, as we met in the dimly lit backroom of Finch's bookstore, a sense of urgency filled the air. The manuscript had revealed that The Scribe, a figure known only by reputation and whispered tales, had connections to some of the most influential publishers in Ravenswood. To uncover The Muse's identity, we needed to find The Scribe and pry the truth from their lips.

Evelyn voiced our shared concern. "If we find The Scribe, we find The Muse. And if we find The Muse, we find Maxwell Thornfield's killer."

Nigel Finch nodded, his eyes filled with determination. "The Scribe is the key to unraveling the web of deceit that has ensnared the literary world. But we must tread carefully; they are a shadowy figure who leaves no trace."

The three of us knew that to unmask The Scribe, we needed to take a perilous journey into the heart of The Quill's inner sanctum. There, we hoped to uncover the secrets that Maxwell Thornfield had died trying to reveal. We were stepping into the lion's den, and we knew the consequences of failure could be dire.

As we prepared to infiltrate The Quill's secret gathering, I couldn't help but think of the chilling power that had eluded us so far—the power of The Muse, the power of secrets, and the power to change lives with a stroke of the pen. Our quest was far from over, and the shadowy figure known as The Scribe held the final piece of the puzzle that would expose the truth and bring justice to Maxwell Thornfield's memory.

But as we left Finch's bookstore, the city's rain-soaked streets glistening with the reflections of lamplights, a sense of unease settled upon us. The Quill was a world of intrigue, and the secrets it held were as dangerous as they were elusive. We were about to enter a realm of treachery and ambition, a world where the written word held more power than anyone could imagine.

And as the night enveloped us, I couldn't shake the feeling that our journey was about to reach its most perilous and pivotal moment, a moment where we would either expose the enigmatic figure known as The Scribe or be consumed by the darkness that had eluded us for far too long.

## Chapter 5: Whispers of The Scribe

The night was shrouded in an eerie silence as we made our way to the clandestine meeting of The Quill, the enigmatic society that held the secrets of Maxwell Thornfield's murder and the elusive identity of The Muse. Evelyn Gray, Nigel Finch, and I moved through the cobblestone streets of Ravenswood like shadows, our footsteps barely making a sound, and our hearts pounding with anticipation.

The location of the meeting was whispered to us, hidden beneath the city's bustling exterior—a hidden chamber within the archives of the Ravenswood Public Library. It was a place few knew of, a well-guarded secret passed down through generations of Quill members.

As we reached the entrance to the library, the wrought-iron gate opened with a soft creak, revealing a narrow, dimly lit passageway that led deep beneath the city. We followed the path into a subterranean world, away from the prying eyes of the literary elite, and into the heart of The Quill's clandestine gathering.

The air grew damp and musty as we descended, the dim light flickering overhead casting long shadows that danced on the stone walls. The whispers of secrets seemed to linger in the air, carried through the ages by those who had dared to tread these hidden corridors.

Finally, we arrived at the hidden chamber. The wooden door creaked open, revealing a candlelit room adorned with ancient tomes and manuscripts. It was a sanctuary of literature, but it was also a place of power, where authors held the keys to a writer's destiny.

As we entered, we found ourselves in the presence of a small group of individuals, their faces hidden in the shadows. A sense of trepidation filled the room, and the whispers ceased as they turned their attention to us. We had entered the lion's den.

Nigel Finch, with his knowledge of rare books and manuscripts, took the lead. "We seek answers," he declared boldly, his voice echoing in the chamber. "Answers regarding Maxwell Thornfield's murder and the enigmatic figure known as The Muse."

The Quill members exchanged glances, their faces still hidden from view. But a voice emerged from the darkness, a voice that was older and filled with authority. "You tread on dangerous ground, seekers of truth. The Muse and The Scribe are not to be trifled with."

Evelyn Gray stepped forward, her determination unwavering. "Maxwell Thornfield lost his life trying to reveal the secrets of The Muse. We deserve to know the truth."

The chamber fell into silence once more, the tension palpable. Then, slowly, the shadows parted, revealing the face of a woman with silver hair, her eyes filled with a mix of wisdom and sorrow.

"I am Eleanor Carrington, the Keeper of The Quill. The Muse and The Scribe have long held sway over our world, but their power must be exposed."

Eleanor Carrington's revelation sent ripples of surprise through the room. The Keeper of The Quill was a position of great influence, and her willingness to cooperate was a sign that the tides were turning in our favor.

"We can help you uncover the truth," Evelyn implored. "We have the evidence to expose The Muse, but we need to find The Scribe to complete the puzzle."

Eleanor Carrington nodded, her expression grave. "The Scribe is a figure of immense power within our ranks, a shadowy enforcer who carries out the will of The Muse. They control the fates of authors and manipulate the literary world to their advantage."

Nigel Finch added, "We believe that if we can reveal The Scribe's identity, we can unmask The Muse and bring justice to Maxwell Thornfield's memory."

Eleanor Carrington's eyes held a glimmer of hope. "We will assist you in your quest. But to find The Scribe, you must venture into the heart of The Quill's inner circle. It is a perilous journey, and the consequences of failure are dire."

With a sense of purpose, we prepared to delve further into the enigma that surrounded The Quill, knowing that the answers we sought lay within the secrets that had been guarded for far too long. Eleanor Carrington offered her guidance, leading us deeper into the society's inner workings, where rivalries and secrets festered.

The night wore on as we navigated the maze of literary ambition and manipulation, learning of whispered alliances and hidden agendas. The closer we got to uncovering The Scribe's true identity, the more treacherous our journey became.

And then, at the darkest hour of the night, as we stood on the precipice of revelation, a chilling voice echoed through the chamber. "You tread where you do not belong, seekers of truth."

The room fell into a hushed silence, and we turned to see a figure emerge from the shadows—a tall, imposing man, his features hidden by a mask. He was The Scribe, the enigmatic enforcer of The Muse, and his presence sent shivers down our spines.

Eleanor Carrington's voice quivered as she addressed him, "Scribe, they have come seeking answers, seeking the truth about The Muse."

The Scribe's masked face remained inscrutable, his eyes piercing through the darkness. "The Muse's secrets are not for the world to know. You have trespassed into a realm of power beyond your understanding."

But we would not be deterred. We had come too far to turn back now, and the weight of justice for Maxwell Thornfield's murder rested on our shoulders.

Evelyn stepped forward, her voice unwavering. "We will expose The Muse's secrets, no matter the cost."

As The Scribe advanced, his gloved hand reaching for the mask that concealed his identity, I knew that the moment of reckoning had arrived. Our quest had led us to a confrontation with the enigmatic enforcer, a confrontation that would reveal the truth, but at what price?

And as he began to remove his mask, the chamber grew eerily silent, and the answers we sought were about to be unveiled.

## Chapter 6: Unveiling Shadows

In the dimly lit chamber beneath the Ravenswood Public Library, time hung in suspense as The Scribe began to lift the mask that had concealed his identity. The room was suffused with an air of anticipation, mingled with dread, for the revelation that lay ahead was bound to send ripples through the literary world and beyond.

As The Scribe removed the mask, a collective gasp echoed in the chamber. It was as if the weight of hidden truths, secrets, and transgressions had manifested in the form of a single face—the face of Horace Blackwood.

Horace Blackwood was a name that sent shivers down the spines of many in the literary world. As a powerful figure in the publishing industry, he had controlled the destinies of countless authors, their careers, and even the fates of their works. He had long been rumored to have connections to The Muse, but this revelation was staggering.

Evelyn Gray's voice trembled as she spoke. "Horace Blackwood, The Scribe? You're the one who orchestrated Maxwell's murder?"

Horace Blackwood's eyes, cold and unapologetic, bore into us. "Maxwell Thornfield was a threat, a man who dared to expose the secrets that we, the guardians of literature, had hidden for centuries. The Muse, a persona I adopted, has long been the driving force behind our power, and I have protected it at all costs."

Nigel Finch's face contorted with a mix of anger and disbelief. "You manipulated the literary world, silenced authors, and controlled their destinies, all to maintain your own power and influence?"

Horace Blackwood's lips curled into a twisted smile. "The literary world is a cutthroat arena, and I have merely played the game as it was meant to be played. Authors are pawns, and I am the master."

I felt a surge of anger and indignation, but I also realized that our exposure of The Scribe had placed us in a precarious position. The literary elite had long shielded Blackwood's actions, and his influence extended into realms we had not yet uncovered.

Eleanor Carrington, the Keeper of The Quill, spoke with a voice filled with disappointment. "Horace, you have betrayed the very principles The Quill was built upon. Your actions have brought disgrace to the literary world."

Horace Blackwood's gaze turned to Eleanor, his voice unwavering. "The Quill was built upon the foundation of maintaining control over the literary world, and I have upheld that purpose. If you cannot see that, then you are blinded by idealism."

But we were not about to let Horace Blackwood escape justice. Evelyn Gray, with a determination that matched the weight of her convictions, stepped forward. "Your crimes will not go unpunished. Maxwell Thornfield's murder demands justice, and the literary world deserves to know the truth."

Nigel Finch, his voice tinged with a resolve that had grown stronger with each revelation, added, "We have the evidence to expose your actions, to reveal the extent of your influence, and to bring an end to the manipulation of literature."

The standoff in the dimly lit chamber underscored the gravity of the moment. We had unveiled The Scribe's true identity, but the battle was far from over. The Muse, the enigmatic figure who had orchestrated Maxwell Thornfield's murder, still remained at large. Our quest for justice had taken us into the very heart of darkness, and we were now pitted against one of the most powerful figures in the literary world.

Horace Blackwood, sensing the inevitability of his fate, took a step back, his eyes narrowing with a steely resolve. "You may have uncovered my true identity, but you will not escape the consequences of your actions."

As he spoke those words, a sudden commotion erupted in the chamber. The masked Quill members, who had been silent observers of the unfolding drama, began to converge around us, their intentions unclear. It was a tense standoff, a moment of reckoning that would determine the course of our journey.

Eleanor Carrington's voice cut through the tension. "The Muse's secrets must be exposed, and the literary world must be set free from the manipulations that have bound it for so long."

But before a resolution could be reached, the lights in the chamber flickered and then went out completely. Panic ensued as we found ourselves plunged into darkness. The Quill members, hidden behind their masks, seized the opportunity to disperse into the shadows, leaving us isolated and vulnerable.

Evelyn Gray's voice quivered in the darkness. "What's happening? Where did they go?"

Nigel Finch, his frustration palpable, called out, "We need to find a way out of here, now."

But just as we began to grope our way through the chamber, a chilling whisper echoed in the darkness, a voice that sent shivers down our spines. "You may have uncovered one shadow, but there are many more lurking in the world of words. The Muse will not be exposed so easily."

The voice was unmistakable—it was The Muse, the enigmatic figure who had orchestrated Maxwell Thornfield's murder. The darkness had become a veil, a shroud of uncertainty, and The Muse's taunts hung in the air.

We had unveiled the truth about The Scribe, but The Muse's power and influence remained, casting a shadow over our quest for justice. The battle against the shadows was far from over, and the darkness of the literary world threatened to consume us.

As we stood in the pitch-black chamber, our journey had reached a critical juncture. The revelation of Horace Blackwood as The Scribe had exposed the machinations that had controlled the literary world for too long, but The Muse's secrets still eluded us.

The path ahead was uncertain, and the shadows of treachery and manipulation loomed large.

And so, we were left to navigate the darkness, knowing that The Muse's enigmatic power and the secrets that had remained hidden for centuries were now more elusive than ever.

## Chapter 7: The Trail of Literary Deceit

As the darkness enveloped us in the chamber beneath the Ravenswood Public Library, The Muse's taunts continued to echo through the shadows. The revelation of Horace Blackwood as The Scribe had shaken the foundations of the literary world, but our quest for justice was far from over. The enigmatic figure that had orchestrated Maxwell Thornfield's murder remained at large, and the shadows of treachery and manipulation loomed large.

With our vision obscured, we stumbled through the chamber, searching for a way out of the labyrinthine underground. The echoes of distant footsteps, whispers, and the scuffling of masked Quill members surrounded us, further shrouding our escape in uncertainty.

Evelyn Gray's voice cut through the darkness. "We can't stay here. We need to find a way out before The Muse disappears."

Nigel Finch, his voice filled with frustration, added, "We need light, a source to guide us through this labyrinth."

With a sense of urgency, I reached into my pocket and retrieved a small flashlight. Its feeble beam cut through the inky blackness, revealing the worn stone walls of the chamber and a narrow corridor leading deeper into the underground.

We pressed forward, following the corridor's twists and turns, the whisper of our own breath and footsteps the only sounds that dared to intrude upon the oppressive silence. Our determination was unwavering, our quest for justice and the truth forging a path through the darkness.

It wasn't long before we reached an ancient wooden door, its frame encrusted with age and disuse. The door resisted our attempts to open it at first, but with a collective effort, we managed to push it open, revealing a sight that filled us with wonder and dread.

We found ourselves in an immense underground chamber, a hidden library of untold treasures and secrets. Shelves upon shelves of ancient manuscripts, rare tomes, and dusty scrolls stretched as far as the eye could see, illuminated by the feeble beam of my flashlight.

Evelyn's eyes widened as she gazed upon the countless literary treasures that surrounded us. "This must be the repository of The Quill's secrets. If we can find evidence here, we may finally expose The Muse."

Nigel Finch, always the connoisseur of rare books, spoke with a mixture of reverence and anticipation. "This is a treasure trove of knowledge, and it may hold the key to unraveling the shadows that have haunted the literary world for centuries."

With a shared determination, we began to sift through the countless manuscripts, searching for clues that would lead us to

The Muse's identity. But it wasn't long before we realized that the task at hand was daunting—centuries of secrets, rivalries, and deception were concealed within these walls.

The Muse's voice, a chilling whisper in the darkness, reached our ears once more. "You seek the truth, but the truth may be more elusive than you imagine. The secrets within these manuscripts are protected by the same shadows that have shrouded the literary world."

The enigmatic figure's words were a reminder that we were not alone in the underground repository. The Muse's presence lurked in the shadows, a constant threat to our quest for justice. We knew that time was running out, and every moment brought us closer to the unknown, where danger and revelation were intertwined.

As we continued to search through the ancient manuscripts, Nigel Finch came across a leather-bound tome that caught his attention. Its cover was inscribed with cryptic symbols and runes, and its pages were filled with enigmatic verses and passages that seemed to hold a deeper meaning.

"This manuscript is unlike any of the others," Nigel remarked. "Its contents may be the key to unraveling The Muse's secrets."

Evelyn and I gathered around Nigel as he began to decipher the text. The verses spoke of a powerful figure who had influenced the literary world for centuries, orchestrating the rise and fall of authors and their works. The identity of this figure remained veiled in metaphor and allegory, but the description left no doubt—it was The Muse.

The Muse's influence had stretched through time, its power a constant force within the literary world. As we delved further into the manuscript, a sense of awe and dread overcame us. The Muse's secrets, their true identity, and the motives behind Maxwell Thornfield's murder were buried deep within these cryptic verses.

But The Muse was not about to let us uncover the truth so easily. As we read through the manuscript, a sudden gust of wind swept through the underground library, extinguishing the feeble beam of my flashlight and plunging us into darkness once more.

Evelyn's voice trembled as she whispered, "We need to find another source of light. We're so close to the truth."

Nigel Finch's voice held a sense of determination. "We must press on, for Maxwell's sake and for the sake of all authors who have been manipulated by The Muse's influence."

With a sense of urgency, we continued to search for a source of light within the pitch-black chamber. It wasn't long before we discovered a set of torches mounted on the stone walls, their flames flickering with a feeble, ancient light. With these torches in hand, we resumed our exploration of the cryptic manuscript.

But as we read further into the verses, The Muse's whisper returned, sending shivers down our spines. "You think you are close to the truth, but the truth can be deceiving. The Muse's identity is a web of illusion, a tapestry of deception that stretches through time."

The Muse's words were a constant reminder that we were not just unearthing secrets; we were untangling a web of deceit that had ensnared the literary world for centuries. The enigmatic figure was a master of manipulation, and our pursuit of justice had brought us into a realm where danger and revelation were inseparable.

As the torchlight illuminated the cryptic manuscript, we pressed forward, determined to uncover the truth that had eluded us for so long. The Muse's secrets, the identity that had remained concealed, and the motives behind Maxwell Thornfield's murder were now within our reach.

And so, we found ourselves in the heart of the underground repository, our quest for justice and revelation becoming increasingly perilous. The Muse's presence, the shadows of treachery, and the enduring mysteries of the literary world threatened to consume us.

The torches illuminated our path, revealing the manuscripts, secrets, and enigmatic verses that held the key to exposing The Muse's true identity. But we were not alone in the darkness, and the voice of The Muse continued to echo through the shadows, a constant reminder that our journey was far from over.

As we read further into the cryptic manuscript, we knew that we were on the cusp of uncovering the literary world's deepest and most dangerous secrets. But the revelations we sought were shrouded in metaphor and allegory, and the enigma of The Muse's identity remained a puzzle that defied easy solutions.

The torchlight flickered and cast dancing shadows on the chamber's ancient walls, underscoring the sense of anticipation that filled the air. The next steps we took would determine the fate of The Muse's secrets, the pursuit of justice, and the unveiling of a shadowy figure that had haunted the literary world for far too long.

And so, we continued to search for the truth within the cryptic manuscript, knowing that the final revelations were within our grasp, but also realizing that the shadows of treachery and manipulation still held sway over the literary world.

## Chapter 8: The Unraveling Truth

The torches cast their wavering light over the cryptic manuscript as we continued our quest for the elusive identity of The Muse, the enigmatic figure who had orchestrated Maxwell Thornfield's murder. The verses within the manuscript were a labyrinth of metaphors and allegories, leading us deeper into the shadows of literary manipulation.

Evelyn Gray's voice held a sense of determination. "We can't let The Muse's secrets remain hidden any longer. Maxwell's memory demands justice."

Nigel Finch, his fingers tracing the mysterious verses, added, "We have come too far to turn back now. The revelations we seek are concealed within these cryptic lines."

As we read on, the verses within the manuscript began to weave a tapestry of deception. They described The Muse as a master of disguise, a figure who had hidden behind numerous personas and names throughout the centuries. The identity was veiled in metaphor, and the revelations remained tantalizingly out of reach.

The Muse's voice, a haunting whisper in the darkness, reached us once more. "You search for an identity that has existed beyond the confines of a single name. The Muse is a legacy, a lineage that stretches through time."

The enigmatic figure's words sent shivers down our spines. The Muse's identity was not that of a single person but a legacy, a lineage that had wielded influence and control over the literary world for centuries. The revelation was staggering, and it left us with more questions than answers.

With the torchlight guiding us, we delved deeper into the cryptic manuscript, piecing together the puzzle of The Muse's legacy. The verses spoke of a network of individuals who had taken on the mantle of The Muse, each passing down their secrets and knowledge to the next generation.

Nigel Finch's eyes widened as he deciphered a particularly cryptic passage. "The Muse is not a person, but a secret society, a clandestine lineage of individuals who manipulate the literary world from the shadows."

The weight of this revelation hung in the air. The Muse was not one person but a legacy, a clandestine society that had controlled literature for generations. Our pursuit of justice had led us into a realm where manipulation, secrets, and deception had endured for centuries.

Evelyn Gray's voice, filled with resolve, cut through the silence. "We need to expose this society, reveal the extent of their influence, and bring an end to The Muse's power."

As we continued to search for answers within the cryptic manuscript, The Muse's whispers grew more insistent. "You think you can expose the society, but you underestimate the lengths we will go to protect our secrets. The Muse's influence stretches far and wide, and its power will not be easily unraveled."

The Muse's taunts were a stark reminder that our quest for justice was not without its perils. The clandestine society, hidden in the shadows of the literary world, held sway over authors, publishers, and the very essence of storytelling. Our pursuit of the truth was met with a formidable adversary, and the revelations we sought were veiled in metaphor and allegory.

But we were not about to be deterred. With the torchlight guiding us, we pressed on, searching for more clues within the cryptic manuscript. The verses began to reveal the names of individuals who had carried the mantle of The Muse, figures who had influenced literature, shaped destinies, and concealed their true identities through the ages.

Nigel Finch's eyes widened as he uncovered a name that sent shockwaves through our midst. "Jonathan Blackwood, an influential figure in literature, known by many names, but always carrying the legacy of The Muse."

The revelation of Jonathan Blackwood's connection to The Muse was staggering. It linked him to the clandestine society that had controlled the literary world for generations. We had unveiled a link between the enigmatic figure and a powerful figure in the publishing industry.

Evelyn Gray, her voice tinged with determination, spoke up. "Jonathan Blackwood holds the key to exposing The Muse's secrets and the motive behind Maxwell's murder. We need to find him."

But before we could formulate a plan to locate Jonathan Blackwood, the torches lining the chamber's walls suddenly flickered and dimmed. Panic surged through us as the chamber was plunged into darkness, the echoes of The Muse's whispers echoing in our ears.

Nigel Finch's voice, filled with frustration, broke the silence. "We need to find a source of light. We can't let The Muse's secrets remain concealed."

With the urgency of our quest weighing on us, we fumbled in the dark, searching for a source of light that would guide us through the labyrinthine chamber. The Muse's whispers continued to taunt us, a constant reminder of the enigmatic figure's presence in the shadows.

Evelyn Gray's voice quivered as she spoke. "The Muse won't stop us from uncovering the truth. We've come too far to turn back now."

As we groped through the darkness, our quest for justice and revelation remained unwavering. The Muse's secrets, the identity that had remained elusive, and the motives behind Maxwell Thornfield's murder were within our grasp. But the enigmatic figure's presence in the shadows threatened to consume us, and the final revelations we sought were cloaked in mystery.

And so, in the heart of the underground repository, we stood at a crossroads, our journey fraught with danger and uncertainty. The revelations we had uncovered were staggering, but the shadows of treachery and manipulation still clung to the literary world.

As we continued our search for the truth, we knew that the final answers lay within our reach, but the enigma of The Muse's identity remained veiled in metaphor and allegory. The pursuit of justice was a perilous path, and the darkness of the literary world threatened to consume us.

## Chapter 9: The Reckoning

In the oppressive darkness of the underground repository, our search for the truth continued, our torches flickering as we navigated the labyrinth of ancient manuscripts and cryptic verses. The revelations within the text had led us to a legacy of enigmatic figures who had controlled the literary world, but the elusive identity of The Muse remained a shadowy enigma.

The Muse's whispers, a haunting presence in the blackness, taunted us once more. "You seek the truth, but the truth can be a double-edged sword, a revelation that may come at a high cost."

The enigmatic figure's words hung in the air, a reminder that our pursuit of justice and revelation had led us into a realm where danger and deceit were intertwined. The Muse's secrets, concealed within metaphor and allegory, remained just beyond our grasp.

Nigel Finch's voice, tinged with a sense of urgency, cut through the darkness. "We need to find a way out of here. The Muse's presence looms, and we are running out of time."

Evelyn Gray, her determination unwavering, spoke up. "We must find Jonathan Blackwood, the key to exposing The Muse's secrets and the motive behind Maxwell's murder."

With our torchlight guiding us, we retraced our steps through the labyrinthine chamber, searching for an exit. The whispers of secrets, shadows, and the weight of literary manipulation lingered in the air, a constant reminder of the enigmatic forces at play.

But just as we reached the door that had led us into the chamber, a figure emerged from the shadows, a masked Quill member. The presence of The Muse's enigmatic society was a chilling reminder that our pursuit of justice had brought us into the heart of darkness.

The masked figure's voice held an air of authority. "You have delved too deep into the shadows, seekers of truth. The Muse's secrets are not to be revealed."

With a sense of determination, we attempted to move past the masked figure and continue our search for Jonathan Blackwood, but our path was blocked. The masked Quill member stepped forward, and as the torchlight revealed the glint of a concealed weapon, a tense standoff ensued.

Evelyn Gray's voice, unwavering, broke the silence. "We seek justice for Maxwell Thornfield's murder. We will not be deterred."

The masked figure's response was a chilling warning. "The Muse's secrets are our duty to protect, and we will stop at nothing to preserve the status quo."

As we stood at the precipice of confrontation, the weight of our quest bore down on us. The revelations we had uncovered, the enigmatic legacy of The Muse, and the desire for justice had brought us to this critical juncture, a moment of reckoning that would determine the fate of literature's darkest secrets.

But before a resolution could be reached, the chamber's torches suddenly extinguished, plunging us into an abyss of absolute darkness. Panic surged through us as the masked Quill member seized the opportunity to retreat into the shadows, leaving us isolated and vulnerable.

Nigel Finch's voice, tinged with frustration, broke the silence. "We need to find another source of light and continue our search for Jonathan Blackwood."

Evelyn Gray, her determination unwavering, added, "The Muse's secrets will not remain hidden. We have come too far to turn back now."

With a collective sense of urgency, we groped through the darkness, searching for another source of light that would guide us through the underground labyrinth. The Muse's whispers continued to echo in our ears, a constant reminder that we were not alone in the shadows.

As we stumbled forward, our fingers brushed against a hidden switch on the stone wall, and a concealed door creaked open, revealing a narrow passageway. The faint glow of distant torchlight beckoned to us, and we followed the corridor into a new chamber, shrouded in shadows.

The chamber revealed a collection of rare artifacts, relics of literature's storied past. The flickering torchlight illuminated ancient typewriters, inkwells, and quills, their presence a testament to the enduring power of words and storytelling.

Nigel Finch, his voice filled with reverence, spoke up. "This chamber is a sanctuary of literary history, a testament to the enduring power of words. Perhaps it holds the key to uncovering The Muse's secrets."

We began to search through the artifacts, looking for clues that would lead us to Jonathan Blackwood and the motive behind Maxwell Thornfield's murder. The answers, we believed, were concealed within these relics, within the echoes of literary history.

Evelyn Gray, her voice tinged with anticipation, remarked, "We need to piece together the puzzle, to find the link between The Muse and the artifacts that have shaped literature."

As we continued to examine the relics, The Muse's whispers returned, a chilling presence in the darkness. "You may have found the chamber of literary history, but the legacy of The Muse transcends time and artifacts. The truth may remain elusive."

The enigmatic figure's taunts were a stark reminder that our pursuit of justice and revelation was not without its challenges. The Muse's secrets, the identity that had remained concealed, and the motives behind Maxwell Thornfield's murder were veiled in metaphor and allegory.

Nigel Finch, undeterred, continued to search through the artifacts, uncovering a hidden compartment within an antique typewriter. Inside, he found a letter, a correspondence that hinted at the link between Jonathan Blackwood and The Muse's clandestine society.

"This letter," Nigel exclaimed, "reveals that Jonathan Blackwood had knowledge of The Muse's society, and he had been a willing participant in their activities."

The revelation was staggering, and it linked Jonathan Blackwood to The Muse's clandestine society. The motives behind Maxwell Thornfield's murder were becoming clearer, and our pursuit of justice had brought us closer to the truth.

Evelyn Gray's voice, filled with determination, cut through the darkness. "We have the evidence we need to expose Jonathan Blackwood and bring an end to The Muse's manipulation of the literary world."

But as we prepared to leave the chamber of literary history, a sudden tremor shook the ground, causing us to stumble. The walls of the chamber began to crumble, and the torches flickered dangerously.

Nigel Finch's voice, filled with alarm, cried out, "The chamber is collapsing! We need to find a way out!"

With the ground shaking beneath us and the chamber of literary history crumbling, we raced to find an exit, a sense of urgency pushing us forward. The echoes of The Muse's whispers still lingered in the air, a constant reminder that our quest for justice was fraught with danger and uncertainty.

As we reached the corridor that led us back to the underground repository, the walls of the chamber continued to crumble, sending debris and dust into the air. The torches sputtered, casting eerie shadows on the crumbling stone walls.

Evelyn Gray's voice, filled with determination, shouted, "We can't let the chamber collapse with the evidence we've found. We need to find a way out, now!"

But as we pressed forward, the corridor leading back to the underground repository suddenly collapsed, blocking our path. Panic surged through us as we realized that the way back was sealed, leaving us trapped in the chamber of literary history as it crumbled around us.

The Muse's voice, a haunting whisper, echoed through the chamber. "You may have uncovered the past, but the future remains uncertain. The Muse's secrets will not be so easily exposed."

The weight of our predicament hung in the air. Trapped in the crumbling chamber of literary history, with the evidence that could expose Jonathan Blackwood and The Muse's secrets, our journey had taken a perilous turn. The darkness of the literary world threatened to consume us, and the revelations we sought were on the cusp of being lost forever.

## Chapter 10: A New Chapter

As the chamber of literary history crumbled around us, the echoes of The Muse's taunts still reverberating in our ears, panic surged through our hearts. The weight of the falling debris and the sense of impending doom pressed upon us. The revelations we had uncovered, the link between Jonathan Blackwood and The Muse's society, and the evidence that could expose the enigmatic figure's secrets were now at risk of being buried forever.

With the torchlight flickering and the ground shaking beneath our feet, there seemed to be no way out. But in that moment of dire uncertainty, an unexpected turn of events unfolded, offering a glimmer of hope.

Evelyn Gray's voice, filled with determination, broke through the chaos. "We can't let the evidence be lost. We must find a way out of here."

Nigel Finch, his gaze scanning the crumbling chamber, added, "There must be another exit, a path that will lead us to safety."

With a shared sense of urgency, we scoured the chamber for any sign of an alternate route. The torches cast wavering light over the crumbling walls and the artifacts of literary history. It was then that I noticed a hidden lever, partially concealed behind a toppled bookshelf.

With a surge of hope, I called out, "I think I've found something!"

I pulled the lever, and with a grinding sound, a concealed door creaked open. A narrow passageway was revealed, leading to an unknown destination. Without hesitation, we rushed toward the passage, leaving the crumbling chamber behind.

The tremors grew more violent, but we pressed forward, guided by the feeble torchlight and the hope of escape. The echoes of The Muse's whispers gradually faded, and the sense of danger gave way to the anticipation of what lay ahead.

As we emerged from the passageway, we found ourselves in a hidden courtyard bathed in moonlight. The sound of the city beyond the library's walls filled the air, a stark contrast to the darkness and danger we had just escaped.

Evelyn Gray's voice, filled with relief, echoed our sentiments. "We made it out. The evidence is safe, and The Muse's secrets will not remain concealed."

Nigel Finch, catching his breath, added, "We need to expose Jonathan Blackwood and bring an end to The Muse's manipulation of the literary world."

Our journey for justice and revelation had taken us to the brink of danger, but we had emerged from the shadows with the evidence we needed to expose the clandestine society and its enigmatic figure. The weight of Maxwell Thornfield's murder, the manipulation of literature, and the legacy of The Muse would no longer haunt us.

In the days that followed, we gathered the evidence we had uncovered, including the cryptic manuscript and the letter linking Jonathan Blackwood to The Muse's society. The revelations we had sought were now in our hands, and the literary world was poised for transformation.

Our pursuit of justice led to a thorough investigation by the authorities, exposing Jonathan Blackwood's connection to The Muse's clandestine society. The influence that had bound authors and the world of publishing was dismantled, and the legacy of The Muse began to unravel.

Jonathan Blackwood, faced with the weight of his actions, chose to cooperate with the authorities. He revealed the extent of The Muse's influence, the motives behind Maxwell Thornfield's murder, and the secrets that had remained concealed for centuries.

As the truth came to light, the literary world was reshaped. Authors found newfound freedom in their creative endeavors, unburdened by the shadow of manipulation. The power that had been wielded by The Muse's society was dispersed, and a new era of transparency and collaboration began.

Evelyn Gray, Nigel Finch, and I found solace in knowing that Maxwell Thornfield's memory had been honored, his legacy one of justice and change. The weight of literary manipulation was lifted, and the pursuit of storytelling could now thrive without the dark shadows that had lingered for so long.

In the midst of the transformation, a bond had formed between us, a shared experience that had shaped our lives. The mysteries we had unraveled, the revelations we had uncovered, and the pursuit of justice had forged a connection that ran deep.

As the days turned into weeks, and the weeks into months, a sense of closure settled over us. The literary world had been reborn, and the echoes of The Muse's enigmatic legacy had faded into obscurity.

And so, our journey came to an end, a chapter in our lives that had been filled with tension, suspense, and revelations. The weight of Maxwell Thornfield's murder had been lifted, and the world of literature had found a new beginning.

In the end, the power of storytelling had triumphed, and the pursuit of truth had brought light to the darkest corners of the literary world. As we gazed at the moonlight that bathed the courtyard where our journey had reached its conclusion, we knew that a new chapter awaited us, one filled with the promise of a brighter, more just literary world.

THE END

# Relics of the Eclipse

## Chapter 1: The Disappearing Act

The Mojave Desert, a vast expanse of sand and rock, stretched out beneath the relentless sun. Heatwaves danced across the horizon like spectral mirages, distorting the line between reality and illusion. In this arid wasteland, where the landscape seemed frozen in time, I found myself at the heart of a mystery that would challenge my very understanding of reality.

I am Victor Kane, a private investigator with a penchant for the unexplained. Desert Mirage, as they called it, was a town tucked away in the Mojave, a place where the silence was so profound that it almost felt like a living entity. I'd come here to solve a disappearance that had been gnawing at me for weeks. A cryptic letter had arrived at my office, one filled with desperation and intrigue, signed with a name I'd never heard before: Lorraine Holloway.

As I stood in front of her last known address, a dilapidated trailer at the edge of town, the rusty door creaked open, revealing a gaunt figure with hollow eyes that mirrored the despair in the letter. Lorraine was middle-aged, her once-vibrant hair now faded and matted, and her hands trembling as she clutched the letter in her skeletal grip.

"Mr. Kane," she whispered, "I need your help. My daughter, Sarah, she's gone, and I fear she's become entangled in something...sinister."

"Please, come in," I replied, guiding her into the dimly lit trailer. The air inside was heavy with the scent of incense, an incongruous presence in this barren landscape. Lorraine's walls were covered in faded tapestries depicting ancient symbols and arcane rituals, a stark contrast to the stark surroundings.

She recounted the tale, her voice shaking with fear and determination. Sarah, her only child, had been researching a cult, the "Eclipse Seekers," who were rumored to possess ancient relics with supernatural powers. Her obsession with the cult led her to this desolate town, and she'd vanished without a trace.

I nodded, my curiosity piqued. The Eclipse Seekers were known for their enigmatic beliefs and their isolationist tendencies. They had a reputation for guarding their secrets fiercely, and their presence in the Mojave had stirred up rumors of a hidden power struggle between modern science and ancient mysticism.

As Lorraine spoke, my thoughts were interrupted by a sudden commotion outside. The trailer trembled as if an earthquake were ripping through the desert. I rushed to the window and was met with a sight that defied explanation. The very ground was quaking, and in the distance, a massive sandstorm was brewing.

"What's happening?" I asked, my voice filled with alarm.

Lorraine's face turned pale, and she muttered, "The Eclipse Seekers...they're summoning the storm. They believe it's a sign, a harbinger of great change."

I watched in awe and terror as the sandstorm swept closer, swallowing everything in its path. The cult's influence over the elements was a force to be reckoned with, and I could feel the tension and suspense build as I contemplated the challenges that lay ahead.

I knew this was only the beginning of a complex mystery that would test my wits, my morality, and my understanding of the world. The enigmatic Eclipse Seekers, the disappearance of Sarah, and the supernatural forces at play in the Mojave Desert had all woven a web of intrigue that I couldn't escape. It was a battle between the known and the unknown, the mundane and the mystical.

With a determined look in my eyes, I turned to Lorraine and said, "I'll find your daughter, no matter the cost."

But as I stepped out into the brewing sandstorm, a chilling thought gripped me. In this town of secrets and hidden beliefs, where ancient relics held the power to shape reality, was I prepared to confront the darkest corners of my own beliefs and morality?

## Chapter 2: Whispers in the Desert

The sandstorm swallowed me whole, a relentless force of nature that blurred the line between the real and the surreal. I wrapped my coat tightly around me, shielding my face from the stinging grains of sand that whipped through the air. The howling wind seemed to carry with it the whispers of secrets long buried beneath the desert's surface.

As I stumbled forward, disoriented and nearly blinded by the tempest, I knew I had ventured into something far more complex and mysterious than any case before. The Eclipse Seekers, with their supposed control over the elements, were more than just a fringe cult—they held ancient knowledge and artifacts that defied conventional wisdom.

It felt like hours, but it was probably only minutes before I glimpsed a flicker of light amidst the sand. It was a dim, eerie glow that drew me closer, guiding me through the heart of the storm. As I approached, I realized it was an ancient, ornate lantern perched on a makeshift stone altar. Its soft, ethereal light cast eerie shadows, revealing symbols etched into the surrounding rocks. The lantern seemed to be both a beacon and a warning.

I cautiously reached out and touched the lantern, and the wind subsided as if granting me passage. The sandstorm relented, retreating into the distance, and the desert was revealed once more. I knew I had to find Sarah and uncover the truth behind the Eclipse Seekers' power, but the question that plagued my mind was whether I could trust Lorraine's desperate plea or if her involvement in this dark world was deeper than she let on.

The trail led me to the heart of Desert Mirage, a town unlike any I'd ever encountered. Its streets were lined with faded neon signs advertising fortune tellers, palm readers, and occult shops. Murmurs of a hidden realm of mysticism and supernatural phenomena reverberated through the alleys, accompanied by the unsettling sound of distant chants.

I approached an enigmatic shop with a sign that read "Oracle's Whispers," its windows veiled with curtains of deep purple and amethyst. A brass bell jingled softly as I entered, revealing a small space adorned with countless crystals, tarot decks, and ancient scrolls. The shopkeeper, a woman in her fifties with a penetrating gaze, regarded me with a mix of curiosity and caution.

"Welcome, traveler," she said, her voice a soft, melodic whisper. "What brings you to Desert Mirage?"

I knew I had to tread carefully, revealing as little as possible. "I'm searching for someone—a girl named Sarah. I've heard she may have come to this town."

The shopkeeper's eyes seemed to penetrate my very soul. She nodded slowly and said, "The Eclipse Seekers, they are a force to be reckoned with, harnessing power that lies beyond our comprehension. To find Sarah, you'll need guidance. Let the cards reveal the path you must follow."

With a sense of unease, I agreed, and she laid out a tarot deck, the cards pulsating with an otherworldly energy. As she dealt the cards, the images seemed to come alive, telling a story of deception, power, and a perilous journey ahead.

The cards revealed a cloaked figure, the High Priestess, who concealed hidden knowledge. The Wheel of Fortune, indicating fate and destiny, and the Tower, a symbol of sudden upheaval, stood side by side. The Chariot depicted a journey filled with determination, and the Two of Cups suggested a connection to someone unexpected.

The shopkeeper's eyes never left mine as she interpreted the cards. "You're on a path filled with danger, Mr. Kane. The Eclipse Seekers guard secrets that must not fall into the wrong hands. Sarah holds a key to their power, and the line between science and the supernatural is blurring in their presence. Be cautious, and trust no one completely."

As I left the shop, the weight of the revelation hung heavily on my shoulders. Sarah's connection to the cult ran deep, and my journey into the unknown was far from over. I had more questions than answers and no idea where the trail would lead me next.

The sun dipped below the horizon, casting long shadows across the mysterious streets of Desert Mirage. My footsteps echoed through the darkness as I ventured deeper into the heart of the town, determined to unravel the enigma of the Eclipse Seekers, find Sarah, and confront the moral and ethical dilemmas that lay ahead.

But then, in the distance, I heard the haunting melody of a song—a song that seemed to transcend time and space, pulling me toward it. It was a tune that resonated with power, danger, and the promise of revelation.

As I followed the melody through the labyrinthine streets, I knew that the town held more secrets than I could have ever imagined, and the tension and suspense were building to a crescendo that threatened to shatter my reality. The Eclipse Seekers were no mere cult; they were the guardians of a hidden world, and I was now a part of it, whether by choice or fate.

## Chapter 3: Song of the Eclipse

The haunting melody led me through the labyrinthine streets of Desert Mirage, each note hanging in the air like a ghostly presence. It was a song of ages, one that seemed to echo from the depths of time, and it drew me closer to its source. The night had wrapped the town in an eerie, otherworldly aura, and the sense of foreboding only deepened as I ventured further.

I came upon a rundown building, its façade cracked and weathered by the unforgiving desert winds. The dilapidated sign above the entrance read "The Crescent Veil," and beneath it, a shadowy figure stood, silhouetted by a dim, flickering light.

As I approached, the figure turned to face me, and I was met with the piercing eyes of a woman, her face painted with intricate patterns of dark ink. Her voice, both alluring and chilling, cut through the night. "You've followed the song," she said, her words laden with an inexplicable power.

I nodded, my curiosity mixed with a growing sense of unease. "Who are you, and what is the meaning of that melody?"

She extended a hand, and the notes of the song lingered in the air. "I am Aria, a guardian of the Eclipse Seekers. Our song is a key to the ancient relics, a power that transcends the boundaries of science and mysticism. You seek Sarah, do you not?"

Aria's words were a revelation, confirming the connection between the Eclipse Seekers, the melody, and Sarah's disappearance. I had no choice but to confide in her, revealing my quest to find the missing girl and unravel the mysteries surrounding the cult.

Her eyes bore into mine, and she spoke in a hushed tone, "You must prove your worth, Victor Kane, if you wish to follow the path of the Eclipse. The relics we guard are powerful, and only those who are truly attuned to their energy can harness their might."

Aria led me into the heart of The Crescent Veil, a place where ancient symbols adorned the walls, and a captivating tapestry of colors, incense, and candlelight enveloped the room. At the center lay an ornate table adorned with curious objects—a crystal ball, a deck of tarot cards, and an intricately carved staff. She gestured toward them.

"Choose a path, Mr. Kane," Aria said, her voice filled with an enigmatic blend of promise and challenge. "Each object will reveal an aspect of your destiny. Your choices will shape your journey and determine your connection to the Eclipse Seekers."

I surveyed the options, knowing that my selection would be more than just a simple choice. It would be a test of my character and a reflection of the mysteries that awaited me. The crystal ball spoke of visions and foresight, the tarot cards of destiny and fate, and the staff of power and influence.

I reached for the tarot cards, feeling a strange pull towards them. As I drew a card, I saw the image of a crowned figure holding a scepter—the Emperor. It was a symbol of authority and leadership, a reminder of the responsibility I bore in this quest.

Aria's eyes gleamed with approval, and she nodded. "You have chosen well. The path of the tarot will guide your way, and the cards will unveil the secrets hidden within this town. But remember, your destiny is your own to shape."

The revelation of the Emperor card set the tone for the journey ahead. It was a responsibility I couldn't shirk, and it signaled a connection between Sarah's fate and the hidden knowledge of the Eclipse Seekers. I knew I had chosen a path that would demand more than mere detective skills—it would require an understanding of the supernatural, a willingness to navigate treacherous waters, and the ability to confront the moral and ethical dilemmas that lay ahead.

Aria's gaze never wavered as she whispered, "The Eclipse Seekers hold their meeting tonight, deep in the heart of the desert. It is there that you will find Sarah and the answers you seek. But be warned, Mr. Kane. The line between science and the supernatural is thinner than you imagine, and the Eclipse has a way of blurring it further."

As the time for the cult's gathering drew near, I felt a rising tide of tension and suspense. The mysteries of Desert Mirage were converging in an intricate web, and I was at the center of it, guided by the tarot's enigmatic hand.

Aria escorted me to the town's outskirts, where the desert awaited, bathed in moonlight. She handed me a small vial containing a peculiar, luminescent substance. "This will lead you to their gathering," she explained. "But be cautious, for the Eclipse Seekers guard their secrets with fervor. The sands of the Mojave hold more than you can fathom."

With a solemn nod, I set off into the desert, my heart pounding with a mixture of anticipation and dread. The song of the Eclipse still echoed in my mind, a reminder of the power that awaited me.

As I followed the path illuminated by the vial's eerie glow, I couldn't shake the feeling that I was hurtling toward a revelation that would challenge the very core of my beliefs, and the resolution and closure I sought might be harder to attain than I had ever imagined. The stakes were high, the unknown loomed in the darkness, and the true nature of the Eclipse Seekers was yet to be uncovered.

## Chapter 4: The Cult of Shadows

The desert stretched endlessly before me, an unforgiving wasteland that whispered secrets with every gust of wind. I followed the ethereal glow of the vial through the shifting dunes, each step taking me deeper into the heart of the Mojave's mysteries.

As the night wore on, the eerie radiance grew brighter, leading me to a hidden encampment. Tents and makeshift altars emerged from the shadows, bathed in the ghostly light. I watched from a concealed vantage point, hidden amidst the rocks, as the Eclipse Seekers gathered around a central fire, their faces obscured by robes and hoods.

The air buzzed with anticipation as their leader, a figure shrouded in a billowing, deep crimson cloak, approached the fire. His voice was a low, commanding whisper that reached my ears as he began to speak.

"Tonight, we stand on the precipice of a new era," he declared, the flames casting eerie shadows on his face. "The relics we protect have shown us the way, and the time of reckoning is near."

The Eclipse Seekers listened with rapt attention, and I strained to hear every word. The leader's speech was a proclamation of power, an ode to the ancient relics and their supposed control over the elements. It was a testament to the blurred line between science and mysticism, and the grip that these beliefs held over the cult.

Sarah was among them, her presence confirmed as she stood among the followers, her gaze fixated on the leader. It was clear that the Eclipse Seekers had ensnared her, and her involvement ran deeper than I'd imagined.

As the leader's speech continued, the tension and suspense in the air grew palpable. It was a moment of reckoning, a culmination of forces beyond my comprehension. The moral and ethical dilemmas that lay ahead seemed insurmountable.

My heart pounded as I contemplated my next move. The relics held within the encampment were a source of power that could tip the balance between the known and the supernatural. But to intervene in the Eclipse Seekers' rituals would be perilous, and the consequences were uncertain.

The choice weighed heavily on me, but my determination to find Sarah and unravel the mysteries that had entwined her fate gave me the resolve to proceed. With each step toward the encampment, I knew I was descending further into the abyss of the unknown.

The shadows deepened as I neared the central fire, the Eclipse Seekers oblivious to my presence. I had to act quickly and discreetly, my every movement calculated to avoid detection. My hand reached for the vial Aria had given me, its eerie light still guiding my way.

As I approached, I saw that the relics lay on a stone altar near the fire—an ancient chalice, a jeweled amulet, and a weathered tome. These artifacts were the keys to the Eclipse Seekers' power, the embodiment of their belief in the supernatural.

I carefully replaced the amulet with a replica I'd brought, one that I hoped would go unnoticed. But the real challenge lay in securing the chalice and the tome, both of which were deeply entwined in the cult's rituals. It would require a delicate touch and unwavering focus.

My heart pounded as I reached for the chalice, the vial's glow reflecting off its ancient surface. Just as my fingers grazed its edge, a sudden hush fell over the gathering. The leader had finished his speech, and all eyes turned toward the altar.

A gasp of realization echoed through the crowd as the leader spoke, "The relics! They have been tampered with."

Panic rippled through the Eclipse Seekers, and their attention shifted to the stolen amulet. I seized the opportunity, snatching the chalice and the tome, my heart racing as I retreated into the desert night.

The vial's glow guided my escape, but I could hear the cult's fervent pursuit, their footsteps and desperate chants following close behind. The sand beneath my feet shifted and gave way, my every step a perilous dance with the unforgiving terrain.

The Eclipse Seekers' power was real, their belief in the supernatural a force to be reckoned with. The line between science and mysticism had never been more blurred, and I was now in possession of the keys to their dominion.

With the stolen relics clutched tightly in my hands, I knew that the cult's vengeance and the resolution and closure I sought were both elusive and treacherous. The moral and ethical dilemmas I would face in the desert's unforgiving embrace were only beginning to reveal their complexity.

As I pressed forward, the vial's glow waned, and the path ahead grew shrouded in darkness. I was caught in the vortex of the Eclipse Seekers' power, and the consequences of my actions remained uncertain. The next chapter of my journey was a descent into shadows deeper than any I had ever encountered.

## Chapter 5: The Relics Unveiled

The desert night had swallowed me, the vial's eerie glow fading to mere pinpricks of light in the inky darkness. I clutched the stolen relics—the chalice and the ancient tome—close to my chest as I navigated the treacherous terrain. The echoes of the Eclipse Seekers' chants still hung in the air behind me, a haunting reminder of the power that had compelled them.

As I ventured further into the Mojave, I couldn't escape the feeling that I had ventured into an abyss where the line between science and mysticism had been obliterated. The stolen relics in my possession held the key to the Eclipse Seekers' enigmatic power, but understanding their true nature remained an elusive challenge.

I needed answers, and the only path forward lay in deciphering the ancient tome. Its pages were covered in intricate symbols, a cryptic language that defied easy interpretation. I huddled beneath the cold, starlit sky, the soft glow of the vial providing just enough light to begin my investigation.

The first page revealed an illustration of the chalice, surrounded by celestial symbols and cryptic runes. It was a key to their power, but its true significance remained hidden. The second page hinted at a ritual, one that involved the chalice, the amulet, and a song—an incantation of tremendous power.

My heart quickened as I realized that I had uncovered the Eclipse Seekers' most guarded secrets. They believed that by combining the relics and singing the ancient song, they could wield a force capable of reshaping reality itself. The blurred line between the known and the supernatural had become starkly evident, and the consequences of their beliefs were far-reaching.

The moral and ethical dilemmas I now faced were daunting. What was the nature of this power, and how did the relics fit into the equation? Could they truly control the elements, or was it all a mere illusion born of fervent belief?

The weight of the unknown pressed upon me as I studied the tome's pages, deciphering symbols and transcribing incantations. With each revelation, I moved closer to understanding the Eclipse Seekers' purpose and the fate of Sarah. But the answers remained fragmented, like pieces of a jigsaw puzzle waiting to be assembled.

As the night wore on, I realized that I needed expert assistance. A name from my past came to mind—a brilliant archaeologist who specialized in ancient languages and relics. Dr. Evelyn Simmons was a woman with an insatiable thirst for knowledge, and she might hold the key to unraveling the cult's mysteries.

With the stolen relics and the tome in tow, I set out on a journey to find Dr. Simmons. She resided in the heart of the academic world, a world where the blurred line between science and mysticism was constantly debated and explored. I hoped that she would shed light on the true nature of the Eclipse Seekers' power.

Upon my arrival at Dr. Simmons' office, the relics and the ancient tome in hand, I was met with a warm but inquisitive smile. Her office was a sanctuary of knowledge, filled with dusty tomes, maps, and artifacts from distant lands.

"Victor Kane," she said, "what brings you to my doorstep with such extraordinary treasures?"

I wasted no time in recounting my encounters in Desert Mirage—the cryptic letter from Lorraine Holloway, the enigmatic Aria and the Eclipse Seekers, and the stolen relics that held the key to a power that defied explanation. Dr. Simmons listened attentively, her eyes widening with each revelation.

"These relics," she said, her voice filled with a mix of fascination and concern, "they bear the mark of ancient civilizations, each with a unique power of its own. The chalice, the amulet, and the tome were believed to be lost to history. Their reappearance in the hands of the Eclipse Seekers is a conundrum that defies all reason."

She examined the stolen amulet and the tome, her fingers tracing the symbols etched into the ancient silver. "The power of these artifacts is no mere illusion, Victor. They hold the key to a force that transcends the known laws of science. But using them comes at a great cost."

As she continued to unravel the secrets of the relics, the blurred line between science and mysticism became more intricate than ever. The moral and ethical dilemmas surrounding their use were impossible to ignore, and I knew that the Eclipse Seekers' rituals and beliefs had consequences far beyond the cult itself.

Dr. Simmons leaned closer, her voice hushed. "The Eclipse Seekers are not the only ones who seek these relics. There are factions within the academic and scientific world who would stop at nothing to harness their power. The battle between modern science and the supernatural has never been more real, and the consequences of their discovery could change the course of history."

My resolve was further tested as I grappled with the implications of her words. The stolen relics and the knowledge I now held were a double-edged sword, capable of immense power and destruction. The line between the known and the unknown had become a tightrope, and I was now a pivotal player in a game where the stakes were higher than ever before.

As I left Dr. Simmons' office, the weight of the relics in my possession served as a reminder of the challenges that lay ahead. The blurred line between science and mysticism was a complex, multifaceted tapestry, and I was caught in its intricate threads, where the moral and ethical dilemmas were no longer black and white.

The true nature of the relics, the power they held, and the consequences of their use remained elusive. The next chapter of my journey would test my determination and resilience as I ventured further into the heart of the Eclipse Seekers' beliefs and the dangerous world that surrounded them.

## Chapter 6: Dance of Shadows

The drive back to Desert Mirage was fraught with unease. Dr. Simmons' revelations had set the stage for an even more complex and perilous journey. The weight of the relics in my possession seemed to increase with every passing mile, as if their power pulsed beneath their ancient surface.

The town emerged from the desert like a mirage, its eerie stillness a stark contrast to the turmoil that lay beneath its surface. I had no doubt that the Eclipse Seekers were aware of the theft, and their pursuit would be relentless.

Lorraine Holloway's trailer, my point of contact and the place where this enigmatic journey had begun, remained a sanctuary of secrets. I had to reach out to her for more information about Sarah, the Eclipse Seekers, and the blurred line between science and mysticism. But I couldn't shake the feeling that Lorraine's involvement ran deeper than a mother's desperation to find her daughter.

As I approached the trailer, the wind howled through the desert, carrying with it the distant echoes of the Eclipse Seekers' song. It was an eerie, haunting melody that seemed to bind the town in an enchantment of secrets and shadows.

Lorraine answered the door with a haunted look in her eyes, as if she had been expecting me. Her frail form seemed even more delicate under the dim light, her hands trembling as they reached for the letter I had taken from the stolen amulet. I had a feeling that this letter held the key to understanding the true nature of the cult and Sarah's involvement.

As I handed her the letter, Lorraine's eyes filled with tears. "I wrote that letter to Sarah, Mr. Kane," she whispered. "It was my desperate plea for her to return, to break free from the Eclipse Seekers' grasp. But she never received it."

The revelation sent shivers down my spine. It meant that Sarah's initial contact with the Eclipse Seekers had been independent of her mother's influence. She had willingly entered their world, seeking answers that remained hidden in the blurred line between science and mysticism.

Lorraine continued, her voice filled with a mix of sorrow and resolve. "The Eclipse Seekers, they hold knowledge beyond our comprehension. They believe that their rituals can unlock the power of the relics and reshape reality itself. But they are a force that can no longer be contained, and the line between science and the supernatural has been blurred to a dangerous degree."

The moral and ethical dilemmas surrounding the Eclipse Seekers and the relics had far-reaching consequences, and I had become a player in a dangerous game where the blurred line between knowledge and power was more precarious than ever.

Lorraine handed me a faded photograph of Sarah, a poignant reminder of the girl whose life had become entangled in the mysteries of Desert Mirage. "Please find my daughter, Mr. Kane. She's lost in a world of shadows and secrets. The line between the known and the unknown has become a maze that she may never escape."

With a promise to Lorraine to bring her daughter back, I left her trailer and headed deeper into the heart of Desert Mirage. The Eclipse Seekers' gathering had revealed a complex and mysterious world, one that demanded my complete understanding.

My next destination was Aria and the Crescent Veil, the source of the haunting melody that had led me to the cult. As I approached the shop, I couldn't help but wonder about Aria's true allegiance. She had guided me to the relics and the Eclipse Seekers' secrets, but her motives remained enigmatic.

The shop was shrouded in a veil of purple and amethyst, and the same brass bell jingled softly as I entered. Aria, with her cryptic eyes and intricate inked patterns on her face, was waiting, as if she had known I would return.

"Mr. Kane," she said, her voice a soft, melodic whisper. "You've seen the Eclipse Seekers' power and the relics' potential. Their rituals are a dance with the unknown, and you hold the key to deciphering their true nature."

The moral and ethical dilemmas surrounding the relics had taken on a new dimension, one that placed me at the center of a world where the line between science and mysticism had been obliterated. Aria's words hinted at the power of the relics and the consequences of their use.

As I questioned her about Sarah's fate, Aria revealed that she had been the one who sent the cryptic letter, an attempt to lure me into the world of the Eclipse Seekers. Her motives remained unclear, but she spoke of the importance of Sarah's role in their rituals, a role that held the key to the blurred line between science and mysticism.

The shadows deepened around us as Aria admitted that the power of the relics was real, a force that transcended the laws of science. The Eclipse Seekers' beliefs were no mere illusion, and their rituals were a testament to the blurred line between the known and the unknown.

Aria's eyes bore into mine as she whispered, "You hold the relics, Mr. Kane. You possess the power to shape the destiny of Desert Mirage and its secrets."

With her revelation, the weight of the relics in my possession became even more significant. The line between the known and the supernatural had never been more blurred, and the moral and ethical dilemmas I faced were a reflection of the power and responsibility that had fallen upon me.

As I left the Crescent Veil, I knew that the next chapter of my journey was a dance with shadows deeper and more mysterious than ever before. The Eclipse Seekers held the key to a power that transcended the boundaries of science, and the consequences of their beliefs were far from being resolved.

The night in Desert Mirage was an intricate tapestry of secrets and shadows, and the blurred line between science and mysticism had never been more enigmatic. The moral and ethical dilemmas I confronted were no longer a matter of choice but a reflection of the forces at play in this enigmatic town, where the unknown and the supernatural danced in a perilous balance.

# Chapter 7: Veil of Deception

The desert night had taken on an eerie quality as I ventured deeper into the enigmatic world of Desert Mirage. The relics I carried in my possession—the chalice and the ancient tome—seemed to pulse with a life of their own. Their power, as revealed by Aria and Dr. Simmons, was both fascinating and perilous.

As I navigated the labyrinthine streets of the town, I couldn't help but ponder the blurred line between science and mysticism that had consumed my journey. The Eclipse Seekers' rituals and beliefs had cast a shadow over Desert Mirage, blurring the boundaries between the known and the unknown. The moral and ethical dilemmas that surrounded their power were a heavy burden to bear.

The Crescent Veil had revealed Aria's ambiguous allegiance, her role in luring me into the world of the Eclipse Seekers, and the potential of the relics I held. It was a place of secrets, shadows, and mysteries that were deeper than I could have imagined.

I knew I needed to return to the Eclipse Seekers' encampment, to find Sarah and to understand her role in the cult's rituals. But the blurred line between the known and the supernatural had become more complex than ever, and the consequences of my actions remained uncertain.

As I approached the encampment, the echoes of the Eclipse Seekers' song seemed to grow louder, an ethereal melody that enveloped the desert. The cult had gathered once more, their presence a testament to the power they believed in.

I hid amidst the rocks, watching the gathering unfold. The leader, shrouded in crimson, stood before the fire, his voice carrying an aura of authority and mysticism. The cult members, robed and hooded, listened with fervent devotion.

Sarah was among them, her face painted with intricate symbols, her gaze fixated on the leader. She was a puzzle within a puzzle, a part of the enigma I needed to unravel.

The leader's words, as before, were a proclamation of power, a declaration of the Eclipse Seekers' beliefs. The chalice, the amulet, and the tome were the key to their rituals, a force that transcended the boundaries of science and mysticism. The blurred line between the known and the unknown had never been more evident.

The moral and ethical dilemmas that confronted me grew heavier with every revelation. What was the true nature of this power, and how could it be harnessed? Could the Eclipse Seekers control the elements, or was their power merely a manifestation of their collective belief?

I couldn't remain hidden any longer. I had to confront the cult, to find Sarah, and to understand the full scope of their rituals and beliefs. The relics in my possession were the catalyst for this enigmatic journey, and I had to use them to unlock the mysteries that lay before me.

With the stolen chalice and the ancient tome, I approached the encampment. The vial's eerie glow illuminated my path, drawing the attention of the cult members. The leader, his crimson cloak billowing in the desert wind, locked eyes with me. There was a moment of recognition, as if he had been expecting my return.

The Eclipse Seekers reacted with a mixture of curiosity and apprehension. It was a perilous moment, where the line between science and mysticism blurred into uncertainty. The moral and ethical dilemmas that confronted me were at the forefront of my mind.

The leader extended a hand, and I placed the stolen chalice and the ancient tome before him. The relics seemed to resonate with power, their symbols glowing with an otherworldly light.

He spoke, his voice a blend of command and reverence, "You have returned, Mr. Kane, bearing the key to our power. The relics belong to us, a force that transcends the known boundaries of science. But their potential is a double-edged sword, and their use comes at a cost."

The revelation was like a revelation of shadows lifted. The Eclipse Seekers' power was no mere illusion. The blurred line between science and mysticism was a complex web of beliefs and rituals, and the relics were the key to their understanding.

As the leader continued to speak, I couldn't escape the moral and ethical dilemmas that confronted me. The consequences of my actions were unclear, and the power I had uncovered was a force that could change the course of history.

The Eclipse Seekers' gaze never wavered as they welcomed me into their fold, their chants taking on a new depth of meaning. I had become a part of their world, where the line between science and mysticism had been irrevocably blurred. The journey I had embarked upon was no longer a quest for answers but a descent into the heart of shadows and secrets.

The next chapter of my journey held the promise of revelation and reckoning. The consequences of my actions were uncertain, and the moral and ethical dilemmas I faced were a reflection of the blurred line between knowledge and power. The relics I had uncovered held the key to the Eclipse Seekers' beliefs, and their true nature remained elusive.

As the night in Desert Mirage enveloped me, the shadows deepened, and the line between the known and the supernatural seemed to vanish completely. The next chapter would be a dance with the Eclipse Seekers, a dance that held the power to reshape reality and unlock the enigma that had consumed my journey.

## Chapter 8: The Eclipsed Revelation

The Crescent Veil had become my sanctuary in Desert Mirage, a place where secrets and shadows converged. Aria's enigmatic presence had drawn me deeper into the mysteries of the Eclipse Seekers, a world where the blurred line between science and mysticism held me captive.

As I stood amidst the amethyst and purple hues of the shop, Aria's cryptic eyes bore into mine. Her voice, like a soft melody, carried the weight of revelations and decisions that lay ahead.

"Mr. Kane," she whispered, "you have entered the heart of the Eclipse Seekers, a world where science and mysticism are no longer distinct. The relics you possess hold the key to power and consequence. It is a dance with the unknown, and your role in this intricate performance is pivotal."

Aria's words weighed on me, and the moral and ethical dilemmas surrounding the relics and the Eclipse Seekers seemed insurmountable. The consequences of my actions were unclear, and the power that had been revealed held the potential to reshape reality itself.

My thoughts drifted to the stolen chalice and the ancient tome, both of which had revealed the Eclipse Seekers' rituals and beliefs. The blurred line between science and mysticism had never been more enigmatic, and my understanding of this world was still fragmented.

Aria had a role to play in this enigmatic dance, and her motives remained shrouded in mystery. She had lured me into the world of the Eclipse Seekers, but to what end? Her cryptic letter to Sarah and her guidance had set me on a path that had led to power, danger, and revelation.

As I questioned Aria about Sarah's involvement in the cult, she revealed that the Eclipse Seekers considered Sarah to be the key to their beliefs and rituals. The moral and ethical dilemmas that surrounded her fate were inextricably linked to the blurred line between science and mysticism.

The shadows deepened around us, and Aria's eyes held secrets that she had yet to share. "The Eclipse Seekers hold knowledge that transcends the boundaries of science, Mr. Kane," she said. "Their rituals are a dance with the unknown, and the consequences of their beliefs extend beyond what we can fathom."

With her revelation, I knew that I held the power to unlock the enigma that had consumed Desert Mirage. The stolen relics, the chalice, and the tome were the key to understanding the Eclipse Seekers' power, a power that had blurred the line between the known and the supernatural.

As I left the Crescent Veil, I felt the weight of the relics in my possession. The line between science and mysticism had been obliterated, and I had become a pivotal player in this intricate dance of shadows and secrets.

The next chapter of my journey was a descent into the heart of the Eclipse Seekers' world, a world where the consequences of their beliefs and the moral and ethical dilemmas that surrounded them held the power to reshape my understanding of reality.

The desert night enveloped me as I returned to the encampment of the Eclipse Seekers, the echoes of their song drawing me closer. The cult had gathered once more, their rituals and beliefs casting an aura of mysticism over the desert.

The leader, shrouded in crimson, stood before the fire, his voice a blend of authority and reverence. The relics, the chalice and the tome, were laid before him, their symbols glowing with otherworldly light.

Sarah's presence among the cult members was a haunting reminder of the role she played in their beliefs. Her face painted with intricate symbols, she gazed at the leader with a mixture of devotion and apprehension.

The leader's words were a declaration of power, a testament to the Eclipse Seekers' beliefs. The blurred line between science and mysticism was more evident than ever, and their rituals were a dance with the unknown.

The moral and ethical dilemmas that confronted me seemed insurmountable. What was the true nature of their power, and how could it be harnessed? Could the Eclipse Seekers control the elements, or was their power a mere manifestation of their collective belief?

I couldn't remain hidden any longer. I had to confront the cult, to find Sarah, and to understand the full scope of their rituals and beliefs. The relics in my possession were the catalyst for this enigmatic journey, and I had to use them to unlock the mysteries that lay before me.

With the stolen chalice and the ancient tome, I approached the encampment. The vial's eerie glow illuminated my path, drawing the attention of the cult members. The leader, his crimson cloak billowing in the desert wind, locked eyes with me. There was a moment of recognition, as if he had been expecting my return.

The Eclipse Seekers reacted with a mixture of curiosity and apprehension. It was a perilous moment, where the line between science and mysticism blurred into uncertainty. The moral and ethical dilemmas that confronted me were at the forefront of my mind.

The leader extended a hand, and I placed the stolen relics before him. The chalice and the tome resonated with power, their symbols glowing with an otherworldly light.

He spoke, his voice a blend of command and reverence, "You have returned, Mr. Kane, bearing the key to our power. The relics belong to us, a force that transcends the known boundaries of science. But their potential is a double-edged sword, and their use comes at a cost."

The revelation was like a shadow lifted. The Eclipse Seekers' power was no mere illusion. The blurred line between science and mysticism was a complex web of beliefs and rituals, and the relics were the key to their understanding.

As the leader continued to speak, I couldn't escape the moral and ethical dilemmas that confronted me. The consequences of my actions were unclear, and the power I had uncovered was a force that could change the course of history.

The Eclipse Seekers' gaze never wavered as they welcomed me into their fold, their chants taking on a new depth of meaning. I had become a part of their world, where the line between science and mysticism had been irrevocably blurred. The journey I had embarked upon was no longer a quest for answers but a descent into the heart of shadows and secrets.

The next chapter of my journey held the promise of revelation and reckoning. The consequences of my actions were uncertain, and the moral and ethical dilemmas I faced were a reflection of the blurred line between knowledge and power. The relics I had uncovered held the key to the Eclipse Seekers' beliefs, and their true nature remained elusive.

As the night in Desert Mirage enveloped me, the shadows deepened, and the line between the known and the supernatural seemed to vanish completely.

# Chapter 9: Whispers of the Relics

The desert night embraced me as I stood amidst the Eclipse Seekers, the stolen relics—the chalice and the ancient tome—laid before their leader. The eerie glow of the vial illuminated the encampment, casting strange shadows that danced to the rhythm of the cult's fervent chants.

The leader extended a hand, his crimson cloak flowing like a river of blood. "You have returned, Mr. Kane, with the relics that hold the key to our power. Their potential transcends the known boundaries of science, and their use is both a blessing and a curse."

As the leader's words hung in the air, the moral and ethical dilemmas I faced weighed heavily upon me. The consequences of my actions were unclear, and the relics, with their otherworldly symbols, were the linchpin of the Eclipse Seekers' beliefs. The line between science and mysticism had vanished, leaving me with a profound sense of trepidation.

Sarah's presence among the cult members, her face painted with intricate symbols, was a haunting reminder of her role in their enigmatic rituals. Her eyes were both lost and resolute, caught in a world where the blurred line between knowledge and power had become a treacherous path.

The leader's gaze never left me, and it was clear that he expected something from me. I felt like a pawn in a game I could not fully comprehend, a game where the Eclipse Seekers held the cards and the rules remained elusive.

"What is it that you seek, Mr. Kane?" the leader inquired, his voice a hypnotic melody. "The relics are in your possession, and their power is yours to unlock. But the path you tread is fraught with shadows and secrets."

I couldn't deny the allure of the relics, the potential they held to reshape reality itself. But the consequences of their use, the blurred line between science and mysticism, and the moral and ethical dilemmas that surrounded them were a heavy burden to bear.

I hesitated, caught between the enigma of the Eclipse Seekers and the promise of power. The relics held answers I sought, not just about the cult but about the blurred line between the known and the unknown that had become my obsession.

The leader's eyes bore into mine, his silent command growing stronger. "The relics," he said, "hold the secrets of the ancients. It is through them that we seek to shape reality. The chalice, the amulet, and the tome are the keys to our destiny. Will you help us unlock their potential?"

The question hung in the air like a ghostly specter, a choice that would define the next chapter of my journey. To aid the Eclipse Seekers was to delve deeper into a world where the line between science and mysticism was obliterated. To refuse was to confront the consequences of their power and the moral and ethical dilemmas that confronted me.

As I hesitated, Sarah's eyes locked onto mine, a plea for understanding and salvation. Her role in the cult's beliefs was a mystery I needed to solve, and the relics were the key to her fate.

The weight of the blurred line between the known and the unknown seemed insurmountable.

In a moment of resolve, I made a choice that would shape the path ahead. "I will help you unlock the potential of the relics," I said. "But in return, I demand answers about the Eclipse Seekers, their beliefs, and the true nature of the power we hold."

The leader's face contorted in a twisted smile, a mixture of satisfaction and anticipation. "You have chosen wisely, Mr. Kane. The relics hold the secrets of the ancients, a power that transcends the boundaries of science. But their use comes at a cost, and their potential is both a blessing and a curse."

With that, the cult began to gather around the stolen relics—the chalice and the ancient tome. Their chants intensified, their voices rising in a hypnotic crescendo. The blurred line between science and mysticism became even more tenuous as I watched the cult members embrace their rituals with unwavering devotion.

The vial's eerie glow grew brighter, its light intermingling with the cult's fervent incantations. I could feel a surge of power, a force that seemed to emanate from the relics themselves.

As the rituals unfolded, the desert night became a surreal dreamscape, where the line between the known and the supernatural dissolved completely. The power that I had unlocked was beyond comprehension, and the moral and ethical dilemmas surrounding its use seemed insurmountable.

Aria's cryptic presence and Dr. Simmons' warning echoed in my mind, as did the desperation in Lorraine Holloway's eyes when she had begged me to find her daughter. The next chapter of my journey held the promise of revelation and reckoning, but the consequences were still unknown.

The cult's chants grew louder, and the stolen relics pulsed with a life of their own. The blurred line between science and mysticism had become a chasm, a void where reality itself seemed to warp and shift.

The leader's voice, a whisper that seemed to come from the depths of the unknown, intoned the ancient incantation. The vial's eerie glow intensified, casting strange shadows that danced with a life of their own.

And then, as if a dam had burst, a surge of power cascaded through the encampment. The desert night seemed to quiver, and the world around me blurred and shifted. The very elements themselves—earth, air, fire, and water—bowed to the power of the relics.

I watched in awe as the chalice's contents transformed into a shimmering liquid, the amulet's jewels emitting a radiant light, and the ancient tome's pages revealing cryptic symbols that seemed to rewrite reality itself. The cult's chants reached a deafening crescendo, their voices now one with the elements.

The blurred line between science and mysticism had become a cataclysmic event, a dance with the unknown that threatened to unravel the very fabric of existence. The moral and ethical dilemmas that had consumed me were now a raging tempest, and the consequences of my choice were a storm that had just begun.

As the power of the relics continued to surge, the leader's eyes met mine. "This is the true nature of our beliefs, Mr. Kane. The relics hold the power to shape reality itself. But with great power comes great responsibility, and the consequences of our actions are a force that cannot be controlled."

The desert night had transformed into a surreal dreamscape, and I was caught in a maelstrom of power and consequence.

## Chapter 10: Echoes of Consequence

The surreal dreamscape of power and consequence continued to swirl around me as the Eclipse Seekers' rituals reached their zenith. The relics—the stolen chalice, the ancient tome, and the amulet—had unleashed a force that transcended the boundaries of science and mysticism. The blurred line between the known and the supernatural had become a chasm, a void that threatened to unravel reality itself.

The cult members chanted with unwavering devotion, their voices merging with the elements as they paid homage to the power of the relics. The desert night seemed to quiver and warp, and I found myself at the epicenter of an enigmatic dance with the unknown.

As I watched the chalice's contents transform into a shimmering liquid, the amulet's jewels emitting a radiant light, and the ancient tome's pages revealing cryptic symbols that rewrote reality itself, I felt a surge of awe and trepidation. The moral and ethical dilemmas that had consumed me were now a tempest, and the consequences of my choice loomed like a gathering storm.

The leader's voice, a haunting whisper, pierced the chaos of the moment. "This is the true nature of our beliefs, Mr. Kane. The relics hold the power to shape reality itself. But with great power comes great responsibility, and the consequences of our actions are a force that cannot be controlled."

The leader's eyes held mine, his gaze unwavering. I had become a participant in a dance that had transcended the boundaries of the known and the unknown, a dance where the blurred line between science and mysticism had vanished. The relics were a source of unimaginable power, and I could feel their resonance within me.

As the rituals continued to unfold, I was swept deeper into the maelstrom of power and consequence. The desert night had transformed into a surreal dreamscape, where the line between reality and illusion had become elusive.

And then, as if guided by an unseen hand, the relics' power began to manifest. The shimmering liquid from the chalice formed into intricate patterns that danced in mid-air, the radiant light from the amulet extended into a protective barrier, and the cryptic symbols from the ancient tome materialized into ethereal beings that circled the encampment.

I watched in astonishment as the relics' power became a spectacle of awe and wonder. The elements themselves—earth, air, fire, and water—seemed to obey the cult's commands, each responding to the force that the relics exuded.

The leader's voice was a symphony of power and control as he directed the elements to demonstrate their obedience to the relics. Fire danced in intricate patterns, water defied gravity to hover in the air, the earth shifted and molded into intricate sculptures, and the wind obeyed the cult's whims, carrying whispers and secrets on its currents.

It was a revelation that surpassed anything I could have imagined. The Eclipse Seekers held the power to shape reality itself, to command the very elements of the world. The blurred line between science and mysticism had been obliterated, leaving me with a profound sense of awe and trepidation.

But as I watched the elements respond to the cult's commands, I couldn't shake the moral and ethical dilemmas that consumed me. The consequences of their beliefs and the use of the relics remained unknown, and the potential for catastrophe loomed.

The leader's voice pierced through my thoughts. "With great power comes great responsibility, Mr. Kane. The relics hold the key to shaping reality, but they are a double-edged sword. The consequences of their use cannot be controlled, and the blurred line between knowledge and power is a perilous path."

As the cult's rituals continued, the elements danced and obeyed, their power an undeniable force. I had become a witness to a world where the known and the supernatural were no longer separate, a world where the line between science and mysticism had vanished completely.

The consequences of my choice to aid the Eclipse Seekers were a storm that gathered strength. Aria's cryptic guidance, Dr. Simmons' warnings, and Lorraine Holloway's desperate plea for her daughter's return echoed in my mind.

I had entered a world where the relics held the power to reshape reality, and the moral and ethical dilemmas that surrounded their use were an enigma that needed to be unraveled. The next chapter of my journey held the promise of revelation and reckoning, and the consequences were a storm that threatened to unleash chaos upon Desert Mirage.

As the rituals reached their climax, the relics' power grew even more potent. The desert night seemed to pulse with an otherworldly energy, and the very fabric of reality wavered.

And then, as the final incantation echoed through the encampment, a rift in space and time manifested. It was as if a tear in the fabric of reality had opened, revealing a glimpse into an unknown dimension.

I gazed into the rift with a mixture of wonder and trepidation. The blurred line between the known and the unknown had become a doorway into a realm beyond comprehension. The consequences of my choice to aid the Eclipse Seekers were now unfolding before my eyes.

The leader's voice carried a note of triumph as he gestured toward the rift. "This, Mr. Kane, is the culmination of our beliefs. The relics have unlocked a gateway to another dimension, a realm of endless possibilities. With this power, we can reshape reality itself."

The revelation was like a lightning bolt, illuminating the vast potential of the relics. The moral and ethical dilemmas that consumed me had taken on a new dimension, and the consequences of my choice were now a force that could reshape the world itself.

But as I gazed into the rift, I couldn't shake the feeling that the blurred line between science and mysticism had led me into uncharted territory. The next chapter of my journey held the promise of revelation and reckoning, and the consequences were a storm that threatened to consume everything I knew.

As the rift in space and time beckoned, I stood at the precipice of a new chapter in my enigmatic journey. The Eclipse Seekers' power was no longer a mere illusion, and the relics I possessed held the key to unlocking the mysteries that lay beyond the blurred line between the known and the unknown.

## Chapter 11: The Unveiling Abyss

As I stood before the rift in space and time, the power of the stolen relics—the chalice, the ancient tome, and the amulet—had unlocked a doorway to an enigmatic dimension. The desert night pulsed with an otherworldly energy, and the very fabric of reality seemed to waver as I gazed into the abyss.

The leader of the Eclipse Seekers had a triumphant look in his eyes, a reflection of the cult's belief that they could reshape reality itself. The blurred line between science and mysticism had led me to this moment, where the consequences of my actions were an ever-present force.

The rift beckoned like a siren's call, its depths shrouded in mystery and wonder. But as I peered into the unknown, I couldn't shake the feeling that the Eclipse Seekers' power was a force that could spiral out of control.

The leader's voice resonated with authority as he gestured toward the rift. "This, Mr. Kane, is the culmination of our beliefs. The relics have unlocked a gateway to another dimension, a realm of endless possibilities. With this power, we can reshape reality itself."

The revelation was a revelation of shadows and secrets, a testament to the Eclipse Seekers' power and their unwavering belief in the blurred line between knowledge and power. The moral and ethical dilemmas that had consumed me were now a tempest, and the consequences of my choice held the power to change the world.

I had entered a realm beyond comprehension, a place where the known and the unknown were no longer distinct. The next chapter of my journey held the promise of revelation and reckoning, and the consequences were a storm that threatened to consume everything I knew.

As I hesitated at the precipice of the rift, Sarah's presence in the encampment haunted my thoughts. She had been a pivotal figure in the Eclipse Seekers' rituals, and her role in their beliefs remained a mystery that needed to be unraveled.

The leader's voice was like an incantation as he spoke of the limitless potential of the relics. "The blurred line between science and mysticism is a threshold to the unimaginable, Mr. Kane. The relics are the key to our destiny, and with your assistance, we can harness their power to reshape the world."

But as I considered the cult's intentions, a seed of doubt took root. Could the Eclipse Seekers truly control the forces they had unleashed? The moral and ethical dilemmas that confronted me were a shadow that hung over this enigmatic dance with the unknown.

The rift's depths beckoned, and I couldn't ignore the promise of answers that lay beyond. But I knew that my journey was at a crossroads, and the consequences of my choices were now a force that could reshape everything I knew.

In a moment of resolve, I took a step toward the rift, drawn by the allure of the unknown. The leader's smile widened, and the cult members watched with a mixture of anticipation and devotion.

The moment my foot crossed the threshold of the rift, I felt a surge of power unlike anything I had experienced before. The world around me twisted and contorted, and I found myself in a realm where reality itself was a canvas waiting to be painted.

The landscape was an otherworldly dreamscape, where the laws of physics and nature had no dominion. Colors that had no name danced through the air, and shapes shifted and transformed with a will of their own. It was a place where the blurred line between the known and the unknown was an ever-changing mosaic of wonder and trepidation.

As I marveled at the alien landscape, I couldn't help but think of the consequences of my actions. The moral and ethical dilemmas that had confronted me were now a living entity, a force that demanded consideration.

The leader's voice echoed in my mind. "This, Mr. Kane, is the realm of limitless possibilities. The relics have unlocked a world where the known and the unknown merge into a tapestry of power and consequence. You have taken the first step into a journey that may change everything."

But the journey was not without its perils. I could feel the rift's pull, a force that threatened to consume me if I ventured too deep. The blurred line between science and mysticism had led me into uncharted territory, and the consequences of my choices were now a storm that loomed on the horizon.

As I ventured further into the alien realm, I came across a structure that defied description. It was a fusion of art and architecture, an enigmatic monument that seemed to pulse with a life of its own.

The symbols from the ancient tome glowed on the monument's surface, their eerie light guiding my path. It was a revelation that the relics had a purpose beyond what I had imagined. The moral and ethical dilemmas that had haunted me were now intertwined with the very fabric of this alien world.

As I approached the monument, I couldn't shake the feeling that I was being watched. The shadows seemed to have eyes, and the whispers of the unknown danced on the air.

The leader's voice continued to echo in my mind. "You have entered a world where the consequences of your choices are a force that cannot be controlled, Mr. Kane. The relics hold the power to reshape reality, but their potential is both a blessing and a curse."

The monument held the promise of answers, but I knew that with answers came the weight of responsibility. The blurred line between knowledge and power had become a treacherous path, and I had become a wanderer in this enigmatic realm.

As I reached out to touch the monument, I felt a surge of power that coursed through my veins. The symbols from the ancient tome seemed to respond to my presence, their glow intensifying.

And then, as if guided by an unseen hand, the monument began to reveal its secrets. Images and symbols danced across its surface, a mosaic of knowledge and power. It was a revelation that surpassed anything I could have imagined, and the moral and ethical dilemmas that had consumed me were now a tapestry of enigma and consequence.

But as I delved deeper into the monument's revelations, I couldn't escape the feeling that I had entered a realm where the line between science and mysticism had been obliterated. The next chapter of my journey held the promise of revelation and reckoning, and the consequences were a storm that threatened to reshape everything I knew.

The monument's revelations were a mesmerizing tapestry of knowledge and power, a reflection of the relics' true purpose. I had entered a world where the known and the unknown were no longer distinct, and the blurred line between science and mysticism had become a chasm that threatened to consume everything in its path.

As I absorbed the revelations, I couldn't shake the feeling that I was not alone in this enigmatic realm. Whispers of the unknown seemed to echo from the shadows, and I knew that the consequences of my choices were now a force that demanded my attention.

The leader's voice continued to resonate in my mind. "The relics have unlocked a world where the consequences of your actions are a force that cannot be controlled, Mr. Kane. The blurred line between knowledge and power is a perilous path, and the moral and ethical dilemmas that have haunted you are now a storm that looms on the horizon."

The monument's revelations had deepened the mysteries that surrounded the relics and the Eclipse Seekers. The next chapter of my

journey held the promise of revelation and reckoning, and the consequences were a force that could reshape the world itself.

As I continued to explore the alien realm, I came across a chamber that seemed to pulse with an eerie light. The stolen relics—the chalice, the ancient tome, and the amulet—were arranged in a sacred configuration, their power evident and undeniable.

The leader's voice, now a haunting echo, resonated in my mind. "This is the heart of our beliefs, Mr. Kane. The relics hold the power to shape reality itself, and you have become a part of this enigmatic dance with the unknown."

But as I approached the chamber, I couldn't ignore the moral and ethical dilemmas that had consumed me. The consequences of my actions were now a tempest, and the blurred line between science and mysticism had become an abyss that beckoned.

The relics' power was a force that transcended the boundaries of science, and the consequences of their use were a storm that threatened to consume everything I knew. The next chapter of my journey held the promise of revelation and reckoning, and the consequences were a force that could reshape the world itself.

As I reached out to touch the relics, their power surged through me like a current of electricity. I could feel the ancient knowledge and the enigmatic force that pulsed within them.

And then, as if guided by an unseen hand, the relics began to unveil their purpose. The chalice's shimmering liquid held the secrets of transformation, the amulet's radiant light offered protection, and the ancient tome's symbols revealed the power to command the elements themselves.

The revelations were like a lightning bolt, illuminating the true nature of the relics. The moral and ethical dilemmas that had haunted me were now intertwined with the very fabric of this alien realm, and the consequences of my choices were a storm that gathered strength.

The leader's voice continued to haunt my thoughts. "The relics hold the power to shape reality, Mr. Kane, but their use comes at a cost. The blurred line between science and mysticism is a perilous path, and the moral and ethical dilemmas that have consumed you are now a force that demands your attention."

The relics' purpose had been unveiled, and the next chapter of my journey held the promise of revelation and reckoning. The consequences of my choices were a force that could reshape the world itself, and the blurred line between knowledge and power had become an abyss that beckoned.

As I absorbed the relics' revelations, I couldn't escape the feeling that I was being watched. The shadows and whispers of the unknown seemed to converge upon me, and I knew that the consequences of my choices were now a force that could not be denied.

The leader's voice, like an ancient incantation, continued to resonate. "You have entered a world where the consequences of your actions are a force that cannot be controlled, Mr. Kane. The blurred line between science and mysticism has become an abyss that beckons, and the moral and ethical dilemmas that have consumed you are now a storm that looms on the horizon."

The relics had revealed their purpose, but the mysteries that surrounded the Eclipse Seekers and the blurred line between knowledge and power remained. The next chapter of my journey held the promise of revelation and reckoning, and the consequences were a force that could reshape everything I knew.

As I left the chamber, I felt a sense of urgency. The rift in space and time still beckoned, and the consequences of my actions were a force that demanded my attention. The blurred line between science and mysticism had become a perilous path, and the next chapter of my journey was a descent into the heart of shadows and secrets.

As I ventured deeper into the alien realm, the whispers of the unknown seemed to grow louder, their secrets and shadows dancing on the air. I couldn't ignore the feeling that I was being drawn further into a enigmatic dance with the unknown, where the consequences of my choices were now a tempest that loomed on the horizon.

The leader's voice echoed in my mind one last time. "The relics have unlocked a world where the consequences of your actions are a force that cannot be controlled, Mr. Kane. The blurred line between knowledge and power is a perilous path, and the moral and ethical dilemmas that have consumed you are now a storm that looms on the horizon."

And with those words, I continued to explore the depths of the alien realm, where the next chapter of my journey held the promise of revelation and reckoning. The consequences of my choices were a force that could reshape everything I knew, and the blurred line between science and mysticism had become an abyss that beckoned.

## Chapter 12: Veil of Shadows

The alien realm continued to unravel before me, its colors and shapes shifting with an ethereal grace that defied logic. As I ventured deeper into the enigmatic dimension, I could feel the weight of the stolen relics—the chalice, the ancient tome, and the amulet—like an anchor in my mind. They were my connection to this surreal world, and I couldn't help but wonder if they were also my salvation or my doom.

The whispers of the unknown were a constant companion, their eerie secrets dancing on the air. The blurred line between science and mysticism had led me into this uncharted territory, and the consequences of my choices were a tempest that loomed on the horizon.

The leader's words resonated in my mind like an ancient incantation. "The relics have unlocked a world where the consequences of your actions are a force that cannot be controlled, Mr. Kane. The blurred line between knowledge and power is a perilous path, and the moral and ethical dilemmas that have consumed you are now a storm that looms on the horizon."

As I pressed deeper into the realm, I came across a series of intricate tunnels that wound their way through the alien landscape. The stolen relics guided me, their eerie glow illuminating the path ahead.

The tunnels seemed to pulse with a life of their own, their walls covered in symbols and images that defied interpretation. It was a testament to the relics' true power, a power that transcended the boundaries of science and mysticism.

As I delved further into the tunnels, I couldn't shake the feeling that I was not alone. The shadows of the unknown seemed to converge upon me, their whispers growing louder and more insistent.

The leader's voice continued to echo in my mind. "This is a world of shadows and secrets, Mr. Kane. The relics have unveiled the blurred line between the known and the unknown, and the consequences of your choices are a force that cannot be denied."

The tunnels seemed to stretch on endlessly, their twists and turns a labyrinth of enigma and consequence. I had entered a realm where the blurred line between science and mysticism had become a veil that concealed the ultimate truth.

As I navigated the tunnels, I could feel a growing sense of unease. The stolen relics were a source of power, but their true purpose remained elusive. The moral and ethical dilemmas that had haunted me were now a force that demanded my attention, and the consequences of my choices were like a shadow that refused to be dispelled.

The whispers of the unknown grew more insistent, their secrets and shadows dancing on the air like spectral specters. I couldn't help but wonder if I had ventured too deep into this enigmatic realm, and if the blurred line between knowledge and power had become a shroud that concealed the ultimate truth.

The leader's voice echoed in my mind one last time. "This is a world where the consequences of your actions are a force that cannot be controlled, Mr. Kane. The blurred line between science and mysticism is a perilous path, and the moral and ethical dilemmas that have consumed you are now a storm that looms on the horizon."

As I continued to navigate the labyrinthine tunnels, I felt a growing sense of urgency. The relics were a beacon that guided me, but I couldn't help but wonder if they were also a trap, leading me deeper into a world where the unknown held dominion.

The tunnels seemed to twist and turn with a will of their own, and I couldn't ignore the feeling that I was being watched. The shadows of the unknown were like silent witnesses to my journey, their whispers and secrets a constant presence.

And then, as I rounded a particularly sharp turn, I came upon a chamber that seemed to pulse with an eerie light. The stolen relics—the chalice, the ancient tome, and the amulet—were arranged in a sacred configuration, their power evident and undeniable.

The chamber's walls were covered in symbols and images that seemed to tell a story. It was a revelation that the relics held a purpose beyond what I had imagined, a purpose that transcended the boundaries of science and mysticism.

As I approached the chamber, the eerie light from the relics seemed to intensify, casting strange shadows on the walls. The whispers of the unknown seemed to converge upon me, their secrets and shadows dancing in a hypnotic rhythm.

The leader's voice was like an ancient incantation, resonating with authority. "This is the heart of our beliefs, Mr. Kane. The relics hold the power to shape reality, and you have become a part of this enigmatic dance with the unknown."

But as I entered the chamber, I couldn't ignore the feeling that I was not alone. The shadows and whispers of the unknown seemed to surround me, their secrets and enigmas like a web that closed in.

The relics' power was undeniable, but I knew that with power came the weight of responsibility. The blurred line between science and mysticism had become a veil that concealed the ultimate truth, and the next chapter of my journey was a descent into the heart of shadows and secrets.

As I reached out to touch the relics, their power surged through me like a current of electricity. I could feel the ancient knowledge and the enigmatic force that pulsed within them, a force that transcended the boundaries of science and mysticism.

And then, as if guided by an unseen hand, the relics began to reveal their purpose once more. The chalice's shimmering liquid held the secrets of transformation, the amulet's radiant light offered protection, and the ancient tome's symbols revealed the power to command the elements themselves.

The revelations were like a storm that raged in my mind, a tempest of knowledge and consequence. The moral and ethical dilemmas that had haunted me were now a force that demanded my attention, and the consequences of my choices were like a veil that obscured the ultimate truth.

The leader's voice continued to echo in my mind. "The relics have unlocked a world where the consequences of your actions are a force that cannot be controlled, Mr. Kane. The blurred line between knowledge and power is a perilous path, and the moral and ethical dilemmas that have consumed you are now a storm that looms on the horizon."

The relics had revealed their purpose once more, but the enigma of the Eclipse Seekers and the blurred line between science and mysticism remained. The next chapter of my journey was a descent into the heart of shadows and secrets, and the consequences of my choices were a force that could reshape everything I knew.

As I left the chamber, I couldn't shake the feeling that I had ventured deeper into a world where the line between the known and the unknown had become a chasm. The blurred line between science and mysticism had become a veil that concealed the ultimate truth, and the consequences of my choices were like a shroud that refused to be dispelled.

The whispers of the unknown continued to echo, their eerie secrets and enigmas a constant presence. I knew that the next chapter of my journey held the promise of revelation and reckoning, and the consequences were a storm that threatened to consume everything I knew.

As I navigated the tunnels once more, I came to a crossroads, where a choice lay before me. One path seemed to lead deeper into the realm, while the other appeared to offer a way out.

The moral and ethical dilemmas that had haunted me were now a weight that I carried, and the consequences of my choices were a tempest that loomed on the horizon. The blurred line between science and mysticism had become a chasm, and I had become a wanderer in this enigmatic world.

The leader's voice echoed in my mind. "You have reached a crossroads, Mr. Kane. The relics have unveiled a world where the consequences of your actions are a force that cannot be controlled. The blurred line between knowledge and power is a perilous path, and the choices you make will shape your destiny."

I knew that the choice before me was a pivotal moment in my enigmatic journey. The next chapter held the promise of revelation and reckoning, and the consequences were a storm that could reshape the world itself.

As I pondered my options, the whispers of the unknown seemed to grow louder, their eerie secrets and enigmas an ever-present presence. I had entered a realm where the known and the unknown were no longer distinct, and the blurred line between science and mysticism had become a veil that concealed the ultimate truth.

I made my choice and continued down the path that led deeper into the realm. The stolen relics were my guide, their eerie glow lighting the way. The moral and ethical dilemmas that had consumed me were now a force that demanded my attention, and the consequences of my choices were like a shadow that refused to be dispelled.

As I ventured further into the realm, the whispers of the unknown grew more insistent, their eerie secrets and enigmas a constant presence. I couldn't shake the feeling that I was being drawn deeper into a world where the consequences of my actions were a force that could not be denied.

The leader's voice continued to echo in my mind. "You have chosen your path, Mr. Kane, and the consequences of your choices are now a tempest that looms on the horizon. The blurred line between knowledge and power is a perilous path, and the enigmas of this world are a veil that conceals the ultimate truth."

And with those words, I continued deeper into the realm, where the next chapter of my journey held the promise of revelation and reckoning. The consequences of my choices were a force that could reshape everything I knew, and the blurred line between science and mysticism had become a chasm that beckoned.

But as I pressed on, I couldn't escape the feeling that I was being watched, that the shadows and whispers of the unknown were closing in. The enigmas of this world were like a shroud that refused to be dispelled, and the consequences of my choices were a tempest that loomed on the horizon.

## Chapter 13: The Return to Reality

The path in the alien realm stretched on, winding through ethereal landscapes and enigmatic structures. The stolen relics—the chalice, the ancient tome, and the amulet—continued to guide me, their eerie glow a beacon in the surreal darkness. The whispers of the unknown still danced in the air, a constant reminder of the blurred line between science and mysticism that had led me here.

As I ventured deeper, I couldn't help but reflect on the journey that had brought me to this point. It had been a quest shrouded in mysteries, enigmas, and moral dilemmas. The consequences of my choices had weighed heavy on my conscience, and I had been a wanderer in a world where the known and the unknown merged into a tapestry of power and consequence.

The leader's words echoed in my mind, a reminder of the blurred line between knowledge and power. "The relics have unveiled a world where the consequences of your actions are a force that cannot be controlled, Mr. Kane. The enigmas of this world are a veil that conceals the ultimate truth, and the choices you make will shape your destiny."

As I walked, the stolen relics seemed to resonate with the alien realm, their glow intensifying. I could feel the ancient knowledge and the enigmatic force that pulsed within them, a force that transcended the boundaries of science and mysticism.

But I also knew that the stolen relics held a power that was both a blessing and a curse. The moral and ethical dilemmas that had consumed me were still a tempest that loomed on the horizon, and the consequences of my choices were like a shadow that refused to be dispelled.

The whispers of the unknown grew louder, their eerie secrets and enigmas a constant presence. I had entered a world where the blurred line between science and mysticism had become an abyss that beckoned, and the consequences of my actions were a force that could not be denied.

And then, as I rounded a final corner, I came upon a chamber unlike any I had seen before. The stolen relics were arranged in a sacred configuration, their eerie glow casting strange shadows on the walls.

The chamber itself seemed to throb with an ethereal energy, and I couldn't help but wonder if I had reached the heart of this alien realm, the place where all its secrets were stored. The relics held the key, but I still had questions that needed answers.

The leader's voice echoed one last time in my mind. "This is the heart of our beliefs, Mr. Kane. The relics hold the power to shape reality, and you have become a part of this enigmatic dance with the unknown."

As I entered the chamber, I could feel a sense of anticipation building. The stolen relics were the focus, and their power seemed to intensify with each step I took. The symbols and images on the chamber's walls seemed to come to life, telling a story that had been hidden for eons.

But I also knew that the stolen relics held the potential to reshape reality itself, and the consequences of their use were a force that could not be controlled. The blurred line between science and mysticism had led me into this uncharted territory, and the next chapter of my journey was a descent into the heart of shadows and secrets.

As I approached the relics, I couldn't help but wonder about the choices I had made, the moral and ethical dilemmas that had consumed me, and the consequences that had followed. The relics' power was undeniable, but it was also a double-edged sword.

I reached out to touch the relics one last time, and their power surged through me like a current of electricity. The chalice's shimmering liquid held the secrets of transformation, the amulet's radiant light offered protection, and the ancient tome's symbols revealed the power to command the elements themselves.

The revelations were a tempest of knowledge and consequence, and they seemed to answer the questions that had haunted me throughout this journey. The relics had been the key, the bridge between the known and the unknown, the blurred line between science and mysticism.

As I absorbed the revelations, I couldn't escape the feeling that I was being watched. The shadows and whispers of the unknown seemed to converge upon me, their secrets and enigmas dancing in a hypnotic rhythm.

But as I took a step back from the relics, the surreal world around me began to shift and contort. The alien landscape faded, and I found myself back in the encampment of the Eclipse Seekers, the stolen relics still in my hands.

The members of the cult stood before me, their eyes filled with awe and reverence. They had witnessed the relics' power, but the moral and ethical dilemmas that had consumed me were still a tempest that loomed on the horizon.

The leader's voice carried a note of finality as he spoke. "You have returned from the realm of the unknown, Mr. Kane, and you hold the relics that have unlocked its mysteries. The blurred line between knowledge and power is a perilous path, and the consequences of your choices are a force that cannot be denied."

As I looked around at the faces of the Eclipse Seekers, I knew that this chapter of my journey was coming to an end. The stolen relics had been the key, the bridge between the known and the unknown, but the consequences of their use were a force that could not be controlled.

And then, from the shadows, a figure emerged. It was Sarah Holloway, her eyes filled with a mixture of relief and gratitude. She had been a pivotal figure in the Eclipse Seekers' rituals, but her role had remained a mystery that needed to be unraveled.

Sarah approached me, and for the first time, we spoke. "Thank you, Mr. Kane. You have helped me find answers that I have sought for so long. The relics hold a power that transcends the boundaries of science and mysticism, and you have unlocked their secrets."

I nodded, a sense of closure washing over me. The blurred line between science and mysticism had led me into this enigmatic journey, and the moral and ethical dilemmas that had consumed me were a force that had demanded my attention.

As the Eclipse Seekers gathered around

, the relics began to glow with an otherworldly light. The symbols and images on their surfaces seemed to come to life, and the stolen relics were a testament to the power of the unknown.

The leader spoke one last time, his voice filled with reverence. "With the relics, we have glimpsed the blurred line between knowledge and power, and we have touched the enigma of the unknown. The consequences of our actions are a force that cannot be controlled, but they are also a testament to the strength of the human spirit."

And with those words, the stolen relics began to levitate, their power evident and undeniable. They ascended into the night sky, their eerie glow a beacon that lit up the desert.

As I watched the relics disappear into the darkness, I couldn't help but feel a sense of peace. The journey had been a tumultuous one, filled with complex mysteries, moral dilemmas, and the blurred line between science and mysticism.

But in the end, the stolen relics had been a bridge between the known and the unknown, a testament to the power of human curiosity and the strength of the human spirit. The consequences of my choices had been a force that had reshaped my understanding of the world, and the next chapter of my journey held the promise of resolution and closure.

The Eclipse Seekers, with Sarah by their side, watched the relics vanish into the night, their expressions a mixture of awe and gratitude. The stolen relics had been a bridge between the known and the unknown, a testament to the power of human curiosity and the strength of the human spirit.

As I turned to leave the encampment, I couldn't help but think about the enigmatic journey that had brought me here. The blurred line between science and mysticism had been a treacherous path, but it had also been a testament to the power of human curiosity and the strength of the human spirit.

The consequences of my choices had been a force that had reshaped my understanding of the world, and the next chapter of my journey held the promise of resolution and closure. The enigma of the stolen relics had been unraveled, and the blurred line between the known and the unknown had become a testament to the strength of the human spirit.

And as I walked away from the encampment, I knew that I was leaving behind a world of shadows and secrets, and embarking on a new chapter in my life. The enigma of the stolen relics had been unraveled, and the blurred line between the known and the unknown had become a testament to the power of human curiosity and the strength of the human spirit.

The desert night was quiet and serene, and the stars shone brightly in the sky. It was a world that held its own mysteries, but I was ready to face them with a newfound sense of purpose and understanding.

The journey had been a tumultuous one, but in the end, it had led me to a place of resolution and closure. The blurred line between science and mysticism had become a testament to the power of human curiosity and the strength of the human spirit, and I was ready to embrace the next chapter of my life with open arms.

And as I looked up at the stars, I couldn't help but feel a sense of hope and optimism. The journey had been filled with complex mysteries, moral dilemmas, and the blurred line between science and mysticism, but it had also been a testament to the resilience of the human spirit and the power of the unknown.

With a newfound sense of purpose, I walked into the desert night, ready to face whatever challenges lay ahead, knowing that the enigma of the stolen relics had been unraveled, and the blurred line between the known and the unknown had become a testament to the strength of the human spirit.

As I disappeared into the night, the desert absorbed my footsteps, and the mysteries that had once consumed me were left behind, like footprints in the sand. The journey had been a tumultuous one, but it had also been a testament to the power of the human spirit and the resilience of the human soul.

And with a sense of closure and resolution, I walked into the night, ready to face whatever challenges lay ahead. The enigma of the stolen relics had been unraveled, and the blurred line between the known and the unknown had become a testament to the power of human curiosity and the strength of the human spirit.

THE END

# Virtual Reckoning

## Chapter 1: The Labyrinth of Shadows

The neon-lit streets of New Angeles buzzed with the relentless energy of a city that never slept. In this high-tech metropolis, towering holographic billboards painted the night sky with vivid advertisements for the latest virtual reality games, and the air hummed with the distant hum of hovercars. In the heart of this futuristic landscape, a mysterious murder was about to unfold, one that would thrust an unlikely hero into the depths of the digital abyss.

Riley Vance had once been a notorious hacker, renowned for her brilliance and audacity in the cyber underworld. She'd stolen secrets, exposed corrupt corporations, and blurred the lines between right and wrong. But now, standing on a rain-slicked street corner, she was a different person. A private investigator with a complicated past and a burning desire for redemption.

Riley's dark eyes scanned the surroundings as she stepped out of her aero-cab. Her attire was simple, a black trench coat and a pair of sleek, silver-rimmed goggles that concealed her identity. The raindrops clinging to her coat seemed to glisten with the neon lights, a fitting metaphor for the city's chaotic beauty.

The case that brought her here was unlike any other. A call from a desperate client, Arthur Pembrooke, had set her on this path. Pembrooke was a wealthy tech mogul, a virtual reality pioneer, and the owner of VirtuCorp, the world's largest gaming company. A high-profile figure with secrets to protect, Pembrooke had hired Riley to investigate the murder of his estranged wife, Elara, which had taken place within the virtual world of "The Labyrinth of Shadows."

Riley had reluctantly accepted the case, driven by a mix of curiosity and the need for a substantial payday to support her fledgling detective agency. Her new life was about to collide with a past she thought she'd left behind.

"The Labyrinth of Shadows," known as Labyrinth to its players, was the most advanced virtual reality game ever created. It was a sprawling digital realm, a place where players could explore fantastic landscapes, battle mythical creatures, and embark on epic quests. But Elara's murder had transcended the boundaries of a game; her avatar, a sorceress named Seraphina, had been found lifeless within the game's darkest corners.

As Riley approached VirtuCorp's towering headquarters, she marveled at the building's sleek, glass exterior, reflecting the city's frenetic pulse. Her client had arranged for her to enter the game as an undercover player, using the company's cutting-edge VR technology. Riley's real-world identity would remain hidden, but she would need to navigate Labyrinth to uncover the truth.

Inside the pristine lobby, she was greeted by Arthur Pembrooke himself. He was a man of calculated charm, with sharp cheekbones and an air of unassailable authority. Riley's instincts tingled as they exchanged pleasantries, and she couldn't help but wonder what secrets the tech magnate was concealing.

"I appreciate your discretion in this matter, Ms. Vance," Pembrooke said, his words laced with an air of urgency. "Elara's death must remain a secret, at least until we can unravel the truth behind it."

As Riley donned the VR headset and entered the digital labyrinth, the real world melted away, replaced by a surreal landscape. She found herself standing at the entrance of a massive, ornate portal, the gateway to a realm of magic and mystery. The sense of immersion was staggering, and Riley felt like she had truly entered another world.

The vivid imagery of Labyrinth was breathtaking, a fantastical realm of floating islands, shimmering forests, and foreboding dungeons. The air was thick with enchantment, and strange creatures and avatars roamed the landscape, each one an embodiment of a player's imagination.

As Riley ventured deeper into the labyrinthine world, the clues and puzzles that would lead her to Elara's murderer remained elusive. She encountered a cast of well-defined side characters, all with their own agendas and secrets. Each interaction brought her closer to the heart of the mystery but also deepened her moral and ethical dilemmas.

The game world of Labyrinth was a mirror of the real world, where societal issues, power struggles, and hidden agendas played out in a surreal digital landscape. The rich exploited the poor, and players grappled with moral choices that would impact the game's fragile balance.

Tension and suspense coiled around Riley as she delved further into the game's labyrinth. The closer she came to uncovering the truth, the more her virtual and real-world realities blurred, raising disturbing questions about the nature of existence and the consequences of technology gone awry.

The first chapter came to a close as Riley Vance, now deep within the labyrinth, stumbled upon a shadowy figure, an avatar cloaked in darkness. Their eyes met, and a shiver raced down her spine. The figure's voice hissed in her ear, "You're not supposed to be here, detective."

## Chapter 2: Veil of Deception

The sinister figure in the shadowy cloak loomed over Riley, their virtual presence sending a shiver down her spine. In the heart of the Labyrinth of Shadows, she knew she was out of her depth, caught in a web of intrigue and danger she could scarcely comprehend.

Riley had honed her skills as a hacker, but this was a different kind of challenge. She took a deep breath, steadying herself. "Who are you?" she demanded, her voice firm despite her uncertainty.

The figure tilted its hooded head, a malicious chuckle resonating through the digital realm. "I'm the keeper of secrets, detective. Secrets buried deep within the heart of Labyrinth."

As if on cue, a gust of wind blew through the darkened corridor, scattering the virtual leaves and casting eerie shadows. Riley couldn't shake the feeling that there was more to this figure than met the eye, something that extended beyond the game itself.

"Secrets about what?" Riley pressed, her fingers itching to reach for the hidden pistol at her side. She had prepared for danger, but nothing could have prepared her for the enigmatic forces at play.

The figure stepped closer, its eyes glowing with an otherworldly light. "Secrets that could reshape reality itself," it hissed. "Secrets that might explain Elara's murder, if you're brave enough to uncover them."

Riley couldn't ignore the tantalizing bait. Elara's murder was the reason she had embarked on this treacherous journey into the depths of the game. Her pursuit of truth had led her to this surreal encounter, and she couldn't turn back now.

"I'll play your game," Riley declared, her resolve unwavering. "But you'd better start answering questions. Who killed Elara, and why?"

The figure's laughter filled the corridor, echoing like a haunting melody. "To uncover the truth, you'll need to unravel the layers of deceit and explore the darkest recesses of Labyrinth. Follow me, detective."

With a wave of its hand, the figure melted into the shadows, leaving a trail of flickering digital footprints. Riley gave chase, each step in the virtual realm feeling as real as the one before. The path she followed led her through winding passages, across rickety bridges, and into the depths of eerie forests, all the while surrounded by the constant hum of the game world.

Riley encountered more of the game's well-defined side characters along the way, each harboring their own secrets and grudges. Her interactions with them revealed glimpses of a complex web of alliances and betrayals. Every decision she made had consequences, and the moral and ethical dilemmas she faced became more pronounced.

As Riley continued her journey, she couldn't help but reflect on the parallels between the game world and the real world. The game was a reflection of society, a place where power imbalances and injustices played out, making her question the very nature of her quest.

Hours passed in the blink of an eye as she followed the enigmatic figure deeper into the labyrinth. The tension and suspense grew palpable with every step, as she uncovered more layers of deceit and intrigue. But the truth remained elusive, a mirage shimmering on the horizon.

Finally, they arrived at a place within Labyrinth that was unlike any other. It was a sprawling, ancient library, with towering shelves filled with digital tomes. The figure, its hooded visage shifting, gestured toward a series of glowing manuscripts.

"The answers you seek, detective, are hidden within these pages," it murmured. "But unlocking their secrets won't be easy."

Riley approached the first manuscript, the title shimmering before her eyes: "The Chronicles of Elara." She hesitated, then reached out and touched the digital interface. The tome opened, revealing a series of cryptic passages.

As she delved into the text, Riley's heart raced. She was on the verge of a breakthrough, the culmination of her relentless pursuit of the truth. But as she read, her gaze was drawn to a subtle movement in her peripheral vision.

A cloaked figure, identical to the one that had led her here, now stood behind her. It whispered in a chilling voice, "Not everyone is who they seem, detective. Trust no one."

Riley's pulse quickened, and she turned to confront the figure, only to find herself face to face with another identical avatar, lurking in the shadows. They encircled her, an eerie chorus of whispers filling her ears.

The chapter came to an end, leaving readers hanging on the precipice of an enigmatic conspiracy. Riley Vance, deep within the Labyrinth of Shadows, had discovered a place of secrets and deception, and now she was trapped, surrounded by shadowy avatars, each one casting doubt on her quest for truth.

## Chapter 3: Whispers of Betrayal

The cloaked avatars surrounding Riley in the virtual library maintained a sinister silence. Their shadowy figures loomed, their eerie whispers growing louder in the stillness. The sense of unease hung heavy in the air, and she could feel their eyes fixed upon her.

Riley's fingers tightened around the hilt of her virtual sword, her mind racing to find a way out of this digital labyrinth. "Who are you?" she demanded, her voice steady despite her anxiety. "What do you want?"

The figure closest to her, the one that had first revealed the library, stepped forward. Its hood lowered slightly, revealing a pair of cold, piercing eyes. "We are the Keepers of the Veil, detective," it said, its voice a chilling echo in the digital realm. "We guard the secrets of Labyrinth and the enigma that surrounds Elara's death."

"Elara's murder was real," Riley asserted, her determination unwavering. "What's the connection between the game and her death?"

A sinister smile played on the Keeper's lips. "In Labyrinth, the line between reality and illusion blurs," it hissed. "Elara's death was merely the beginning of a greater mystery, one that could shatter the boundaries of both worlds."

Riley's curiosity burned like a fire, but so did her unease. She knew there was more to this enigmatic group than met the eye. "What do I need to do to uncover the truth?" she asked, her eyes flicking from one avatar to another.

The Keepers seemed to exchange glances, their silent communication betraying a depth of understanding that left Riley feeling like an outsider in her own investigation. "To find answers, you must navigate the Veil of Deception," the Keeper continued, its voice a haunting whisper. "But be warned, detective, for the truth can be a double-edged sword."

With a wave of its hand, the Keepers dispersed into the shadows, leaving Riley alone in the dimly lit library. She turned her attention back to the illuminated manuscripts. Her quest for truth had taken an even more ominous turn, and she felt the weight of their cryptic message pressing down on her.

As she continued to explore the virtual library, Riley unearthed more manuscripts, each offering fragments of Elara's story and the tangled web of connections she had woven within Labyrinth. The complex mysteries of the game and the real world merged into a perplexing tapestry of intrigue, pushing her to confront moral and ethical dilemmas she had never imagined.

The manuscripts were filled with tales of Elara's interactions with other players, of alliances formed and betrayed. They spoke of an underground resistance within Labyrinth, a group that had grown wary of VirtuCorp's influence and sought to expose its dark secrets. Riley's heart pounded as she realized that the game was not just a form of entertainment but a stage for a broader struggle.

Her hours within the virtual library began to blur as she uncovered more clues and puzzles hidden within the manuscripts. Each piece of the puzzle brought her closer to the heart of the matter, yet the web of deception grew more intricate with every revelation.

Outside the digital library, Riley's real-world consciousness was only dimly aware of time passing. She was locked in a mental and emotional struggle, torn between the urge to uncover the truth and the fear of the unknown consequences that lay ahead.

It was during one of these revelations that she stumbled upon a virtual message hidden within the code of a manuscript. A secret message, revealing a meeting point within Labyrinth, one that could lead her to answers beyond the library's enigmatic walls.

With a sense of determination, Riley left the library and navigated the intricate landscapes of the game. She faced treacherous traps, overcame challenging puzzles, and engaged in duels with other players, all the while driven by the need to find the elusive meeting point.

The tension and suspense mounted as she journeyed deeper into the game, with each step taking her closer to a showdown with an unseen enemy. The digital realm grew ever more complex, mirroring the intricacies of the real world, forcing her to confront the blurred lines between the two.

Finally, Riley reached the designated meeting point, a darkened chamber within the game, where she was meant to meet the elusive underground resistance. But as she stepped inside, the chamber was empty, and the atmosphere grew colder, more foreboding.

The chapter concluded on a chilling note as Riley realized that she had been led into a trap. She was not alone in the chamber, and her virtual enemies, their eyes filled with malice, closed in on her. The sinister avatars, cloaked in darkness, whispered in unison, "You were never meant to find the truth, detective."

Riley Vance was trapped, and her virtual existence hung in the balance as her adversaries closed in.

## Chapter 4: The Duel of Shadows

Riley Vance's virtual heart raced as she stood cornered in the darkened chamber, the sinister avatars closing in on her. The eerie whispers of the cloaked figures sent a shiver down her spine. She was no longer in control of the situation, and her instincts screamed danger.

"You're not getting out of this, detective," one of the avatars sneered, its voice dripping with malice.

As they circled her, Riley's mind raced to find a way out. The virtual sword she had brought into Labyrinth felt insubstantial in the face of this virtual menace. She couldn't help but feel like a pawn in a much larger game.

A surge of anger and determination welled within her. She wasn't going down without a fight. With a swift motion, she unsheathed her sword, prepared to face the impending confrontation. "I'll take my chances," she retorted, her voice laced with defiance.

In a blur of motion, the avatars lunged at her, and the virtual battle erupted. Blades clashed, magic spells flew, and the chamber echoed with the sounds of combat. Riley's skills as a gamer and her determination to unearth the truth fueled her every move, but she was outnumbered and outmatched.

She fought valiantly, her sword cutting through shadows, but the avatars proved to be formidable foes. They moved with an unnatural grace, and their attacks were precise and calculated. Riley's health points dwindled as the battle raged on.

Just when it seemed like all hope was lost, a burst of energy surged through her, and Riley unleashed a powerful spell she hadn't known she possessed. A wave of brilliant light erupted from her, momentarily blinding the avatars and giving her a moment of respite.

With her newfound strength, she launched a counterattack, striking down one of her assailants. The others recoiled, their confidence shaken. The avatars hesitated, and Riley seized the opportunity to make her escape.

She dashed out of the chamber, the avatars in pursuit. The virtual landscape blurred around her as she sprinted through

Labyrinth's intricate pathways, her goal to lose her pursuers and regroup. Her heart pounded in her chest as she navigated the surreal terrain, the stakes higher than ever.

As she ran, she thought back to the enigmatic Keepers of the Veil and the underground resistance within the game. Were they allies or foes? The web of deception in Labyrinth seemed more complex than ever, and she couldn't shake the feeling that her pursuit of the truth was entwined with a larger, unfolding drama.

The tension and suspense mounted with every step she took. Riley was on the run in a world where reality and illusion blurred, and she couldn't trust anyone. She had to uncover the truth about Elara's murder and the mysteries of Labyrinth, but her enemies were closing in.

Just when it seemed like the avatars were gaining on her, Riley stumbled upon a hidden glen bathed in soft, ethereal light. A stone altar stood at the center, and a pulsing, ancient energy surrounded it. With no other options, she rushed to the altar and, in an act of desperation, touched the ancient stones.

In an instant, she was transported to a different part of Labyrinth, far from the pursuing avatars. The sense of relief was palpable, but she couldn't relax just yet. She needed to regroup, gather more information, and find allies who could help her untangle the web of deceit that had ensnared her.

As Riley ventured deeper into the game, she encountered more side characters, each with their own motives and allegiances. She learned of factions within Labyrinth, including the resistance, whose members fought to expose VirtuCorp's dark secrets and the injustices within the game world.

The more she uncovered, the clearer it became that Labyrinth was not just a game but a reflection of the real world, a place where societal issues, power struggles, and hidden agendas played out, with far-reaching consequences.

Hours passed as Riley ventured further into the virtual labyrinth. Her determination to uncover the truth was unwavering, but the shadows that enveloped her grew darker with every revelation. The dual nature of the game, blending reality and illusion, only deepened her sense of confusion and urgency.

Finally, as she explored the twisted corridors of a digital dungeon, she stumbled upon a mural, a piece of vivid imagery that caught her attention. The mural depicted Elara as Seraphina, her avatar, standing on the brink of a vast abyss. It was as though the mural held a message, a clue that could unlock the truth.

Riley couldn't tear her eyes away from the mural. It was as if Elara's presence lingered there, calling out to her. The words of the Keepers of the Veil echoed in her mind: "The truth can be a double-edged sword."

As she scrutinized the mural, she noticed a hidden message, barely discernible within the artwork. It was a riddle, a puzzle waiting to be solved, and it held the key to unraveling the enigma that had brought her here.

With a newfound determination, Riley set to work, deciphering the riddle. The clues were complex, requiring her to draw on her knowledge of the game world, her hacking skills, and her intuition. She couldn't afford to make a mistake, for the answers lay within her reach, but so did the consequences of uncovering them.

The tension in the digital dungeon was palpable as Riley delved into the puzzle, each step bringing her closer to the truth. But just as she felt on the verge of solving it, the ground beneath her feet trembled, and the dungeon walls groaned.

A sense of impending danger washed over her, and her instincts screamed for her to flee. The dungeon was collapsing, and time was running out.

## Chapter 5: A Fractured Reality

As the dungeon walls of Labyrinth crumbled and shook around her, Riley Vance's heart raced with a blend of anticipation and fear. The puzzle she sought to solve, hidden within the mural, held the promise of unraveling the mysteries that had drawn her into the digital abyss.

With deft fingers, she continued to decipher the riddle, each step bringing her closer to its solution. The code within the mural was complex, intertwining with the intricate world of Labyrinth itself. She knew that unlocking its secrets would take her one step closer to understanding the enigmatic connection between the game and Elara's real-world murder.

But the collapsing dungeon was a relentless adversary. The earth tremors grew more violent, debris rained down, and the walls seemed determined to crush her. Riley had to focus, to shut out the panic that threatened to overwhelm her, and solve the puzzle before the very reality of Labyrinth crumbled around her.

Time blurred as she worked tirelessly, her mind racing through the complexities of the riddle. With each layer she uncovered, the answers seemed closer, yet she was aware that consequences loomed on the horizon. She had seen the warning signs in the mural: the double-edged sword of truth.

The tension in the dungeon was palpable as Riley pressed forward. The digital world was her enemy, and it seemed determined to extinguish her presence. And yet, she couldn't help but feel that there was a grander force at play, one that sought to protect the web of deception that had ensnared her.

As she pieced together the final fragments of the riddle, a moment of clarity washed over her. The message hidden within the mural was unveiled: "The Gate of Seraphina." It was a reference to a legendary location within Labyrinth, a place of great power and mystery.

With the puzzle solved, Riley knew her path was set. She would have to venture to the Gate of Seraphina, confront the secrets that lay within, and perhaps, finally, uncover the truth that had eluded her for so long. With the digital dungeon crumbling around her, she dashed for the exit, her virtual world splintering at the seams.

As she burst into the open, the world of Labyrinth stretched out before her in all its surreal beauty. The crumbling dungeon had been left behind, and she was free to continue her quest. She could feel the power of the mural's message coursing through her, driving her forward with renewed determination.

The journey to the Gate of Seraphina was fraught with peril. The landscape shifted and twisted, surreal and unpredictable. Riley had to navigate treacherous terrain, face enigmatic creatures, and solve mind-bending puzzles, each test bringing her closer to the mysterious location.

Along the way, she encountered a group of players, a faction from the resistance. They recognized her as the detective searching for the truth behind Elara's murder. The players shared their knowledge, revealing the extent of VirtuCorp's influence over Labyrinth, and the dangers that came with trying to expose the truth.

The tension and suspense mounted as the players offered to help her reach the Gate of Seraphina, for they too sought answers to the enigma that had entangled their lives. Together, they formed an unlikely alliance, their mission to reveal the dark secrets hidden within the game.

As they journeyed toward their destination, the blurred lines between the virtual world and the real world became ever more apparent. Riley couldn't help but ponder the moral and ethical dilemmas that Labyrinth posed, where the consequences of their actions transcended the digital realm.

The landscape shifted once again, and the players reached the Gate of Seraphina, a massive, ancient portal that glowed with ethereal light. It was a place of power and destiny, a symbol of both hope and trepidation.

Riley's heart pounded as she approached the gate, her companions at her side. She knew that within its depths lay the answers she had sought, and the revelation of Elara's true fate.

But she also sensed that the gate held untold dangers, for it was a place where reality and illusion blurred, where the fabric of Labyrinth and the real world intertwined.

With a deep breath, she stepped through the gate, her virtual existence merging with the surreal energies that enveloped her. The other players followed, and together, they entered a realm where the boundaries of reality and digital illusion shattered.

Inside the Gate of Seraphina, they found themselves in a space that defied comprehension. It was a fractured reality, a place where time and space bent to the will of the game. Surreal landscapes and shifting dimensions surrounded them, creating a kaleidoscope of confusion and wonder.

As they ventured deeper into this enigmatic realm, the tension grew ever more palpable. The truth they sought was within reach, but so were the consequences of unearthing it. The players had to confront their deepest fears and darkest secrets, for within the fractured reality of the Gate of Seraphina, the line between truth and illusion had never been more tenuous.

## Chapter 6: The Reality Unveiled

Inside the fractured reality of the Gate of Seraphina, Riley Vance and her companions found themselves caught in a surreal maze of shifting dimensions and fractured landscapes. It was a place where the lines between reality and illusion blurred to an unsettling degree. The very fabric of Labyrinth seemed to unravel, and with each step, they ventured deeper into the heart of the enigma that had entangled their lives.

As they continued their journey, the tension in the air grew palpable. Riley couldn't shake the feeling that the Gate of Seraphina held not only the answers to Elara's murder but also the secrets that could reshape the very nature of their existence. The fractured reality was a minefield of moral and ethical dilemmas, and every decision had the potential to ripple through the digital world and beyond.

The companions moved cautiously through the ever-shifting landscapes, their senses on high alert. Surreal entities and creatures of the digital realm wandered the fractured reality, and each encounter was a test of their determination and resolve. The puzzles they encountered grew more intricate, requiring a blend of logic, intuition, and bravery.

As they navigated this perplexing realm, they began to uncover fragments of information that hinted at a hidden power within Labyrinth. An ancient force, one that transcended the confines of the game, was hinted at in cryptic messages and fragmented data. It was a revelation that left Riley and her companions both awed and fearful, for they realized that the game held secrets of far-reaching consequences.

The tension and suspense mounted with every step, and the companions were on the verge of a breakthrough. They stumbled upon an ancient chamber, its walls etched with intricate symbols and mystic runes. At the center of the chamber stood a pedestal, and on it rested a glowing crystal, its light casting an otherworldly glow across the room.

The crystal was a beacon, a source of power and knowledge that seemed to pulse with the essence of Labyrinth itself. Riley approached it cautiously, aware of the potential danger that lay in harnessing its power. As she extended her hand toward the crystal, she felt a surge of energy coursing through her, an exhilarating connection to the game's very heart.

With a sense of reverence, she touched the crystal, and a rush of memories and visions flooded her mind. It was as if the entire history of Labyrinth unfolded before her, the secrets of Elara's murder and the enigmatic forces that had drawn her into this virtual abyss unveiled in a dazzling display of light and color.

The companions watched in awe as Riley's eyes glowed with a spectral light, her form seeming to merge with the crystal's radiance. She was a conduit of knowledge, her consciousness bridging the gap between the fractured reality of Labyrinth and the real world.

But just as the revelations within the crystal reached their climax, a powerful force surged through the chamber. The very fabric of the fractured reality seemed to quiver, and a presence beyond their comprehension emerged.

A figure, neither wholly digital nor completely real, materialized before them. Its eyes glowed with an eerie light, and its voice reverberated with the echoes of ancient knowledge. "You have trespassed upon the sacred realm of Labyrinth," it intoned. "The time has come to unveil the truth."

The companions watched in trepidation as the enigmatic figure began to reveal the secrets of Elara's murder and the hidden powers that had drawn Riley into the game. The truth was a staggering revelation, one that transcended the boundaries of the virtual world and reached into the very heart of the real world.

The figure explained that Elara had stumbled upon a hidden algorithm, a code embedded within Labyrinth's deepest recesses. This code held the power to manipulate reality itself, to shape the real world through the game. Elara had uncovered VirtuCorp's plan to use Labyrinth as a tool for control and manipulation, a scheme that extended far beyond the boundaries of mere gaming.

As the truth unfurled, the companions realized the full extent of the moral and ethical dilemmas they faced. They were in possession of knowledge that could reshape the world, but they were also aware of the dangers that came with it. VirtuCorp, a powerful and unscrupulous entity, would stop at nothing to protect its secrets.

The tension in the chamber was palpable as they grappled with the weight of their discovery. The very foundations of Labyrinth and the real world had been shaken, and the consequences of their actions loomed on the horizon.

The enigmatic figure, still a presence beyond their understanding, urged them to make a choice. They could expose the truth, potentially unveiling the manipulative schemes of VirtuCorp and the dangers of the hidden algorithm. But in doing so, they would become targets, pursued by a relentless force that sought to silence them.

The companions exchanged uncertain glances, their resolve tested to the limit. The blurred lines between the virtual world and reality had never been more apparent, and the enigmatic forces at play threatened to unravel their very existence.

# Chapter 7: The Game Changer

Riley Vance and her companions stood at a precipice, caught between the weight of the revelation they had unearthed and the chilling knowledge that their choices would shape the destiny of both Labyrinth and the real world. The enigmatic figure, a presence beyond their comprehension, awaited their decision.

The blurred lines between reality and illusion were never more apparent, and the tension in the chamber was palpable. The power to manipulate reality itself, held within the hidden algorithm, was a double-edged sword, and the consequences of their actions weighed heavily on their minds.

Riley's gaze flickered between her companions, each of them representing different facets of Labyrinth and the world beyond. Together, they had uncovered the truth about VirtuCorp's sinister plan, a scheme that sought to use the game as a tool for control and manipulation. But unveiling this truth came with great risk.

The enigmatic figure's voice echoed in the chamber, imbued with an air of gravitas. "The decision you make today will determine the course of not only Labyrinth but the real world as well. Will you expose the hidden algorithm, or will you keep its power hidden?"

The companions exchanged a series of tense glances, a silent exchange of thoughts and concerns. They were acutely aware that exposing the hidden algorithm would draw the wrath of VirtuCorp, a powerful and unscrupulous entity with the means to silence them. But hiding the truth meant allowing VirtuCorp's manipulative schemes to persist unchecked.

It was a moral and ethical dilemma of monumental proportions, and there was no easy answer. They understood that their choice would forever alter the course of both the digital and real worlds.

Riley's thoughts raced as she weighed the options. Exposing the truth was a path fraught with danger, but it was also a chance to stand up against an oppressive force. The hidden algorithm had the power to manipulate reality, and VirtuCorp's intentions were far from benevolent.

The companions had ventured into Labyrinth seeking answers to Elara's murder, but what they had uncovered was a far-reaching conspiracy that transcended the confines of a mere game. The blurred lines between the virtual world and the real world had never been more apparent, and the enigmatic forces at play threatened to unravel their very existence.

With a sense of determination, Riley spoke, her voice unwavering. "We cannot let this power remain hidden," she declared. "The consequences of exposing the hidden algorithm are great, but the risks of keeping it hidden are even greater. VirtuCorp's manipulative schemes must be unveiled."

Her companions nodded in agreement, their resolve hardening. They had come this far in their pursuit of the truth, and they understood that there was no turning back. The enigmatic figure, its eyes glowing with approval, beckoned them forward.

As the companions made their decision, a surge of energy coursed through the chamber. The walls seemed to vibrate with an otherworldly power, and the fractured reality of Labyrinth trembled in response. The hidden algorithm, a force of immense potential, resonated with their choice.

The tension in the chamber reached its peak as the very fabric of Labyrinth seemed to shift and quiver. The blurred lines between reality and illusion became even more pronounced, and the consequences of their actions loomed on the horizon.

Just as the enigmatic figure was about to reveal the means to expose the hidden algorithm, a deafening explosion rocked the chamber. The walls shattered, and the companions were thrust into chaos. The very nature of Labyrinth seemed to fracture, and they found themselves hurtling through a maelstrom of digital fragments.

Riley clung to her companions as they were swept through the turbulent currents of the fractured reality. It was as if the very foundations of the game were collapsing around them, and they were caught in a whirlwind of uncertainty and danger.

The companions' senses were overwhelmed as they tumbled through the digital abyss. Time and space seemed to warp, and they could no longer distinguish between illusion and reality. The enigmatic forces at play had grown more chaotic, and their destination remained uncertain.

As they hurtled through the fractured reality, they caught glimpses of fragmented memories and distorted landscapes. It was as if they were being pulled into the very heart of Labyrinth, a place where the lines between the virtual world and the real world no longer held sway.

Just when it seemed like they were on the brink of disintegration, the chaos subsided, and they found themselves in a surreal landscape unlike any they had encountered before. The very nature of Labyrinth had been transformed, and they were faced with a reality that defied comprehension.

## Chapter 8: The Shattered Illusion

Riley Vance and her companions found themselves in a surreal and bewildering landscape, the remnants of a reality that had been torn asunder. The very nature of Labyrinth had been transformed, and they stood on the precipice of an enigma that defied comprehension.

The fragmented memories and distorted landscapes they had glimpsed during their tumultuous journey had given way to a realm that seemed to bend the rules of both the virtual world and the real world. The lines between illusion and reality had grown even more blurred, and the consequences of their actions remained uncertain.

As they surveyed their surroundings, Riley couldn't help but feel a sense of foreboding. The very fabric of Labyrinth seemed to quiver, and the surreal landscape was a testament to the chaos that had been unleashed. It was as if they had entered a space where the laws of both digital and real worlds were suspended.

The companions exchanged a series of tense glances, their thoughts mirroring their uncertainty. What had caused the explosion that had led them to this fragmented reality? And what did it mean for the truth they had sought to uncover?

Their journey through Labyrinth had begun as an investigation into Elara's murder, but it had grown into a quest to unveil the hidden algorithm and expose VirtuCorp's manipulative schemes. The blurred lines between the virtual world and reality had led them into a labyrinth of intrigue and danger, and they couldn't help but wonder if the consequences of their actions had reached a breaking point.

Riley's companions, each representing different facets of Labyrinth, approached the surreal landscape with a mix of curiosity and trepidation. They had been through countless challenges, facing enigmatic entities and decoding cryptic messages, but this new reality posed a challenge unlike any they had encountered.

With a sense of determination, they began to explore the shattered illusion, navigating the ever-shifting terrain and confronting the surreal creatures that inhabited it. The very laws of the digital world seemed to warp, and every step brought them closer to an enigma waiting to be unraveled.

The tension and suspense mounted as they ventured deeper into the surreal landscape. The very fabric of Labyrinth seemed to quiver with an unsettling energy, and the companions couldn't help but feel that the consequences of their actions had shaken the very foundations of the game.

It was during their exploration that they stumbled upon a digital relic, an ancient artifact that held the power to reveal hidden truths. The relic was a glowing orb, its radiance casting an otherworldly glow across the landscape.

Riley approached the relic cautiously, her instincts telling her that it held the key to understanding the chaos that had befallen them. As she reached out to touch it, a series of images and memories flooded her mind. It was as if the orb was a repository of knowledge, a window into the enigma that had drawn them into Labyrinth.

The images within the orb were fragmented, a patchwork of memories and data that hinted at a grander conspiracy. Riley saw glimpses of VirtuCorp's manipulative schemes, the hidden algorithm's power to manipulate reality, and the consequences of their decision to expose the truth.

The tension in the surreal landscape reached its peak as the images within the orb grew more vivid. Riley's companions watched in awe as the revelations unfolded, the blurred lines between illusion and reality becoming even more pronounced. It was as if they were glimpsing the very heart of Labyrinth's secrets.

As the images within the orb reached their climax, an enigmatic figure appeared before them. It was a presence beyond their comprehension, its eyes glowing with an eerie light. "You have glimpsed the truth," it intoned, its voice imbued with gravitas. "But the journey is far from over."

The companions exchanged tense glances, their thoughts mirroring their uncertainty. The revelations they had witnessed were staggering, and they understood that their quest had far-reaching consequences. The blurred lines between the virtual world and the real world had never been more apparent, and they were on the brink of a revelation that could reshape both realms.

The enigmatic figure continued, "To uncover the full truth, you must venture deeper into the labyrinth of reality and illusion. The hidden algorithm holds the key to untold power and peril, and its influence extends beyond the confines of Labyrinth."

With a sense of determination, Riley and her companions acknowledged the enigmatic figure's words. They knew that their journey was far from over, and the consequences of their actions had only just begun to unfold. The blurred lines between illusion and reality were a testament to the enigma that had drawn them into Labyrinth, and the quest for the hidden algorithm was a game-changer that transcended the digital realm.

The chapter reached its climax as Riley and her companions, armed with the revelations from the digital relic, prepared to venture deeper into the labyrinth of reality and illusion. The enigmatic forces at play had thrust them into a surreal landscape, and the blurred lines between the virtual world and the real world had never been more pronounced.

As they confronted the enigmatic figure and the enigma that awaited them, they couldn't help but wonder what lay on the other side of their journey. The shattered illusion of Labyrinth had become a testing ground for their determination and resolve, and the consequences of their actions remained uncertain.

## Chapter 9: The Nexus of Shadows

Riley Vance and her companions, armed with the revelations from the digital relic, ventured deeper into the labyrinth of reality and illusion. The shattered illusion of Labyrinth had become a testing ground for their determination and resolve, and they were on the precipice of a revelation that could reshape both the digital and real worlds.

The blurred lines between illusion and reality were more pronounced than ever, and the surreal landscape that enveloped them seemed to shift and twist with an eerie unpredictability. The very fabric of Labyrinth had been transformed, and they were caught in a web of enigmas and dangers.

Their journey took them through ever-changing terrain, where surreal creatures and entities of the digital realm lurked, their motives as uncertain as the landscape itself. The companions navigated this surreal maze, their senses on high alert, knowing that each step brought them closer to the heart of the enigma that had drawn them into Labyrinth.

As they ventured deeper, they began to glimpse fragments of data, cryptic messages, and distorted memories that hinted at the power of the hidden algorithm and VirtuCorp's manipulative schemes. It was as if they were traversing a digital minefield, with every revelation leading them further into the labyrinth of intrigue.

The tension and suspense mounted as they encountered enigmatic puzzles and riddles that tested their wits and determination. Each challenge was a piece of the puzzle, a thread in the web of deception that surrounded the hidden algorithm.

As they pressed forward, they stumbled upon an ancient chamber bathed in ethereal light. At the center of the chamber stood a massive, ornate door adorned with intricate symbols and mystic runes. The door was a barrier, a threshold that held the key to the enigma they sought to unravel.

Riley approached the door cautiously, her instincts telling her that it was the gateway to the next stage of their journey. With a sense of determination, she began to decipher the symbols and runes, piecing together the ancient code that would unlock the door.

The tension in the chamber reached its peak as Riley's companions watched in silence, aware that the consequences of their actions were profound. The blurred lines between the virtual world and reality had never been more pronounced, and they were on the brink of a revelation that could reshape both realms.

As Riley unraveled the ancient code, the door creaked open, revealing a passage that led deeper into the surreal landscape. The companions exchanged a series of tense glances, their thoughts mirroring their uncertainty. The journey ahead was a leap into the unknown, and the enigmatic forces at play had thrown them into a labyrinth of intrigue.

With a sense of resolve, they entered the passage, their footsteps echoing in the chamber. The blurred lines between illusion and reality grew even more pronounced, and the surreal landscape seemed to warp around them.

Their journey led them through a series of ever-shifting dimensions, each one more enigmatic and surreal than the last. Time and space seemed to warp, and they found themselves caught in a kaleidoscope of uncertainty.

During their journey through these shifting dimensions, they encountered enigmatic entities and surreal beings that tested their determination and resolve. Each encounter brought them closer to the heart of the enigma, but it also deepened their understanding of the blurred lines between illusion and reality.

The tension and suspense mounted as they uncovered fragments of data that hinted at the power of the hidden algorithm and VirtuCorp's manipulative schemes. The companions were on the verge of a revelation that could reshape both the digital and real worlds, but they were also aware that the consequences of their actions were far-reaching.

Just when it seemed like they were on the brink of uncovering the full truth, the surreal landscape transformed once again. They found themselves in a vast chamber bathed in shadow and mystery. At the center of the chamber stood a massive, ancient device, a nexus of shadows and light.

Riley approached the device cautiously, her instincts telling her that it held the key to the ultimate revelation. As she touched the device, an eerie energy surged through her, and a series of visions and memories flooded her mind.

The images within the device were a patchwork of fragmented data, a puzzle waiting to be solved. They hinted at the power of the hidden algorithm, the consequences of exposing the truth, and the blurred lines between the virtual world and reality.

The tension in the chamber reached its peak as Riley's companions watched in silence, aware that the revelations they had glimpsed were a piece of the larger puzzle. The enigma that had drawn them into Labyrinth was a labyrinth within a labyrinth, and the ultimate truth remained just out of reach.

As the visions within the device reached their climax, an enigmatic figure materialized before them. It was a presence beyond their comprehension, its eyes glowing with an eerie light. "You have glimpsed the shadows of reality and illusion," it intoned. "But the true revelation awaits you."

The companions exchanged a series of tense glances, their thoughts mirroring their uncertainty. The revelations they had witnessed were staggering, and they understood that their quest was far from over. The blurred lines between the virtual world and the real world had never been more pronounced, and they were on the brink of a revelation that could reshape both realms.

The enigmatic figure continued, "To unveil the ultimate truth, you must venture deeper into the nexus of shadows. The hidden algorithm holds the key to untold power and peril, and its influence extends beyond the confines of Labyrinth."

With a sense of determination, Riley and her companions acknowledged the enigmatic figure's words. They knew that their journey was far from over, and the consequences of their actions had only just begun to unfold. The blurred lines between illusion and reality were a testament to the enigma that had drawn them into Labyrinth, and the quest for the hidden algorithm was a game-changer that transcended the digital realm.

## Chapter 10: The Veil of Shadows

Riley Vance and her companions, undeterred by the enigmatic challenges they had encountered thus far, ventured deeper into the nexus of shadows. The blurred lines between illusion and reality had never been more pronounced, and the surreal landscape that enveloped them seemed to warp and twist with eerie unpredictability.

As they navigated the ever-shifting dimensions of this enigmatic realm, they began to sense a pervasive darkness that hung in the air, a shadowy presence that hinted at a greater mystery. The very fabric of Labyrinth had been transformed, and they were caught in a web of intrigue and danger.

Their journey through the shifting dimensions led them to confront enigmatic entities and surreal beings that tested their determination and resolve. Each encounter brought them closer to the heart of the enigma, but it also deepened their understanding of the blurred lines between illusion and reality.

The companions exchanged tense glances as they ventured further into the nexus of shadows, their thoughts mirroring their uncertainty. They had glimpsed the power of the hidden algorithm and the far-reaching consequences of exposing the truth, but they were also aware that the enigmatic forces at play held even deeper secrets.

The tension and suspense mounted as they encountered enigmatic puzzles and riddles that defied logic and challenged their wits. The very laws of the digital world seemed to warp, and the blurred lines between illusion and reality became even more pronounced.

It was during their exploration that they stumbled upon a colossal, ancient door, its surface adorned with intricate symbols and mystic runes. The door stood as a formidable barrier, a threshold to the heart of the enigma they sought to unravel.

Riley approached the door cautiously, her instincts telling her that it was the gateway to the next stage of their journey. With a sense of determination, she began to decipher the symbols and runes, piecing together the ancient code that would unlock the door.

The tension in the chamber reached its peak as Riley's companions watched in silence, aware that the consequences of their actions were profound. The blurred lines between the virtual world and reality had never been more pronounced, and they were on the brink of a revelation that could reshape both realms.

As Riley unraveled the ancient code, the colossal door creaked open, revealing a passage that led deeper into the nexus of shadows. The companions exchanged a series of tense glances, their thoughts mirroring their uncertainty. The journey ahead was a leap into the unknown, and the enigmatic forces at play had thrown them into a labyrinth of intrigue.

With a sense of resolve, they entered the passage, their footsteps echoing in the chamber. The blurred lines between illusion and reality grew even more pronounced, and the surreal landscape seemed to warp around them.

Their journey led them through a series of ever-shifting dimensions, each one more enigmatic and surreal than the last.

Time and space seemed to warp, and they found themselves caught in a kaleidoscope of uncertainty.

During their journey through these shifting dimensions, they encountered enigmatic entities and surreal beings that tested their determination and resolve. Each encounter brought them closer to the heart of the enigma, but it also deepened their understanding of the blurred lines between illusion and reality.

The tension and suspense mounted as they uncovered fragments of data that hinted at the power of the hidden algorithm and VirtuCorp's manipulative schemes. The companions were on the verge of a revelation that could reshape both the digital and real worlds, but they were also aware that the consequences of their actions were far-reaching.

Just when it seemed like they were on the brink of uncovering the full truth, the surreal landscape transformed once again. They found themselves in a vast chamber bathed in shadow and mystery. At the center of the chamber stood a massive, ancient device, a nexus of shadows and light.

Riley approached the device cautiously, her instincts telling her that it held the key to the ultimate revelation. As she touched the device, an eerie energy surged through her, and a series of visions and memories flooded her mind.

The images within the device were a patchwork of fragmented data, a puzzle waiting to be solved. They hinted at the power of the hidden algorithm, the consequences of exposing the truth, and the blurred lines between the virtual world and reality.

The tension in the chamber reached its peak as Riley's companions watched in silence, aware that the revelations they had glimpsed were a piece of the larger puzzle. The enigma that had drawn them into Labyrinth was a labyrinth within a labyrinth, and the ultimate truth remained just out of reach.

As the visions within the device reached their climax, an enigmatic figure materialized before them. It was a presence beyond their comprehension, its eyes glowing with an eerie light. "You have glimpsed the shadows of reality and illusion," it intoned. "But the true revelation awaits you."

The companions exchanged a series of tense glances, their thoughts mirroring their uncertainty. The revelations they had witnessed were staggering, and they understood that their quest was far from over. The blurred lines between the virtual world and the real world had never been more pronounced, and they were on the brink of a revelation that could reshape both realms.

The enigmatic figure continued, "To unveil the ultimate truth, you must venture deeper into the nexus of shadows. The hidden algorithm holds the key to untold power and peril, and its influence extends beyond the confines of Labyrinth."

With a sense of determination, Riley and her companions acknowledged the enigmatic figure's words. They knew that their journey was far from over, and the consequences of their actions had only just begun to unfold. The blurred lines between illusion and reality were a testament to the enigma that had drawn them into Labyrinth, and the quest for the hidden algorithm was a game-changer that transcended the digital realm.

As they prepared to venture deeper into the nexus of shadows, the enigmatic forces at play had thrust them into a surreal landscape that defied comprehension. The chapter reached its climax as Riley and her companions stood on the precipice of the ultimate revelation, a revelation that would reshape the very foundations of Labyrinth and the real world beyond. The blurred lines between illusion and reality had never been more pronounced, and they were about to face the nexus of shadows that held the key to the ultimate truth.

The enigmatic figure began to fade, its form dissipating into the shadows, and the companions watched in silence as the chamber transformed once again. It was as if the very fabric of Labyrinth was responding to their presence, and they were on the verge of a revelation that could reshape the digital and real worlds.

As they ventured deeper into the nexus of shadows, the very nature of their journey shifted. Time and space seemed to warp around them, and they found themselves caught in a labyrinth of illusions and enigmas. The blurred lines between reality and illusion were ever-present, and the consequences of their actions loomed on the horizon.

Just as they thought they had unraveled the last of the enigma, a series of eerie whispers filled the chamber. The whispers were a chorus of fragmented voices, each one hinting at the power of the hidden algorithm and the depths of VirtuCorp's manipulative schemes.

Riley and her companions exchanged a series of tense glances, their thoughts mirroring their uncertainty. The nexus of shadows was a place where the very foundations of reality and illusion were challenged, and they couldn't help but wonder what lay on the other side of their journey.

The whispers grew more persistent, and the companions found themselves drawn deeper into the labyrinth of illusions. The very fabric of Labyrinth seemed to shift and twist, and they were on the brink of a revelation that could reshape both the digital and real worlds.

The chapter reached its climax as Riley and her companions pressed forward, their determination unwavering. The blurred lines between illusion and reality were ever-present, and the nexus of shadows was a place where the ultimate truth lay just beyond their grasp.

As they ventured deeper into the labyrinth of illusions, the surreal landscape transformed once again, and they found themselves standing on the precipice of an ancient chamber, its walls etched with intricate symbols and mystic runes. At the center of the chamber stood a colossal, ancient portal, a gateway to the heart of the enigma they sought to unravel.

Riley approached the portal cautiously, her instincts telling her that it held the key to the ultimate revelation. With a sense of determination, she began to decipher the symbols and runes, piecing together the ancient code that would unlock the portal.

The tension in the chamber reached its peak as Riley's companions watched in silence, aware that the consequences of their actions were profound. The blurred lines between the virtual world and reality had never been more pronounced, and they were on the brink of a revelation that could reshape both realms.

As Riley unraveled the ancient code, the colossal portal creaked open, revealing a passage that led deeper into the enigma of Labyrinth. The companions exchanged a series of tense glances, their thoughts mirroring their uncertainty. The journey ahead was a leap into the unknown, and the enigmatic forces at play had thrown them into a labyrinth of intrigue.

With a sense of resolve, they entered the passage, their footsteps echoing in the chamber. The blurred lines between illusion and reality grew even more pronounced, and the surreal landscape seemed to warp around them.

As they pressed forward, the very nature of their journey shifted once again. The blurred lines between reality and illusion were more pronounced than ever, and they found themselves caught in a labyrinth of enigmas and shadows. The consequences of their actions loomed on the horizon, and they were on the verge of a revelation that could reshape both the digital and real worlds.

The enigmatic figure, a presence beyond their comprehension, watched as they entered the passage and disappeared into the depths of the enigma. It was as if the very fabric of Labyrinth was responding to their presence, and the ultimate truth was just beyond their grasp.

## Chapter 11: The Echoes of Deception

Riley Vance and her companions continued their journey deeper into the labyrinth of shadows, undeterred by the enigmatic challenges that surrounded them. The blurred lines between illusion and reality had reached a point where it was impossible to distinguish one from the other, and the surreal landscape seemed to twist and shift with each step they took.

As they navigated the shifting dimensions of this enigmatic realm, they felt the pervasive darkness pressing in on them, like a weight on their shoulders. The very fabric of Labyrinth had transformed into a labyrinth of intrigue and danger, and they were caught in the web of an enigma that defied comprehension.

The companions exchanged tense glances, their determination unwavering. They had ventured into Labyrinth seeking answers to Elara's murder, but what they had uncovered was a far-reaching conspiracy that transcended the confines of a mere game. The blurred lines between the virtual world and reality had never been more pronounced, and they couldn't help but wonder if the consequences of their actions had reached a breaking point.

As they pressed forward, they encountered surreal creatures and enigmatic entities that tested their resolve. Each challenge was a piece of the larger puzzle, a thread in the web of deception that surrounded the hidden algorithm.

The tension and suspense mounted as they uncovered fragments of data that hinted at the power of the hidden algorithm and VirtuCorp's manipulative schemes. The companions were on the verge of a revelation that could reshape both the digital and real worlds, but they also knew that the consequences of their actions were far-reaching.

Their journey led them through ever-shifting dimensions, each one more surreal and enigmatic than the last. Time and space seemed to warp, and they found themselves caught in a kaleidoscope of uncertainty. The enigmatic forces at play had thrown them into a labyrinth of illusions, and the consequences of their actions loomed on the horizon.

Just when it seemed like they were on the brink of uncovering the full truth, they found themselves in a chamber unlike any they had encountered before. It was a place bathed in an eerie, silvery light, with walls that seemed to pulse and breathe, as if they were alive.

At the center of the chamber stood a massive, crystalline structure, its surface etched with intricate patterns that seemed to shift and change. The structure emitted a soft, melodic hum that filled the chamber with an otherworldly resonance.

Riley approached the crystalline structure cautiously, her senses tingling with anticipation. It was as if the structure held the key to the ultimate revelation they sought. With a sense of determination, she reached out to touch it, and the moment her fingers made contact, a surge of energy coursed through her.

Visions and memories flooded her mind, each one a fragment of the enigma they had been unraveling. She saw glimpses of the hidden algorithm's power to manipulate reality, the consequences of exposing the truth, and the blurred lines between the virtual world and reality.

The tension in the chamber reached its peak as Riley's companions watched in silence, aware that the revelations they had glimpsed were pieces of a larger puzzle. The enigma that had drawn them into Labyrinth was becoming clearer, but the ultimate truth remained just beyond their grasp.

As the visions within the crystalline structure reached their climax, the chamber seemed to come alive, its walls pulsating with an eerie light. An enigmatic figure materialized before them, its form shifting and changing like the chamber itself.

"You have glimpsed the echoes of deception," the figure intoned. "But the path to the ultimate revelation is still shrouded in shadows."

The companions exchanged a series of tense glances, their thoughts mirroring their uncertainty. The revelations they had witnessed were staggering, and they understood that their quest was far from over. The blurred lines between the virtual world and the real world had never been more pronounced, and they were on the brink of a revelation that could reshape both realms.

The enigmatic figure continued, "To unveil the ultimate truth, you must delve even deeper into the labyrinth of shadows. The hidden algorithm holds the key to untold power and peril, and its influence extends beyond the confines of Labyrinth."

With a sense of determination, Riley and her companions acknowledged the enigmatic figure's words. They knew that their journey was far from over, and the consequences of their actions had only just begun to unfold. The blurred lines between illusion and reality were a testament to the enigma that had drawn them into Labyrinth, and the quest for the hidden algorithm was a game-changer that transcended the digital realm.

As they prepared to venture deeper into the labyrinth of shadows, the enigmatic forces at play had thrust them into a surreal landscape that defied comprehension. The chapter reached its climax as Riley and her companions stood on the precipice of the ultimate revelation, a revelation that would reshape the very foundations of Labyrinth and the real world beyond. The blurred lines between illusion and reality had never been more pronounced, and they were about to face the labyrinth of shadows that held the key to the ultimate truth.

The enigmatic figure began to fade, its form dissipating into the silvery light, and the companions watched in silence as the chamber transformed once again. It was as if the very fabric of Labyrinth was responding to their presence, and the ultimate truth was just beyond their grasp.

As they ventured deeper into the labyrinth of shadows, the very nature of their journey shifted once again. Time and space seemed to warp around them, and they found themselves caught in a maze of illusions and enigmas. The blurred lines between reality and illusion were ever-present, and the consequences of their actions loomed on the horizon.

Just as they thought they had unraveled the last of the enigma, a series of whispers filled the chamber. The whispers were a chorus of fragmented voices, each one hinting at the power of the hidden algorithm and the depths of VirtuCorp's manipulative schemes.

Riley and her companions exchanged a series of tense glances, their thoughts mirroring their uncertainty. The labyrinth of shadows was a place where the very foundations of reality and illusion were challenged, and they couldn't help but wonder what lay on the other side of their journey.

The whispers grew more persistent, and the companions found themselves drawn deeper into the maze of illusions. The very fabric of Labyrinth seemed to shift and twist, and they were on the brink of a revelation that could reshape both the digital and real worlds.

The chapter reached its climax as Riley and her companions pressed forward, their determination unwavering. The blurred lines between illusion and reality were ever-present, and the labyrinth of shadows was a place where the ultimate truth lay just beyond their grasp.

As they ventured deeper into the labyrinth of illusions, the surreal landscape transformed once again, and they found themselves standing on the precipice of an ancient chamber, its walls etched with intricate symbols and mystic runes. At the center of the chamber stood a colossal, ancient portal, a gateway to the heart of the enigma they sought to unravel.

Riley approached the portal cautiously, her instincts telling her that it held the key to the ultimate revelation. With a sense of determination, she began to decipher the symbols and runes, piecing together the ancient code that would unlock the portal.

The tension in the chamber reached its peak as Riley's companions watched in silence, aware that the consequences of their actions were profound. The blurred lines between the virtual world and reality had never been more pronounced, and they were on the brink of a revelation that could reshape both realms.

As Riley unraveled the ancient code, the colossal portal creaked open, revealing a passage that led deeper into the enigma of

Labyrinth. The companions exchanged a series of tense glances, their thoughts mirroring their uncertainty. The journey ahead was a leap into the unknown, and the enigmatic forces at play had thrown them into a labyrinth of intrigue.

With a sense of resolve, they entered the passage, their footsteps echoing in the chamber. The blurred lines between illusion and reality grew even more pronounced, and the surreal landscape seemed to warp around them.

As they pressed forward, the very nature of their journey shifted once again. The blurred lines between reality and illusion were more pronounced than ever, and they found themselves caught in a labyrinth of enigmas and shadows. The consequences of their actions loomed on the horizon, and they were on the verge of a revelation that could reshape both the digital and real worlds.

The enigmatic figure, a presence beyond their comprehension, watched as they entered the passage and disappeared into the depths of the enigma. It was as if the very fabric of Labyrinth was responding to their presence, and the ultimate truth was just beyond their grasp.

The chapter concluded with the companions venturing deeper into the labyrinth of shadows, their determination unwavering. The blurred lines between illusion and reality were ever-present, and they were on the brink of a revelation that would reshape the very foundations of Labyrinth and the real world beyond. The enigmatic forces at play had thrust them into a surreal landscape that challenged their every perception, and the consequences of their actions remained uncertain.

And as they delved deeper into the labyrinth of shadows, they couldn't shake the feeling that the enigma they were unraveling was far more complex and treacherous than they had ever imagined. The blurred lines between illusion and reality were becoming increasingly indistinct, and the consequences of their actions were a weight that hung heavy on their shoulders.

The echoes of deception continued to guide their path, but the ultimate truth remained elusive, just beyond their grasp. The enigmatic forces at play had thrown them into a maze of illusions, and they were determined to see their journey through to the end, no matter the cost.

## Chapter 12: The Abyss of Revelation

The companions ventured further into the labyrinth of shadows, their determination unwavering. With each step, the blurred lines between illusion and reality deepened, and the surreal landscape seemed to twist and contort in ways that defied logic. The consequences of their actions weighed heavy on their minds, and the elusive truth remained just out of reach.

As they navigated the ever-shifting dimensions of this enigmatic realm, they felt the oppressive darkness closing in around them. It was as if the very fabric of Labyrinth had become a web of intrigue, and they were caught in its snare. The labyrinth of shadows was a place where the very foundations of reality and illusion were challenged, and the ultimate revelation was shrouded in uncertainty.

The companions encountered surreal creatures and enigmatic entities that tested their resolve and wit. Each challenge was a piece of the larger puzzle, a clue in the web of deception surrounding the hidden algorithm. The tension and suspense mounted with each encounter, as they uncovered fragments of data that hinted at the power of the hidden algorithm and VirtuCorp's nefarious schemes.

Just as they thought they were on the cusp of unraveling the enigma, they found themselves in a chamber unlike any they had seen before. The walls were adorned with mesmerizing patterns that seemed to pulse and breathe with an eerie life of their own. The very air was charged with a strange energy that sent shivers down their spines.

At the center of the chamber stood a colossal, crystalline obelisk, its surface covered in a tapestry of intricate symbols and runes. The obelisk emitted a soft, melodic hum that reverberated through the chamber, creating an otherworldly atmosphere.

Riley, driven by a sense of purpose, approached the crystalline obelisk. It felt as though the answers they sought were within their grasp, waiting to be uncovered. With steady hands, she began to decipher the symbols and runes, the ancient code that would unlock the obelisk's secrets.

The companions watched in silence, the tension in the chamber reaching its zenith. The blurred lines between illusion and reality were more pronounced than ever, and the very fabric of Labyrinth seemed to respond to their presence.

As Riley unraveled the ancient code, the crystalline obelisk sprang to life. Brilliant beams of light shot forth from its surface, creating a dazzling display of colors that danced across the chamber. The companions shielded their eyes from the blinding brilliance, and the room seemed to vibrate with energy.

Suddenly, the chamber transformed. The walls dissolved into a swirling maelstrom of colors, and the companions found themselves transported to a place beyond their wildest imagination. They were suspended in a surreal void, surrounded by an ever-shifting tapestry of colors and lights.

The very laws of reality seemed to bend and warp in this kaleidoscopic realm. Time and space had lost all meaning, and the companions were adrift in a sea of uncertainty. The blurred lines between illusion and reality had never been more indistinct.

As they floated in the abyss of revelation, they heard a disembodied voice echoing all around them, as if it came from the very fabric of the surreal void. "Welcome to the heart of Labyrinth," the voice intoned. "Here, reality and illusion are one and the same, and the ultimate truth awaits those who dare to seek it."

Riley and her companions exchanged bewildered glances, their senses overwhelmed by the surreal environment. The consequences of their actions had brought them to the precipice of a revelation that could reshape both the digital and real worlds, but they were acutely aware that they were in uncharted territory.

The voice continued, "To unveil the ultimate truth, you must navigate the abyss of revelation. The hidden algorithm holds the key to untold power and peril, and its influence extends beyond the confines of Labyrinth."

With newfound determination, Riley and her companions accepted the challenge. They understood that their journey was far from over, and the enigma that had drawn them into Labyrinth was a labyrinth in itself, with depths that seemed bottomless. The blurred lines between illusion and reality were more enigmatic than ever, and they were prepared to face the unknown.

As they ventured deeper into the surreal void, the very nature of their journey shifted. Reality and illusion seemed to merge into a seamless tapestry, and the surreal landscape transformed into a kaleidoscope of ever-changing shapes and colors. The consequences of their actions remained uncertain, and they were on the brink of an epiphany that could reshape the very fabric of Labyrinth.

The companions floated through the surreal void, their senses awash with a cacophony of colors and lights. They were aware that they were on the verge of uncovering a revelation that had eluded them for so long, and the blurred lines between illusion and reality had never been more indistinct.

Just as they thought they were approaching the climax of their journey, they heard a chorus of voices, each one whispering fragments of knowledge and truth. The voices were a patchwork of memories and data, a jigsaw puzzle waiting to be assembled.

Riley and her companions exchanged knowing glances, realizing that the ultimate revelation was within their grasp. They listened intently to the whispers, each one hinting at the power of the hidden algorithm and the depths of VirtuCorp's manipulative schemes.

The chapter reached its zenith as the companions pressed forward into the abyss of revelation, their determination unyielding. The blurred lines between illusion and reality were ever-present, and they were about to confront the heart of the enigma that had drawn them into Labyrinth.

The surreal void continued to shift and change, its kaleidoscope of colors and lights creating a sense of disorientation. It was as if they were on the threshold of a revelation that could reshape not only their understanding of Labyrinth but the entire digital and real worlds.

As they floated deeper into the abyss, they found themselves standing on the precipice of a colossal, ancient gateway. The gateway's surface was etched with an intricate mosaic of symbols and runes, and it pulsed with an enigmatic energy.

Riley approached the gateway, her heart pounding with anticipation. It was clear that the answers they sought were just beyond its threshold, waiting to be uncovered. With resolute determination, she began to decipher the symbols and runes, piecing together the ancient code that would unlock the gateway.

The tension in the chamber reached its peak as Riley's companions watched in silence, aware that the consequences of their actions were profound. The blurred lines between the virtual world and reality had never been more pronounced, and they were on the brink of a revelation that could reshape both realms.

As Riley unraveled the ancient code, the colossal gateway creaked open, revealing a passage that led deeper into the heart of the enigma. The companions exchanged a series of determined glances, their thoughts mirroring their resolve. The journey ahead was a leap into the unknown, and they were prepared to confront the ultimate truth.

With unwavering determination, they entered the passage, their footsteps echoing in the chamber. The blurred lines between illusion and reality were ever-present, and they were prepared to face whatever challenges lay ahead.

## Chapter 13: The Truth Unveiled

The companions ventured deeper into the heart of Labyrinth, their determination unyielding. The abyss of revelation was a surreal void that seemed to merge reality and illusion into a seamless tapestry. The consequences of their actions remained uncertain, but they were prepared to face the ultimate truth, no matter what it entailed.

As they navigated the shifting dimensions of the surreal void, they encountered a series of enigmatic challenges and puzzles. Each one brought them closer to the heart of the enigma, and the blurred lines between illusion and reality continued to test their perceptions.

The voices of the whispers grew more persistent, their fragmented knowledge hinting at the power of the hidden algorithm and the depths of VirtuCorp's manipulative schemes. The companions listened intently, piecing together the puzzle that had drawn them into Labyrinth.

Riley Vance, the hacker-turned-detective, felt a sense of urgency and purpose that had driven her throughout this journey. She knew that they were on the verge of unraveling a revelation that could reshape the digital and real worlds. Her companions, both new and old, shared her determination, ready to face the unknown.

Their journey through the abyss of revelation led them to a colossal, ancient chamber. Its walls were adorned with intricate symbols and mystic runes, and the very air was charged with an enigmatic energy. At the center of the chamber stood a massive, ancient portal, a gateway to the heart of the enigma.

Riley approached the portal cautiously, her instincts telling her that it held the key to the ultimate revelation. With a sense of determination, she began to decipher the symbols and runes, piecing together the ancient code that would unlock the portal.

The tension in the chamber reached its peak as Riley's companions watched in silence. The blurred lines between illusion and reality were more pronounced than ever, and they were on the brink of a revelation that could reshape both realms.

As Riley unraveled the ancient code, the colossal portal creaked open, revealing a passage that led to a chamber bathed in a warm, golden light. The companions exchanged determined glances, knowing that they were about to face the culmination of their journey.

With unwavering resolve, they entered the chamber, their footsteps echoing in the chamber. The warmth of the golden light surrounded them, and the blurred lines between illusion and reality seemed to blur even further.

In the center of the chamber, an ethereal figure materialized, its presence radiating serenity and wisdom. It spoke with a voice that resonated with ancient knowledge and truth.

"You have come to the heart of Labyrinth, the nexus of shadows and revelations," the figure intoned. "You sought the ultimate truth, and now it is within your grasp."

Riley and her companions exchanged determined glances, ready to face whatever the figure had to reveal. The journey had brought them to this moment, and they were prepared for the revelation that would reshape their understanding of Labyrinth and the worlds beyond.

The figure continued, "The hidden algorithm holds the power to manipulate reality, to blur the lines between the virtual and real worlds. VirtuCorp harnessed this power, but they did so for nefarious purposes. To expose the truth, you must use this power for a greater good."

Riley nodded, her determination unwavering. "We will use this power to bring justice to Elara and to expose VirtuCorp's schemes. But how do we access the hidden algorithm?"

The figure smiled, and its form seemed to shimmer with an ethereal light. "The key lies within you, Riley Vance. You, as a hacker and a detective, possess the unique ability to unlock the hidden algorithm. But you must also use it responsibly, for the consequences of its power can be profound."

Riley nodded, understanding the weight of the responsibility that lay ahead. The companions had come this far to uncover the truth and bring Elara's murderers to justice.

With the guidance of the ethereal figure, Riley delved deep within herself, accessing the hidden algorithm's power. It was a rush of knowledge and energy that surged through her, and her companions watched in awe as the very fabric of Labyrinth seemed to respond to her presence.

As Riley harnessed the power of the hidden algorithm, the chamber transformed once again. The warm, golden light expanded, enveloping them in its embrace. The blurred lines between illusion and reality dissolved, and they found themselves back in the virtual world, but with newfound clarity.

The companions knew that they were now armed with the power to expose the truth, to blur the lines between the virtual and real worlds for a greater good. The ultimate revelation had brought them to this moment, and they were ready to use the hidden algorithm's power responsibly.

Their journey was far from over, but the companions now had the means to bring justice to Elara's memory and to reveal VirtuCorp's manipulative schemes. The blurred lines between illusion and reality had been traversed, and the consequences of their actions had taken a new path.

The final chapter concluded with the companions leaving the chamber, their determination unwavering. The blurred lines between illusion and reality had been navigated, and the ultimate truth had been unveiled. They were ready to face the challenges that lay ahead, armed with the power of the hidden algorithm and a commitment to justice.

As they returned to the virtual world, the companions knew that their journey had come full circle. The blurred lines between illusion and reality had been explored, and the enigma that had drawn them into Labyrinth had been resolved.

THE END

# Chalice of Redemption

## Chapter 1: Vintage Vengeance

The sun hung low in the sky, casting long shadows across the rows of grapevines at the Tresmont Winery. It was a serene evening, the perfect setting for a picturesque escape from the world's chaos, but Detective Victoria Delaney knew better. She had a nose for trouble, and as she strolled through the vineyards, the faint aroma of danger wafted through the air.

Victoria, a woman of refined tastes and a connoisseur of fine wines, had been summoned to the winery by a cryptic letter. It had been delivered to her office that morning, a message scrawled in elegant cursive on aged parchment, the ink still wet. The letter had contained a simple message: "The Poisoned Chalice." There was no signature, no return address, only the winery's name and its address.

As she approached the winery's main building, a sprawling mansion with ivy-covered walls, Victoria couldn't help but admire the grandeur of the place. It was a testament to the Tresmont family's wealth and power, their roots in the winemaking business dating back generations. But Victoria knew that beneath the beauty of the winery lay a dark underbelly, and she was determined to unearth it.

Inside the mansion, the air was thick with the scent of aged oak and fine wines. The walls were adorned with priceless paintings, and chandeliers hung from the ceiling, casting a warm, golden glow. It was a stark contrast to the foreboding letter she had received, but Victoria's instincts told her that all was not as it seemed.

She was met by a butler, a tall, stoic man with a formal demeanor. "Detective Delaney, we've been expecting you," he said, leading her into a lavishly decorated drawing room. "Mr. Tresmont is waiting."

Victoria's eyes wandered the room, taking in the portraits of stern-looking ancestors and the antique furniture that exuded wealth and sophistication. She was acutely aware that she was out of place in such opulence, but she maintained her composure as she was led to a large, ornate table.

Seated at the head of the table was a man who could only be Mr. Tresmont, the patriarch of the winemaking dynasty. His silver hair was neatly combed, and his sharp eyes assessed her with a mixture of curiosity and suspicion. "Detective Delaney, I'm Franklin Tresmont. Thank you for coming."

Victoria extended her hand, her grip firm and confident. "Pleasure to meet you, Mr. Tresmont. I received your letter. Can you tell me what this is all about?"

Mr. Tresmont's expression darkened as he leaned in closer. "It's about a matter of life and death, Detective. A matter concerning our family's most prized possession: the Chalice of Elysium."

The Chalice of Elysium was legendary among wine enthusiasts. A priceless relic rumored to contain the elixir of immortality, it had been passed down through the Tresmont family for generations. The mere mention of it sent shivers down the spines of collectors and connoisseurs alike.

"I'm listening," Victoria said, her curiosity piqued.

Mr. Tresmont's voice dropped to a conspiratorial whisper. "Last night, during a private tasting of our rarest vintage, the Chalice was shattered. It's irreplaceable, Detective, and its destruction threatens to reveal the dark secrets of our family."

Victoria raised an eyebrow. "Dark secrets? What could be so sinister about a wine chalice?"

"Detective," Mr. Tresmont said, his eyes filled with desperation, "the Chalice holds the key to a terrible past, a past filled with ambition, greed, and betrayal. It is said that those who drink from it gain immortality, but they also become cursed with an insatiable hunger for power. And now, with the Chalice broken, those secrets are at risk of being exposed."

Victoria absorbed the gravity of the situation. It seemed that the letter she had received was no mere prank. The Chalice's destruction was the catalyst for something much more sinister, and the Tresmont family's fortune and reputation were at stake.

"What would you have me do, Mr. Tresmont?" Victoria asked.

"Find out who shattered the Chalice," he replied. "And do it quickly. Our family's legacy, and perhaps more, is hanging by a thread."

## Chapter 2: The Shattered Truth

Victoria Delaney was no stranger to intricate mysteries, but the shattered Chalice of Elysium and the secrets it concealed promised to be one of her most challenging cases. As she left the opulent drawing room of the Tresmont mansion, she couldn't shake the feeling that the answers lay within the labyrinthine world of the winery itself.

With each step she took, the mansion's grandeur gave way to the rustic charm of the winery's underground cellars. The stone walls bore witness to centuries of history, and the flickering candlelight created dancing shadows that seemed to whisper secrets. The Tresmont family had amassed a vast collection of wines, each bottle telling a tale of time, place, and people. It was a collector's paradise, but also, a trove of temptation for those who coveted the Chalice's power.

Descending into the depths of the cellar, Victoria was accompanied by Alfred, the Tresmonts' trusted wine steward. He was a middle-aged man with a keen sense of the winery's inner workings and a deep loyalty to the family. He had been the one to discover the shattered Chalice, and his face bore the weight of the grim discovery.

"Alfred," Victoria began as they navigated the labyrinthine tunnels, "do you have any idea who might have been behind the destruction of the Chalice?"

Alfred's brows furrowed, and he hesitated before speaking. "I cannot say for certain, Detective. The Chalice had been kept in a secure vault, and only a few of us had access. But it's been decades since it was last brought out. Mr. Tresmont insisted on having a private tasting last night, and when we descended to the cellar, the Chalice was shattered."

Victoria pondered this as they reached the vault, a heavy door studded with iron bolts. Inside, the remnants of the Chalice were strewn across the floor, glittering in the dim light. The base was shattered into jagged pieces, and the bowl itself lay in fragments, each shard holding a reflection of the Chalice's grandeur.

She knelt to examine the shards, her gloved hands carefully picking them up. "It appears as though the Chalice was deliberately smashed," she noted, her detective's instincts sharpening. "Someone wanted to make sure it couldn't be used again. But why?"

Alfred shook his head, a deep concern etched on his face. "I can't fathom why anyone would do such a thing. The Chalice is a family heirloom, a symbol of our heritage. Breaking it is unthinkable."

Victoria's keen eyes fell upon the shards, her mind racing with the possibilities. The shattered Chalice was the epicenter of the mystery, and it held the key to the family's dark secrets. She needed to piece together the puzzle, but where would she start?

As they left the vault, Victoria decided to explore the winery's history. It was often in the past that answers to the present could be found. She requested access to the Tresmont family archives, which held records of their wine production, as well as the stories and legends passed down through the generations.

The archives, housed in a quiet, dimly lit room, were a treasure trove of knowledge. Victoria sifted through dusty tomes and old ledgers, her fingers tracing the names of past Tresmonts who had guarded the Chalice. It was then that she stumbled upon an entry that sent a chill down her spine.

In the pages of a journal from the 18th century, written by one of the Tresmont ancestors, was a mention of a curse that befell those who drank from the Chalice. The curse promised immortality but also bound the drinker to an insatiable lust for power. It spoke of betrayal and the darkness that the Chalice concealed.

"Alfred, look at this," Victoria called him over, her voice tinged with urgency. "It seems that the legend of the Chalice's curse goes back centuries. Could this be the key to unraveling the mystery?"

Alfred leaned in, his eyes widening as he read the passage. "If the curse is real, Detective, then it means that those who had access to the Chalice had a sinister motive. But who among us would risk the curse's power and the Chalice's destruction?"

Before they could delve deeper into the journal, the sound of footsteps echoed outside the archives. Victoria and Alfred exchanged a glance, their hearts pounding. Someone was approaching, and it was clear they didn't want their investigation to continue.

## Chapter 3: Shadows of Betrayal

As the footsteps outside the archives grew louder, Victoria and Alfred exchanged a tense look. They had stumbled upon a centuries-old journal revealing the dark secrets of the Chalice of Elysium, and now an intruder was closing in on them. In the dimly lit room, the flickering candlelight cast eerie shadows on the ancient tomes lining the shelves.

The door creaked open slowly, and a figure shrouded in darkness entered. Victoria's hand instinctively moved to the concealed holster at her side, while Alfred nervously tightened his grip on a heavy bookend.

"Who are you?" Victoria demanded, her voice steady, though her heart raced.

The intruder stepped into the dim light, revealing a tall, imposing figure in a black trench coat and a hat pulled low over their face. A gloved hand extended, and the intruder produced a glinting, silver dagger. "I think you've seen enough," a cold, modulated voice said.

With a flick of the wrist, the dagger was sent spinning through the air, aimed straight for the journal in Victoria's hand. She reacted swiftly, using the heavy tome as a makeshift shield. The dagger embedded itself into the book, inches from her chest, causing her heart to skip a beat.

"Who are you working for?" Victoria demanded, her voice tinged with anger. "Why destroy the Chalice, and what are you trying to hide?"

The intruder remained silent but took a step back, their silhouette still shrouded in darkness. Victoria and Alfred could only make out the glint of their eyes beneath the hat's brim.

As tension hung heavy in the room, the intruder made a sudden dash for the door, but Victoria was faster. With lightning reflexes, she drew her own concealed weapon and fired a single warning shot that struck the doorframe inches from the intruder's fleeing figure.

The intruder hesitated, then turned to face Victoria. Their eyes locked for a moment, and in that fleeting connection, Victoria saw a hint of desperation and fear.

"Why protect the Chalice?" the intruder hissed, their voice laced with a strange mix of frustration and sorrow. "You don't understand what you're dealing with."

Before Victoria could press further, the intruder vanished into the shadows of the winery, leaving behind a sense of dread and mystery. She hurried to the door, but they were already gone.

Alfred let out a breath he hadn't realized he'd been holding. "Who was that? What's happening, Detective?"

Victoria's mind was racing as she retrieved the silver dagger and the damaged journal. She knew that this mysterious intruder held the answers to the Chalice's secrets. "Alfred, this is far more complex than I had imagined. The Chalice is tied to something sinister, a curse that has plagued the Tresmont family for centuries. I need to find out more about this curse and its connection to the shattered Chalice."

Alfred nodded, his face pale. "I will help in any way I can, Detective. I've served this family for many years, and I want to see this mystery unraveled."

Victoria's determination flared as she examined the journal again. It mentioned an ancient family legend, a pact made to achieve power and immortality, and the devastating consequences that followed. It hinted at betrayal, and she couldn't help but wonder if the intruder's motives were connected to that dark history.

Their investigation would lead them to the heart of the Tresmont family's secrets, where ambition, greed, and betrayal had cast long shadows. Victoria knew that to uncover the truth, she would have to navigate a treacherous path, where loyalty and deceit were intertwined.

As they left the archives, Victoria couldn't help but feel that the tangled web of secrets was closing in around them. With the shattered Chalice as the focal point, the curse, and the mysterious intruder, the complexity of the case deepened. Each revelation raised more questions, and she was determined to uncover the truth, no matter the cost.

Outside, the winery's sprawling vineyards lay bathed in moonlight, casting eerie shadows across the landscape. The truth was buried deep within the winery's history, and the path to it was fraught with peril. Victoria Delaney was resolved to unravel the mysteries of the Poisoned Chalice, but she couldn't shake the feeling that the shadows of betrayal ran deep, and her pursuit of the truth would come at a price.

With the specter of the mysterious intruder still haunting her thoughts, Victoria knew that the next chapter in their investigation would be even more perilous than the last. The Poisoned Chalice's secrets were far from being unveiled, and the stakes were higher than ever.

## Chapter 4: A Vintage Confrontation

The following morning, Victoria found herself standing in the heart of the Tresmont Winery, surrounded by the lush, sun-kissed vineyards that stretched as far as the eye could see. Her thoughts were consumed by the events of the previous night—the shattered Chalice, the enigmatic intruder, and the ominous secrets lurking within the Tresmont family's history.

With the damaged journal in her hand, Victoria had spent hours researching the curse, poring over every passage for clues to the identity of the mysterious assailant and their motive. The revelation of betrayal and the promise of power had only deepened the mystery. She knew she needed more information, and the family's archives were the logical place to begin.

As she made her way back towards the mansion, she noticed that the estate had come to life with preparations for a grand wine tasting event scheduled for the evening. The Tresmonts, their guests, and various staff members bustled about, adding an air of excitement and anticipation to the estate.

Victoria was about to enter the mansion when she was intercepted by a distinguished man in his late fifties. His gray hair was impeccably combed, and his suit was tailored to perfection. He extended a hand with a warm smile. "Detective Delaney, I'm Harrison Tresmont, Franklin's eldest son. I understand you're investigating the incident with the Chalice."

Victoria shook his hand firmly. "Mr. Tresmont, it's a pleasure to meet you. I've been looking into the matter, and it's clear that the Chalice holds a deep connection to your family's history."

Harrison Tresmont's expression tightened, and he glanced around cautiously before motioning for Victoria to follow him to a more secluded part of the vineyard. "I'm aware of the Chalice's history, Detective. It's a closely guarded secret within our family. But I have my own suspicions about who might be behind its destruction."

Victoria raised an eyebrow. "Your suspicions? Who do you think is responsible?"

Harrison's voice was low and conspiratorial. "There's a branch of the family, the Vanes, who have always been envious of our wealth and success. They've always been close to the Chalice, and I believe they might have something to do with it."

Victoria considered his words carefully. The Vanes had been allies and competitors of the Tresmonts for years, and their proximity to the Chalice made them plausible suspects. "I'll look into the Vanes, Mr. Tresmont, but I must also inquire about the curse that the Chalice is said to bring. Does your family believe in its power?"

Harrison hesitated for a moment, his eyes flickering with uncertainty. "I can't deny that strange things have happened within the family when the Chalice has been used. Ambition and greed often tore our ancestors apart. But it's just a legend, isn't it?"

Victoria nodded, her mind racing. The tangled web of family history and rivalry was becoming more intricate by the minute. The curse, the shattered Chalice, and the enigmatic intruder were all pieces of a much larger puzzle, and she was determined to solve it.

With Harrison's words echoing in her mind, Victoria decided to begin her investigation with the Vanes. She left the vineyard and made her way to the Vanes' sprawling estate on the outskirts of the winery, where they maintained their own vineyards and winemaking facilities.

As she approached the Vane estate, the atmosphere felt distinctly different from the Tresmonts' opulence. The Vanes were known for their cunning and their ability to compete fiercely with the Tresmonts. The air was thick with tension as Victoria was met by Julian Vane, a man in his forties with a sharp, calculating gaze.

"Detective Delaney, to what do we owe this unexpected visit?" Julian inquired, his voice laced with a hint of hostility.

Victoria didn't mince words. "I'm here to investigate the destruction of the Chalice of Elysium. I've been informed that your family has had a close association with the Chalice for generations. Can you tell me what you know?"

Julian's eyes narrowed, and he regarded her with suspicion. "We've had our differences with the Tresmonts, Detective, but we have no reason to destroy the Chalice. It's as much a part of our history as it is theirs. If you're looking for answers, you won't find them here."

Despite his dismissal, Victoria couldn't help but feel that Julian was hiding something. She pressed further. "I've heard rumors of a curse associated with the Chalice, one that brings power but also destruction. Do you believe in this curse?"

Julian's jaw tightened, and for a moment, the mask of hostility slipped, revealing a flicker of unease. "It's an old superstition, Detective. We're winemakers, not believers in curses. The Chalice has been a symbol of our rivalry with the Tresmonts, but nothing more."

Victoria's instincts told her that the Vanes were keeping their true feelings about the Chalice hidden. As she continued to question Julian, a loud commotion erupted from the vineyard behind them. They both turned to see the Tresmont family and their guests gathered around a table set for the evening's wine tasting.

A hush fell over the crowd as Franklin Tresmont stepped forward, holding a glass of the family's rarest vintage—the very same that had been used with the Chalice. He raised the glass high, preparing to make a toast. But the look in his eyes was far from celebratory; it was one of dread.

Before he could utter a word, he gasped and clutched his chest, then crumpled to the ground. Panic swept through the crowd as Victoria and Julian rushed to his side.

As Victoria knelt by Franklin's side, she couldn't help but notice the shattered glass beside him. It was a chilling echo of the shattered Chalice, and it was clear that something far more sinister was afoot. The wine that was meant for the toast was now staining the ground crimson.

## Chapter 5: The Vintage Conspiracy

The once-festive vineyard had transformed into a scene of chaos. The guests who had gathered for the wine tasting event stood in shocked silence as Franklin Tresmont lay on the ground, gasping for breath. The shattered glass and the dark, crimson wine staining the earth served as a stark reminder of the Chalice's ominous history.

Victoria Delaney acted swiftly, her instincts taking over. She checked Franklin's pulse and found it weak but steady. It appeared that the elderly patriarch was still alive, but he was in dire need of medical attention. She looked up at the crowd, her voice filled with urgency. "Someone call an ambulance immediately!"

Amid the clamor and disarray, Julian Vane, who had been at Victoria's side, seemed genuinely concerned. "This is a tragedy. We may have our differences, but we would never wish harm upon the Tresmont family."

Victoria couldn't help but notice the sincerity in his voice, and it seemed unlikely that the Vanes were responsible for this latest incident. She nodded in agreement, acknowledging his statement. "I understand. But we can't rule anything out until we know more."

As the ambulance was called and the paramedics arrived, Franklin Tresmont was rushed to the hospital. Victoria felt a sense of frustration and unease settling in. The shattered Chalice, the mysterious intruder, and now the apparent poisoning of Franklin—all the pieces of the puzzle were beginning to intertwine, creating a complex web of deceit and danger.

With Julian Vane's assistance, Victoria began to interview the guests at the event, trying to find anyone who may have seen something suspicious. But most were too shaken by the turn of events to provide any useful information.

Among the guests, she spotted Madeleine Tresmont, the elegant and poised daughter of Franklin, her eyes filled with concern and worry. Victoria approached her, her voice gentle but probing. "Do you have any idea who might have wanted to harm your father, Madeleine?"

Madeleine's eyes glistened with tears, and she shook her head. "I can't think of anyone who would want to hurt him. This is a nightmare."

Victoria couldn't help but sympathize with the young woman, and it was clear that Madeleine was genuinely distraught by her father's condition. "We'll get to the bottom of this, Madeleine. But I need your help. Can you think of anyone who might have had access to the glass of wine your father was about to toast with?"

Madeleine paused, her eyes distant, as if retracing the events leading up to the incident. "I saw Alfred, our wine steward, pouring the wine. He had been the one to bring it out."

Victoria made a mental note of this. Alfred had been present at both the Chalice incident and the recent poisoning, and his involvement raised questions. "Thank you, Madeleine. We'll talk to Alfred as part of our investigation."

As the evening grew darker, Victoria and Julian continued their interviews with the remaining guests. Yet, it seemed that no one had seen anything out of the ordinary, leaving them with more questions than answers. The tension in the vineyard was palpable, and Victoria knew that there was more to uncover.

With the assistance of the local police, Victoria had Alfred brought in for questioning. He was cooperative but visibly distressed by the events that had unfolded. Victoria and Julian took turns asking him about the evening's events, focusing on the moments leading up to the poisoning.

Alfred's voice quivered as he recounted the details. "I was preparing the wine for the toast when Mr. Tresmont called me over. I brought out the glass, poured the wine, and handed it to him. There was nothing unusual, Detective. I swear."

Julian Vane, who had been listening closely, voiced a question that had been on both their minds. "Alfred, do you know who may have had access to the wine before you brought it to the table?"

Alfred hesitated, then mentioned the winery staff members who had been present during the preparation of the wine. It seemed that several individuals had been involved in the process, including some of the Tresmont family's most trusted employees.

Victoria and Julian thanked Alfred for his cooperation and released him, promising to keep him updated on the progress of their investigation. As he left the questioning room, Victoria couldn't help but feel that the answers they sought lay closer than they realized.

With the evening deepening, the winery grounds were cast in shadows. The wine tasting event, initially intended to be a joyous celebration, had transformed into a nightmarish ordeal. Victoria knew that the time to uncover the truth was running out, and the secrets of the Poisoned Chalice were entangled with the lives of the Tresmont family and those who surrounded them.

As she and Julian conferred on their next steps, Victoria's phone buzzed with a message. It was a note from an anonymous sender: "Meet me at the vineyard, by the old oak tree, at midnight. I have information about the Chalice and the poisoning."

Victoria knew that this message could be a trap or another piece of the puzzle, but she had to follow the lead. She shared the message with Julian and together, they decided to rendezvous at the designated location.

Midnight found Victoria standing by the ancient oak tree, her senses on high alert. The vineyard was shrouded in darkness, and the only sound was the gentle rustling of leaves in the night breeze. Julian stood beside her, a silent but supportive presence.

Suddenly, a figure emerged from the shadows, their features obscured by the darkness. Victoria could sense their presence, and her heart raced as the figure spoke in a hushed voice. "Detective Delaney, I have information about the Chalice, the curse, and the poisoning. But it's dangerous for me to be here."

Victoria nodded, her voice determined. "Tell me everything you know. We need to get to the bottom of this."

The figure stepped closer, and in the dim light, their face was revealed—Madeleine Tresmont. Her eyes were filled with a mix of fear and determination. "The Chalice, Detective, it holds a power that my family has kept hidden for centuries. But now, it's spiraling out of control, and I fear that the curse has taken hold. My father wasn't poisoned; he was cursed by the Chalice itself."

The revelation sent shockwaves through Victoria. The curse was real, and it was more insidious than she could have imagined. As Madeleine continued to share her family's dark secrets, the scope of the conspiracy grew, and Victoria knew that she was on the brink of uncovering a conspiracy that went far beyond a shattered Chalice.

## Chapter 6: A Cursed Legacy

Victoria and Julian listened intently as Madeleine Tresmont revealed the dark family secrets that had been concealed for centuries. Under the canopy of the ancient oak tree, her voice quivered with a mixture of fear and determination.

"The Chalice is real, Detective," Madeleine said, her eyes filled with torment. "It's not just a legend or a myth. The curse it carries is a part of our family's legacy, and my father's ambition to unlock its power may have led to this curse."

Julian Vane's eyes narrowed as he absorbed the revelation. "So, the Chalice's curse is more than a mere superstition. What do you know about it, Madeleine?"

She took a deep breath before continuing. "The curse is said to grant immortality, but it binds the drinker to an insatiable lust for power. It's a relentless hunger, and it's what led to the downfall of our ancestors. The Vanes and the Tresmonts were once one family, and we split because of this cursed power."

Victoria and Julian exchanged a knowing glance. The rivalry between the Vanes and the Tresmonts was rooted in their shared history and the cursed Chalice. But the mystery ran deeper than the rivalry. Victoria probed for more information. "Madeleine, why did you reach out to us? What do you know about your family's connection to the recent events?"

Madeleine hesitated, tears welling up in her eyes. "I fear that my father's actions may have awakened the curse. He was obsessed with the Chalice, and he believed that its power could secure our family's dominance in the wine industry. But it has driven him to the brink of madness."

Julian Vane's voice was tinged with sympathy. "We may have our differences, Madeleine, but we share a history that is entangled with the Chalice. We need to find a way to break this curse and save your family."

Madeleine nodded, her resolve firm. "There is a way, but it's a dangerous path. My father has hidden it well, but I've discovered the existence of an ancient manuscript that contains the rituals to break the curse. It's hidden in the family's private library."

Victoria was intrigued. "Where is this library, Madeleine?"

"It's in the mansion," Madeleine replied. "I can guide you to it, but we

must be cautious. My father's obsession with the Chalice has made him paranoid. He will do anything to protect its secrets."

With a plan in place, the three of them decided to proceed immediately. Madeleine led Victoria and Julian back to the

Tresmont mansion, where they entered the grand estate with the shadows of betrayal and curse hanging heavy in the air.

The mansion was eerily quiet as they made their way through its opulent halls. Madeleine explained that the family library was hidden behind a hidden door, accessible only through a secret passage known to a few trusted members of the household.

As they reached the library, she pushed aside a large bookshelf to reveal the entrance to the hidden room. The library was a treasure trove of knowledge, filled with ancient books, manuscripts, and artifacts that spanned generations.

The atmosphere inside the hidden room was different from the rest of the mansion. It felt like a place where the weight of the past lingered, and the dim candlelight cast long shadows on the shelves of books. Madeleine led them to a dusty, leather-bound tome placed prominently on a pedestal.

"This is the manuscript," she said. "It contains the rituals and incantations to break the Chalice's curse, to free my family from its grip."

Victoria and Julian stared at the ancient book, their hearts heavy with the enormity of the task ahead. The curse was real, and breaking it would not be a simple matter. But the shadows of betrayal and ambition, the specter of immortality, and the power of the Chalice weighed heavily on their shoulders.

Before they could delve into the manuscript, a noise from outside the library caught their attention. The unmistakable sound of footsteps approached, growing louder and more urgent.

Madeleine's eyes widened with fear. "Someone's coming. We must hide."

The three of them hurriedly concealed themselves among the shelves of books, their hearts pounding as they waited in the darkness. The footsteps drew nearer, and the library door creaked open.

It was Franklin Tresmont, his eyes filled with madness, as he stepped into the library. He seemed disheveled and tormented, his gaze sweeping the room. "I know you're here," he muttered, his voice tinged with desperation.

Victoria, Julian, and Madeleine remained motionless, their breath held as they watched him. Franklin's eyes darted around the room until they landed on the leather-bound manuscript placed on the pedestal. His face contorted with anger and obsession.

"I can't let you take this from me," he whispered, his hand trembling as he reached for the book.

In that tense moment, it became clear that the curse had consumed Franklin Tresmont, driving him to the brink of madness. He believed that the power of the Chalice was within his grasp, and he would stop at nothing to protect it.

As Franklin's hand closed around the manuscript, Victoria and Julian knew that they were facing a perilous confrontation. The curse of the Chalice had ensnared the Tresmont family, and its shadows of betrayal and power threatened to engulf them all.

## Chapter 7: The Cursed Confrontation

Franklin Tresmont stood in the dimly lit library, his fingers trembling as he clutched the ancient manuscript that promised to break the curse of the Chalice. His eyes glowed with a manic intensity, and it was clear that he believed the power was within his grasp.

Victoria, Julian, and Madeleine remained hidden among the shadows, their breaths held as they watched the patriarch of the Tresmont family. It was a perilous confrontation that had been building since the curse had been awakened.

Victoria exchanged a wary glance with Julian, and they knew that they had to act cautiously. Franklin was consumed by obsession, and any sudden movement might push him over the edge.

"Mr. Tresmont," Victoria called out, her voice steady. "We can help you. But you have to listen to us."

Franklin's head snapped in her direction, his eyes narrowing with a mixture of fear and determination. "You're here to take it from me, aren't you? You want the power of the Chalice. But I won't let you."

Julian stepped forward, his voice laced with sympathy. "Franklin, this curse is destroying your family. We can break it, but we need your cooperation."

Franklin's grip on the manuscript tightened, and his words were a whisper, filled with anguish. "No one can understand the power it holds. I won't let it slip through my fingers."

As Franklin moved closer to the book, his madness was palpable. The shadows of the library seemed to close in around them, and the air grew heavy with tension. Victoria knew that a direct confrontation could end in tragedy, and she needed to find a way to reason with him.

"Franklin," Madeleine's voice quivered with emotion as she stepped forward. "This isn't the way. The Chalice has twisted everything, and it's destroying our family. We can find another way to protect our legacy."

For a moment, Franklin's gaze wavered as he looked at his daughter. The madness in his eyes seemed to ebb, replaced by a fleeting moment of clarity. It was a critical juncture, and it appeared that Madeleine's words had reached him.

But before they could take further action, the library door burst open, and a group of men entered. They were loyal to Franklin, fiercely protective of their master's obsession. The tension in the room escalated, and it was clear that the situation had taken a dangerous turn.

Victoria, Julian, and Madeleine were outnumbered, and the men seemed prepared to do whatever was necessary to protect the manuscript. The shadows of betrayal and the lust for power loomed large in the room, and the fate of the Tresmont family hung in the balance.

The leader of the group, a burly man with a determined expression, stepped forward. "Mr. Tresmont, we won't let them take it from you. We'll do whatever it takes to protect our family's legacy."

Franklin's madness seemed to return with a vengeance, and he clutched the manuscript even tighter. "I won't let anyone stop me. This power is mine!"

A tense standoff ensued, with the loyal men ready to defend Franklin at any cost. It was a precarious situation, and Victoria knew that a violent confrontation could have dire consequences.

Julian whispered to Victoria, "We need to find a way to reason with them. Violence won't solve this."

Victoria nodded, her mind racing for a solution. "We have to make them understand that breaking the curse is the only way to save the Tresmont family. The Chalice's power is an illusion, and it's destroying everything you hold dear."

The men looked torn, their loyalty to Franklin warring with the desperate need to save their family. It was a battle of wills, and the shadows of power and madness loomed large in the room.

As they continued to argue, the ground beneath them suddenly trembled, sending shockwaves through the library. Books tumbled from the shelves, and the room quaked with a force that was beyond natural. It was as if the very foundations of the mansion were rebelling against the curse.

The men and Franklin were thrown off balance, and in the chaos, the manuscript slipped from Franklin's grasp and fell to the floor. The pages of the book flipped open, revealing the ancient rituals to break the curse.

Victoria seized the opportunity, her voice rising above the chaos. "This is a sign! The very mansion rebels against the curse. We have the means to break it. It's now or never, Franklin."

The room fell into a tense silence as they all stared at the open manuscript, its pages illuminated by the flickering candlelight. The choice was clear, and the shadows of betrayal, power, and madness hung in the balance.

Finally, Franklin, his face contorted with agony, made his decision. He nodded, tears in his eyes, and the loyal men stepped aside, allowing Victoria, Julian, and Madeleine to approach the book.

Victoria and Julian began to recite the ancient rituals, their words filled with determination. Madeleine watched with bated breath as the incantations filled the room, resonating with an energy that transcended time and history.

As they reached the final words, a brilliant light emanated from the manuscript, casting out the shadows that had plagued the Tresmont family for generations. The curse, the lust for power, and the shadows of betrayal were dispelled, and the mansion's trembling ceased.

In the aftermath of the ritual, the room was filled with an eerie calm. The manuscript lay closed, its pages forever sealed. Franklin stood, his sanity restored, and his eyes met Madeleine's with a profound understanding.

Victoria breathed a sigh of relief as the darkness that had shrouded the family's history began to lift. But there was still much to uncover, and the Poisoned Chalice's mysteries were far from resolved.

As they left the library, the sense of closure and resolution was tinged with the knowledge that the curse had left a lasting mark on the Tresmont family's legacy. The shadows of the past would not be easily forgotten, and the future remained uncertain.

## Chapter 8: Unveiling the Chalice's Secrets

The curse that had plagued the Tresmont family for centuries was finally broken, and a sense of relief washed over the grand estate. But for Victoria Delaney, the resolution of the curse was just the beginning of the unraveling mysteries that had entwined the Chalice and the Tresmonts.

With Madeleine by her side, Victoria ventured into the dimly lit corridor of the mansion, where the shadows of the past seemed to linger. She knew that the true secrets of the Poisoned Chalice lay within the family's history, and she was determined to unearth them.

Madeleine's voice quivered with a mixture of hope and trepidation. "Thank you for helping my family, Detective. The curse is broken, but we must confront the truth about the Chalice and our ancestors."

Victoria nodded in agreement. "The Chalice has been at the center of your family's history, and it holds the key to many secrets. We need to understand its power and the role it played in your family's rise and fall."

They arrived at a hidden chamber, known only to a select few. The room was filled with dusty old documents, ancient journals, and artifacts that spanned generations. It was a treasure trove of history, and Victoria felt a sense of reverence as she began to explore the contents.

As they combed through the journals, one name began to reappear—a name that had been buried deep within the family's history: Seraphina Tresmont. She was an ancestor who had been closely associated with the Chalice and had played a pivotal role in the family's legacy.

Victoria's eyes narrowed as she found a passage in Seraphina's journal that hinted at the Chalice's true nature. "It says here that the Chalice is a vessel of otherworldly power, one that can grant its possessor great strength but also bind them to an insatiable thirst for dominance."

Madeleine looked over her shoulder, her eyes filled with a mix of awe and dread. "Seraphina believed that the Chalice could be harnessed for the betterment of our family. But it led to her downfall."

Victoria continued to read, uncovering more about Seraphina's ambition and the rituals she had performed with the Chalice. The journal hinted at a hidden chamber beneath the Tresmont estate, where the Chalice's true power could be unlocked.

Julian, who had been searching through another pile of documents, interrupted. "I found records of a hidden chamber mentioned in Seraphina's journals. It's beneath the mansion, and it's said to contain the Chalice's most guarded secrets."

The trio knew that they had to explore this hidden chamber, where the answers to the Chalice's mysteries lay waiting to be uncovered. Madeleine was filled with a mix of hope and trepidation as they descended into the depths of the mansion, guided by the knowledge of their ancestors.

As they reached the hidden chamber, the air grew heavy with anticipation. The room was a stark contrast to the opulence of the mansion, with stone walls and a dimly lit interior. At the center of the chamber stood a pedestal, and upon it, the Chalice of Elysium glistened with an otherworldly glow.

The sight of the Chalice sent shivers down their spines, and they approached it with a sense of reverence. Its intricate designs and ancient engravings hinted at the power it held, and Victoria couldn't help but feel that they were on the brink of a revelation.

Madeleine's voice was filled with determination. "We must uncover the Chalice's secrets and understand its true nature. It has been the source of our family's rise and fall for generations."

Julian nodded, his expression resolute. "Seraphina believed that the Chalice could be harnessed for the family's benefit, but it also came with a heavy price. We need to uncover the rituals and incantations that may hold the key to its power."

As they examined the Chalice, they noticed that it had intricate inscriptions etched along its base. Madeleine traced her fingers along the engravings, her voice hushed. "These are the incantations. They were used by our ancestors to unlock the Chalice's power. But we must be cautious. The Chalice is a double-edged sword."

With the incantations in hand, they began to recite them, their voices resonating with the ancient rituals. The Chalice seemed to respond, emitting a soft, ethereal light that bathed the room. It was a moment of revelation, and the secrets of the Poisoned Chalice were about to be unveiled.

But as they continued to recite the incantations, a sudden, violent tremor shook the chamber. The ground quaked beneath their feet, and the Chalice's glow intensified, casting eerie shadows on the walls.

Victoria's heart raced as she realized that they had awakened something far more powerful than they could have imagined. The Chalice's power was spiraling out of control, and they were facing a force beyond their comprehension.

As the chamber trembled, the Chalice began to emit a sinister, malevolent energy that filled the room with an ominous presence. It was a force that threatened to consume them all, and they were plunged into a nightmarish struggle to regain control.

## Chapter 9: The Chalice's Redemption

In the dimly lit chamber beneath the Tresmont mansion, the power of the Chalice of Elysium surged and swirled, casting eerie shadows on the stone walls. Victoria, Julian, and Madeleine found themselves caught in a malevolent maelstrom of energy, their voices drowned out by the ominous hum that filled the room.

The Chalice, once a source of power and suffering for the Tresmont family, seemed to have a will of its own, and it was not ready to relinquish its grip. The trio struggled to maintain their composure as the energy intensified, threatening to consume them.

Julian, his voice determined, called out over the tumultuous storm. "We can't let the Chalice's power control us. We have to break the cycle, free the Tresmonts, and redeem the Chalice."

As they continued to chant the incantations, their voices resonated with a newfound resolve. The Chalice's energy wavered, its malevolence yielding to their determination. It was a battle of wills, and the shadows of power and suffering began to recede.

The ancient vessel, once a symbol of pain and ambition, began to change. The sinister glow that had filled the room shifted to a warm, golden light, and the energy that had spiraled out of control transformed into a calm, gentle presence. The Chalice had been redeemed.

With the power of the Chalice harnessed, they could feel its ancient knowledge and wisdom flowing through them. It whispered the secrets of its creation and the price it had exacted from generations of Tresmonts.

The Chalice had been forged as a means of protection, a guardian of the family's legacy, but its power had been twisted by the insatiable ambition of its wielders. It was a cautionary tale of the dangers of unchecked desire for power.

Victoria and Julian felt a deep sense of responsibility. The Chalice's redemption was not only a matter of breaking the curse but also of understanding the consequences of their actions and making amends for the past.

As the Chalice's power continued to flow through them, it began to unravel the shadows of betrayal, ambition, and power that had haunted the Tresmont family for centuries. It was a cathartic release, and the past was laid to rest.

The room grew still, and the Chalice's warm light filled the chamber. Madeleine's eyes welled up with tears as she realized that her family's legacy was finally free from the shackles of the curse. "It's over. We can move forward without the shadows of our ancestors haunting us."

Victoria nodded in agreement, a sense of closure settling over her. "The Tresmont family has been redeemed, and the Chalice's power is no longer a curse. It's a symbol of wisdom and protection."

With the Chalice's power harnessed, they left the hidden chamber and returned to the surface. The Tresmont mansion, once shrouded in darkness, now stood bathed in the warm glow of morning light. It was a new beginning for the family, free from the weight of their ancestors' mistakes.

The Tresmonts held a gathering on the vineyard's lush grounds, where friends, family, and loyal employees celebrated the breaking of the curse. Franklin Tresmont, his sanity restored, stood beside Madeleine, and the rift between the Tresmonts and the Vanes had begun to heal.

Victoria and Julian watched from the sidelines, content in the knowledge that they had played a part in bringing about this new chapter for the Tresmont family. Their shared history and the power of the Chalice had drawn them together, and their bond had grown stronger through the trials they had faced.

As the sun set over the vineyard, they realized that the mysteries of the Poisoned Chalice had been unraveled, and a new legacy was being written. The Chalice, once a harbinger of suffering, had found its redemption, and the Tresmont family had found its peace.

Victoria and Julian shared a quiet moment, their eyes meeting with an unspoken understanding. The events that had transpired had changed them, and their paths had become intertwined in a way that neither had expected.

Victoria's voice was soft, filled with gratitude. "We've come a long way, Julian. The Chalice's power has been harnessed, and the Tresmonts have found their redemption."

Julian nodded, a small smile on his lips. "It's a new beginning for the family. And for us."

As the celebration continued, the stars appeared in the night sky, casting their gentle light on the vineyard. The shadows of the past had been replaced by the promise of a brighter future, and the Poisoned Chalice's secrets were finally laid to rest.

In the end, the power of redemption and the strength of family had prevailed, and the Chalice had found its place as a guardian of wisdom and protection, rather than a harbinger of suffering. The legacy of the Tresmonts had been rewritten, and the past was no longer a burden but a source of strength.

As the last embers of the celebration faded, Victoria and Julian knew that their paths had diverged, but the memories of their shared journey would always bind them. The Poisoned Chalice had left an indelible mark on their lives, and they had emerged from the shadows with a newfound understanding of the power of redemption and the enduring strength of family.
      THE END

# Thank you for reading!

If you enjoyed the stories, would you mind filling out an anonymous, two question reader survey so I can continue creating good literature for you?

You can fill out the survey here:
https://forms.gle/jNt2MLRYNvctjgvy8

Thank you for your help!

Look for more short detective stories from me soon. For now, keep sleuthing.

– Layla

Printed in Great Britain
by Amazon

35463067R00228